"You can't marry Lean Elk."

"I must! You have known this all along."

"Swan Necklace." James yanked her against him and crushed her soft lips with his mouth. She made no struggle to get away from him. He felt her mouth open, felt the surrender in her kiss, and his blood flamed. "You belong to me, Swan Necklace," he whispered, raining kisses on her cheeks and brow and finally on her mouth again. "You can never belong to another man. I love you. You love me."

Tears streamed down her cheeks, yet she made no sound. "I belong to Lean Elk," she said in a small voice that cut him more painfully than any knife ever had. "I cannot belong to you...."

By Peggy Hanchar
Published by Fawcett Books:

THE GILDED DOVE
WHERE EAGLES SOAR
CHEYENNE DREAMS
FANCY LADY
WILD SAGE
SWAN NECKLACE

SWAN NECKLACE

Peggy Hanchar

FAWCETT GOLD MEDAL • NEW YORK

A Fawcett Gold Medal Book
Published by Ballantine Books
Copyright © 1995 by Peggy Hanchar

Library of Congress Catalog Card Number: 95-90344

ISBN 0-449-14865-3

Manufactured in the United States of America

First Edition: September 1995

10 9 8 7 6 5 4 3 2 1

Chapter 1

"**Y**ESSIRREE! RIGHT THIS way for a genu-wine Indian princess. What am I bid for her, gents?" The crowd of grizzled, sweating men moved closer to the narrow makeshift stage. T. J. Nichelby McHoney, acting auctioneer at this questionable affair, pushed forward the pitiful flesh-and-blood wares he hawked for the perusal of potential buyers. His eyes glittered with greed as he measured the crowd. A gap-toothed grin split the fuzzy, graying beard, erasing any claim to credibility he might have claimed.

"Yes, sir, gents. Brought her myself all the way from the dangerous Indian territory to the west. Nearly lost my scalp for my trouble." He doffed his dirty knit cap, displaying a nearly bald head. The onlookers laughed.

"Like I said, gents, she's the daughter of a great chief, a genu-wine Indian princess, and you can have her for just a few of the coins jangling in your money pouches."

Swan Necklace heard the hoarse cry of the slave trader and bowed her head in shame. Her long, glossy hair, black as a raven's wing, fell forward, partially covering her bare breasts. From behind its silken veil she peered out at the greedy, lustful faces of the men who would buy her, white men, once thought to be friends to the Cree Indians, men who'd smoked the peace pipes and traded goods for rich, thick beaver pelts. But these were not friends. Friends did

1

not capture Indians and sell them far away from their people. Her delicate features remained stoic, giving no hint to the turmoil she felt within.

She was Swan Necklace, daughter of Red Hawke, chief of the Cree Indian nation, destined to be the bride of Lean Elk, war chief of the Chipewyans. Memory of her proud heritage kept her slim young body ramrod-straight, her shoulders back, her chin high. Coarse men, bewhiskered Scottish trappers in rough woven breeches and greatcoats, cold-lipped English gentlemen in their fine vests and braided tricorn hats, and glib, smiling French boatmen, *voyageurs de bois*, garbed in their red blanket jackets, luxurious whiskers, and colorful bandannas, stared with hot, salacious eyes at the curve of her naked buttocks and long, slim, brown legs. Their lechery was a wall between her and freedom. She closed her eyes against the sight of them.

Hearing the ripple of interest from the onlookers, the slave trader took pains to extol her virtues, sweeping aside the silken black curtain of hair to expose the slim, strong, young back and snatching away the dirty, ragged skin with which she'd modestly tried to hide her final nakedness. Seeing the silken, black nest of hair at the juncture of her soft thighs, the men called out prices, each vying for the privilege of owning her.

"Come on now," the slave trader jeered at his bidders. "I tell you, she's a true princess, and a virgin at that. No red-skinned buck has rested between them thighs, and no white man either. I seen to that personally meself. Me, T. J. Nichelby McHoney." He rolled the syllables off with a great relish.

Swan Necklace shuddered at the coarse, unfamiliar words and fixed her gaze on some distant point above the heads of the onlookers. She'd been on her way to the village of her bridegroom when her small wedding party had been overtaken by a hostile band of Indians led by a handful of French trappers.

She and her wedding party were taken captive, beaten and half-starved, made to carry heavy loads of furs from the interior. By night some of the women had been made to bed down with the Frenchmen. Some of them, herself included, had been closely guarded and left alone at night. She could remember still the burly, foul-smelling Frenchman who had come to examine her, his hot gaze holding her own as he thrust his dirty fingers into the private cavities of her body until she'd shrunk away in pain and disgust.

"Another virgin," he'd shouted in glee, and shoved her toward the other young women of her bridal party. No one had touched them after that. Dimly she perceived they were being kept separate because they were still virginal, but to what avail, she wondered as her gaze dipped to the lust-filled faces around her. So she might bring a higher price? All her friends and kinswomen had been sold away on the trek to Montreal, some sold at the Fort *d'Étroit*, some at the small trading stops along the way. Only she had been saved and brought to this ugly town. She felt the sting of tears behind her lids, and blinked. She would not show weakness here in front of these white eyes. She would concentrate on her *manitou*, her vision spirit, and pray the Kitchi-Kitchi Manitou, the Great-Great Spirit, would deliver her.

She closed her eyes, willing herself away from the sights and sounds and stink of this white man's town to a place far away in the prairies where the wildflowers grew and the mighty rivers churned into the greater basins of the big lakes, where the Mother Earth lent her strength to all who walked upon her and the Father Sun warmed their blood and made well his wounded children. Swan Necklace felt wounded in spirit. In her vision she returned to the prairie and lay against the new sweet earth and felt Mother Earth's nurturing touch and was well again.

She roamed the plains, feeling the Father Sun upon her face and the wind in her hair. The Mother Earth was firm and good beneath her feet, then the ground shook as with the thunder of buffalos of a number too great to count. Dust rose around her feet, blocking the sun and wind, blocking the sight of the sky. Great bodies rushed by on either side of her, not quite touching her, yet she felt them and grew frightened. Above the thunder of their hooves, she cried out in fear, and suddenly from out of the spinning golden vortex of the sun came the shadow of a mighty bird, a great white falcon. Its long, pointed wings moved slowly and gracefully, yet its flight was swift. Its large head was regal and magnificent against the glow of the sun, and it called to her in short, loud notes, urging her to be brave and courageous. Dipping low, the falcon caught hold of her in its mighty golden talons. Its widespread wings fluttered and they rose above the thunder and dust of the swiftly flowing bodies. She heard the whir of its powerful wings as it carried her over the plains and set her down on the shores of a mighty lake. The falcon had brought her home.

"Yessiree, she's the daughter of a Cree chief from way out yonder in that vast wilderness as yet unexplored by the white man." With a start, Swan Necklace opened her eyes. She was not home. She was still here in this ugly white man's town. The Great Spirit had not heard her cry. The falcon had not brought her home.

The slave trader swiped his dirty hands over her breasts, tweaking one nipple cruelly. Disconsolate, Swan Necklace lashed out at him. "See that, gentlemen?" he cried. "She's a fiery little thing. She'll need some taming, but then, what man is there among you who don't feel up to the task?" He cackled gleefully.

Swan Necklace put one hand over her aching, violated breast and stood with her head bowed, shoulders slumping. She would never return to the Mother Earth, never be healed of the white man's painful touch. A silent tear rolled along one rounded cheek.

"Ain't much of a town, I think," Angus McDougall said to his new friend, James McLeod. The huge Scotsman with his bushy beard and barrel chest, his flashing smile and piercing blue eyes, had taken a liking to this younger countryman and had joined forces with him. Angus had spent the past two winters in the Northwest Territory trapping beaver for the Hudson Bay Fur Company. James had just arrived from Scotland, apprenticed by Lord Percival Ogden, who had spent a holiday hunting in the Scottish Highlands. He'd been impressed by the young Scotsman's character and woodlore. Mindful of a letter he'd received from the governor of Albany requesting a better caliber of men than those recruited from the streets of London, he'd at once engaged James McLeod. James had left his homeland in pursuit of the dreams Ogden had promised could be fulfilled in the service of the company.

Now Angus and James would work as a team over the coming winters, and the older trapper would teach the younger one all he needed to survive here in the dangerous Northwest country.

James and Angus stood out even in a place filled with such eccentric inhabitants as those in the square. There were men from myriad countries and backgrounds, rough-hewn men dressed in skins, sporting shaggy beards and long hair, driven from their winter isolation in the vast wilderness by the need for a taste of civilization; strangely painted red men offering the obvious wares of their willing squaws in return for a coin or two to buy a keg of whiskey or a copper kettle, and swarthy Frenchmen, ex-patriots who'd stayed behind when their country surrendered Montreal. Even here, in a town with such a colorful history, Angus McDougall and James McLeod had gained fame.

Angus, whose strong arm and unerring eye earned him any respect his breadth and height had failed to do, strolled along the square like a conquering infidel of old, while his companion, younger and lighter, taller and leaner of muscle, commanded the same degree of deference based on his cool demeanor.

Not one man who'd come up against James McLeod doubted he'd met a skilled fighter and a stubborn opponent, so many thought carefully before choosing to side against him. Craggy face, burned brown by exposure to the salt-tainted sea winds and Highland sun of Scotland, keen gray eyes that could narrow to sharp slivers of rage in warfare, black glossy hair that fell in careless disarray across a wide, thoughtful brow, did not make a reassuring picture to the faint of heart. One had only to note the straight, narrow nose, the firm, molded mouth and high cheekbones, to know that this man's character had been chiseled from the harsh climate of his Scottish Highlands as surely as had his big, rugged body.

He was built to endure hardships, conditioned by the soul-seeping poverty of his homeland, driven by his proud Scottish heritage to overcome whatever barriers this new land offered. He'd come to the Northwest Territory looking to make his fortune in the icy beaver streams and wild tumbling rivers, after which he would return to Scotland, buy a wee plot of land, and live happily as a squire watching o'er his sheep and his rowdy offspring. Such was the dream of most Scotsmen who came to the fur company. Such was the dream of James McLeod. He walked this new land fearlessly and with purpose. He brought with him his reputation as a peerless fighter, an honest man, and a dependable ally.

Two weeks before, James had arrived on the transport *Pallus*, bringing with him sealed instructions from the company's committee chairman to the firm's Montreal governor, Lydell Amherst. Having made his presence known to the governor and having delivered the aforementioned papers, James had quickly joined the free-wheeling, brawling life of this rough port town, partaking generously of the ale, the boisterous rhetoric, and the betting games of horse racing and fisticuffs. It was during such a skirmish that James and Angus had come face-to-face, and after some effort on both their parts resulting in bleeding gashes and loosened teeth, had recognized themselves as equals. Being men of some intelligence as well as physical attributes, they had accepted the futility of continuing, finally calling the battle a draw. Shaking hands, they clamped arms around battered shoulders, stumbled to the nearest tavern, and refreshed themselves over mugs of ale while they drew new measures of each other and became fast friends.

Now James stood looking around the Place Royale. The

square was also called *Le Berceau de Villa Marie*, or the cradle of Montreal. Behind the town walls lay a low mountain, Mount Royal. From the waterfront, streets rose in steps along the mountain terraces. Great virginal forests pressed in on either side of the walled town, but the men within the square paid their surroundings no heed. They were too busily engaged in their trade of goods, liquor, and furs to notice much of anything else. Their wrangling, executed in the tongues of their mother countries, raised such a babble, James was at once reminded of his Bible lessons and understood how diversely God had made man.

Down on the wharfs lay great pressed bundles of beaver furs waiting to be loaded onto one of the merchant ships and taken back to London, where they would become fine top hats and rich trims for ladies' capes. Crates of incoming goods had been unloaded onto the wooden piers, barrels of beads, blankets, copper kettles, musket loaders, whiskey, and any other commodity that had proven successful in trading with the Indians.

"Right this way, gentlemen." The slave trader's shrill voice had penetrated the din, reaching James McLeod's ear. He glanced at the knot of men and slowly made his way down the street.

"Where are ye going now, lad?" Angus grumbled, and ambled after his friend toward the rabble around the trader's platform. "'Tis aught but a hobbleshew." James paid him no heed, but pushed his way through the crowd. Angus followed. He liked the way the young Scotsman moved, the quick-quiet way he had of setting his foot down as if stalking an enemy.

In a few long strides, James drew alongside the make-shift platform on which stood several young Indian girls. His glance was captured by one who stood apart from the others, her head bowed, her slender arms curving so one hand cupped a small breast and the other lay against the silken mound of her womanhood. So eloquent was her pose, so abject the misery expressed by her sagging shoulders, that he was automatically touched by her innocence and shame.

"She's naught but a child," he cried to Angus.

"Aye, maybe back in Scotland, lad, but here a woman is full-grown when she reaches her menses."

"Three pounds, eight," the man beside him called out.

"That's three pounds well spent," his friend snickered. "You'll have three times that back afore the day's out."

"I won't be hirin' her out, though, till I've busted her maidenhead meself," the bidder allowed. He was a thin, dirty man whose ragged skins smelled. He winked and with a dirty hand scratched at his scraggly beard.

James looked at the pitiful young girl on the makeshift stage. She was too young for what the men had in mind for her. He thought of his sister, Abigail, back home. She was about the age of this girl, with budding breasts and an awkward pride in her change from girl to woman. James had carried her on his shoulders when she was a toddler and given her a kitten when she was older. Something of this girl reminded him of Abigail, and he couldn't turn his back on her. Some emotion possessed him, possibly a temporary bout of homesickness, possibly a thin trill of human kindness. Whichever, he stepped forward and raised his hand.

"Four pounds," he called out before he was even aware he was about to bid. The man beside him jerked around and glared at him with a malevolent eye.

"Heah, now. I've been biddin' on 'er. Ye wait fer the next bitch w'at goes up."

"I want this one," James said evenly without even looking at the man who'd addressed him. Across the gaggle of men another buyer called out.

"Four pounds, three."

James grinned at the first bidder. "Four pounds, five."

The thin, dirty little man sputtered. "Four pounds, six."

The bidding grew lively then. T. J. Nichelby McHoney cackled with anticipation. He'd known this sweet little red-skinned bitch would bring the weight of coin to his bag. He slipped behind the girl known as Swan Necklace and swept her long, glossy hair up away from her body so that her face and one breast was bared. James McLeod drew in his breath.

Her face was delicate, with each feature precisely and lovingly molded. Her small nose was perfectly straight, her mouth sweetly curved, the full lower lip pouty, the upper lip full and sensuous, but it was her eyes, dark and wide and glittering with hatred and temper, that arrested his attention most of all. Glossy, arching brows, delicate nostrils flaring with distaste, defined her spirit as readily as did the proud tilt of her chin. Then he noticed how her ribs showed beneath the smooth brown skin, and the bruises on her buttocks and thighs. She'd not been treated well of late, he guessed.

Caught up in the need to titillate his audience still further, T. J. Nichelby McHoney slapped the girl on her smooth buttocks, so hard that the red outline of his hand was left on her skin. The men in the crowd guffawed; some rubbed at their crotches. None save James McLeod saw the girl's muscles bunch as she turned, one arm outstretched as she brought her foot in its thin, ragged moccasin up to kick the little slave trader strategically between his legs. His howl was heard round the square so that vendors, traders, and suppliers halted for a heartbeat in their bartering before once again resuming.

T. J. Nichelby McHoney landed on his back on the makeshift stage, one hand bunched protectively around his aching flesh, but he was not so incapacitated as to let go of his hold on the slave girl's hair. He'd dragged the girl down with him as he fell, and now she crouched on her knees, her head resting on the wooden planks, her eyes scrunched shut in pain as the trader howled and yanked at her hair. The onlookers exchanged reluctant glances, laughed at the comedy upon the stage, and shuffled their feet. Though a rough and hearty lot, none of them had a wish to buy an Indian woman who might rise in the night and slay them in their sleep. Why take such a risk when there were so many willing ones available? Not even her youth and beauty were temptation enough.

As the pain receded, T. J. Nichelby McHoney saw that he was losing his crowd. He staggered to his feet, hoisting the girl to hers by her hair.

"What was my last bid for this bitch?" he cried.

The dirty little man who'd last bid shuffled his feet and edged away.

"Right here," his friend called out. "Four pounds, six."

"Four pounds, six," called out the trader. "Going once, going twice—"

"Four pounds, seven," James said, barely raising his voice, but T. J. Nichelby McHoney heard him.

"Sold to the good Scotsman in the back for four pounds, seven," he cried out before anyone else could change his mind. His assistant came onstage and took hold of the Indian girl's arm. She jerked away from him and pulled the ragged, dirty skin over her head and settled it around her hips. Then, giving the assistant a dark glare that made him quail in his boots, she walked off the stage with the regal air of a queen going to a ball.

"Coo, she's a bonny one," Angus McDougall said admiringly. "She'll keep yer nights lively enough, that one."

"I didn't buy her for myself," James said, shelling out the four pounds seven pence.

"Then why, lad?" Angus roared. "She'll jest git in yer way."

"I didn't want to leave her for this rabble," James said, pocketing his leather bag, considerably lighter now, and turning to face the girl. She was even more beautiful up close, but as Angus said, he had no need for a woman. She'd just get in his way.

"You're free now," he told her. "You can go on your way."

The girl only stared at him, uncomprehending.

"Ye kinna mean that, lad," Angus said. "Ye kinna buy the girl and let her go amid this rabble. She'll be a permanent guest of a back-street crib before nightfall."

"A crib?"

"A whorehouse. A place where every man has use of her for a coin or two. You dinna save her for that."

"But I don't want her," James said. "I just didn't want that dirty trader to have her."

Angus shook his head. "You're stuck with her now, lad. Ye kinna let her loose in this town with no sponsor. It would be crueler than if you'd let her be bought at a goodly price."

"What has that to do with it?" James snapped.

"The higher price a man pays for his merchandise, the better he values it," Angus said, shrugging one big shoulder and turning a critical eye on the slip of a girl who stood listening to them and waiting. "Hear now, d'you understand English?" he asked the girl.

His burr was so thick that Swan Necklace looked at him blankly. In truth she understood French very well and had also come to know some of the clumsy, unyielding English words from the Jesuit priests who flooded the country. But she could not understand this bear of a man who loomed over her. Without comprehension she turned to the younger man, the one who'd bought her. He would be her master now. He was the one she must learn to please.

"My name is Swan Necklace," she said in her native language, and when the man seemed not to comprehend, she repeated it in French.

James shook his head to show he didn't understand. Patiently she repeated her words in English. James looked at Angus in some delight.

"She speaks English," he said with obvious relief. "We'll just take her with us to Governor Amherst. He'll know what to do with her." He looked back at the Indian girl. "Your name is Swan Necklace?"

She nodded. "Your name is . . . ?" She nudged the air with her head as if encouraging a bashful child to speak, much in the same impatient manner he'd used.

"James McLeod," he said. "And this is Angus McDougall."

"James McLeod," she repeated carefully and seriously. Her dark gaze was direct as she submitted to his perusal.

"Where are your people?" he asked.

Silently she pointed to the west.

"I think she's Cree, Jaimie, lad," Angus said. "They have the most comely women. Them and the Chipewyans." He pronounced the name of the second Indian tribe the way the Canadians said it.

"I am Cree," Swan Necklace said proudly, indicating herself. "My father is Red Hawke, chief of the Cree."

"Chief?" Angus said, looking at her and then at James. "Do you know what that means, Jaimie?" he asked. "Her father'd be mighty glad to get this little gal back."

"You'd think so, wouldn't you?" James said, eyeing Swan Necklace. Finally he sighed and shifted his broad shoulders. "Let's take her with us to see the governor. He'll know what to do."

The two men turned up a side street leading to the first of several mountain terraces, upon which the town was built. Beaver Hall Hill climbed from one terrace to the other, and perched along its steep inclines were the John Forbicher residence and the long, low walls of the Château de Ramezay. Dormer windows, neatly and uniformly placed, and turrets at either end broke the otherwise austere lines of the plain two-story building that the French governors had once used as their residence. Now that Governor Francois de Rigaud had surrendered and the Truce of Paris had been signed, relinquishing Montreal and all the Canadian provinces to English control, Governor Amherst had taken over the building for his apartments and offices.

Now Angus and James climbed the hillside and made themselves known to Governor Amherst's assistant. Within a short while the three of them were shown into the governor's office.

"Good day, McLeod," the tall, aristocratic-looking Englishman said, coming to greet them. "What have you here?" His tone was slightly disapproving, his eyebrows raised in eloquent commentary on their companion. Swan

Necklace hung her head, letting her loosened hair fall forward to hide her face. However, nothing in her stand could be misconstrued as humbleness.

"Sir." James shook hands with the governor. This was not his first visit to these offices. When he'd first made himself known to Amherst immediately upon arrival in Montreal, he'd been greeted here in these very rooms. He'd sensed the Englishman had taken a liking to him. He was here today at a summons from the governor. "This is my partner, Angus McDougall."

"McDougall." Amherst nodded his head at the big man. "I've heard about you."

Angus's rough features lit in a broad smile and he flexed his shoulders just the slightest bit. "Thank you, sir," he growled good-humoredly.

"And this?" Amherst asked, waving an elegant hand toward the Indian girl in the dirty, tattered skins. He was too well bred to comment upon the odor emanating from her, but he did unobtrusively open a small, gilt-edged box and hold a pinch of snuff to his nostrils.

"This, sir, is Swan Necklace," James explained. "We've just bought her from the slave trader who calls himself McHoney."

"Ah, yes, I've heard of that good man's activities as well," the governor said. "It seems the Frenchmen and their Indian allies were in the habit of taking captives from among their enemies and selling them off as slaves. Now that we've taken over the territory, the renegade trappers still persist in such an abominable practice."

"So Angus has told me," James said.

"What do you intend to do with the girl?" Lydell asked, then waved his hand negligently. "Aside from the obvious."

"No, sir, I didn't buy her with that in mind," James said quickly. A slight redness stained his raw cheekbones, but his gray eyes were direct and unwavering, so the governor had little doubt of his sincerity. "I just felt sorry for her, sir. She's little more than a child."

"She says she's Chief Red Hawke's daughter," Angus interposed.

"Chief Red Hawke?" Governor Amherst asked, raising one eyebrow expressively. "And what Indian nation does he command?"

"My people are the Cree nation," Swan Necklace spoke up, her chin tilting proudly. If the governor was surprised at her grasp of English, he made no comment on it.

"I am also promised as the wife of Lean Elk, war chief of the Chipewyan nation."

Even the governor's well-bred features could not contain the show of surprise at her revelations.

"She didn't tell us that, sir," Angus said, looking at her.

"I think this is a most fortuitous purchase you've made, Mr. McLeod."

"How is that, sir?" James asked.

"I've just finished reading the mail you brought from the London committee, and they've finally agreed to a change. You may not be aware of our past policies; certainly Mr. McDougall should be. It has been the practice of the company to build its trading posts around the Hudson Bay and in the mouths of some of the rivers that feed into the bay. And we've waited for the Indians to come to us with their pelts. The Northwesterners, those rabble peddlers without moral consciences, have gone into the interior right to the hunting grounds, taking their whiskey kegs and creating all sorts of havoc among the tribes. Naturally they get the pick of the beaver pelts and we get what's left over." Amherst's expression registered outrage at the unfair practices of the unscrupulous Northwestern Fur trappers.

"No longer will we wait for the Indian tribes to bring us leftovers. From now on, we're going to establish posts in the interior. I've been ordered to send a party west of the Great Lakes to the Red River Basin to set up and maintain an outpost for us there. Ordinarily this would go to a man with more experience of our countryside, but since you seem to have allied yourself with Mr. McDougall here, whose reputation in the field is flawless, and with M— ah,

Swan Necklace here, you would seem to be the one who would have the greatest success in achieving our goals."

"Yes, sir," James said. He and Angus grinned at each other.

"You will build a fort, man it, and winter over there. From this base fort you will trade with the Indians and send out our own trappers. Eventually we'll want these forts to sustain themselves and supply food to the trappers. You will, in short, be our wintering partners. In return . . ." He paused as if to signify the importance of the announcement he was about to make. "In return, you will be made chief factor of the new fort."

"Thank you, sir," James said, his set features hiding his elation. He would be one of the youngest chief factors the company had, and a Scotsman besides. He'd been given the difficult task of establishing a post deep inland. The company had other posts along its main waterways, but never had they tried to penetrate into the wilderness as the Northwestern Fur Company agents did.

Angus seemed to be thinking along the same lines. "Excuse me, sir," he growled. "But seems to me the Northwestern Fur Company has their own factory already set up out there in Red River country."

Amherst drew himself up. "I'm told it's a big country out there, McDougall. There should be plenty of room for both companies. If there's not—" he shrugged "—make room for yourselves. If there's a question of survival between the two fur companies, we plan to be the survivors."

His brooding gaze fell on the young girl who had stood quietly while the men talked. Yet the alertness of her gaze showed she was aware of the consequence of much they had said. Now she stepped forward.

"My people live north of the Red River," she said. "I will guide you there and my father will reward you for returning me to him. He will make you his blood brother and trade his richest furs with you."

James and Angus turned to look at the girl.

"She's right, of course," Governor Amherst said. "She can be an important liaison for you."

"Are you sure you can find your way back from here?" James asked.

"I know the way," she said quietly, her dark eyes sparkling as her gaze moved from one white face to the other.

"It's pretty far, lass," Angus said doubtfully.

"I know the way," she repeated with more determination. "When the trader brought me over the mountains and plains, I watched and I made images in my head. The Great Spirit will show me the way back to my people."

"They are rather uncanny, these women," Angus said. "They can lead the way through the most god-awful wilderness."

"Though the overland trail is more difficult than going by way of Hudson Bay," Amherst said thoughtfully, "I'm convinced this is best. You'll establish contact with some of the southern tribes we haven't yet reached. The Northwest Fur Company have already made friends with many of these tribes. We have to beat them at their own game. You'll be using voyageurs and Montreal canoes to carry as many supplies with you as you'll need for your first winter out there."

"Well, then," James said in a tone that said all was settled.

"You will take me with you?" Swan Necklace asked.

James McLeod nodded. "You must guide us and our men through the waterways to the Red River Basin. You can do this?"

"I, Swan Necklace, daughter of Red Hawke, will guide the White Falcon and his men through the plains to the land he seeks."

"Why do you call me White Falcon?" James asked.

She gazed at him, her dark eyes serious. "When I stood naked before the white men and they sought to buy me as their slave, I thought I would never see my people again. I feared I would never lay my face against the Mother Earth and feel her healing power. I prayed to the Great Spirit for my deliverance and he sent a vision to me. The vision was that of a bird of prey, a mighty white falcon, and then you came."

"But I'm not a falcon, I'm just an ordinary man," James protested.

Angus slapped him on the shoulder. "Dinna fight it, lad. The Indians believe in their visions. You were her white falcon, and she'll never think of you any other way."

James glanced at Swan Necklace. She might have grinned shyly or been coy. He'd seen other Indian women behave in such a manner when they'd caught the attention of the white men, but this strange, self-contained young girl did none of that. She looked back at him with an intelligent directness as any man might have done. She was not afraid of him, he perceived, of any of them, though they held the power of her future in their hands ... or did they? Was it not she who held their future in her small brown hands? Had they not given themselves over to her in leaving her to guide them into the wilderness?

She saw his hesitation and guessed that this was not a man used to depending on others. He was used to handling his own destiny. Now he stood weighing the consequences of their future plans, accepting the importance of the role she was about to play. She waited until the reality of it had sunk in, and when he understood it and accepted it, she smiled for the first time, not a coy or timid smile, but as one equal smiles at another.

In that moment the three men understood that this was not just any dirty Indian maiden. This was truly an Indian princess, a woman of virtue and high value among her people, and by the strength of her very being, such would she be among the white people as well. She was Swan Necklace, daughter of the Cree nation.

Chapter 2

"**J**AIMIE, I KEN we need six canoes," Angus said.

"Nine," said James McLeod, crouching over the supplies they'd assembled along the wharf. Barrels and packets of trading goods sat waiting to be loaded in the big *canots de maître*, the eleven-meter-long birchbark canoes that had come to be known as "Montreal canoes" for their ability to carry a dozen crew hands as well as several thousand pounds of merchandise and food supplies. Six men, six feet in height, could lie end to end in one of these deep-seated crafts, which were used on the Great Lakes and the larger rivers and lakes beyond. Later, in the smaller streams, they would switch to the shorter, more maneuverable Indian canoes.

James McLeod studied the bales of cargo and wondered how his newly hired men, experienced voyageurs every one, would fit all the cargo into the canoes, and what might be left behind. The trouble was, nothing must be left, they needed it all. This wealth of goods was necessary for survival during the harsh winter months ahead. Within those tightly laced packets and bundles were thick woolen blankets, gunpowder, ice chisels, animal traps, brass pans and kettles, heavy cast-iron pots, finely steeled knives, flints and fire steels, pipes and tobacco, and guns and ammunition. What wasn't actually needed by the trappers themselves would be traded to the Indians for their furs, game, wild rice, and other foodstuff necessary for the months ahead.

"Each birchbark canoe handles three thousand pounds, not counting the crews," James calculated to himself.

"Boss? You want us to load, eh?" called a burly, bewhiskered man with a flashing smile.

Garth Buckley was one of the first voyageurs James had hired. An affable Frenchman, he had at once assumed an easy authority over the rest of the crew, offering names of other experienced hands for James to hire.

"Get to it," James called, and stood watching as the packets of goods were loaded. These were not ordinary voyageurs hired only to row the canoes. These men had signed on to go all the way west to the Red River Valley and to help establish a new fort before returning to Montreal.

"A colorful lot, eh?" Angus commented as he observed the men, with their broad chests, muscular arms, and short bandy legs.

"Aye," James answered. "They're a hardy bunch, and they'll have to be if they're to stay through the winter out there." Long lines slashed his thin cheeks, and his glance was shrewd and measuring as he touted the worth of each man.

They wore a vibrant array of costumes: red blanket coats, multicolored sashes, and calico shirts and bandannas. Most wore moccasins with intricate bead designs worked into them. Bright caps or bits of colorful calico or even an occasional fur hat covered their heads. Most of them sported longish hair down to their shoulders, and some bore full beards and mustaches.

They were short men by most standards, standing no higher than five and a half feet, and each one blessing the saints who had made them thus. Taller men would have found no room in the canoes for their longer legs and so could not have joined this elite corps of boatmen.

Like their oarsmen, the canoes sported bright ornamentations as well, with pictures of animals or flowers or Indian designs emblazoned on their white birch prows.

Under James's critical eye and Garth Buckley's cheerful orders, the supplies were soon loaded in the broad-beamed crafts, packing them to the gunnels and leaving room only for the oarsmen to seat themselves with their legs crossed.

"Like this, boss?" Buckley called. He stood knee-deep in the shallow water, one hand gripping the lead canoe.

"That's fine," James called.

He glanced at Swan Necklace. She looked vastly different from the ragged, dirty slave girl who'd been purchased just days before. Her long, silken hair was caught back in a neat braid and lay against her back. She no longer wore the torn, smelly skins she had during captivity. An Indian dress of soft doeskin and new beaded moccasins had been purchased from one of the Indian women who traded at the fort. Her soft brown skin glowed, clean and healthy. She was more beautiful than ever.

Not only was she beautiful, but James had discovered a keen intelligence behind her impassive gaze. She'd been of immense help in determining what supplies they needed to pack into the interiors, in reassuring them as to what food subsidies to expect from the Indians, and in understanding the terrain and the hostile tribes they must pass through. Now she stood watching the readying of the canoes with the same intensity as James and Angus.

"Do you like this man Buckley?" she asked now, nodding toward the burly oarsman. "Do you think he is a good man?"

"Good enough for what we're wantin'," James replied.

"He has a reputation as a bordellar, and some say he suffers the barrel fevers," Angus replied.

"What is a bordellar?" Swan Necklace asked. James and Angus exchanged glances. How should they explain such things to a woman, and an attractive, innocent young woman at that? Angus shrugged.

"A man who goes to the cribs too often," he mumbled.

"And the barrel fevers come up on a man when he drinks too much."

"I see this possibility in him," Swan Necklace answered. "Many white men are like this."

"I expect these men would earn such a name after being in the field all winter," James said quickly, trying to be fair to the men who would labor under him for the next months.

"As to the fevers," Angus said, and shrugged diffidently, "on the trails there's no extra barrels for overindulging. We're not carrying more than we need for the rowers."

James nodded in acceptance of this. He knew the way of men who labored long and hard amid untold dangers and hardships with few rewards. They were expected to get out of hand when the time came. Back on the trail they would be the same hardworking men they'd always been.

"Mr. McLeod!" A voice hailed them from the riverbank and all hands turned to see the governor's carriage had rolled to a stop. Amherst stood up and waved to them. James ran lightly along the wharf and shook hands with the governor. They stood talking for some time and a soft leather case was passed to James. Angus nodded with satisfaction and went back to checking the lacings on his own canoe.

Unabashed, Swan Necklace observed the tall, lean Scotsman, the easy slouch of his shoulders, the self-respecting lift of his dark head. He showed little deference to the superior position of the governor. Swan Necklace liked this about him. He was a proud and handsome warrior, and she was pleased to be leading one such as he back to her people. She turned to the river and was startled to see that she was not the only one intent on what was happening between McLeod and the governor. Garth Buckley stood watching them as well, his dark eyes speculative, his thick lips drawn back from his large teeth in a grin. Fascinated, she stared at the man until he felt her gaze, then he threw back his head and laughed in a jolly manner. His black eyes glittered with passions she recognized too readily in the eyes of white men. Swan Necklace's cheeks flushed, which only caused him to laugh harder. Abruptly she turned away.

James McLeod was loping down the riverbank now, his booted feet sounding sure and unwavering along the thick board wharf. His long, blue-black hair flashed in the sunlight.

"All is as it should be?" Angus asked, straightening as he came near.

"Aye," James said, holding up the leather pouch for all to see. "Here is our commission to go forth and claim land for the Hudson Bay Company and set up a post." The whole crew cheered, raising their red cedar paddles in a salute. The black and green markings flashed handsome and bold against the red-painted oars.

"There is one thing I should tell you men now," James said, facing his crew. "As you may have heard, the Ottawa and some of the other hostile tribes have captured eight small posts all along the lake route. Sir William Johnson has invited the tribes of the Upper Lakes to come to Niagara for a grand council sometime this summer, but the most hostile tribes have refused. There's bound to be fighting along the lake route. We'll take the northern route to bypass Forts Niagara and *d'Étroit*, but conflict with the hostiles is bound to be met somewhere along the way. If any of you want to change your minds about going, now's the time to do it." His level gaze swept around the wharf.

No man turned away from him. Many of them would have shown the same disregard for danger no matter who led them where, and their enthusiasm would have been as exuberant and unwavering even if they were leaving on a junket for the Northwestern Fur Company. A fiercely independent lot, their loyalties lay with whoever paid them. James and Angus knew this and accepted the standard. Now, with the jingle of coins in their pockets and full barrels of rum aboard, the crew was amenable. Their future loyalty would be tested by hardships and dangers along the trail and by the iron-fisted ability of the man who led them.

James McLeod stuffed the pouch inside his shirt next to his skin.

"Let's get going," he called.

Quickly the voyageurs scrambled into their canoes, three on one side, four on the other. The middlemen with their shorter three-foot-long paddles settled in the center positions, and the *gouvernail* or bowmen with their longer five-foot-long oars took their place in the stern, where they never sat, but often rode for hours with their weight resting on their knees. James helped Swan Necklace into the lead canoe and climbed in himself. Angus would ride one of the follow-up canoes.

A cry went up and was repeated. *"Voilà tout! Voilà tout!"* That is all! They were on their way. There was an answering cheer from the riverbank. Swan Necklace looked back to see the governor still seated in his carriage. Behind him rose the walled city of Montreal. She turned away, hoping never to see this white man's town again. It held many bad memories for her. Gazing ahead, she saw James McLeod's bare sleek head. It was the head of a falcon, and so she would call him from now on. Her animosity for the white man's town eased a little bit, for it was here that the White Falcon had come to her.

The voyageurs dipped their oars and the canoes glided away from the wharf. Once again a great shout went up from boatman and townsman alike. Swiftly the town was left behind them. Suddenly the voyageurs began to sing, strong, lusty male voices, raised in joyful, rhythmic praise of sky, water, boat, and man. They sang "En Roulant Ma Roule" and "La Belle Lisette" with wild exuberance, their paddles dipping and flashing in the cold, clear river water. All who listened heard the joy of communication between man and God, if not in the ribald words, then surely in the robust voices. Their songs kept the strong, steady beat, their oars cut a swath through the tumbling water at forty strokes a minute. They would travel thus from sunup to sundown, with only periodic ten-minute rests.

Swan Necklace sat in the prow of the lead boat, her face

turned to the west, toward the place of her people. She was
going home, she thought, and her heart was filled with elation. The morning sun spilled on the rippling water, its light
reflected in brilliant prisms. Seabirds scudded across the
water, a fish hawk emitted a staccato bark of warning before wheeling off in pursuit of his prey. From the banks of
the river came the sweet smell of wildflowers and sunbaked
grasses. Fish darted from beneath the cool, dark shadows of
the canoes into the clear, sunlit waters of the Ottawa River.
Swan Necklace drew in a deep breath. Here, away from the
odors and walls of the white man's town, she could begin
to smell the breast of the Mother Earth, and her anxieties
were eased.

James set a brisk pace. They turned away from the Saint
Lawrence into the western tributary of the Ottawa River.
Swiftly and surely, the canoes glided over the water, covering four miles in an hour. When the voyageurs tired of
singing, one of them called out the count so their rhythmic
motion continued. Though it was only May, the sun remained warm and constant on their backs. At noon they
paused for a short meal of warmed-over mush and pork,
and very soon were back on the water.

There were no problems on this first leg of their journey.
They traveled the well-known "fur artery," the route used
by Indians and later by trappers and voyageurs. The atmo-
sphere was easy and confident. There were no dangers of
marauding Indians here, no impassable rapids. Even the
portages were easy enough for the seasoned voyageurs.
Only darkness drove them off the water, for they could not
risk ramming into an unseen log or snagging and ripping
away the fragile bellies of their canoes.

The voyageurs drew the birchbark crafts onto the riverbanks, unloaded the supplies, and turned the canoes bottom
up. They would provide shelter for the night. Everything
was bustle and quiet flurry. The cook set about warming
another repast of cornmeal mush and pork while the voyageurs inspected the seamed ribbing of their canoes, looking
for any sign of weakness in the pitch seals. When one was

found, it was quickly plugged with pine pitch. After their chores were attended to and supper eaten, one of the rum barrels was brought out and unplugged, and drinks passed around to one and all. The voyageurs greeted this offering with hearty cries. Swan Necklace sat on the sidelines, close enough to the fire to feel its warmth against the evening chill, yet far enough away as to be lost in its shadows.

"Come, lass, come sit by the banefire," Angus urged her, but she shook her head, and as the men drank their rum rations and grew more boisterous, she edged away, having already experienced the mood swings that occurred when men drank their devil's brew. Crouching beside the lead canoe, preparing her bedroll, she was suddenly aware of a looming shadow and remembered the bold glances of some of the men.

With a muffled outcry, she sprang to her feet, her hand already reaching for the small, sharp knife she'd acquired and now carried in her waistband. Her experiences thus far with the white men had taught her to distrust them.

A rough hand shot out and clasped her thin wrist in a painful grip. Swan Necklace cried out. Her numbed fingers dropped the knife. The shadowy figure moved and now the light played across the chiseled features and stern gray eyes of James McLeod. Stooping, he picked up her knife and held it out to her.

"You have no need of this, Swan Necklace," he said quietly. "I will not harm you."

She stared into his eyes and heard the simple sincerity of his words and found it strange that she could trust this white man when she trusted no other. Thoughtfully she returned the knife to its sheath.

"Swan Necklace does not fear the man who shows himself as the White Falcon," she answered, "but not all men are as honorable as he."

James heard her words and was strangely pleased at her trust in him. "You need fear no man while you are in my charge," he promised. "I will see you are returned to your father unharmed."

"This was revealed to me in my vision," Swan Necklace answered.

James regarded her serene face, curious about her and her ways. "You had a vision about me?" he asked.

Silently she nodded.

"My old baba used to have second sight," he mused. "In my country, the old women stare into the peat fires and see visions."

"Among my people the shaman has this gift of second sight. If a warrior or a young person wishes to have a vision, they must fast and go alone to a solitary place and they must pray for their vision quests to come to them."

"Did you do this when you had your vision?" James asked. He liked to hear her speak, so carefully did she form the words of his language, yet still with a charming little accent that was disarming.

Swan Necklace shook her head slightly, so the silvered black braid of hair swept forward, casting mysterious shadows over her face. "I did not fast or prepare," she said. A smile played at the corners of her mouth. "At least I didn't choose to fast. The white men made that decision for the prisoners. They gave us only enough food to keep us alive. That alone would cause us to have hallucinations, but this was not a dream. It was a promise made by the Great Spirit. I was taken away from the slave trader and returned to my people by a great white falcon." Her gaze turned back to him.

"I am not that falcon," James said quietly.

"You are my vision," Swan Necklace answered. "You and you alone will see me safely back to my people." Her dark eyes regarded him somberly. He was touched by her unwavering trust in him.

"So be it, then," he said, and recognized the solemnity of the moment. "You need not fear for your safety tonight or any other night. If it is my destiny to be your protector, then I will fulfill that destiny."

Swan Necklace smiled an enchantress's smile, a luminous smile of innocence and coquetry all at once, the smile of a child, trusting and uninhibited. With a graceful, fluid motion she lay down upon her pallet, rolled onto her side, and pulled her furs high about her chin. James was left to ponder the lingering image of her smile and the hollow feeling it left in the pit of his stomach. The boisterous noise around the campfire was dying down now. Men who'd spent fourteen hours rowing drifted off to their bedrolls.

James unrolled his own beneath the lead canoe, unbearably conscious of the small bundle that was Swan Necklace. Long after the men had settled around him, he lay awake thinking of the beautiful young Indian girl. She couldn't be more than Abby's age, he reasoned, and Abby was only fourteen. He'd been here in this wild country long enough to know that Indian girls were often taken as wives as early as twelve years of age or upon the showing of their first menses. Such an early age was one way of ensuring a man had a virgin. But James had never favored such an early alliance. When he'd turned to the Indian prostitutes to still his own wild yearnings, he'd chosen someone a little less childlike. Now here he lay mooning over a young girl barely out of childhood, a girl the same age as his sister.

He thought of Abby. He'd been a boy of ten himself when his mother gave birth to the mewling red-haired babe who had stirred their hearts and laughter over the next years. Now he longed for Abby so that he might pull her braid and see her bright blue eyes flash with anger at his taunts. That was why he was so susceptible to this Indian girl, he thought. He was longing for hearth and family and his beloved sister. Relieved that all his feelings were nothing more than homesickness, James settled himself deeper into his bedroll. He knew how he'd behave around Swan Necklace from now on. He'd treat her as he did his little sister. He fell asleep instantly, a man with his world orderly and in place, all puzzles solved, all mysteries breached, all uncertainties conquered.

They were up before the first light of dawn. After a hurried cup of coffee, the voyageurs checked their repairs from the night before, then righted their canoes in the shallows where they reloaded the supplies. In little time the cry went up and everyone boarded the canoes, oars were dipped and the birchbark vessels glided out on the mirror surface of the river.

For several days they followed the Ottawa River westward. The sunshine was warm and splendid on their backs, an omen to them that their venture was blessed. Near the mouth of the French River they met up with a returning brigade of voyageurs who shouted out greetings. When all information had been exchanged about journeys begun and journeys ending, the headman of the other crew spoke up.

"Have a care, *mon ami*," he said. "Rumor came down the trail that the Fauk and the Chippewa have turned hostile. They've attacked some of the outposts."

"I thought Pontiac and his Ottawas were the danger," James said.

The head voyageur shrugged. "Pontiac and his tribe started it, the bloody devils, but the hostility has spread all along the Great Lakes."

"I heard Johnson had called a powwow at Fort Niagara," James revealed.

"Don't depend on that, brother," the headman answered. "There's too much unrest among the tribes." His gaze fell on Swan Necklace. "If thet little gal ye've got there has any clout with a tribe, use it. Elsewise, ye'll lose a few scalps."

"Thanks for the warning," James called.

"Good luck to you, brothers." The other men pulled away, swiftly paddling their birchbark canoes, heavily loaded with sleek beaver plews. James and his party pushed on, taking the westward branch of the French River. They were far north of the Lakes Huron and Erie, but that was no guarantee of safety. James warned his men and they proceeded warily.

As if in recompense for the beautiful sunshine they'd enjoyed thus far, rain began to fall, at first lightly, then with increasing intensity. It continued throughout the day, a cold, sleeting curtain of water that beat against their hunched shoulders and slowly and inexorably chilled them to the bone. James passed an oiled skin up to Swan Necklace, and gratefully she wrapped it around her head and shoulders. Beneath it, she remained dry and relatively warm.

Darkness came early to the river that night, and in disgust his voyageurs steered their canoes to the shallows. Upon finding a suitable place for the night, they disembarked, pulling their canoes high up on the banks. Despite the stiffness brought on by hours crouched in the canoe and the chilled rain, they ignored their own discomfort and set to work at once, unloading the supplies and beginning the careful inspection of the birchbark seams.

Supper was a somber affair with each man huddled in his oilclothes, his dish cradled against his chest to avoid rain falling into his food. Swan Necklace took her dish to one side and sat on a slick, wet log. The white man's food was cold and tasteless with a dreary sameness to it, and she had little appetite. Still, she forced herself to eat, knowing it would be noon tomorrow before more food could be had. Surreptitiously she glanced at the man who served as their cook, wondering if she might offer him some suggestions. There were spices that could be added to make the cornmeal porridge more palatable, and game and berries in the woods about that could add some variety to their diets. Perhaps, when she had the chance, she would gather some of the special leaves and herbs her mother had taught her about and she would offer them to the cook. Now she set her nearly full bowl aside and gathered the oiled skin closer about her, shivering a little. James McLeod noticed and crossed the small clearing to her.

"You are cold?" he said, gazing down at her.

She shrugged. "It is nothing. The rain is cold. Winter does not want to let go of the land, but it knows it must, so it sends us this final day of defiance. Next time the rains must be obedient. They will be warmer for us."

James smiled and seated himself on the wet log beside her. The drum of the rain closed them off in an intimate,

separate world. "How do you know so much about the
rain? You're just a bairn."

"A *bairn*?" she asked, staring at him with wide eyes.

James grinned again, feeling every inch the man, and she
the wee bairn he'd called her.

"I called you a child," he said.

At first Swan Necklace's face went blank, and he sensed
he had offended her. Her chin came up sharply and her dark
eyes flashed. "Swan Necklace is not a child," she said adamantly. "Swan Necklace is to be the bride of Lean Elk,
war chief of the Chipewyan nation. This is not an honor
given to a child."

"You're right," James said quickly. "I misspoke."

She paid him little attention. Her blood was stirred to anger. "If the white man sees Swan Necklace as a child, then
why did those of his kind make her a slave and try to sell
her for the bedding of other white men?"

"It shouldn't have happened to you, Swan Necklace,"
James said. "That is why I have purchased you and will see
you returned to your father safely."

"Then it is James McLeod who thinks Swan Necklace a
bairn?" she asked flatly.

"Aye, a bairn." He repeated the word gently. "You are
the age of my sister at home. Abby is a child who teases
me to vexation and I pull her braids until she cries and runs
away."

"I see," Swan Necklace said, thinking of the games
played among her friends and families back in the lodge of
her father. "Do you like this sister called Abby?"

James sighed, a long, soft sound that echoed her own
feelings since her capture. "I like her very much," he replied softly.

"I would like to know this sister of yours," Swan Necklace observed. "Her name is strange to me. Abby."

James laughed. "That's not her real name. Sometimes I
call her Gabby Abby to tease her. Her name is Abigail and
she's a bonny lass. Soon the lads'll come down from the
hills a-courtin' her. Then she'll have a cottage full of bairns

herself and the laughter will die from her blue eyes. Life is very hard for women in my country."

"Life is hard for the women of my people. Some of the white trappers make life easier for our women. That is why so many of our women are willing to go to the white men, but sometimes the union is not a happy one. The white men beat the Cree women and sell them to other men."

James glanced at her. "Why do you go to be Lean Elk's bride, then?" He asked the question that had needled him for some nights now. "He is Chipewyan and you are Cree. Why do you not choose a brave from your own tribe?"

"My father has given his word, and I cannot dishonor him," she said softly. Suddenly he wanted her more intensely than he'd ever longed for a woman. He wondered how it would be to hold her tight to his chest and feel her beneath him all *carie* and giving. His gaze met hers and she read the desire in his eyes. The intensity of her gaze shocked him clear down to his toes, yet he knew he must make no move. She felt no anger or fear at this passion in his eyes. Her own heart beat loudly in her breast. Quickly she looked away. One day she must stand before Lean Elk and she must do so with a pure heart. She'd been pledged to him, and if she lay with another man now, she could be killed or disfigured for infidelity.

"The trees tell me about the rain," she said, primly lowering her gaze to the muddy ground.

"The trees?" James struggled to regain his calm. Think of her as one of Abigail's friends, he warned himself. Deliberately he made a scoffing noise in the back of his throat. "First you tell me of vision quests and now you reveal you talk to trees. What's a man to think of a strange lass like you?"

"That I speak the truth," she answered. "Swan Necklace does not lie about the ways of her people or her gods. To do so would bring the anger of the spirits down on her head. I have no wish to do this." She got to her feet. "Perhaps it is best I do not speak of these things to the white man who scoffs at our ways."

James took hold of her wrist to halt her flight. He was surprised at the delicate bones beneath the smooth, brown skin and the hint of strength in her fragile limbs. "I'm sorry, lass, I've offended you yet again," he said softly. His voice was deep with only a hint of the Scottish burr Angus McDougall showed. She relented and turned to face him, a tremulous smile lighting her features.

"Trees talk to each other and to the Indian," she revealed. "They would talk to the white man, too, but the white man thinks himself too important to listen to the trees."

James was silent for a moment, his wide mouth curved in a bemused smile. "You do not think well of the white men."

Her glance was suddenly wary, secretive. "The white man does not think well of the Indians. They pretend to be our friends, but they are not."

"Most of us are," James said, aware of his future task as an emissary among the Indian tribes. He must convince Swan Necklace of their friendly intentions, and she would tell her father, Red Hawke. "Why do you think we are not friends to the Indians?"

Swan Necklace's lips tightened. "Because I do not see the white man sell other white men off as slaves, even when they are enemies as the French and English have been, yet they sell the women of the Indian tribes who have befriended them."

James was silenced. "What you say is true," he answered finally. "Some white men are very bad, but you mustn't judge us all by the bad ones."

"That is what our chiefs have said to the white men about our people. Still, they do not listen, just as they do not listen to the trees." She looked at his hand on her wrist. "Perhaps one day the white man will learn to listen to trees and the other voices of the Mother Earth, and then they will understand many things about the Great Spirit."

"I would like to hear them. I'd like to understand their

messages to the people. Can you show me how, teach me to listen and hear?"

Swan Necklace turned to study his face in the darkness.

"There is much danger for us here, McLeod," she said, and he felt her small body stiffen. Instantly his hand went to the knife at his belt, and he looked this way and that. When he saw no one was near, he glanced at her.

"We carry the danger here," she said, touching her left breast, and then he understood.

"I would not do anything to bring danger to Swan Necklace," he said fervently. "I have made my pledge to return her unharmed to her people."

"That is what you must do," she answered. She pulled away from him then, drawing the slicker around her shoulders and over her head, so it hid her face and form from him. With calm, even steps she walked away from him and made her bed beneath the canoe. He stood watching her for a long time, but she didn't glance over her shoulder at him, nor did she move once she'd rolled herself into her furs. It was as if, just that quickly, she'd put him out of her mind.

But what was he to do? He couldn't put her out of his mind so easily. Cursing to himself, he walked along the river, listening to the steady downpour of rain against the great, unmoving stretch of water and against the leaves of the trees. He thought of Scotland, of the Highlands with their summer heather and the cold winter rains that fell against the trees just so. He crouched beneath an oak tree, choosing it because it towered over the river and scrub. There was no such tree like this specimen in the scrubby Highlands. This one stood like a proud sentinel.

Wrapping his oiled slicker about himself, leaving only his eyes uncovered, he settled himself at its base and stared out at the blue-black darkness. This was a strange country he'd come to, and he felt its challenge in the very flowing of his blood. He felt alive and whole as a man here. He felt like that oak towering over him.

He turned his shoulder in to the tree trunk, settling his hips in a place between the thick roots, and lay thinking of the tree, making himself a part of it. Hadn't the old ones revered the oak once? He remembered a tale brought by a wanderer of an oak copse at Loch Siant on the Isle of Skye that was held so sacred that no man was brave enough to cut even the smallest branch from the trees. Perhaps there was something to all this after all. Perhaps he should try to listen to the trees and see what message they rendered him.

Swan Necklace had already called him a falcon, but if he were to take a name of this place, he would rather it be of the oak, for he was sure he could outlive the mighty tree itself. Fitfully he dozed in his wet, woodsy bed. Near morning, he was brought awake by the impatient call of a bird. He opened his eyes and saw a great white falcon hovering over the river. The rain had stopped and the moonlight gilded the mighty bird's wings. The bird called to him and he rose from his cold bed and followed, wading through the river water to reach the bird. Once he was there, the falcon took him upon his back and flew across the land. James saw rivers and great bodies of water that must be the lakes of which he'd heard so much, and beyond, the Indian villages sprawled along the riverbanks.

"These will be your people," a voice said to him, and he listened with his heart because a little Indian girl had told him he must learn to do so. He listened and he heard the message and he believed it. Now the falcon took him back to the mighty oak tree, where James woke and looked around in bemusement. Had he been dreaming? Yet deep within himself he accepted this vision that had come to him. Slowly he made his way back to camp. The rain had ceased falling and the moon lit the westward passage of the river like a shiny ribbon luring men onward to unknown destinies.

James looked at the small tumble of furs that would be Swan Necklace and wondered what role she might play in his future here in this magnificent land. He would have to be patient and see. He would have to be patient and listen to the trees as Swan Necklace had told him to, for by listening to the trees, he'd brought the great white falcon to him. Tired, he slumped in his own bedroll and closed his eyes. Immediately he fell asleep with no hint of anxiety over what the morrow might bring.

In her warm nest of furs, Swan Necklace had dozed and been awakened by a strange whirring of wings. She had waited, stiff and uncertain. At last she heard James return to camp and understood why she'd waited and been afraid. She knew the great falcon had come to him, just as it had once come to her. It had taken him on a journey and she had been fearful he might not return. Now he lay in his bedroll only a few feet from her, so she could hear his even breathing and knew he slept. She had never thought a white man could have a vision just as the people did. Yet he'd warned her that his grandmother had second sight. Swan Necklace peered into the dark shadows, wondering what all this meant to her and her people.

Chapter 3

JAMES AND SWAN Necklace kept apart in the days that
followed. Though they rode in the same canoe, their
eyes never once met, nor did their faces turn toward each
other. The voyageurs appeared not to notice, all save
Buckley with his quick-darting, speculative eyes. He saw
everything and chuckled to himself that James did not press
his suit upon the little Indian maiden. If James did not, he
determined, then he himself would do so at the first opportunity. So it was, as James withdrew from Swan Necklace,
Garth Buckley pushed forward, his leering smile and bold
glances greeting her at every turn, until she was filled with
a chilling fear.

As they left the Ottawa River and pushed westward
along the French River, rumors became more rampant of
hostile Indians ahead. They'd left behind them the country
designated as belonging to the white man and entered Indian land. The new proclamation line was part of the uneasiness between white man and Indian. In defeating France
and gaining control of land on the new continent, the British had sought to establish boundaries for the southern col-
onists. Likewise they'd created this dividing line with the
intention of permanently separating the white men and Indians. The white men crossed the line with impunity; the
Indians were punished if they did so. Resentments had

grown. Tempers flared. Travel was not as safe as it once might have been.

Still the voyageurs sang as they rowed, still raised their paddles with the same old flourish, but their faces were often grim and watchful as their canoes glided deeper through cool, shadowy forests. One afternoon as they pushed their oars deep into the quiet waters and sent their canoes sailing along the mirrored surface of the river, Angus became aware of movement on the shoreline. Immediately he sent out a short, shrill whistle. In the lead canoe, James heard him and raised his arm in signal to the men. At once the paddles stilled. Not a sound came from the men, not even that of breathing. They were all suspended in a time of wariness. The canoes glided onward, carried by momentum as if propelled by some unseen hand.

"There!" hissed Maurice Byron, one of the middlemen. He was a sharp-witted man with a quick eye and a calm manner. Now he pointed toward the riverbank. All gazes turned in the direction he indicated. A handful of Indians showed themselves on a bluff and quickly disappeared.

"I see 'em, too, the bloody bastards," cried a man called Brody. The men turned back to James for instructions.

"Go easy, lad." Angus had maneuvered his canoe alongside James's, and now he grasped the gunnel and leaned forward so he might speak in a low voice, heard only by James. "They mayna mean us harm. Just go easy like you don't see 'em."

"What tribe are they?" James asked quietly.

Angus shook his head. "Dinna get a good enough look at them."

"Ottawa," Swan Necklace said. "They are the enemy of my people. They make war when there is no need. They hate the white man." She sat gripping the sides of the canoe, her insides quavery. Glimpses of shadowed bronze skin could be seen through black and green leaves. She'd recognized the war paint the warriors wore. It was the same as for her people, black and white and red, the colors of war and death. All in the canoes seemed to be holding their breaths. James's face was all hard angles and unyielding lines as he contemplated their dilemma. If the voyageurs fired, the warriors would retaliate in a shrieking, frenzied rage. If they did not, the savages might attack anyway. Swan Necklace saw the veins throb in James's forehead as he weighed their chances.

"Angus, signal the men to bring out their weapons and put them in plain view, but not to fire."

"Aye, Jaimie," Angus grunted, and let his canoe drift back among the others. Slowly and silently, the men did as they'd been requested, leaning their long rifles against the sides so the canoes bristled with arms.

"Buckley," James called, his voice ringing out in the silent stillness. "Signal the men to take up their paddles."

"Aye, sir," Buckley called, and relayed the orders. Once again the bright red paddles dipped into the opaque gray water and the canoes shot ahead. No one looked to the right or the left, but kept their faces turned forward, their paddles dipping rhythmically. All expected to hear the swish of an arrow or the report of a rifle at any moment.

Swan Necklace felt the muscles in her back stiffen in anticipation of a musket ball, but there was no sound or movement from the riverbank. The woodland warriors remained hidden to all save the most trained eye until the voyageurs were past and out of danger. Then they darted away like some small game creature, intent on their own pursuits. "It's a war party, no doubt about that," Angus said, cutting off a large chunk of tobacco and passing it around. When everyone had his jaws filled with the evil-smelling stuff, he looked around the gathering and spat. "Like as not, they're intent on hitting some lonely outpost or private farmer. We was too fearsome-looking for them."

The other men laughed and allowed as how they'd run off the skunks, but they grew more watchful. None were as careful as Angus and James. Their long rifles were always at the ready, always primed and capped, ready to fire. Whether in camp bent over the cooking fire, or helping to paddle the big canoes through the shallow passes, they were quietly alert to the terrain around them and to any sound or movement that might denote the presence of hostile Indians.

Their meat supply grew low, for they'd meant to supplement it with fresh game along the way. Since their near escape from the Ottawas, the cook had pulled heavily on his supplies and the voyageurs had stayed in camp. This was not fear on their part, but common sense. There was safety in numbers, and they readily acknowledged, if they were masters on the waters and in their canoes, then the woodland Indians were masters of their own forested terrain. James and his men made uneasy allowances for this and remained in camp. Finally, though, they grew impatient, whether from the sameness of their pork-laden meals or from the tension and inactivity instead of meeting their fears head-on.

"We want to go huntin', eh!" one man demanded. He was one of several who'd come in a group to talk to James. "We will take our rifles and go into the woods and bring back a fine deer."

"You are courting an attack by the savages, you know that, dinna ye?" James snapped, glaring around at the circle of hardened men.

"*Mais oui,* boss, we know this. We are not afraid," Garth Buckley spoke up. "We are voyageurs. We are used to danger."

"All right, go ahead, then," James said, knowing he couldn't have held them in camp anyway. "We'll rest up today, mend the canoes and hunt for fresh meat."

"*Bon,* Captain. *C'est bon,*" Buckley said expansively. His small eyes twinkled behind his fat cheeks, but there was no real humor in their depths. Thoughtfully James watched Buckley as he walked away toward his canoe.

"You know, the more I see of that fellow, the less I like him," Angus said.

"He bears watching," James agreed. His attention was caught by Swan Necklace walking up from the river, a filled pouch of water in one hand, her other arm thrown out to balance her heavy load. She was as graceful and beautiful as the snow geese that sailed across the sky and settled their plump bodies on the river water. James felt his breath catch in his chest and looked away.

"Aye, she's a bonny one," Angus said, nodding his head in appreciation as he watched Swan Necklace's slender figure bend and the soft doeskin tighten across her buttocks as she lowered the water bag to the ground. A warning rumble sounded deep in James's chest, and Angus laughed before turning away and picking up his rifle.

"Come on now, lad," he said to James. "No need to stand mooning after a wee slip of a lass like a great *bluntie*. 'Tis best we hunt."

"Aye," James said, and took up his own rifle. Silently the men left the camp. Though Swan Necklace gave them no notice when they stood at the edge of the camp, she had, in fact, been blatantly aware of White Falcon's eyes on her. Now she pressed one small brown hand against her chest to ease her breathing, then set about heating the stones that she would drop into the filled birchbark container to make the water boil.

While the men were in the woods hunting, Swan Necklace took up her knife and, from the slender willows along the riverbank, fashioned a spear, carving one end to a sharp point. Then, slipping out of her leggings and moccasins, she waded into the shallow cold waters of the river and patiently waited for the quick silver flash of fish beneath the water's surface. Time and again her arm flashed through the air, sometimes with success, sometimes without. Still, by the time she heard the first rustle of underbrush signifying the men were returning, she had a goodly pile of river trout lying on the grassy bank. The men came along the edge of the river and she could tell by the lilt of their voices that they'd brought back fresh game. For a moment, standing there, it was as if she were back in her village and her father and his men were returning after a successful hunt. The smell of campfires tickled her nose and she knew there would be plenty of food to eat that night and much laughter and exchanging of tales both old and new as the hunters related how they'd overcome the spirit of the fleet-footed deer and brought it down.

"Aye, what have we here?" called someone, and Swan Necklace felt a tingle as she recognized the deep voice of White Falcon, for such she thought of him now. His tone was light with laughter and good cheer. He had not yet noticed Swan Necklace standing down in the river behind a screen of willows. "The gods have truly blessed us," he called to his men. "Look, the river has cast up its fish for us. If we'd known, we could have waited patiently in camp, resting on our backsides, while the river gave us food." The men laughed and marched on to the camp, carrying their booty. Swan Necklace perceived they would have laughed at anything at this moment, so cheerful were they.

"How can this be?" James said, coming to a halt and peering into the bushes. "Has some river sprite found favor with us?"

"Dinna tease the fairies of the river," Angus called, coming to a stop beside James. "They are fickle and can be easily offended. Ye wouldna have them angered w'ye."

"Nay, I'd not have that," James said. "But I'm wondering, Angus, are the river sprites as pretty as they say? Can they woo a man's soul with but a smile?"

"Come away quick, lad, afore she shows herself, and then you'll be a-knowin' and all the sorrier for it," Angus teased. The eyes of both men were fixed on the ripple of water near the edge of the bushes. Suddenly caught up in the lighthearted play of the men, Swan Necklace repressed a giggle and stepped forward into view.

"The saints be w'us, then," Angus exclaimed. " 'Tis a river sprite."

"And a pretty one at that," James cried. Suddenly he laid aside his long rifle. "Shall we catch it, then, Angus?" he cried, and before Swan Necklace was sure what he was about, he leaped forward into the river, his long, rangy body spread-eagled as he jumped far beyond Swan Necklace and landed in the deeper water. He disappeared beneath the surface and rose at once, sluicing water, so she was forced to dodge to keep from becoming soaked herself.

"White Falcon is like a dog of but a few moons," she cried playfully as he shook himself, sending more droplets of water to fall into the shallows at her feet. "He shakes himself to be dry, never thinking of others. When we have such a disobedient dog, we drive him from the river with our sticks." So saying, she turned her spear so the sharp end was pointed away from him and, raising it high above her head, brought it down on his shoulders. James yelped at the sharp sting and turned with a menacing scowl toward the girl, but she had already gained the bank and was primly gathering her fish, her small nose in the air, her pink lips curved sweetly in a barely repressed smile.

James stood in the water watching her gather her bounty into a newly woven flat basket of green reeds, and something died and came aborning again within him as he noted her tidy braids and slender figure. Then she raised her head and smiled at him. Her dark eyes sparkled beneath the sweep of dark lashes.

By God, she's flirting with me, he thought, and felt elation spread throughout his being. In the meantime, with a last playful glance, Swan Necklace disappeared down the path toward camp, leaving the two men staring after her.

"Aye, lad, ye havena a chance," Angus sighed.

"She's already taken for a wife," James said, as much for himself as for any other.

"And there's the danger," Angus said. "Some of these Indian tribes have mighty funny ways. One minute they're offering you their wives for the night, and get miffed if you turn 'em down. But let 'em think you're dallyin' wi' their wives on your own and they'll kill you and punish their wives, too."

"D'you mean if Swan Necklace and I were to make love, her husband-to-be could harm her?"

"Aye, he could cut off her nose or an ear or just plain kill her," Angus answered, and spat tobacco juice into the river.

"It's barbaric," James said.

"Aye, but it's their law and the one she has to live with," Angus said imperturbably. "I guess that means ye have to live with it, too, lad." Angus walked away down the path, leaving James to stare after him. Some of the warmth and laughter had left the day. In the distance he could see Swan Necklace stooping beside a log, cleaning fish. Her fine head was bent gracefully to the task at hand, her slender young shoulders were high and proud. He imagined her dishonored and mutilated before her people, her face disfigured with the stamp of an adulteress. Her pride would be destroyed. Those young shoulders would drop in shame, greater shame than that from which he'd saved her as a slave.

Why should it matter? he asked himself. He'd determined before she was but a child. No more a woman than Abigail, who'd have to see at least three more summers pass before she'd be choosin' a husband. What did it matter to him that Swan Necklace was already taken by some savage? It was their way. Still the image of her standing in the river, her tunic pulled high, her brown thighs wet and gleaming, her small breasts pressing against the soft doeskin, haunted him all the way to the camp. When he passed the log where she worked and she called to him, he pretended not to hear and went to join his men where they'd opened the rum barrel and passed around the daily rations of drink.

Swan Necklace watched him stalk away and felt hurt that he'd not answered her call. She was certain he had heard her. She'd seen it in the sudden tightening of his shoulders. Why, then, had he chosen not to speak to her when only a short while ago he teased her? Had she offended him with her gibe? No, he'd laughed outright at her impudence, seemingly pleased at her sassy air. She turned her gaze toward him as he sat among his men, drinking and bragging of the deer they'd downed. They were not so different from the warriors in her tribe, who gathered and relived the kill. Yet she knew that White Falcon was different from every warrior she'd ever known, and she understood that he was also different from his own kind. He was a man who stood alone. He truly was a falcon.

Troubled, she bent her head to her task of cleaning the fish. The men had gathered around their kill, hoisting it into a tree to drain and bragging on its size. Eagerly they cast glances back along the river. Some of the men had not yet returned, and they were loath to begin butchering the animal until they'd shown it off to their friends.

"Where did Buckley and his group say they were going?" James called to Brody.

"They was heading further inland," Brody answered. "I warned 'em not to get too far away lest they run into some Indians. They said they wouldn't."

"Maybe they've gotten something, too, and are having trouble bringin' it in," a man called Lyle said. "Maybe we should go look for them."

James glanced at the sloping sun. "We'll give them another hour, then if they're not back, we'll go looking for them," he said.

The men nodded in agreement and set about mending their boats and equipment. But Swan Necklace could tell their hearts weren't in it. They were wondering about their colleagues. She remained busy, deboning her fish and chopping it into fine pieces, then adding some wild onions and herbs she'd gathered near the forest's edge. She was tired of the bland fare of the voyageurs. She would make a dish her mother often made for them. She wished she had some flour made from the acorns such as her people used, but no matter. She would use the coarse brown flour of the white man. It would not be as tasty, but it would do. She scooped a handful and mixed it with her fish, and once again her thoughts turned to White Falcon. She didn't admit it to herself, but she was making the dish as much for his enjoyment as anyone's.

An hour had passed when James signaled to the men and they put aside their tools and gathered up their weapons. He glanced around the camp, his gaze falling on Swan Necklace.

"We don't know what we'll find when we go out there," he began thoughtfully. "We must be prepared for the worst." The men tightened their grips on their weapons.

"Brody, take three good men and stay here to guard the camp."

"Yessir," Brody answered, and quickly picked out three men. They fell out of ranks and stood to one side.

"The rest of you men, follow me," James ordered. His face was grim, his granite features set. At the edge of the camp he glanced back at Swan Necklace, and she felt his worry for her like a protective arm around her shoulders. She sprang to her feet wanting to call out and tell him she would be on guard, that he himself must be careful, but he didn't pause in his long-legged stride out of camp, and though he stood taller than all the other men, their broad bodies soon blocked him from sight.

"We'll skin the deer," Brody said to his three men. They nodded in agreement. All thoughts of pride and rivalry were gone from them now. Two of the men stepped forward with knives and began skinning the animal, while the other took up a position to watch the paths they'd made into camp. No words were spoken. All were tense and went about their business with a singular attitude.

Swan Necklace placed some flat stones at the edge of the fire and went off to gather more wood, taking care not to go too far away from the camp. Dark shadows were creeping up from the river. She had no idea what the men might find out there in the woods, but one thing they all knew for certain: They couldn't get into their canoes and flee this place, at least not tonight. To attempt to negotiate the river at night was foolhardy, for a log or river snag could rip away the bottom of a canoe. When she was certain the stones she'd placed by the fire were heated through, she returned and, taking up her fish mixture, made patties and put them to bake on the hot stones. Carefully she tended them, starting at every sound coming from the forests. When the men had skinned the stag, they cut away pieces of meat, and Swan Necklace helped skewer them on sticks over the fire. The smell of cooking made her stomach clench with hunger, for like the men, she hadn't eaten all day, yet she couldn't think of taking a bite of food until she knew the fate of the men in the forest. Suddenly a noise sounded from among the bushes.

"Who goes there?" Brody called, taking up his rifle and setting the flintrock to full cock. "Call out or I'll shoot!"

"Don't—don't shoot," a voice called, and Garth Buckley staggered out of the dark trees. His face and head were covered with blood and he dragged one leg as if it were broken. Brody rushed forward and Buckley collapsed in his arms. Quickly Brody lowered him to the ground. The other men crowded around.

"*Mon Dieu*, mun, where have you been?" Brody exclaimed. "They're out looking for you." He peered into the darkness. "Where are the rest of your men?"

"Dead, all dead," Buckley gasped. "Injuns. Ottawas, the bleedin' bastards. They caught us unawares."

Swan Necklace had come forward to examine the injured man. His clothes were stiff with drying blood, yet he appeared not to be badly hurt. Only a blunt gouge on one side of his head needed attention. Swan Necklace hesitated, then straightened his leg, testing it to see if it had been broken as well. Buckley didn't even flinch when she rotated it. He was guzzling down a cup of rum, which Brody held for him.

"Tell us what happened, mun," Brody demanded, sitting back on his heels and fixing Buckley with his gaze.

"We were huntin' inland from the river," he said. "Thinkin' we'd be more apt t'find game that way. We were spread out when I heard Marlin down the line. *Mon ami,* you have never heard such a scream, like the man was meetin' the devil himself." There was a rattle of bushes and the people huddled around the injured man jumped and looked around. Brody and his men readied their rifles.

"Who goes there?" Brody cried out.

"Brody, it's Jaimie and the rest of us," Angus McDougall called out. Quickly the men entered the lighted camp circle.

Several of them were intent on carrying a man on a make-shift travois. When they saw Buckley lying beside the campfire they halted.

"Thank God, man, you're alive," James cried, and knelt beside the injured man. "Who else made it back?"

"Just me, Chief, and by the skin of my teeth," Buckley said, and began coughing, clutching at his chest. He stopped abruptly and looked at James. "Someone else escaped the bloody devils. Who was it?"

"Marlin," James said. "I'm afraid he's pretty bad."

"Marlin," Buckley said, and laid his head back in the dirt. His eyes rolled upward and he closed his lids.

"Buckley!" James said, tapping his face to rouse him.

"Is he dead, then?" Angus asked. He had knelt over Marlin, his big hands gently examining the man's wounds. Swan Necklace had hurried to his side to help.

"No, he's just resting," James said, staring down at his voyageur with perplexed eyes. He glanced at Angus. "Wonder how he made it back here when the other men were so badly mutilated."

"He was mighty lucky," Brody said.

"God, look at him. He looks like he's had a bloodbath."

"His only injury was to his head," Brody said.

James shook his head. "He must have fought them." He glanced at Angus. "How's Marlin doing?"

"He's bad, Jaimie. Hard to say if he'll make it through the night. Swan Necklace and me have packed his wounds with some poultices, but he needs a heap of doctoring and a stitch or two."

"Can you do it," James asked, "or shall I?"

"Swan Necklace and me can handle it," Angus said. He smiled at the little Indian girl and she nodded back.

"There's food on the fire for your men," she said.

James nodded curtly and stood up. "We've lost four men and we have two who are gravely wounded. We'll take turns with watches through the night. There's food cooked on the fire. Eat and try to get some sleep while you can. The rest of you take up your guns and stake out a lookout.

Someone will bring you a bite to eat. You'll be relieved in three hours. You'll have three hours to sleep, if you're lucky. After that, we'll pack up. At first light, I want to be out on the water. Any questions?"

No one spoke. Their silence was confirmation of their willingness to do as he'd ordered.

"Put out the fire," James ordered, and someone sprang forward to do as he bid. Now in darkness the exhausted men nibbled the venison they'd so joyfully shot that day and thought of the dead friends whose bodies hadn't been recovered. Other men rolled themselves into their sleeping robes and wondered if they'd make it through the night.

Swan Necklace watched as White Falcon took up his rifle and moved into the dark shadows to find a strategic lookout. Swiftly she gathered up some meat and fish patties and followed him. She found him hunkered down behind a log. He jerked around when her foot snapped a small twig.

"Swan Necklace, go back with the others," he whispered. "It's not safe out here away from camp."

"I have brought you food, White Falcon," she said quietly, and settled herself beside him and held out the repast. He took the meat. He was grateful she was here. They had found no one other than Marlin, no bodies, no sign that the other men had even existed. He was certain as to their fate and he grieved for his fallen comrades. Now with Swan Necklace here, he could force himself to think of something else, force himself to remember there was more to life than terror and death and betrayal.

"You called me White Falcon," he said, surprising her with his observation.

"That is how I think of you," she said. "When we are with others I shall call you James, but when no one is near, I will call you White Falcon. This I have decided."

"You are very quick to decide things," he said.

"My people have learned to do this," Swan Necklace said. "It is best to make the decision at once and go on with the next task in your life. When you are faced with an enemy, you cannot debate about what you must do. You must simply do it."

"That's a good lesson to learn out here," he observed. "Life is so quickly gone from a man." He turned his attention to the dark forest and she knew he thought of his dead men.

"It is better that a man dies this way," Swan Necklace said, "with his weapon in his hand and his face turned to the Great Spirit."

"You take death lightly," James said, his voice bitter with loss.

"Not so lightly as the white men," she answered serenely. "We have learned to accept death as part of our time on Mother Earth. We grieve for our dead, but we rejoice that they will travel the trail to the Great Hunting Grounds. Perhaps your men have gone there, too."

"Great Hunting Grounds!" James repeated. "A fool's death."

Swan Necklace was hurt by his scornful words, but she held her anger in check. "The white man is unable to accept that which must be accepted," she said, and raised her gaze to the star-studded night sky. "The white man does not see that we are part of the earth and sky, the rivers and forests. We are here for only a short time. The Great Spirit allows us to walk the earth, to have power over the animals and fish so we might eat of their flesh and live. The Great Spirit gives us strength to meet our enemies with honor, and if we are unable to overcome our enemies, the Great Spirit guides our spirit back to him. The white man thinks of himself alone. He thinks he is in charge of the fate of his fellow men. In this way, he makes himself a God. Perhaps for this reason your men fell. You have angered the spirit that rules the land."

"Your gods are not mine, Swan Necklace," James said wearily.

She was silent for a moment. "Did you not believe the vision of the great white falcon who came to you?" she asked finally.

James jerked his head around and glared at her. "How did you know?" he demanded.

"I heard the whir of wings and knew the falcon had taken you," she answered. When he made no response, she got to her feet and turned toward the camp.

"It wasn't a dream," she heard him say, but she didn't pause to answer him. There were many things the white men must learn about this land they'd invaded. Some of it they must learn by themselves.

Swan Necklace returned to the fire and checked on her two patients. Buckley was sleeping deeply, his breathing even and untroubled. Marlin's sleep was ragged and shallow. Swan Necklace moved her bedroll close to the injured men and crawled inside, but she was awake for a long time. Just as she had become foggy with sleep, she heard a sound, a grunt of pain, and raised her head to look around. No one stirred except Garth Buckley, who had sat up and was now pulling his covers around himself. As she watched, he lay down again and soon was asleep. Swan Necklace listened for a sound from Marlin, but he was resting peacefully as well. She lay back in her robes and closed her eyes.

Chapter 4

A SOUND WOKE her. She opened her eyes. Darkness shrouded the campsite. To the side there were whispers and movement. Swan Necklace sat up and peered through the darkness. She perceived men moving about in the shadows. Down by the river, the canoes had been tipped aright and the goods were being reloaded. She turned back to the blackened circle that had once been a campfire, to the pallets that held the wounded men. Someone knelt over them.

"Wake up, Buckley," James said brusquely. With a snort Buckley sat up.

"What is it?" he demanded.

"Marlin's dead," James said. "Did you hear anything during the night?"

"No," Buckley said. "I never woke up once." The burly oarsman glanced at his dead companion. "Poor Marlin," he said softly. "I heard him scream, you know. He must have seen the devils comin' and tried to warn us."

James looked at him sharply. "You say he called to you?"

"He called out once and then he screamed," Buckley said. "I got to him as fast as I could, but he was down already and the savages was upon me, like bees after pollen, a-jabbin' at me and cuttin'."

51

"Yet you sustained no cuts or injuries except the bump on your head," James pressed him.

Buckley's eyes got big and round. "*Sacrebleu!* I thought they'd lifted m'scalp," he yelped. "I went down next to Marlin, half-unconscious, and knew enough to play like I was dead. I thought they might take my scalp, but they went screaming off after the next man." Buckley looked from James to Angus. "That's all I remember. I passed out. When I come to, I was alone. Marlin was gone. I figured they'd taken him and was comin' back for me, so I crawled off through the brush. When I thought I was far enough away from 'em, I got up and ran like the very devil himself was after me, 'cause in truth, I think he was."

"All right, Buckley," James said to still his flow of words. "God knows we're grateful you're back." He looked at Marlin, and the lines of his face deepened with regret. Then he glanced at Swan Necklace and some of their conversation came back to him, releasing him from the self-anger he felt. The darkness with all its hidden dangers pressed around them.

"We won't take time to bury him now," James said.

"You can't leave him here, Jaimie, for the animals to get at. It won't set well with the other men."

"We'll take his body with us," James said, and before any protest could be voiced over that, he stood up. "We've been lucky that the savages haven't found our campsite already. We dare not take the risk to stay longer. Have Marlin wrapped in a fur robe and put him in the last canoe."

"Aye, Jaimie," Angus said, and waved a couple of men forward to care for their fallen companion. Silently the men readied the canoes, and by the time the first gray light streaked the horizon, they pushed off from the bank and made their way to the middle of the river, where there was less danger of being shot at from the banks and less danger of snags and floating logs. There were no songs, no cheerful cries. The men were silent, dark, silver-edged silhouettes gliding silently on the quiet water. No one drew an easy breath until the sun had come up and they were many miles down the river.

May had long since passed into June as the rowers labored under the hot sun, pressing their canoes deeper into Indian territory, moving ever westward toward the Great Lakes that lay curled and graceful in their beds. They buried Marlin one night along the riverbank in a deep grave of sand and shells, then moved on.

Eventually they took up their songs again and their teeth flashed white in quick grins; ribald jokes were called back and forth. Life went on. Buckley recovered quickly from his wounds and soon took up his paddle and his assumed mantle of authority. There were no further incidences with renegade Indians, so they began to relax again, believing the danger behind them. Then one afternoon when the sunlight lay sparkling on the water and the bird calls were sweet and clear, a cry sounded from the riverbanks. They'd stumbled across a hunting party.

"Keep low," James called. "They can't reach us as long as we stay in the middle of the river."

Still the Indians followed them, running along the riverbank and sending shafts of arrows and musket balls into the air. Most fell short of the line of canoes, but some found their marks, thudding into the birchbark sides. A cry sounded along the line of canoes.

"Boss, someone's hit," Buckley called.

"Keep rowing," James ordered. The canoes moved along swiftly. No one felt any real dread. In the canoes they could outrun the Indians on foot. Then they rounded a bend in the river and caught a glimpse of several canoes awaiting the Indians' return.

"Christ Almighty," Angus swore. "We're in for it now."

"Keep paddling, men," James shouted. "We have a head start."

"It won't mean much when they reach their canoes," Angus hollered from his canoe. "They ain't loaded down like we are. They can go faster."

"We have no other choice," James bellowed. "Move."

He'd taken up a paddle as well, and the water hissed in white rebellion at his mighty thrusts. The laden canoes raced down the river. Swan Necklace looked back at the Indians who'd gained their lighter, smaller crafts and were now pushing them out into the main current. High-pitched yelps accompanied their actions as they leaped into the painted and decorated birchbark vessels and took up their paddles. Their pursuit was swift and purposeful.

"They're gaining on us," Swan Necklace cried.

"Faster," James shouted. The men redoubled their efforts, but the larger, heavily laden canoes couldn't outrun the Indian rigs. The water churned around them and it took some time before Swan Necklace became aware that the current of the river had become swifter and white water churned around them.

"Rapids ahead," Angus yelled.

"Keep the boats moving," James hollered, and not one paddle faltered. In the head of each man was the memory of his comrade left behind on the riverbank. If this hostile band overtook them, they could hope for little mercy.

The raging white water caught hold of the heavily laden crafts, propelling them forward with greater speed than the men could have garnered with their paddles. Now the voyageurs used their paddles to deflect the boats from the rocks that jutted treacherously from the shallow river bottom.

"James!" Angus shouted. His voice could barely be heard above the racing water. "The boats kinna last in this."

"Don't stop," James roared back. The lead canoe led the way through the rapids, pitching and roiling like a child's toy in the great wash of water. Swan Necklace clung to the sides of the boat, her eyes wide and fearful, yet accepting, for she knew they had no other choice. The other crafts followed, the men doing their best to keep the vessels turned straight ahead.

The first waterfall was shallow, yet the canoe rocked dangerously before resettling itself in the river. Before they had time to think of the damage the boat had sustained, they were racing toward the next one. Swan Necklace felt her heart stop beating as the canoe bow pushed forward into empty air, then they dropped, lurching and slapping the water with stunned force, so she was nearly thrown over the side. Despite his preoccupation with the rocks, James looked back and gave her a tug to right her on her seat.

"Hold on," he ordered, and so compelling were his words that she nodded her head and determined that nothing other than death itself would dislodge her from her seat. The next waterfall was shallow and sloping. They rode down it like a sleek brown Indian boy sliding down a bank on a sunny summer day, then they were at the bottom.

"Paddle," James ordered, and the men set their oars in the water, pushing away from the rapid spillway of the waterfall and the slapping arrival of the next canoe. When they were several feet away, James ordered his men to a halt and they waited in a shallow backwash, watching as the other canoes shot over the final rapid and settled into the river.

"Paddle. Keep going," he called. "We'll rendezvous downriver."

"Our canoes are leaking," Brody called. "We need to do repairs."

"We can't risk it now," James called back.

"The Indians didn't follow us," Lyle called. "I saw them pulling in to shore before we hit the first waterfall."

"They'll be coming around by land thinking to pick up the pieces," James shouted. "Head downriver." The men picked up their paddles and glided away.

James waited until every canoe was over the falls. Two didn't make it. Their birchbark sides splintered against the rocks, sending their supplies to the bottom of the river and catapulting the rowers into the water.

"Let's pick them up," James called, and paddled his canoe back into the main river. The extra men were taken into the last two canoes, where they sat looking sheepish at their loss.

"What about our supplies?" Maurice called. War whoops

sounded along the bluffs of the river, but no Indians were in sight yet.

"Leave them," James ordered. "Maybe the savages will be satisfied with what they find down here."

The canoes, overly laden now with extra men, limped downriver several miles before James dared to pause and look at the damage they'd sustained.

"We've lost most of our food supplies," Maurice said with some disgust. He was the one who prepared most of their meals, and he was normally a jovial man with snapping, laughing eyes.

"We lost some of our trade goods, beads and axes and whatnot," Lyle called.

"What about our extra ammunition and our firearms?" James inquired.

"Gone," Angus said somberly. "We have only what we carry here, and some of the men lost their rifles in the river. What powder we have is wet through. We're in pretty bad shape." The men looked at each other speculatively, but no one spoke. James knew they were all wondering if they would have to retrace the dangerous miles they'd crossed to return to Montreal, or go on to even more dangers where the lack of proper food, arms, and trade goods would leave them vulnerable to the whims of the Indian tribes.

"Tend to your canoes," James ordered, and grim-faced, the men turned to their tasks. Maurice and his assistant, a round-faced young voyageur of twenty or so, affectionately called Wye, made a fire and began drying out things. Toward evening they prepared a skimpy meal from what food supplies they could find. No one suggested hunting for fresh game. James ordered an extra allocation of rum to be passed around that evening. Ironically, the rum barrels had come through the ordeal unscathed.

Gratefully the men accepted this extra portion and settled themselves by the fire to talk and rest. This had been a hard trip, they agreed among themselves, and they'd met far more difficulties than normal. They began to speculate among themselves that the expedition was cursed.

"Iffen I'd known at the beginning, I wouldna have signed on," one man said.

"*Enfermez!*" cried Lyle. "Shut up. This talk is no good now. We are here and we must do what we must do. Our leader is a good man. He is strong and brave. We will be safe."

"*Oui,* Lyle is correct. We must not lose our courage now," Maurice said, and several of the men nodded in agreement. All of them liked the tall, young Scotsman who led them.

Later, James came to hunker down beside them and talk. His gray eyes studied each man in the lighted circle, weighing what he'd come to know in these past weeks about each man's loyalty and steadfastness.

"We have come a long way," he said at last. "To turn back will do us little good, for we must run the gamut of the hostile renegades we've already encountered. I think it's best for us to go forward. Swan Necklace tells me the Chippewa will help us replenish our food supplies against the winter. When we push on to the Red River area, we should meet up with some more friendly Indians. The girl's family tribe will be in the area. She assures me we will be welcomed and given shelter."

"We're with you, Chief," Buckley called, and the other men nodded and vowed their allegiance. With a final nod, James rose and walked down toward the river. Swan Necklace left her place by the fire and glided along the trail behind him. He'd gone to a place that was quiet, far enough from the camp to lose the sounds of others, yet close enough so he could quickly return if there was any trouble. Swan Necklace paused on the bank, studying the silvery river and the dark outline of trees on the distant shore.

"You did very well today," James said from the shadows. "You were courageous."

"Could I be anything else when the White Falcon and his men acted so bravely?"

"I'm surprised you think us brave, when we fled the weapons of your enemies."

"Sometimes it is best to flee and fight again another time," Swan Necklace said. "We were outnumbered and these were not the warriors of the Ottawa. These were renegades, troublemakers who are not welcomed even in their own villages. They have been corrupted by the white men. They are no longer true children of the Great Spirit."

"Are you saying the Ottawa would welcome us if we should arrive in their midst?"

"The Ottawa are angry with the British soldiers, for they do not honor their own agreements. That is why their chief Pontiac has attacked your forts and villages."

"It has been the same in my country. My ancestors fought the English, who wished to take over our lands. Much blood was spilled there. I wonder if this fighting will ever be done."

"And in my country as well, White Falcon. Once, these were the lands of the Indians; now they belong to the men in red coats who come from a faraway land of their own. They come for the bounty of the Mother Earth, but they desecrate her and do much dishonor to her. For this reason alone they should not be here."

"Yet you and your people help the white eyes to take foothold here. Why do you do this, Swan Necklace?"

"Because we have come to want the things of the white men."

"Do you mean the beads and wampum?" James asked softly.

"Our warriors desire the firearms and the firewater of the white father," Swan Necklace said softly.

"And what do the women desire of the white man?" His voice was soft yet unyielding. Swan Necklace felt tongue-tied before the directness of his question. He stepped forward out of the shadows and put his arm around her shoulders, drawing her back against him. She felt the long, sinewy hardness of his body and remembered the stamina and endurance he'd shown on the river. He was a man among men and he spoke to her heart in a way no other had. Her pulse raced and she leaned against him, melding her body to his.

"The women of my people must be the same as your own women," she whispered. "We desire the things of a woman's heart, things that are secret and not easily spoken of." His head lowered. She felt his hot breath against her cheek, then his lips touched her temples. His hands slid downward, seeking and finding the soft mounds of her breasts. His long fingers closed around her flesh, caressing it through the soft deerskin.

"A woman's secret desiring is not so different from a man's," he said. His breath was hot and quick against her ear. Her heartbeat thundered in answer. He turned her to him then, pulling her against him, lowering his mouth to plunder hers. His firm lips were cool and demanding against her own, his tongue dark and probing. Her thoughts were lost to her. When he lifted her in his arms and carried her up the riverbank to a place of privacy, she made no demur. She sought what he sought, a surcease from the raging desire that burned through her veins.

James placed her on a mat of grass and bent over her, his gray eyes sweeping over her face. "You are so beautiful," he whispered. "You are in my thoughts all through the day."

"I think of you as well, White Falcon," she whispered. Her small, brown hand came up to smooth along the edge of his jaw. His bones were long and heavy. Even in his face they showed strength more than beauty. He lowered himself to her, pressing her back against the grass, kissing her with fierce passion. His hands fumbled beneath her doeskin dress, gliding across her soft flesh until he once again found her virginal nipples. His hands were gentle on her, soothing even; his mouth was not. His tongue swirled over her nipples, raising them to hard peaks, and his teeth closed over the dark aureola, suckling until she whimpered from pain and desire.

"Have I hurt you?" he whispered, drawing back.

"No," she answered, smiling in the darkness at his gentle

concern. "It is just that I am not yet used to a man's touch."
She hugged him to her, but she felt the desire drain from
him. He lay stiff and unmoving for a long time, then slowly
pulled her buckskin back into place.

"What is wrong, White Falcon?" she asked softly, her
small hands smoothing back the thick black hair from his
brow. "Have I said something to displease you?"

"Swan Necklace," he cried, and she felt his pain coming
from some deep well. Slowly he rolled away from her. "I
cannot dishonor you in this manner," he said.

She remained silent beside him. She knew what he said
was right. She risked Lean Elk's rage. She should be grateful to him, but disappointment ran deep.

"You are a child," he said in weary anguish. He was
tired of fighting this battle within himself. "You are promised to another. Angus has told me what your husband
could do to you if you were unfaithful to him."

Swan Necklace bowed her head in shame. "It is true,"
she said. "Even now, I have dishonored him by my willingness to lie with you, White Falcon. You must think me a
woman of low morals."

James was startled by the sophistication of her words.
"What do you know of morals?" he asked.

"Just because my skin is not the same as yours does not
mean I have not laws that must be followed," she said
primly.

"I spoke unwisely. Angus has told me something of your
laws. I do not judge you lightly, Swan Necklace. It is myself I blame. I've shown little character and have not kept
my pledge not to bring harm to you. Come, I will walk you
back to the fire."

Swan Necklace rose and stood before him. Their bodies
swayed as if drawn together, but they turned away and
walked apart back to the camp without saying another
word. The rest of the men had already turned in, save for
those on sentry duty. James waited in the shadows until she
had settled into her bedroll, then he turned back to the river,
pausing to speak briefly with the sentry on duty. He did not

see the gleam of eyes that watched Swan Necklace as she readied herself for bed.

Garth Buckley watched the little maiden, imagining what she might have been doing out in the darkness with James. Then he thought of her small body, nude and pliant beneath his own, and his member hardened and throbbed in anticipation. One day very soon, he would have the girl, he promised himself.

They left the Ottawa River behind them, moving into the narrower French River, then portaging overland to the Georgian Bay and thus into Lake Huron itself. South lay Fort d'*Étroit*, but James and his party had no desire to go there. They turned westward toward the northernmost of the five lakes. For the first time in weeks, they felt free of the threat of an attack. The Indians here were known to be friendly to the white traders.

The first night they camped along a sandy shore, stopping early enough for the men to hunt for game. Swan Necklace set snare traps and returned to camp with three rabbits, not enough to feed such a large gathering of hungry men, but she made herself a digging stick and gathered some groundnuts, or wild bean vines, as they were called by some tribes. They were not as tender as those gathered in the spring, but they would do well for a stew. She gathered the potatolike pods and scrubbed them in a nearby stream and pulled wild onions from the riverbank. When she'd assembled all her supplies, she took up a bark utensil that she'd made early on in their voyage, filled it with water, put in the rabbit meat, groundnuts, and onion, and dropped in hot stones to start it boiling. By the time the men had returned to camp with their venison, her pot dish was giving off a delectable aroma.

Now that danger was behind them, the voyageurs returned to their old ways, charming and flirting with Swan Necklace, bringing her a bouquet of flowers or singing her a ballad. All of them knew she was being returned to her husband and was not available to any of them, but they relished having such a comely Indian maiden in camp. They hadn't forgotten how she'd nursed Buckley and Marlin when they were injured or the extra dishes she'd made to supplement their monotonous fare.

Now, with fresh venison roasting on the fire, a vessel of rabbit stew, and a mug of rum, they settled around the fire, jovial and of natural good cheer. They exchanged tales, and each tried to outdo the other in brave deeds or narrow escapes from hostile Indians.

Talk flowed, laughter came easily. The fire hissed and spit, sending up plumes of smoke and great orange sparks that drifted upward and dissipated in the night air.

Sitting across the fire, James surreptitiously studied Swan Necklace, noting the curve of her cheek, the glossy sheen of her blue-black braids, the slender shoulders. He remembered the surprising fullness of her breasts on one so small and dainty. The memory of them filling his hand caused a response that was near pain.

He glanced away and for the first time encountered the lust-filled gaze of Garth Buckley as he sat staring at the young Indian girl. James's hands balled into fists and he fought the urge to leap across the flames and beat the other man's face to a pulp. Something in Buckley's expression warned James to pay closer attention to Swan Necklace's safety in the days ahead.

As if drawn by James's anger, Buckley turned his head and met the Scotsman's gaze. Buckley read the rage in the other man's eyes and knew a moment's fear. To come up against James McLeod was something he wouldn't relish. Quickly Buckley turned away and said something to his companion, engaging him in conversation, but long after the moment passed, he felt the probing gaze of the White Falcon against his back.

From her place by the fire, Swan Necklace saw the interchange between White Falcon and Garth Buckley, and she shivered a little. The voyageur had become bolder over the past few days, deliberately crossing her path so closely that their shoulders brushed. Often she was forced to come to a halt to keep from walking right into him, for he planted himself in her path. When she withdrew, her eyes wide and uncertain, he would laugh, an ugly sound meant to reassure her, but it had the opposite effect. Now she wished ardently that Buckley would be warned by White Falcon's expression that he was not to approach her.

The talk of the men flowed around the fire circle, but she'd lost her interest in it. Getting to her feet, she walked down to the lakeshore to watch the moonlight on the water. It lay all golden and shimmery. The air was sweet, filled with promises for young lovers, making her restless for things she could not have. She heard a sound behind her and whirled, gasping in fear that it might be Buckley, but the moonlight shone on broad shoulders and a lean torso, and instinctively she knew it was White Falcon.

"Swan Necklace?" he said in a low voice, and she heard his longing, as deep and untouched as her own.

"White Falcon," she cried, and ran to him. His arms closed around her and he held her tight. He made no attempt to claim her in any other way. There was contentment in just holding one another. They stood wrapped in each other's arms, looking at the moon on the water, until the night air cooled and a mist crept over the lake, then slowly they walked back to the campsite and went to their lonely separate beds.

The camp rested, secure in the knowledge that it had left all dangers behind. No one heard the occasional slap of a paddle against water or the scrape of a birchbark canoe being drawn across sand. No one knew the enemy was in the camp until the red men stood over them in the clear gray dawn.

Exhausted, James had fallen into his bedroll and closed his eyes, striving to shut out the image of Swan Necklace as she bent to a task or the sweetness of her in his arms. He made his mind blank and slept heavily. Only well-served instincts saved him from the stone ax that descended toward him. He sensed someone stood over him before he was fully awake. Without thinking, he rolled and heard the

thud of a weapon against the covers where moments before
his head had lain. Lashing out with his legs, he connected
with something solid. He heard a grunt and the warrior who
stood over him fell to the ground.

Dashing sleep from his eyes, James leaped to his feet,
fixing his mind on the enemy who strove to kill him. All
around him was noise and confusion of a one-sided battle
as his men tried to fight off the surprise invaders. The warrior was on his feet, his club in one hand, a knife in the
other. His face was painted and fierce, his black eyes red-
rimmed and unwavering in their promise of death. James
circled, his empty hands held in front of him. He watched
the warrior's face and braced himself when he saw signs he
was about to attack.

With a wild, abandoned cry, the Indian brave sprang forward, his sharp club raised high, his knife low and deadly.
James advanced, one hand up to ward off the warrior's
blow, the other low to grab hold of the knife hand. He
clasped the warrior's strong wrists and arched his lean
body, struggling to bring the warrior down. The two men
pitted their strength for a moment, then James feinted a
move to the right and rolled, carrying the savage with him.
When they stopped rolling, James was on top and the warrior's hand that carried the knife was clasped against his
chest, the point scant inches from his own neck. The warrior's eyes widened with the knowledge of his own death.
James leaned against the hand and the point drove deep
into the warrior's throat. He gave a final death rattle and
went slack beneath James.

James didn't wait to see the death of his adversary. All
around him were the cries of his men as they died or fought
back. James grabbed the stone club from the dead Indian's
hand and stood up. Automatically he struck out, killing
another warrior and grappling with another before bringing him down. The sounds of battle had lessened. James
threw himself across the body of a dead Indian and reached
for his long rifle. He managed to get off one shot before a
brave raced toward him. James stood up and met the attack,

using his rifle to bludgeon the Indian. The warrior fell to the ground.

James's sharp gaze swept around the campsite, looking for Swan Necklace. She was nowhere in sight. Already warriors were tearing into the packs of supplies, while the voyageurs were being herded to one side as prisoners. Angus was among them. James let out a rallying cry, the cry that Highlanders used before they leaped into battle, but his men were too disheartened and unprepared for the attack.

Swan Necklace had slept fitfully, so when the first alien cry sounded, she sprang up and looked around. The campsite was surrounded by the enemy. She saw their death masks, their war paint, their weapons of death, and she cried out. The sound was lost in the cries of the men around her.

She looked across the fire ring and saw White Falcon rise from his pallet, his strong, sinewy body arching against the strength of an enemy brave. She saw the two warriors struggling and instinctively turned to do what she'd been taught since childhood. While the warriors fought off the enemies, the women and children fled and hid along the river bluffs. There were no bluffs here.

Swan Necklace crawled into the brush. From there she could see the battle raging between the voyageurs and the renegade Indians. Wye, that gentle young man who'd been teased so by his comrades, fought valiantly but was soon overpowered; a stunning blow to his shoulder sent him to the ground. Swan Necklace pressed her hands to her mouth to keep from crying out. She'd liked the young voyageur with his sparkling brown eyes and shy smiles, and she prayed to the spirits that he had not been killed.

A man screamed in pain and she crawled forward to peer into camp, her gaze automatically seeking White Falcon. He stood tall and unscathed, legs anchored in a wide stance as he swung an Indian club. Dead warriors lay at his feet. He had laid aside his shirt while he slept, and now she saw his smooth skin rippling over taut muscles. Beneath his shirt, he was very white, she noted, like all the white men when they took off their shirts. She'd never been so aware of their racial differences until this moment, but the thought spiraled away from her as she watched him fight. Never had she seen such a fierce, brave warrior. Her heart exalted in his triumphs.

She was so engaged in watching White Falcon, she forgot her own safety, unaware an enemy warrior had spotted her until he leaped forward and gripped her arm, pulling her from her hiding place with a triumphant cry. She fought against him, struggling to free herself, but he pulled her forward into the melee.

"Swan Necklace!" She heard White Falcon's cry. He leaped forward trying to get to her, but a warrior ran forward, blocking his way. James swung the club round his head as he'd seen the warriors do and let it go. It smashed into the warrior's face, crushing all features to a bloody mass. Swan Necklace saw White Falcon struggling to reach her. The light in her dark eyes flared with hope, then died as she glimpsed another enemy warrior spring up behind him and raise his weapon. She screamed a warning, but too late.

James felt the fiery pain as something hit him across the back of the head. He felt the warm river of blood, his blood, pour down his neck and shoulders. The ground seemed a long way down, and before he felt it meet him, he saw Swan Necklace being dragged toward the enemy canoes.

"Swan Ne—" he shouted before darkness claimed him.

Chapter 5

WHEN HE WOKE, he felt the crushing weight of pain in his head. He lay still, not moving, keeping his breathing as shallow as possible while he assessed what went on around him. He could hear the crackle of the fire and guttural voices around it. The Indians were availing themselves of the leftover venison and rabbit stew.

He raised his lids halfway and cautiously watched the renegades. They had indeed built up the fire and were seated around it, relaxed and laughing. Their faces still bore the black war paint. Only white circles had been left around their eyes, making their bloodshot eyes appear more fearsome. They wore leggings and loincloths, decorated with porcupine quills. Their heads had been shaved save for the topknots in which feathers and beads had been tied with strips of rawhide. Even their bare chests and arms had been blackened with the charcoal and grease mixture.

James wondered if all his men had been killed. Where was Swan Necklace? Swan Necklace! He groaned at the thought of her. Immediately one of the Indians rose from his place at the fire and walked over to him. James didn't move as the man stood peering down at him for a long moment. Finally shrugging, the Indian kicked James in the chest and moved back to the fire.

"Jaimie, boy, is that you? Are you alive?" Angus called from someplace on the other side of the fire. A warrior

67

rose, shouting an ugly curse in the direction of Angus's voice. James felt relief flood through him. Angus had been kept alive, and if he had, so had some of the other men. Swan Necklace was not here. He knew that as surely as he knew that he'd been dismissed as dead. Before unconsciousness had claimed him, he'd seen a warrior dragging her toward the canoes. So why hadn't the rest of the band followed? Why were they still here? What would they do with their captives?

He lay listening to the guttural language, wishing he could translate. By listening carefully, he could pick out some things, words that Angus had taught him. From what he heard, he surmised that Swan Necklace and the bounty they'd captured had been taken away to a neighboring village. These warriors were to bring the rest of the prisoners and the barrels of rum. They'd paused long enough to imbibe of the white man's firewater. As they sat passing the jugs, their voices became more belligerent and they began to quarrel among themselves.

Desperately James felt around, seeking some form of weaponry. He must rescue his men and find Swan Necklace. A terrible rage at his helplessness caused a roaring in his head. His hand encountered the head of a war club dropped by a fallen warrior. Slowly he began working it from beneath the dead man's body.

The voices became louder and coarser. One Indian called Wawatam seemed more hotheaded than the others. Leaping to his feet, he shouted at his comrades, as if prodding them toward something they did not themselves desire. Finally another warrior rose and left the circle of warriors, passing out of James's field of vision, but soon he could hear a shout of protest from one of the voyageurs.

"Leave him be, you heartless buggers," Angus cried out. The sound of a blow made James clench his teeth and pray that the burly Scottish trapper would keep his mouth shut and not bring more retribution down on his head. The chosen captive was brought to the fire pit. James barely opened his lids. He had to see what was about to happen to his men and who was the first to be chosen for the torture that was sure to come.

They'd picked a man named Travis, a quiet, hardworking man, James remembered, not given to the braggadocio of the other voyageurs. Now he stood with his head down like some defeated animal who dumbly awaited his fate. James saw the bloody wound in his side and guessed the man was too weak to offer resistance and for this reason had been selected.

With a cruel grin, the hotheaded warrior called Wawatam stepped to the fire and took up a small glowing brand before approaching the wounded man. James worked frantically trying to free the club. He had to do something. Travis was a good man. He didn't deserve what was about to happen to him.

The warriors around the fire called out comments to the weaving man and laughed uproariously. With a wild yell, Wawatam danced around the fire, shouting and waving the flaming brand menacingly.

Travis's eyes were dull with pain as he regarded the leaping, screaming savages. Suddenly, amid a cloud of sand, Wawatam threw himself across the clearing at the captive. Travis fell to the ground and the Indian was upon him, straddling him, his brand raised.

James's muscles bunched beneath him as he fought the urge to spring up and throw himself, weaponless, at the savage. Discipline alone made him stay where he was. He needed a weapon or he would be their next victim of torture. James could hear the wounded man's sobs.

James yanked at the handle of the war club, felt it break free, and in one mighty lunge, sprang to his feet. His head roared with pain, and dried blood crackled and flew away from his shoulders with each movement. None of this mattered. He thought only of rescuing Travis, of ending another human being's suffering. With a wild Highland cry, he swung the war club around his head and let it go, aimed directly at Wawatam.

Startled, the other warriors turned to look at this fierce

warrior risen from the dead. In that moment of confusion James's war club struck the warrior standing next to Wawatam directly in the head and he fell at their feet dead. The stunned Indians looked at their fallen comrade and back at the white spirit that could not be killed. With a wild cry of fear and superstition, they fled away from the fire, running this way and that. Wawatam and his closest comrades gained their canoes and pushed off toward the center of the lake. Other warriors ran along the lakeshore and into the water, swimming with long strokes toward the departing canoes.

"That a lad," Angus cried. "I knew ye wasna dead, Jaimie."

James took no time to answer or to loosen the other captives. He knelt at once beside Travis, who cried out in anguish. His wound was fatal; his dying would be long and painful. Mutely the hapless voyageur gazed up at him, unable to voice his plea. James hesitated only a moment and raised the war club. His arm had to be strong, his aim true, to save this man from more suffering. When it was finished he sat with his head bowed over the dead voyageur.

"Quick, Jaimie, unloosen us before the devils come back," Angus cried, for already the Indians were creeping back to the campsite to see what the white spirit was doing. James leaped across the clearing and fumbled with the knots, but Wawatam had rallied his men and again they entered the camp, overwhelming the voyageurs as soon as James had freed them. James raised his club and uttered his homeland cry as he had before, but this time the Indians would not be frightened by him. They faced him, their weapons at the ready, their gazes wary but determined.

"It's na use, lad," Angus called. "Ye might as well give y'self up. Ye'll be na good to us dead."

James gazed about the ring of warriors and thought of Travis. For what they had done to him alone, he wanted to fight on, but common sense prevailed. Angus was right. They had to try and live. Reluctantly he dropped the war club. At once the Indians sprang on him, beating him with

their fists and even their clubs, but no blow was hard
enough to bring him death. In the midst of that beating,
James understood he was to be kept alive. He thought of
Swan Necklace and, for the first time since their capture,
felt hope.

They carried her away in a canoe. When White Falcon
fell beneath the weapon of the renegade warriors, she
stopped struggling, going limp in the hands of her captors.
Surprised, they released her, staring at her in puzzlement. A
swaggering warrior came forward. His markings were
fierce and he carried himself with authority. The other warriors called him Shemung.

"What are you doing here? Why are you with the white
men?" he demanded roughly, and she understood his words,
for the Ottawa and Cree languages were not so different.

"The white men rescued me and were returning me to
my village," she answered haltingly.

"What is your village?" the tall, fierce warrior demanded.

Suddenly she realized they had been unable to determine
her tribe, for her skins were bought in Montreal and did not
bear the markings of her people. She drew her shoulders up
and faced the warrior proudly.

"I am Cree," she answered. "My father, Red Hawke, is
chief of the Cree. I am to be the wife of Lean Elk, war chief
of the Chipewyan. My father will reward you if you release
my friends, the white men, and let us go on our way." White
Falcon was dead, but many of his men were not. She would
show the brave warrior honor by trying to help his men.

"She lies!" A warrior stepped forward, his weapon raised
as if he might strike her. "She sleeps with the white chief.
I saw this myself when we trailed the white men." His eyes
held a cruelty to which she was not accustomed among her
own people. Wawatam reminded her of Lean Elk.

She edged away from him, but the warriors on either
side jerked her back. Stoically she stood before him. "I

have not been dishonored by the white man," she replied, her gaze unwavering in its innocence.

Shemung regarded her with dark, measuring eyes. "How did you come to be with the white men, if you are to be the wife of a Chipewyan chief?" he demanded.

"On the way to my new husband, I was kidnapped by the French and taken to Montreal," Swan Necklace explained. "White Falcon was returning me to my people."

"Who is this White Falcon?"

Swan Necklace was silent for a moment. "He is the white chief," she said in a low voice.

The warrior known as Wawatam smiled, his teeth glistening yellow against his black paint. "I have killed this white warrior known as White Falcon," he bragged.

Shemung nodded in approval before turning back to his captive. "What are you called?"

"I am Swan Necklace," she cried, and for good measure repeated her kinship to great chiefs, "daughter of Red Hawke of the Cree nation, wife of Lean Elk, war chief of the Chipewyans."

"She lies!" The fierce warrior waved his weapon at her.

"Wawatam!" Shemung called a warning at mention of the Chipewyan war chief. Though their land was farther northwest from the Great Lakes, the ferociousness of the tribe was not unknown. With a vehement slash of his arm, Wawatam moved away. Shemung stood thinking. Swan Necklace could almost see what he was contemplating. She was an important captive. If she were harmed or injured, her father or her future husband would call down the wrath of their nations on these renegades. At last Shemung made up his mind.

"Put her in the canoe. We will take her to our village at Isle du Castor," he ordered several of his men. "We will trade her back to her tribe for much wampum."

The two warriors seized her arms and led her away toward the lakeshore and the waiting canoes. They passed the huddled voyageurs. Swan Necklace met Angus's gaze and peered over her shoulder toward Wawatam. The grip the two warriors had on her shoulders propelled her feet forward.

"What about the white men?" she called back to the war chief. "They are my friends."

Shemung made no answer. The warriors jerked on her arms, making her stumble. She fell to her knees not six feet from Angus and the others.

"Dinna worry about us, lass," Angus said. "Save yerself if ye kin." The other men remained silent, but she could see the hopelessness in their eyes. Wye, the young voyageur who'd brought her flowers, didn't even blink in recognition, merely stared into the distance. His shoulder wound oozed blood.

"I will try to help you, Angus," she whispered in English before she was once again snatched to her feet. The warriors herded her down to the shore. Rudely she was shoved into a canoe and made to lie on the bottom. Three warriors got in and began paddling.

Miserably she huddled in fear for what seemed like hours. The sun rose overhead and burned hotly, parching her mouth. She begged for water and the warrior laughed and pointed to the lake. Swan Necklace sat up and dipped her hand in the cold, clear lake water and drank. The lake water felt good on her dried tongue, but before she could dip a second time, the warrior grunted and kicked at her, forcing her down on the bottom of the canoe again.

She guessed they were trying to keep her from seeing her surroundings, but she'd glimpsed enough. She lay shielding her eyes from the glaring sun with her bent arm, trying to discern where they were taking her. As nearly as she could tell, they were heading southeast through the narrow gorge into the bay that the white men had christened Georgian Bay.

Late in the day, the warriors paused in a secluded outlet and allowed her to sit up. Bread was offered her, cut with the same knives that had slain the voyageurs who had been her friends. One warrior saw the expression of disgust on her face and dipped his bloodied blade in the water and smeared it across the bread before handing it to her. Swan Necklace's stomach churned. She knew it was the practice of some tribes to eat the hearts or even to drink the blood of their enemies, but she could not abide the thought of such barbaric actions now. However, she knew if she refused the bread, more would not be offered. She took the bread and held it in her hand, surreptitiously tearing away the blood-smeared exterior and eating the uncontaminated center. She must keep up her strength.

Once again she drank from the lake, letting the blood-soaked pieces of bread float away from her. When she was done, the warriors forced her to lie down in the bottom of the canoe again. They traveled until darkness lay across the water, then paddled toward land.

Swan Necklace was tied to a small tree and left alone as the warriors built a fire and gathered round it to eat and drink and boast of their exploits. The night air grew chilly and she shivered in her thin deerskins. Rolling herself into a ball, she tried to sleep, but the memory of White Falcon and his valiant battle against the renegades haunted her.

She remembered how brave and tall and invincible he'd seemed, the look on his face when he saw she'd been captured and the sight of his big body falling under the war club of the enemy. She longed to tear at her hair and clothes and mourn his death, but knew it was wiser for her to remain as silent as possible with her captors.

She turned her tearless gaze to the sky and watched the stars cross the heavens. There was no comfort there. The stars of Father Sky no longer shone down upon the White Falcon. She thought of her vision and of the night White Falcon had been visited by a vision as well. She had thought him invulnerable. What had happened? In their love for one another, had they displeased the spirits? Was this their punishment? She wept then, pressing her face into the dried leaves to muffle her sobs.

When morning came the warriors forced her into the canoe and once again took up their paddles. Hours passed. Her muscles cramped from the lack of movement. She half dozed in the heat. When she woke the sun had passed beyond its zenith and was seeking its bed far to the west. A fog had covered the distant horizons, melding water and sky into one. She raised her head high enough to peer over the edge of the canoe.

They could not traverse such a large body of water in a fog. Shemung seemed to recognize this, for he motioned his men to turn and follow the shoreline. She guessed they were too far south to be traveling the northernmost basin of the big water. The voices of her captors held a note of excitement, and she guessed from the things they said that they were approaching a village. Within minutes, several men raised their voices in a shrill warning. When someone answered from along the shore, the warriors laughed and paddled with renewed vigor. The fog had deepened. A bluish haze had settled over the water and land. Swan Necklace could smell the smoke of campfires.

The canoes were paddled close to shore. The warriors disembarked and pulled them upon the sand, then motioned Swan Necklace from the canoe. Obediently she rose and followed them. Other warriors ran to join them as they made their way to the village square. Shemung motioned one of his men to stay with the canoe. At a harshly spoken command, two others got back into a canoe and pushed off from shore.

Around the square sat conical tepees made of sheets of birchbark tied over a frame of sapling poles. Sheaths of reeds were placed around the bottom perimeter of the tepees. Swan Necklace was familiar with these structures, for such were the summer homes of her own people. They were not in an Ottawa village, she realized. The fog had caused them to take refuge with a Chippewa band.

The Crees and the Chippewas were brother tribes of the Algonquin-speaking people. Her fear lessened as she passed among the people. The women and children turned to stare after her as she was led to a lodge that sat apart and was surely that of the chief. The birchbark flap was pushed aside and a tall, well-made man of some years stepped out.

His headdress of feathers and his painted robe showed he was a figure of authority. Swan Necklace cast her gaze down to the ground and waited for him to speak.

"Welcome, my brothers," the old man said slowly and with great dignity as befit his status.

"Greetings to Manitowa, chief of the Chippewa." The Indian struck his chest. "I am Shemung, war chief of the Ottawa."

"Does Shemung come to make war on the Chippewa?" Manitowa asked.

"Shemung comes with a prisoner, which he will trade to the Chippewas."

Manitowa studied Swan Necklace. "She is but a woman. We do not need women slaves," he said finally.

"I have other prisoners as well," Shemung said. "My warriors follow with them. They bring much bounty from the white men."

"The Ottawa are still at war with the white soldiers?" Manitowa asked in some surprise. "It had come to us that Pontiac, chief of all the Ottawa, will smoke the peace pipe with the redcoats."

"Pontiac, pah!" Shemung spat on the ground. "Pontiac has lost his heart to fight the English. We carry the secret war belts from one village to the next. We will drive the English from our land as Pontiac has not been able to do." He smiled at Manitowa. "Perhaps the Chippewa would like to join the Ottawa in their fight against the hated English."

Manitowa shook his head. "We have put down our weapons. We will live in peace with the English."

Shemung made a scoffing noise. Manitowa held up his hand.

"Once, we were friends to the Frenchmen. We helped them to find the beaver in our streams. The Frenchmen and the redcoats fought one another and the Frenchmen surrendered. Now they are at peace with the English, and we must learn to be at peace with them as well."

"We will have no peace with any white man," Shemung cried. "The white men take our lands. They cut down our forests and build fences where once we hunted. Now the Ottawa go hungry. We will drive them from our land and live as we did before the white man came."

"The Chippewa will not fight beside his Ottawa brother," Manitowa said firmly. "We will honor the treaty Pontiac and the other chiefs make with the redcoats." He turned away from Shemung's angry face. "Who is this small woman captive you have brought to us?"

Swan Necklace raised her head and met the old chief's gaze without flinching, but she did not speak. She would if she must, but for now she remained silent.

"She claims she is the daughter of Red Hawke, chief of the Cree nation."

"I remember Red Hawke," Manitowa said. "He is a wise man. What is your name, woman?"

"I am called Swan Necklace," she answered.

"How did you come to be with the white man?" the old chief asked kindly, but his black eyes were lively and intelligent. She knew he waited to see if she spoke the truth. She told him of her betrothal to the Chipewyan war chief and of the Frenchmen who kidnapped her. She explained how White Falcon and his men had befriended her and were returning her to her people. Shemung grew impatient as she spoke of her vision of the White Falcon, but Manitowa nodded his head wisely.

"This warrior known as the White Falcon is a brave and wise man," he commented. "Such a man would speak well between the white man and the red man."

"He was a fair man," Swan Necklace said, and her voice caught so she had to pause before continuing. "Now the White Falcon has been killed by the Ottawa warriors, but his men are alive. They have been my friends and they will take me to my father. He will be most grateful to have his daughter returned to him."

Manitowa nodded. One gnarled hand came up to rub absently at his chin. He glanced at Shemung. "Manitowa will trade for the Cree woman," he said. Swan Necklace's face revealed her relief, then she thought of Angus McDougall and the rest of the voyageurs.

"And the others?" she asked quickly. "They mean no harm to the Ottawa or the Chippewa tribes. They wish only to pass through your lands on their way to the land of the Cree."

"Where are these men?" Manitowa asked.

"My warriors are bringing them," Shemung answered. Swan Necklace glanced at him with dawning hope.

"Then they *are* still alive?" she asked.

Shemung only glanced at her and did not deign to answer.

Manitowa nodded at the war chief. "Come into my lodge. We will smoke the pipe and agree on our trade of the white men." The two men went into the chief's lodge and the flap was closed behind them.

Swan Necklace was left standing in the midst of the villagers, surrounded by Shemung's warriors. She tried to remain calm as she thought that her fate and that of White Falcon's men rested on what the two men inside the birch tepee decreed. The fog had swirled up from the shore now, softening the shapes of the lodges and the faces of the villagers themselves.

Swan Necklace glanced around at the curious faces. One girl, about her own age, smiled timidly. Her eyes danced with good humor and inquisitiveness. Swan Necklace smiled back. She wondered who the girl might be. She was very pretty and her sleek, dark hair was plaited with strips of fur and shells. Her dress was made of three skins and well decorated with dyed porcupine quills of red, yellow, and black. Swan Necklace guessed she was the daughter or wife of an important man in the tribe.

The lodge flap was thrown aside and Manitowa and Shemung stepped out. Swan Necklace studied the faces of the two chiefs, wondering what had been decided about the fate of the voyageurs. Shemung nodded to the old chief and strode from the encampment. At once his men followed, leaving Swan Necklace behind. Without revealing anything of what had occurred, Manitowa returned to his lodge. Now the villagers pressed closer to her. The pretty girl she'd noticed earlier came forward.

"*Venez,*" she said, motioning to Swan Necklace to follow.

"You do not need to use the language of the French. I am Cree. Our tongues are not so different," Swan Necklace said, speaking in the Algonquian-based tongue.

The girl giggled, a sound not unlike that of melting ice against the lake's rocky shore in springtime. Swan Necklace was enchanted.

"There are some differences in our languages," the girl said, "but it will be much easier to speak in our own tongues than that of the bearded white men."

"You do not like the white men?" Swan Necklace asked, which brought another gale of tinkling laughter from the girl.

"The white men are funny-looking with their pale skin and hairy faces," she replied. "And they walk about thus as if they were gods." She strutted a bit, moving her shoulders in an exaggerated parody of the white men's swagger. She halted, dissolving into giggles. "You are called Swan Necklace," she continued. "That is very pretty."

"My mother wished me to be called so," Swan Necklace said. "I came in the spring when the great white swans had returned to the lakes and streams. She thought they were a symbol of good fortune for me."

"And your father allowed your mother to so name you?"

Swan Necklace smiled and nodded. "My mother, Beaver Woman, was wise and well regarded beyond her years. She was my father's first wife and he listened to her advice. He was greatly saddened when she went away to the land of the Great Spirit."

"I am saddened, too," the girl said, her pretty face somber.

"What are you called?" Swan Necklace asked. The girl paused before a tepee, her eyes flashing with laughter again.

"I am called Yellow Leaf," the girl answered. She drew aside the birchbark covering. "Come inside." Swan Necklace bent low and stepped inside the conical dwelling. The lodge was dark and cool. Light filtered in from the smoke hole and the entrance, for Yellow Leaf had left the covering thrown back. A woman sat in the middle of the earthen floor holding a small sleeping child.

"Mama, this is Swan Necklace," Yellow Leaf said. "She is to stay with us. Father has traded for her from the Ottawa warriors."

"Welcome to our lodge, Swan Necklace," the woman said. "I am called Walking Woman."

"I am honored to share your lodge, Walking Woman," Swan Necklace said. She looked around, uncertain of what was expected of her next.

"Please sit down," Walking Woman said. "Yellow Leaf!" She nodded to the girl, who giggled and hurried to one side of the lodge. Very soon she was back with a bone cup filled with water. Gratefully Swan Necklace took the cup and drank.

The water had been sweetened with maple sugar. Greedily she gulped it down, then realized how bad-mannered she had seemed. She hung her head, but Walking Woman grinned in understanding. By that time Yellow Leaf had returned again and placed a bowl of food before her. Swan Necklace's stomach rumbled with hunger. Other than the bread, she'd been given nothing to eat since her captivity. However, she forced herself to nod to her hostess and to use some dignity as she picked up the bowl and began to eat the rice, which had been boiled in a syrup made from the sap of woodbine.

Walking Woman and Yellow Leaf said nothing while she ate, but the small child who'd been napping woke, sat up, and stared at the stranger with large round eyes.

"This is Grasshopper, my little sister," Yellow Leaf said when Swan Necklace had emptied the bowl and set it aside. The little girl smiled shyly and leaned back against her mother.

"Tell me what has happened to you," Walking Woman said. "How did you come to be captured by the Ottawa?"

Swan Necklace told her story again, ending it plaintively with a cry of frustration. "I do not know if Chief Manitowa intends to trade for my friends or not."

Walking Woman smiled. "Like Yellow Leaf, you must learn patience, Swan Necklace," she chided softly. "Manitowa will trade for the white men. He wishes to have peace with the white men. He will be their friend and help them." Her dark eyes glowed softly. Swan Necklace saw that she, too, was a handsome woman, an older version of Yellow Leaf and Grasshopper.

"How can you be so sure?" Swan Necklace asked dubiously. "Manitowa said nothing when he and Shemung left the lodge."

"That is so," Walking Woman replied. "But do not fear for your friends, Swan Necklace. Manitowa will trade for them from the Ottawa and they will be safe in our village. Manitowa will send for Red Hawke and you will be returned to your people. I know this because I know Manitowa. He is a great chief and he is my husband."

Swan Necklace leaned back on her heels and regarded Walking Woman. Something in the other woman's calm demeanor reassured her. For the first time in days, the fear of death or captivity drained from her. She had managed to see to the safety of Angus and the other voyageurs. Her joy was short-lived, however. She thought of White Falcon and silently grieved because the White Falcon had fallen in battle.

Chapter 6

*T*HEY WERE LEAVING! Under Wawatam's watchful eye, the captives were herded down to the canoes. The goods had already been loaded into their own birchbark vessels. The heavier Montreal boats had been smashed and abandoned.

"Why did they destroy our canoes?" James whispered to Angus. "Why didn't they keep them for their own use?"

"Too big and bulky for the Indians' taste," Angus whispered back. His face was scraped and bleeding on one side. One eye was swollen nearly shut. Looking at his friend, James felt rage and pushed it down. He'd tried outright attacking them and had been overpowered. He had to be more subtle and wait for the right time. His lips tightened. He had to wait in the hope that he'd find out something about Swan Necklace.

The captives were shoved into the boats, cuffed and beaten when they didn't move quickly enough, and ordered to take up the oars. Wye shivered and slumped against the side of the canoe, unable to pull himself inside. One of the warriors shouted and kicked him several times before Angus tugged him into the vessel. The burly voyageur glared at the warrior, then saw that James was watching him. Almost imperceptibly James shook his head, admonishing restraint. Without a change of expression, Angus picked up the paddle and waited for the order to cast off from shore. The other voyageurs did the same.

In short order they were paddling away from the sandy shore, heading eastward again.

"Where are they taking us?" James asked Angus in a low voice meant to reach only his ears. Neither man paused in his rowing.

"They're takin' us back to the lands of the Ottawa," Angus grunted between strokes. "They have a village at Beaver Island."

"That's south of where we are," James said in amazement.

"Aye, at the mouth of Lake Michigan."

"Do you think Swan Necklace has been taken there?"

"I dinna know, lad," Angus said sadly.

James fell silent, thinking. They paddled day and night. The Indians seemed unconcerned with hitting snags on the broad expanse of water. James recognized that they'd retraced their route back to the Georgian Bay and turned south almost at once. The canoes moved swiftly, silently, pausing only when a fog crept over the land. Wawatam held up his hand, indicating the canoes were to halt, then conferred with one of the other warriors. They argued heatedly, then pressed on, turning westward along a densely wooded shoreline. He was uncertain how long they traveled. His shoulders ached from the pull of the oar, and thirst nagged at him. He longed to reach over the edge of the canoe and scoop up a handful of water, but he was ever mindful of the warrior seated behind, his knife a constant threat.

A call sounded from out of the fog, and once again Wawatam motioned the canoes to a halt. He sat listening until the call came again, then placing his hand to his mouth, he returned the cry. When it was answered with a series of calls, the Indians chattered excitedly among themselves. James perceived they'd feared becoming lost in the engulfing fog. With renewed purpose, the canoes moved forward, and the Indians uttered loud, piercing cries.

"They're lettin' their friends know how many captives they have," Angus said from farther back in the canoe. One

of the warriors shouted harshly and buffeted him across the
head.

"Don't talk, Angus. I need you alive, not dead," James
said, and didn't flinch when his own captor struck him. The
two men fell silent; only the sound of the paddles dipping
into the murky water could be heard.

Finally a canoe approached from the opposite direction,
appearing out of the fog like a specter. Wawatam spoke with
the new arrivals, shaking his head vehemently. At one point
he cast a glance toward James, and he perceived he was being discussed. He watched them closely, trying to decipher
what was about to happen, but the fog swirled around them.

The two warriors finished speaking. Wawatam nodded his
head and waved his men to follow. The new canoe turned
around and led the way. Now and then the Indians gave a
hoot, which was answered from out of the foggy darkness.
They passed other canoes, which fell into line with them.
They had strung out a line of canoes to act as guides, James
surmised.

A group of warriors ran down from the shore and seized
the front of the canoes, helping to haul them in to shore.
With nudges and cuffs, the prisoners were urged out of
the canoes and herded onshore. James was tense. Now and
then through the drifting fog, he caught glimpses of campfires. Was this the village where they'd brought Swan
Necklace? A warrior shoved him, separating him from the
other men. Wawatam spoke harshly, waving his arms.

"He wants us to follow him," Angus translated. The other
men moved forward, taking turns helping Wye. Buckley
seemed to hang back. James noted no one prodded him. He
started to follow his men, and one of the warriors shouted
something and raised his hatchet in warning. James halted
and stared at him, a feeling of dread washing over him.

"What are you doing with my men?" he cried. Without
answering, the warrior shoved him backward so he sprawled
in the sand. It was pointless to demand answers, James realized. These renegades didn't understand the white man's
tongue, and he hadn't had time to learn theirs. Wearily he got

to his feet, but the warrior clubbed him on the shoulder so he sank to his knees again, then knelt to tie his hands and feet.

James fought back the black shadows that threatened to claim him. He must stay alert. With a great show of nonchalance he sat down in the sand, crossed his hands over his raised knees, and regarded the warrior with a black glare of his own. The warrior looked away first as James knew he must.

Time passed. He heard no cries of torture from the village, so he began to relax, supposing his men to be safe. The warriors who guarded him had relaxed their stance somewhat now. Some stretched out on the sandy shore and soon fell asleep; others lounged on the ground talking and laughing among themselves. Nothing more would happen, James perceived, until morning.

Finally he lay back and closed his eyes. When he opened them, dawn was a gray light over the foggy horizon. Quickly he sat up and looked around. The other warriors were still sleeping. Even his guard leaned against a piece of driftwood, gently snoring. James wriggled and worked at the coarse rope binding his feet. The knot gave and he looked around. No one seemed to have noticed.

He took no time to bite at the knots binding his hands, but got to his feet and crept toward the canoes. Choosing one farthest from his guards, he pushed it into the lake, and when he felt the current tug at it, he clambered in and lay down flat. The canoe floated away from the shore.

James remained where he was for some time, then lifted his head and peered over the side of the canoe. There was no sign of pursuit. He used his teeth to loosen the knotted cord and free his hands. Taking up the paddle, he dipped it in the water and felt the painful protest of sore muscles. But he'd escaped the Indians and he had a canoe. The new freedom was exhilarating until he thought of Swan Necklace and Angus. He must somehow find a way to free them.

White Falcon was alive. Angus had said so! She'd stood at the edge of the village square with Yellow Leaf and watched as Manitowa and Shemung bartered over the white men. Finally they reached an agreement and the pipe was passed between them. Only then did she dare approach Angus. She'd slipped to the side closest to the old trapper and called his name.

"You're alive, lassie," he said, unable to keep the elation from his voice, although his gaze remained straight ahead and his expression revealed nothing. "James will be happy for that."

"White Falcon? Oh, Angus, is he alive?"

"Aye. If he hasn't taken it upon himself to fight the red devils down by the lake and been killed."

"I must go see," she cried.

"Nay, lass. Not now," Angus admonished in a low, urgent voice that caught her up.

"Why?" she whispered with dread.

"Something's going on; I dinna ken what it is. James fought like a wild man back at the campsite. I dinna ken if they fear him or if they want to trade him separately for more goods. They're guardin' him close. Have a care."

"I am grateful, Angus," she whispered, and crept away. She was still uncertain what Manitowa intended to do with Angus and the other voyageurs, but she guessed they were better off with the old Chippewa chief, rather than Shemung. She crept back to the tepee she shared with Yellow Leaf and her family. That night she dozed fitfully and woke with a start.

All was dark within the lodge, but a pale gray light filtered in from the smoke hole. She could just make out the figures of Walking Woman, Manitowa, and Yellow Leaf. Soon the village would stir and her chance to see White Falcon might be lost. Rising, she crept from the lodge and, keeping to the shadows, made her way down to the lakeshore.

Pausing behind a clump of scrub willows, she peered at the figures stretched out on the sand. In the gloom, she couldn't make out which one was White Falcon. Then one of the figures moved and she was able to tell it was he. She had to hug herself to keep from running forward and throwing herself into his arms. He was alive and she must view him from afar. That she would do in order not to further endanger his life. Through her tears she noted that he moved about on the ground, then suddenly threw aside his bindings and got to his feet. She opened her mouth to cry out his name, and as quickly pressed her fingers to her lips. Heart pounding with joy to see he was unharmed, she watched him crouch and look around, then run down to the water to claim a canoe.

Quick and purposeful were his actions; she hardly knew what he was about until the canoe had been shoved into deep water and he'd tumbled inside. He ducked down in the canoe so she could no longer see him and the current swirled past, quickly carrying the light birchbark vessel farther away from shore, until the fog swallowed him up.

"White Falcon!" she whispered behind her hand. Tears poured down her cheeks. He was gone! He'd escaped. She should be grateful that he was alive and free, but she felt disconsolate, abandoned. Wiping at her cheeks, she turned back toward the village.

He didn't know where he was going. He'd never been in a wilderness so vast. Vaguely he remembered the maps he'd seen. They'd just reached the mouth of Lake Superior when they were attacked. The Ottawas had carried them east and then turned south. To the south lay the long body of Lake Michigan, to the north a dark, wooded peninsula. The current had carried him westward, and when he'd begun paddling, he'd continued in that direction.

His memory of the maps he'd seen told him that the shoreline would eventually curve to the south. He would have to put in to shore if he was to find his way back to the village and rescue his men. He had no idea what he could do. His first thought had been to escape. Now he needed to rest and make plans. Besides, if the Ottawa came after him, they could easily overtake him on the water. His best chance was to hide. He angled the canoe toward shore and pulled it behind a clump of scrub willows. A flutter of wings and a nasal birdcry signaled the protest of a black tern that resented this intrusion so close to its nest. James ignored it and peered through the willow brush. There was no sign of pursuing canoes.

The sun had burned away the fog by now. It shone down hot and unrelenting. Clouds of mosquitoes rose from the long grass. James slapped at them, cursing the small insects that had caused his men much discomfort. He found a spot beneath a tree and lay down. He was exhausted and hungry. Without a weapon, he hadn't much of a chance of hunting game, but he could rest and be ready, should Wawatam and the others come after him.

He sprawled in the grass, cradling his head in his arms, and tried to sleep. His thoughts were too full of the Indian attack, concern for his men, and worry over Swan Necklace. A delicate yellow butterfly landed on the pink bloom of a pasture thistle. Its wings moved languidly in the warmth of the sun, and he thought of Swan Necklace bending to dip water from the lake. She was as delicate and beautiful as that butterfly, yet was able to find a place in this savage wilderness. He remembered what she'd said of white men not taking time to see the Mother Earth and all its bounties.

He let his gaze stray to other wildflowers, the slender branch of chicory with its delicate pale blue flowers, the yellow, spiky flower of the goatsbeard, which closed its petals at noon, and the pokeweed bush, heavy with its deep purple berries. Along the lakeshore were patches of purple loosestrife, and tiny white seedpods from the wild lettuce blew in the air and settled on the water. He saw the fragile beauty and thought of Swan Necklace. His mind was emptied of turmoil and he slept.

When he woke, the sun was higher and his mouth was parched. He stumbled down to the lake and dipped his hand in the cold water. A cry from the water brought his head up. He squinted against the glare of the sun. Several Indian canoes were approaching. James could make out the figure of Wawatam in the lead canoe. The Indian shouted again and motioned the canoes toward shore. A hail of arrows fell around James, even as he leaped to his feet and ran toward the woods. Branches tore at his face and clothes as he scrambled through the underbrush. He could hear the savage yelp and cry of the warriors as they leaped out of their canoes and chased after him. At first he ran easily, as if he were not part of the ordinary world and he were not an ordinary man. He felt tireless. He could run forever through the forests, knocking aside the stubby willow scrubs, slender saplings, and thorny berry bushes. He was invincible. The clear air made him heady. His legs churned, his heart pumped blood and oxygen throughout his body, and he believed he could escape.

The land tilted upward in a gradual sloping hill and still he ran on. He could hear the shouts of the warriors behind, like the yowls of a demon over a dark moor. Still he seemed to be drawing away from them. He renewed his efforts, dragging air into his lungs. He crested the hill and came to an abrupt halt, grabbing hold of a sapling to keep from going over. The ground fell away hundreds of feet below. His momentum carried him forward, so his legs left the safety of the cliffside and his body swung sickeningly into space before crashing back against the rock and dirt wall. Stones rattled down on his head and disappeared without a sound into the void below.

James clung to the spindly sapling and waited, hardly daring to breathe. Every muscle quivered with exertion. His grip on the sapling slipped minutely, reminding him he must do something. He couldn't hang there indefinitely. With superhuman effort he began climbing up the side of the cliff and at last threw his leg over the edge. When he was safely back on firm ground, he lay drawing in air, listening to his heart pound. The warriors were upon him. He heard them coming, but could summon no strength with which to fight them. And there was no place left to run.

Triumphantly they fell upon him, kicking and cuffing him before stripping him of his clothes and binding his wrists with a rope of twisted basswood fiber. They marched him back to the canoes, finding great sport in tripping and knocking him down several times along the way. When they thought he lagged, they prodded him with the sharp tips of their arrows. His back and buttocks were soon covered with bleeding cuts. As they neared the canoes where sentries had been posted, a figure sat up in one of the canoes and called.

"Jaimie, lad. You're still alive."

"Angus!" James answered in spite of the blow one of the warriors aimed at his head. "Where are the other men?"

"Back at the Chippewa camp with Swan Necklace," Angus answered. One of the sentries was already leaping toward the trapper.

"Did you see Swan Necklace?" James shouted, dodging another blow. Wawatam was among the warriors. Now he rushed forward and raised his stone weapon and aimed it at James's head. James ducked. The weapon missed his temple but landed on his shoulder, stunning him and driving him to his knees. Wawatam raised his weapon once more, intent upon delivering the killing blow, but another warrior shouted harshly. Wawatam stood with fierce black eyes, his weapon drawn back.

"Wawatam!" The Indian spoke again, and slowly the warrior lowered his weapon. James guessed the first warrior was a chief of some sort. He motioned the warriors back to the canoe. Quickly James got to his feet and took a step forward before they could prod him from behind. Angus was lying down in the canoe, forced there by the sentry who'd sought to shut him up. Blood welled from a blow on his head, but his gaze was fixed on James.

"She's alive!" James whispered. Almost imperceptibly Angus nodded, then flinched as if expecting another blow. When none came, he was emboldened to speak.

"Aye, lad. She's safe in the Chippewa village."

Relief swept over James, so he nearly stumbled getting into the canoe. A sharp blow with a willow stick brought his attention back to his own dire situation. He was unbound and a paddle thrust into his hands.

The warriors filled the canoes and paddled back out into the lake, but they didn't turn back to the village where they'd spent the night, the village where Swan Necklace and his men were.

James cursed under his breath. He longed to talk to Angus, but feared bringing more punishment down on his friend. Throughout the day they rowed, without food or water. James swallowed and ran his tongue around his mouth, seeking any drop of moisture. It seemed especially cruel that neither he nor Angus were allowed to drink when they traveled through clear water.

They approached a tongue of land that jutted into the water, and there sat an Indian village not unlike the one where they'd stayed the night before. The warriors gave two war whoops and an Indian appeared and signaled them to land. James and Angus were dragged from the canoe and paraded through the village by the yelping warriors. The villagers gathered and their shouts were hostile, their eyes unfriendly. Some of the women ran forward with sticks and beat the two captives about the shoulders and head. When one woman would have swung her ax at James, Shemung stepped forward and harshly ordered her away.

After that, the hostility of the villagers seemed to quiet somewhat. They wandered off to their campfires. James could smell the kettles of food, and in spite of the danger, his mouth watered. He'd eaten nothing for two days. Shemung led them to a lodge and shoved them to the ground outside. After tethering them with a rope about the neck, he stalked away, leaving Angus and James alone. Wawatam glared at them from a distance. James glared back, and after a while the menacing warrior went away. For the first time they were able to talk without fear of punishment.

"How are you, lad?" Angus asked immediately.

"Better than you are," James replied, glancing at the blood-encrusted head wound. "It's a wonder the bastards didn't kill you."

"Ach, it'll take more than a red heathen devil to do in

my thick skull," Angus said. "You sure riled 'em up when you took that canoe and made your escape."

"I should have kept going. I was a bloody fool to get caught again." James cursed.

"Dinna say that," Angus said. "You have na knowledge of the land. They do. They would have found you eventually."

"Maybe. Maybe not. I was fearful of getting too far from the village where you and Swa— the men were. I thought I'd go back and rescue you all."

"Seems they're not needin' rescuin'," Angus informed him. "Especially Swan Necklace. Seems like the Chippewa and the Cree are friendly to one another. Manitowa has already sent a messenger north to the Crees informing Red Hawke his daughter is safe with the Chippewas."

"Thank God for that," James said, breathing easier. "What about the other men?"

"That little Indian lass has taken it upon herself to nurse Wye and the others back to health."

"How is Wye? Was he badly wounded?"

"Pretty bad. He'll make it if Swan Necklace has her way. In the meantime, the men are guests of the Chippewa, slaves, you might say, although Manitowa would never admit to it. He's bent on making peace with the English regardless of what the Ottawa do." He glanced at James. "So it's you and me, friend. How do we get out of here?"

"We watch and wait," James said. "And when we get the opportunity, we steal a canoe and escape. In the meantime, we rest." He lay back on the ground, curling himself into a ball against the evening chill. He was still without clothing of any kind.

Angus watched him for a moment, noting the long, heavy bones, the lean muscles bunching beneath the pale skin. Nude as he was, the power of the man seemed more evident. Angus shivered, and guessing that James felt the dropping temperature even more without any covering or clothes, he moved closer to his friend, lending him what body heat he could.

Sometime later, they were awakened by the drunken revelry of the villagers. Both men sat up, feeling uneasy, for both had heard of the atrocities committed by the Indians when they were under the influence of whiskey or rum.

A shadow moved out of the darkness. James leaped to his feet, jerking against the fibrous rope. His fists balled, his leg muscles twitched, as he readied himself for an attack. Wawatam staggered out of the shadows. His eyes were black and unfocused. His expression was ugly and mocking as he stepped toward James. He shouted at James and pulled a knife from the sheath at his waist.

"What did he say?" James asked without taking his gaze off the drunken Indian.

"He said you do not look like a White Falcon," Angus interpreted. "He does not think you are equal to the Ottawa warriors."

"Tell him to cut me loose and we'll see who is the best warrior," James said without breaking eye contact with Wawatam. "Tell him it's easy to be brave when one's enemy is tied." Angus interpreted his challenge, and James saw the warrior's eyes narrow with rage.

Grimacing with evil intent, Wawatam circled the two men. Angus scrambled to his feet, but Wawatam appeared to ignore him. His attention was pinned on James. With a wild cry he sprang toward him, his knife raised. James lunged forward to meet his attack, but the neck tether jerked him backward. He felt his breath constrict, felt the rough fibers tear at his throat. Still he strained to meet Wawatam's attack.

One large hand clamped around Wawatam's wrist, halting the knife in its downward plunge. The men struggled against each other. The rope around James's neck held him back. His head pounded with the need to draw a breath. He jerked backward, falling to the ground in a rolling motion that sent Wawatam flying over his head. The warrior fell on his back with such force, the knife was knocked from his hand. Angus snatched up the knife and hid it beneath his shirt.

Both men leaped to their feet and faced each other. The glare from Wawatam's eyes was murderous. James crouched, his long back sloping, his knees bent ready to meet any further attack. From out of the darkness, Shemung appeared. Scowling, he shouted at Wawatam. The drunken warrior did not back down. For some time they argued. Finally Shemung drew his knife and waved it menacingly. Warily Wawatam backed away. His face was dark with anger. With a final harsh shout, he turned and strode away.

Shemung watched him go, then glanced at his captives. James still stood, his head up, eyes defiant. Shemung disappeared inside the lodge and returned with a pair of worn leather leggings and shirt, which he threw on the ground before James. He also tossed down some pieces of dried jerky at them, much as he would have tossed a few scraps to his dogs. Since a dog was nearby, Angus snatched up the dried meat and held it against his chest. James had said nothing, merely staring at Shemung challengingly. He'd already perceived that the best way to remain alive with the Ottawa was to display bold courage.

Shemung spoke to him in hard guttural words, then turned toward the square and the revelry there. James remained on guard until the chief disappeared from view. Only then did he reach for the cast-off leggings and shirt. When he'd donned them, he sat beside Angus once more and took up a piece of the dried jerky. Angus glanced around. No one in the village paid them any attention. Cautiously he raised his shirt, displaying the Indian knife Wawatam had lost.

"He'll come back for it," James warned.

"Aye, but he'll na find it," Angus said, and used the blade to dig a hole in the ground near the back of the lodge. When it was big enough, he put the knife inside and covered it over, taking care to erase any sign of anyone having dug there. James watched closely, taking note of where the knife was buried.

"What did the great chief, Shemung, say?" he asked.

The burly man shrugged. "He said he has saved your life."

"I wasn't in danger!" James snapped.

"Aye, he knows that," Angus replied. "But Shemung

don't like it that you counted coup against one of his best warriors."

"What is counting coup?" James asked wearily.

"When a warrior wants to count coup against his enemies, sometimes he stakes himself out and fights every enemy who comes near. You've bested Wawatam by taking his weapon. You've counted coup on him. Wawatam will hate you for making him lose face among his people."

"He hated me anyway," James observed cheerlessly. "I may have to kill him before we leave this place."

Angus nodded. He found nothing incongruous about the fact that James spoke thusly when they were both prisoners. He had little doubt the young Scotsman would triumph in the end.

"Shemung said he has heard talk of how you are called the White Falcon and are a great warrior, but he won't hesitate to kill you if you try to escape."

"I'll just have to be sure we're not caught when the time comes," James replied grimly. "Do you know where we are?"

"I heard one of 'em say this is their village of L'Arbre Croche. I figure we're about twenty miles from Fort Michilimackninac."

James nodded thoughtfully. "The Chippewa village is back that way." His tone was more a statement of fact than a need for confirmation. Angus said nothing. He was tired and his wound throbbed interminably. They chewed on the tough dried meat, grateful to have anything at all, and lay down to sleep.

James lay thinking. Swan Necklace and his men were safe in the Chippewa village. She must have been there when he made his escape. If only he'd known! Well, he'd go back for them. He had only Angus and himself to worry about now. He wouldn't give up hope that they could escape Shemung and his renegades. He had to believe he would see Swan Necklace again. The memory of her helped him shut out the discomfort of cold and hunger and find temporary peace in sleep.

Chapter 7

"***D***RINK," A VOICE whispered, and Wye Sheffield's throat convulsed as he tried to sip the sweet, cooling liquid that trickled down his throat. Gentle hands lifted his head. Soft arms supported him until weariness claimed him and he was unable to make the effort to drink.

"You must try to drink and eat something or you will never grow strong again," the voice chided. It was an angel's voice, he was certain of it. He opened his eyes, blinking against the pain of light on his eyeballs, and tried to focus on the face that swam in and out of his dreams.

"Wye!" the angel said. He blinked and her face became clearer. Her lips were soft and sweetly curved, her fine brows like a bird's wing in flight. Her dark eyes were filled with concern for him, and for a moment he thought his mother bent over him.

"Do you remember me, Wye?" the angel asked. "It's Swan Necklace."

Wye swallowed. "Sw-Swan Necklace," he managed.

"You do remember," she said, clapping her small, brown hands together. He hadn't known angels had black hair and small, brown hands; he'd always supposed them to be blond and cherubic. Ah well, he liked this angel better, anyway. The angel went on speaking, and he listened, although her voice fluttered in and out of his consciousness. He was aware of a dull pain in his side, and when he tried to draw

96

a breath, the pain increased, so he was content to lie quietly and not breathe.

"You can't die," the angel said grimly. "The medicine man has prayed over you." Wye closed his eyes and drifted into blackness where he was tending sheep in the gentle Lowland fields and his mother called to him. When he woke, Swan Necklace bent over him and he recognized her at once.

"Where are we?" he whispered.

"You are safe. We're at the summer village of the Chippewa. Chief Manitowa is our friend. He has sent for my father."

"The others?" Wye turned his head on the fur pillow, his gaze sweeping around the darkened interior of some sort of dwelling. Nearby sat a pretty Indian girl, her lively dark eyes watching him intently. When his gaze settled on her, she smiled, showing even white teeth against her copper skin.

"This is Yellow Leaf. She helped me take care of you." The young girl smiled wider, and Wye saw that she was very pretty indeed.

"The rest of the men are here," Swan Necklace went on, "except White Falcon and Angus."

"White Falcon?"

"James," Swan Necklace said in a tone that said he should have recognized the Indian name for his leader. "When White Falcon escaped, the Indians took Angus and went after him."

"Mr. McLeod escaped?" Slowly Wye took in the information. "Why did they take Angus?"

"Shemung said Angus and White Falcon talked together and planned the escape."

"Did they?" Wye asked wearily. This business of talking was tiring.

"I don't know," Swan Necklace said slowly. "But if White Falcon did escape, he will return for his men."

"I hope so."

"Don't count on it," a rough voice said from the lodge

opening. Immediately Swan Necklace's expression changed
to one of distaste and fear. Garth Buckley moved across the
dirt floor to the pallet where Wye rested. Quickly Swan
Necklace moved away as if to avoid any contact with the
burly white man. Buckley knelt beside the young voyageur.
"So you're going to live after all," he snarled.

Wye swallowed and nodded. "I owe my life to Swan
Necklace. She nursed me back."

"Pah, these lazy devils have been shoving all manner of
weeds and roots down your throat."

"We have used hemlock and burr oak to stop the bleeding, and tansy for the fever," Swan Necklace said stiffly.

"It's a wonder you didn't die under their ignorant care,"
Buckley sneered.

"But I didn't," Wye said, the closest he could come to
refuting Buckley's comments. The burly voyageur scared
the younger man. He'd seen him draw a knife on a man for
no other reason than that the man had snickered at some
tall tale of Buckley's. Now Wye turned his head away and
closed his eyes.

"Why do you think White Falcon won't come back to
rescue us?" he asked.

"Pah, White Falcon! McLeod's a coward. He'll run to
save his own neck, him and Angus both."

"That is not true," Swan Necklace cried. "White Falcon
is a brave warrior. I have seen him fight."

"*Mais oui*, he fought. We all did. We fought for our very
lives. This proves nothing, nothing at all," Buckley cried.
His roving black eyes settled on the young Indian girl. She
blushed and looked away. Buckley's eyes gleamed speculatively.

"You would not say these things if White Falcon were
here," Swan Necklace said. Buckley swung around to face
her, his mouth curling into a snarl.

"You'll never know for sure, Miss High and Mighty. He
ain't here. You just might remember that. I'm in charge of
this group now."

"You will not be for long," Swan Necklace answered. "White Falcon will return. I am sure of it."

"You are sure of it," Buckley mimicked, and grabbed hold of one shining braid, tugging on it painfully. Swan Necklace refused to cry out. She sat with her lips pressed together and glared at the burly man. Buckley increased the pain and still she would not acknowledge it. Mutely Yellow Leaf stared at him with wide, terrified eyes. Someone called from the village square and suddenly he seemed to remember that he was surrounded by other Indians. With a laugh, he let go of her hair.

"He is an evil man," Swan Necklace spat out when Garth Buckley had left the tepee. "What he says is a lie. White Falcon *will* come back for us." She was unaware she'd subconsciously grouped herself in with the voyageurs.

Wye smiled. "Aye, he'll come back, if he can."

Swan Necklace made no answer. In her heart she'd feared for his safety as well.

Wye improved greatly in the next few days. The rest of the men were recovering from their wounds and began to relax, realizing the Chippewas meant them no harm. Swan Necklace and Yellow Leaf had become friends and chattered incessantly as they shared their chores. Willingly Swan Necklace joined in the gathering of food and the drying of fish caught by the men in the great lake. Although her mother had died when Swan Necklace was a small child, she'd been well taught by her stepmother. Now she joined her new friend Yellow Leaf in gathering acorns and spreading them to dry in the sun. When the acorns were dried, the two girls settled on the ground beside each other to crack away the shells while they talked. Walking Woman worked nearby with the stone mortar, grinding the acorn meat into a fine flour.

"Wye is a brave, handsome warrior, do you not think so, Yellow Leaf?" Swan Necklace teased. She'd long suspected the young girl was smitten by the young voyageur, and from the way Wye's gaze followed Yellow Leaf, the feelings seemed to be reciprocated. Yellow Leaf blushed and giggled. Walking Woman scowled.

"He is not so handsome or brave as our own warriors," Walking Woman called, scooping the newly ground flour from the mortar and placing it into a finely woven basket that had been placed over a pile of gravel. Bending, she poured clean water over the basket of flour and checked to see that it filtered through satisfactorily. In this manner she would remove the bitter tannic acid and make the flour sweet and wholesome. Nodding her head in approval of her filter, she straightened and looked at her daughter.

"The white men promise many things, but often they break their promises."

"The white men have brought us weapons and metal pots," Yellow Leaf replied. "They are very generous."

"They take our pelts in exchange for these things," Walking Woman replied. "It is the way of our people to trade for those things we do not have."

"Why do you not like the white men, Mother?" Yellow Leaf asked softly.

"They are unclean. They bring disease to our people. They bring their firewater and cheat the Indian when he is drunk." Walking Woman glared at Swan Necklace as if she blamed her for the presence of the white men in their village.

"I am sorry Walking Woman does not wish us to be here," Swan Necklace replied sadly, for she truly liked the dour woman and didn't wish to offend her.

"The daughter of Red Hawke is always welcome in the village of the Chippewa," Walking Woman replied, pausing in her pounding of the flour. "Soon he will be here in our village. He has sent a messenger to say he will be here by full moon. He also brings your husband, Lean Elk."

Startled, Swan Necklace stared at the woman. "Lean Elk is on his way here?"

"Such is the message your father has sent," Walking Woman said. "Your work is finished here. Go now and gather berries." She made a shooing motion and the two girls picked up baskets and turned toward the hillside.

Swan Necklace couldn't help a glance back at the lakeshore. Soon her father and Lean Elk would arrive. She would become Lean Elk's wife then. She thought of White Falcon and wondered where he was. Would he be sad when he returned one day and found she was gone? Troubled, she went up into the woods and helped Yellow Leaf gather wild grapes and chokecherries.

They'd been among the Ottawas for weeks now. There was talk of moving their camp back to their winter home. If they did that, James knew he would have little chance of finding the Chippewa tribe who held his men and Swan Necklace captive. He was desperate to effect an escape.

"Dinna be a fool," Angus warned. "If we escape these varmints and they recapture us, like as not, they'll put us to death."

"We won't be recaptured alive," James answered quietly. His tall body had become even leaner due to the bare sustenance they were given, scraps thrown at them by anyone who happened to remember. At night they were tethered by the neck outside the lodge without furs to cover them against the night air. By day they were led away to do any menial labor that needed doing. They had gathered wood, carried water, hauled loads of skins, helped slaughter the moose and elk brought in by the hunters. They were forced to do women's labor, and in turn, mocked and abused while they worked.

James's face grew more grim every day. Often he lashed out at his tormentors and was whipped or beaten for his defiance. Never was he able to participate in a fair fight, with his hands untied or without being tethered by the neck. The Ottawas seemed intent upon breaking his spirit. He was equally determined they'd never succeed.

Shemung seemed even more mesmerized by the white man known as White Falcon. He regarded him as some other warrior might prize a special weapon, proud of his strength and savagery, yet respectful of it as well. When the men went out to hunt again, James and Angus were allowed to go, too. Usually they were used to carry the game home, but this was a vast improvement on the lowly tasks they'd been set to before.

Angus had also begun to teach James something of the language. James was a quick pupil, and though he missed the finer subtleties of the language, he soon picked up key words. He never revealed to the Ottawas that he understood any word of their tongue. If a warrior came too close when Angus was teaching him, they quickly switched to English. Neither man mentioned it, but they both knew they were only waiting for the chance to escape.

One day as they came upon a herd of elk feeding in a pasture, Shemung silently handed a bow and arrow to James, indicating he was to try his luck. Never having used a bow and arrow before, James bit his inner lip. He knew this was a test, and one he couldn't afford to fail. He thought of the manner in which he'd seen the Indians slot their arrows and aim, and he followed their example. Shemung watched him closely. Wawatam waited nearby, ready to deride him for his failure.

Outwardly James showed no hesitation. He drew the great bow, surprised at its strength, aimed carefully, and let fly. At the last moment something startled the elk at which he'd aimed, so it raised its head. The arrow pierced its neck. If it hadn't moved, the arrow would have sailed over it. The elk fell to the ground and its mates leaped away nervously and ran into the forest.

James glanced at Shemung smugly, as if he'd intended the arrow to land as it had all along. Shemung and his warriors looked stunned.

"Tell them that the Great White Spirit guides the arrows of White Falcon," James instructed Angus. "Tell him I can kill as many elk as they need."

"That was a rare shot, lad. Dinna press your luck."

"Tell them!" James said without looking away from Shemung. Angus relayed the message and Shemung nodded thoughtfully as if he'd already guessed such a thing. Silently he nodded to the other men, who moved forward to track the elk herd.

After that, James was often given a bow and arrow on the hunt, and he seldom missed bringing down game with it. When he was allowed to track off alone, he took the opportunity to practice until he was as proficient as he'd claimed to be. He seemed to have gained special favor with Shemung. Wawatam was further inflamed by this. In his harsh, whispery shout he denounced James time and again at the council fires. Shemung refused to listen and soon the other warriors turned against Wawatam, taunting him for fearing White Falcon. Wawatam's hatred knew no bounds.

A few days later when they were on a hunt, Shemung and James veered away from the other hunters, tracking a deer through the sparse growth. So intent was he upon his prey, James gave no thought to where he was or who might have followed. He sensed that Shemung was somewhere to his right, although he couldn't see him. When he heard the rustle of bushes behind him, he assumed Shemung had rejoined him.

James didn't recognize Wawatam was at hand until the warrior was upon him and the sharp blade of his knife had pierced his shoulder. Automatically James dropped to his knees and rolled away from his attacker. Wawatam leaped forward, intent upon delivering a death blow. James lashed out with his feet, tripping the charging warrior so he fell heavily to the ground. James was upon him at once, struggling to hold on to the hand that held the knife. Wawatam was a powerful warrior, but so was James. Despite his meager diet, his hard life among the Ottawas had further strengthened his muscles and endurance. He arched his back, straining to throw the warrior off him. They rolled on the ground.

James heard the roar of some animal and Shemung's cry. He doubled his fist and beat Wawatam about the head, stunning the warrior. Shemung shouted again, his voice raw with pain. Grabbing up Wawatam's knife, James charged through the trees to a small clearing. Shemung lay wounded and bleeding, the skin on the side of his chest hanging in strips. A large black bear towered over him. James already saw the acceptance of death in Shemung's eyes.

"Hai!" he cried, running forward and plunging the knife in the bear's shoulder. With a roar of pain the great beast turned and knocked him aside as if he were a child. James scrambled to his feet and warily circled, trying to work his way back toward Shemung. He still carried Wawatam's knife, stained now by the bear's blood. The bear seemed uncertain as to which quarry to pursue first.

"Hai!" James shouted again, and the bear turned back to him. "Come on, you monster," he shouted. "Come and get me. I am White Falcon. I'll peck you to death and fly away. Hai! Come on and get me!" He danced around to distract the bear from the wounded man.

Shemung's eyes were glazed and he stared at James in amazement. Suddenly his eyes widened and focused on something behind James.

"Wawatam!" he shouted.

James whirled, but too late to ward off the blow. Wawatam brought the butt of a large stick down on his head. James was driven to his knees, stunned. Feebly he put up a hand to ward off another blow, but Wawatam continued to beat at him with the heavy stick. James felt blood run down his neck and knew he was badly injured. He fell forward onto the ground and lay still. Dimly he perceived the bear's growl. Wawatam dropped the stick and reclaimed his knife before backing away.

"Wawatam!" Shemung shouted. Dimly James perceived the chief was ordering the warrior back, but Wawatam turned and ran, leaving them both to be mauled by the angry bear. The great lumbering beast turned toward Shemung and the chief began his death chant, beseeching the Great Spirit to find him worthy to wander the Great Hunting Grounds beyond.

James tried to push himself up from the ground. Blackness enveloped him and he slumped down again. It would be so good to simply lie there and let all the pain drain away from him into the earth beneath him, the Mother Earth as Swan Necklace had called it. He wouldn't mind dying, but then he thought of Angus and his men and, most of all, Swan Necklace, and he forced himself to his feet.

The bear swiped at Shemung with its great paw. Its sharp claws ripped across the chief's thigh, tearing away flesh, exposing sinew and muscle. James reached for the cudgel Wawatam had used on him and staggered forward, raining blows on the bear's head. With a growl, the bear turned and growled a warning. James swung his club again. The bear charged with greater swiftness than he expected of an animal of such weight and girth. James leaped aside and landed another blow.

Ponderously the bear turned, but James was prepared. Grasping the truncheon with both hands, he swung with his whole weight behind the blow. It hit the bear squarely on the snout. With a high-pitched whine of pain, the bear batted at the club. James hit him again, and as if confused by this attack, the bear lumbered around the clearing, looking for a place to escape. James chased after him, landing more blows, although each impact shook him to his very core. With another cry of pain the bear found a path and lumbered away into the forest.

James stood drawing in air, listening to be sure the creature didn't return. Finally he turned to Shemung. The Indian chief was barely conscious. He'd lost a good deal of blood. James retrieved the chief's weapons and gathered some leaves to pack the wounds. He cut strips from his ragged buckskin shirt to hold them in place. When he was sure he'd done all he could, he took hold of Shemung's arm.

"Wait, White Falcon," Shemung said. "I will not forget what you have done for me today."

James nodded his head. He was able to understand little of what the war chief said, but the gratitude in his eyes said it all.

"Don't thank me until I get you back to the village," he muttered. "Then I'm going to kill Wawatam."

"Kill Wawatam," Shemung said in English, making a stabbing motion with his hand.

"That's right," James nodded, repeating the action. "Kill Wawatam."

Shemung nodded and leaned against James. James lifted him and put him on his back. He could feel the Ottawa's wound begin to bleed again. He'd probably bleed to death before James got him back to the village, but he had to try. Holding Shemung's body with one hand, he took up his rifle with the other and turned back along the trail, running in spite of his burden.

As he made his way back toward the canoes, two warriors came upon him. They had already begun the search for their chief and the captive. Seeing Shemung over his shoulder, wounded and bleeding, they immediately raced forward and claimed their chief's body. When they saw the extent of Shemung's injuries, they grew angry. One warrior rushed forward and dealt James a blow that drove him to the ground.

Other warriors had come by now, and they quickly carried Shemung and James down to the canoes. Their actions were swift, their mood ugly. Silently they paddled back to the tongue of land were their village sat. Once there, they carried their chief to the lodge of the medicine man. James was once again tethered by his neck. In a short while, Angus was brought and tethered as well.

"Why are they doing this to us?" James asked the trapper when the warriors had kicked them and gone away.

"They think you led their chief to his death."

"Shemung is dead?"

"Not yet, and you better pray, lad, that he doesn't die. They'll blame you and, like as not, put us both to death."

James cursed under his breath. "A bear attacked Shemung. I tried to save him. Then Wawatam came along and knocked me out and left us both for the bear."

"That's not what he claims," Angus said. "He told the

others that he saw you knock Shemung unconscious and leave him in the bear's path. He said he fought with you and thought he'd killed you himself, but the bear drove him away before he could scalp you, and your medicine was too strong."

"Did they believe him?"

"They may not like him, but he's one of them. You're the hated white man."

"Damn!"

Through the night and the next day they waited. No one came near them, not even to bring food and water.

"Shemung must be dead," James muttered, "and they're going to kill us by starvation and thirst."

"If Shemung dies, they'll think of a worse death than that," Angus replied.

"Aye, that's true." James nodded.

At dark someone came for them and led them to the village square. The villagers were gathered and all were silent. Wawatam stood at one end of the square, his expression evil and triumphant.

"The chief must have died," Angus said.

"Looks that way," James acknowledged. "I'm not dying without a fight."

"Nor me, lad. We'll go down together."

They steeled themselves against what was to come. They were marched to the end of the square before the shaman's lodge. Pine knots had been lit so the area was bright as day. The shaman came out of his lodge and spoke.

"What's he saying?" James whispered, unable to keep up with the rapid-fire speech.

"He's talking about the Great Spirit."

"Must be consigning Shemung's soul to the Happy Hunting Ground."

"Aye, sounds like it."

The medicine man spoke again, and Wawatam made a strangled sound and leaped forward. His eyes looked wild. The flap of the lodge was thrown back and Shemung limped out. His side and thigh were bound in soft deerhide and he leaned upon one of his warriors, but his eyes were clear as he gazed around the encampment. His glance halted briefly on James and Angus, then hardened as he turned toward Wawatam. He spoke a few words and immediately two warriors sprang forward and grabbed Wawatam. He struggled against them, but was soon subdued. Shemung spoke then at some length, raising his voice so all his village might hear.

"What's he saying now?" James asked. "I can't make it out."

"He's telling how the bear attacked him and how White Falcon came to save him. He's also telling them of Wawatam's treachery."

The villagers muttered among themselves, then turned toward Wawatam. The warrior cried out as they converged on him. Silently the villagers meted out their punishment. Knives flashed. Wawatam screamed time and again and at last fell silent.

"They've killed him," James said, regretful that he himself hadn't been able to perform that deed.

"I don't think so," Angus replied.

The villagers fell back now, and James could see Wawatam writhing on the ground. He was covered with blood. His mouth seemed filled with it. It bubbled forth as he sobbed.

"They cut out his tongue," Angus observed. James was silent as he regarded his enemy. Not only had the villagers cut away his tongue, but he'd been hamstrung as well. He'd never walk right again.

Shemung looked at James and grinned. Making a stabbing motion with his hand, he spoke.

"He says you can kill him now if you want," Angus interpreted.

James regarded the pitiful huddle that once had been an arrogant warrior and slowly shook his head. "No, I wouldn't do him the favor," he said.

Angus repeated the words for Shemung and the chief nodded in agreement. He spoke again and James caught some of the words. Hope blossomed in his chest, but he was afraid to believe what he was hearing.

"What did he say?" he demanded, gripping Angus's shirt.

"He said White Falcon is a brave warrior and he owes his life to you. He says we're free to go," Angus shouted. "They'll give us supplies and a canoe and a scout to take us back wherever we want to go."

"Swan Necklace!" James whispered. "Tell him we want to go back to the Chippewa village where he left my men. Tell him we appreciate his gift. Tell him—he is a great chief."

Angus began to translate, but James interrupted him. "Tell him we want to leave immediately." Angus nodded.

Within an hour they glided away from the Ottawa village of L'Arbre Croche and paddled northward toward the village of the Chippewa.

Chapter 8

"*T*HEY'RE HERE! SWAN NECKLACE, they're here!"

Yellow Leaf's cry was as joyous as if it were her own father approaching in the brightly decorated birchbark canoes. Swan Necklace recognized Red Hawke's proud figure in the prow of the first boat. He was followed by ten other canoes. Her joy at seeing her father was diminished by the thought that Lean Elk traveled with him. Sunlight sparkled over the water and the lake breeze was cool and balmy. The air seemed made for jubilation, yet Swan Necklace's heart was torn. She had no wish to marry Lean Elk, but to back out now would dishonor her father. Besides, there had been no word of White Falcon or Angus. She had no way of knowing if they were dead or alive. It would matter little to her future. She must resolve herself to her fate.

Paddles flashed in the sunlight and the canoes drew to shore. Manitowa went forward to greet his guests. Swan Necklace waited until the men had spoken. Standing beside Yellow Leaf, she felt pride swell through her as she regarded her father. Red Hawke was a handsome, dignified man. Scars testified to his fierceness in battle. He was a wise and well-respected chief as well, and his noble bearing expressed that prominence. He'd dressed with special care for his entrance into the Chippewa village, donning his best moccasins and elk shirt made by his second wife, Red Sky.

Red Sky had embroidered the shirt with shells and dyed porcupine quills. His moccasins were also embroidered in a pattern special to the Cree. Her handiwork was considered the best in the village, and Swan Necklace was grateful to see Red Sky had made her father such splendid clothes as befit a great chief.

"Why do you not go greet your father?" Yellow Leaf whispered, her brow wrinkled in bewilderment.

Swan Necklace shook her head. She hated to admit her reluctance to go forward now in full view of the whole village. "I will greet my father later," she said. She knew there was another reason she hesitated. The other canoes had drawn up onshore and more figures stepped from them. Red Sky had come, as well as other women and children from the village. Lean Elk and his warriors rode in separate canoes, and now when they stepped ashore, the Cree warriors and their women moved aside for him. Without looking to either side, he stalked forward and presented himself to Manitowa.

"Greetings," Manitowa said. "Welcome to the village of the Chippewa."

"We are honored to be among our friends the Chippewa," Red Hawke said, raising his hand in a greeting of peace.

"You have the Cree woman, Swan Necklace?" Lean Elk demanded without acknowledging Manitowa's greeting. The Chippewa villagers drew in their breaths at this breach of manners. Manitowa waited a space of time to signify his awareness of this discourtesy before answering.

"The woman of which you speak is a guest in our village," the old chief said evenly, and turned to Red Hawke before speaking again. "That is the reason I have sent word to Red Hawke. In time, we would have brought your daughter to your village, but she wished to wait."

"Why should she wish to delay here in the Chippewa camp when she can return to her own people and the tribe of her husband?" Lean Elk demanded harshly.

"I do not know the answer to this," Manitowa answered calmly. "But we have made the Cree woman welcome."

"Red Hawke is grateful to his friend, Chief Manitowa," Red Hawke answered. "I have brought my wife and family and some of my warriors. We come in peace and with much gladness to have our daughter returned to us."

"The Chippewa are honored to have Red Hawke and his family. We have prepared a feast." Without glancing at Lean Elk, Manitowa led Red Hawke and his entourage toward the village square. Furious at this slight, Lean Elk stalked after them.

"I demand to see Swan Necklace," he shouted.

Embarrassed at such rude behavior and fearful that Lean Elk might start a war with the Chippewa, Swan Necklace quickly stepped forward.

"I am here," she cried. Lean Elk whirled and barely acknowledged her presence. She perceived that she was less important to him as a woman than she was as a symbol of his own position as a war chief. No one might withhold that which belonged to him. Lean Elk nodded and stalked away toward the canoes with his warriors. Swan Necklace bit back her vexation that he should treat her in such a disrespectful manner. She rushed forward to greet her father and stepmother.

"Father, I did not believe you would come," she cried, embracing him.

"Swan Necklace is our only daughter. When we heard of the attack on your wedding party, we went after the men who did such a thing, but we lost their trails. Then we went to the French chiefs, but they claimed they no longer had any authority since the war. Red Hawke does not believe this, but I could do nothing more."

"I am sorry to have brought such worry to my father," Swan Necklace answered.

"He grieved for you many moons," Red Sky said. "He remembers you are the daughter of Beaver Woman and he was saddened to lose you."

"Red Sky is generous to tell me of this," Swan Necklace

said, taking the woman's hand. Red Sky had taken the place of her dead mother many years before, and their relationship had been filled with trust and laughter. Now Red Sky hugged Swan Necklace.

"I am happy, too, that my adopted daughter has returned," she said shyly. She placed a hand over her stomach. "Soon I hope to have a sister or brother for Swan Necklace."

"Red Sky!" Swan Necklace hugged her stepmother and the two of them giggled with enjoyment of the news. Swan Necklace glimpsed Yellow Leaf's watchful face among the villagers and hurried to introduce her to her father and mother. The stiffness of their arrival was soon lost in the laughter and joy of being with her family again and in introducing them to her new friends. Red Sky and Walking Woman became friends at once. Both were the wives of great chiefs and they sat chattering about events.

During the feast that followed, Swan Necklace sat between her father and Red Sky, relating her adventures from the time she was kidnapped by the French adventurers to the time James McLeod bought her and began the journey to return her to her people.

"Where is this warrior known as White Falcon?" Red Hawke asked. "And how are you so sure he is the White Falcon from your vision?"

"He had a vision too, Father. The great white falcon came to him and showed him the lands of the Cree. Although he escaped from the Ottawa warriors, he has not returned to the Chippewa village. It is for this reason that I have delayed here."

"Perhaps he will never return," Red Hawke said kindly.

Swan Necklace shook her head. "He will return, Father. I know this."

"Then we will stay here for a short while and see if he will come, but soon we must return to our own lands. Winter comes and we must move our village to our winter camp."

"Yes, Father," Swan Necklace said, bowing her head to

hide her elation. They would stay for a while longer. Surely White Falcon would come.

"There is something more," Red Hawke said slowly. "Lean Elk wishes to claim you as his wife. He will not wait long. He has been impatient."

"I do not understand why he should feel this way, Father," Swan Necklace said. "He shows no interest in me and even insults me before the whole village."

Red Hawke's brows drew down in a scowl. "This is true," he mumbled. "Lean Elk wishes to ally himself with the Cree, and he thinks to do this with this marriage."

"He does not respect me, Father, nor do I have affection for him." Swan Necklace spoke in a low voice.

"Lean Elk is not the only one who seeks this alliance," Red Hawke said. "The white men push into our country in greater number every season. If the people are not to be driven from their country as the Ottawa have been, then we must unite. For this reason, I have wanted this marriage."

"I understand, Father," Swan Necklace whispered. She put aside her food. She had no stomach to eat now. She sat beside her father and Red Sky for a while longer, then slipped away to Walking Woman's lodge. Despite the arrival of her father, she didn't feel like joining the festivities.

For three days the Chippewas feasted with their guests. Lean Elk seldom spoke to Swan Necklace during that time, ignoring her as if she counted for little. Swan Necklace longed for him to show some warmth to her, some indication that she would be well regarded once she returned to his tribe. Perhaps then, secure in the knowledge of her position as a chief's wife, she would forget White Falcon and be happy with Lean Elk, but such an understanding did not seem likely. Swan Necklace was further troubled by the comments made among her new friends.

"The Chipewyans are a rough tribe," said Little Bird, a comely girl two winters older than Swan Necklace. "I have heard the winters are very harsh and there is little food. There is no time to sing or dance. One must spend much time gathering roots and bark from the trees in order not to starve."

"Lean Elk is a great war chief," Swan Necklace replied with greater serenity than she felt. "Surely such a man is a great hunter as well. I do not fear for my future with the Chipewyans."

Little Bird shivered. "I am glad it is you who will go to be his wife. He is a man without manners. He seems very ferocious."

"That is because he is such a fierce warrior," Swan Necklace answered. "I would not have a man who is mistaken for an *agokwa*." Little Bird's face fell. Her only suitor was a gentle brave whose womanish ways made him the butt of jokes among the rest of the warriors.

"Netnokwa is a good man," Little Bird said faintly. Swan Necklace was sorry for her unkind remark.

"'He is a good hunter," she said. "His wife will never want for food or hides."

The plain girl brightened at this praise. "He has a funny way. He makes me laugh," she said. "And when the others tease him, he never grows angry with them. He makes fun of himself and laughs with them."

"This is a rare gift," Yellow Leaf said, nodding her approval. Now that the three of them were in accord again, they grinned at each other.

Red Hawke lingered in the camp of the Chippewa. Red Sky and the other Cree women went out with the Chippewa women to gather berries and roots. Swan Necklace and Yellow Leaf joined the women, and many long days were spent in laughter while their hands were busy.

Yellow Leaf, Little Bird, and Swan Necklace joined the other girls who were good swimmers and with long poles dived to the bottom of a pond to dig out the roots of the yellow pond lily. The onion-shaped peppery root of the plant called fireball was gathered and stored in damp sand. It would be used later for winter bread.

While the young girls lolled in the meadow chattering about the unmarried warriors, the women went out to gather leaves of adder tongue, wild mustard, clover, watercress, honeywort, and trillium, which they served as fresh salads with their meals or made into pot herbs used for stuffing game or fish. Every day the girls went out to gather chestnuts, hickory nuts, walnuts, butternuts, and beechnuts. Some of these nuts would be crushed for their oil, which was then used over green leaves to make them more palatable and for frying meats.

The summer was passing swiftly. The season of plenty was upon them. The hunters went out every day and returned with rabbits, grouse, and pheasants. The men fished for sturgeon, and the Cree and Chippewa women vied with each other in preparing them. Fish were left unscaled, birds left unplucked, although their wings and heads were removed, and the whole covered with clay two fingers thick before being placed in the cook fire's embers and covered with ashes and coals. Another fire was built over this mound and the whole left to cook for an hour or so. When the hardened clay was pulled from the embers, broken with a stick, and the casing pulled aside, scales, fur, or feathers came with it.

"Aah!" Red Sky said in approval when she was shown this method by Walking Woman. Not to be undone, she showed her new friend the way to cook vegetables and meat without a fire.

"It cannot be done!" Walking Woman cried. Swan Necklace giggled. She knew Red Sky's secret and eagerly helped her dig a deep hole and light a fire in it. When the interior of the pit was well heated and the earth was heated a considerable distance around the hole, she helped Red Sky clear away the fire and put in their birchbark *mukkuks* filled with meat and vegetables. They covered over the hole with ashes and hot embers.

"Come, we will gather berries," Red Sky said.

"A good cook does not leave her cooking," Walking Woman protested.

"Come, come." Red Sky laughed and motioned Walking Woman to follow. Swan Necklace was proud of Red Sky's skills when they returned later and dug up the *mukkuks*. They were filled with steaming hot and tender food. Walking Woman was suitably impressed, and the pride and skill of the Cree women maintained.

The time passed quickly and happily for all except Lean Elk, who chafed at this idyllic delay. He was anxious to return to his village and he wished to take Swan Necklace with him.

"What will you do?" Yellow Leaf asked one night as she and Swan Necklace lay side by side on their pallets.

"I do not know," Swan Necklace answered. "I have no desire to become Lean Elk's woman. Yet my father would be much pleased if I did this."

"He is very handsome," Yellow Leaf declared, although in truth she thought the war chief looked cruel. She was frightened of him and feared for her friend. "If you go to the lands of the Chipewyan, I shall never see you again."

"I have thought of this as well," Swan Necklace answered. "But I do not wish to disobey my father."

"What of this warrior White Falcon? What if he returns?"

"It would make no difference," Swan Necklace said. "I am promised to Lean Elk."

"Did you love White Falcon very much?" Yellow Leaf asked softly.

For a long time Swan Necklace did not answer her. Tears gathered in her eyes and rolled down her cheeks, so she was glad the tepee was dark and Yellow Leaf could not see.

"Did you love him?" Yellow Leaf repeated.

"No," Swan Necklace said. "I did not love him." She closed her eyes and pretended to sleep. With all her heart she wished White Falcon would return.

Then, as if in answer to her prayer, he arrived at the village. Swan Necklace and Yellow Leaf were at the cook fire of Walking Woman, hulling corn, which would be put into cold water and boiled until the kernels burst open. Since her talk with Yellow Leaf the night before, she'd found little pleasure in the things around her. She'd come to accept the fact that White Falcon was lost to her, then there he was, surrounded by villagers, striding up the bank from the lake, his proud dark head thrown back, his eyes seeking her out. She knew he was looking for her because his gaze settled on her with all the intensity they'd shared on their journey together.

The breath caught in her throat and she grew light-headed. She couldn't take her gaze from him. He was leaner, harder-muscled, browner. He wore no shirt, only a pair of ragged buckskin leggings and a loincloth and dusty moccasins. His movements were vigorous, yet still retained a graceful strength. His lean features were even more prominent, his nose a sharp blade in his face, his cheekbones and jaws chiseled as if by sharp flashes of a sculptor's knife. His black hair was long, held in place by a piece of rawhide.

"What is wrong, Swan Necklace?" Yellow Leaf cried, but Swan Necklace had already leaped to her feet and was running toward the tall man.

"White Falcon!" she cried. Her heart nearly burst from joy. She ran forward, then came to an abrupt halt scant inches away from him. She saw the surprise in his eyes, saw that he meant to take her into his arms and quickly stepped back.

"I am pleased to see White Falcon again," she said stiffly. "We had thought he was dead. Has Angus returned with you as well?"

"Aye, lass. He's coming. Are you not glad to see me?" He held out his arms in a silent invitation again. She remained where she was, unable to meet his gaze.

"Aye, White Falcon. I am pleased. My father is here. So is Lean Elk. They, too, will be happy to see the man who has helped restore me to them."

James took in the meaning of her words and frowned. "Lean Elk is here?"

"Aye!" She couldn't meet his gaze.

"You are his woman now." His voice was flat with disappointment.

"Not yet," she cried. "My father has waited. He wished to have you return so he could reward you for your kindness to me."

"It wasn't kindness," James said gruffly. He stared at her. She'd never looked so sleek and beautiful. Her stay in the Chippewa village had been good for her. She'd regained weight. Her body beneath the soft doeskin was softly rounded. Her cheeks bloomed with health, and her eyes and hair shone. He'd forgotten how tiny she was. She'd loomed so large in his thoughts. An awkward silence fell over them, broken at last by the arrival of two Indian men who, by their dress, could only be chiefs.

"Father," Swan Necklace called. "White Falcon has come."

The tall, stately man approached James, his hand extended in friendship. "It is a great honor to meet White Falcon," Red Hawke said. "My daughter has told me much of your bravery."

"She has told me many times of her wise father," James replied. Introductions were made with Manitowa and courteous greetings exchanged. Angus came up the bank, and feeling no such reserve with him as she had with White Falcon, Swan Necklace threw herself in his arms.

"You are alive, my friend. Every day I prayed to the Great Spirit to guide your footsteps back to us."

"I did a bit of praying myself, lassie," Angus said. The newcomers were welcomed into the village and made to tell all that had happened to them since leaving the village. James and Angus took turns telling of their weeks among the Ottawa. Angus revealed Wawatam's treachery and the brave deed James had performed, which won their freedom.

"White Falcon is indeed a brave man," Red Hawke said, nodding in approval.

Lean Elk had been away with his warriors hunting when James and Angus arrived. Upon returning and hearing that strange white men were in camp, he hurried to Manitowa's lodge and burst in, pulling his knife. James saw him first and leaped to his feet.

"Put away your knife, Lean Elk," Manitowa ordered in a loud voice. "This man, known as White Falcon, is a guest at my campfire, as are you. You should be grateful to him, for he has saved Swan Necklace from a life among the white eyes. He has sought to return her to you and her people."

The two men glared at each other, each taking the measure of the other. Lean Elk was nearly as tall as James. Muscles rippled beneath his coppery skin. His dark eyes were fierce and crafty. James made a mental note not to turn his back on this man if he could help it. Some instinctive cruelty in the war chief's eyes reminded him of Wawatam. He braced himself and waited.

Reluctantly Lean Elk sheathed his knife and took a seat before the campfire. He made no effort to apologize to James or to Manitowa for his rude outburst. Manitowa waved James back to his seat and drew out a pipe.

"Come, we will smoke the pipe and become friends," the old chief said, and began stuffing the pipe with sweet grasses. James seated himself beside Angus and looked across the flames at the man who would claim Swan Necklace. Lean Elk was a big man with coarse features and a curling bottom lip that denoted a quick anger. His dark eyes darted restlessly about the interior of the lodge as if seeking enemies where there were none. He was heavily scarred over his arms and shoulders, testifying to the violence of his life. The land did that to men, though, James thought. If he was lucky, one day he would look like that. If he was not, then he would be buried at an early age.

With great ceremony, Manitowa lit the pipe, made his offerings to the Great Spirit, and drew three puffs before passing it to his right to Red Hawke. Red Hawke repeated the offerings, smoked, and passed it around the circle. When the pipe came to James, Lean Elk reached across the fire and grabbed it from his hands. With a look of superiority he performed the necessary ritual of smoking and handed it to the warrior at his side. Grinning evilly, he glared at James.

"Don't let him bait you, lad," Angus said. "He's not in favor with Manitowa and Red Hawke right now." James clenched his fists and eased back on his haunches. With an angry protest, Manitowa retrieved the pipe and with great dignity offered it to James.

"This is a great honor, Chief Manitowa," James said, and mimicked the ritual he'd seen the other Indians perform, holding the bowl toward the earth and sky and the four corners before drawing on the stem.

Lean Elk could only glare in anger. His behavior had been arrogant and insulting time and again, and he knew the Chippewa chief disliked him. He also guessed that his father-in-law-to-be was fast losing patience with him, but Lean Elk had no caring for the white men who were invading the Indian lands. He'd noted firsthand how they plundered the beaver streams, how they desecrated the Mother Earth's bounty, and how they brought sickness and death to the Indians. He'd seen firsthand how the Indian was made to follow the laws of the white men while the white men ignored those of the people. Many times he'd protested these injustices. Many times he had warred against the white-eyed intruders. He did not understand these southern tribes who grew fat and glossy and dependent on the white traders' goods. His contempt spilled over, plain for all to see.

"I wish to return to the lands of my people," Lean Elk said to the council members.

"May the Great Spirit grant you a safe journey," Manitowa replied serenely.

"I wish to take the Cree woman with me," Lean Elk said.

"She wishes to wait," Red Hawke answered.

"She has been promised to me." Lean Elk leaped to his feet.

Red Hawke did not answer this rebuttal. He sat staring into the flames of the fire. He sat so still and silent that those seated around the fire thought he was meditating and waited patiently—all save Lean Elk, who stirred restlessly.

At last Red Hawke raised his head and regarded the Chipewyan chief.

"Aye, she has been promised," he said in a low voice.

"No!" James cried, half rising from his seat. Angus took
hold of his arm and held him back. Lean Elk turned a hard
gaze on him. Red Hawke and Manitowa gazed at him in
surprise.

"White Falcon has something to say?" Red Hawke asked
mildly. James glanced at Lean Elk. He had no wish to de-
clare his feelings for Swan Necklace before this angry warrior. He would practice patience as the Indians advocated.
He would talk to Red Hawke alone. He settled back in his
seat.

"I have nothing to say at this time," he said.

Red Hawke nodded and turned back to Lean Elk. "We
will speak of this when the moon is round again."

"That is too long," Lean Elk snapped.

"It is but a short time," Manitowa observed.

"So be it," Red Hawke said.

Lean Elk looked from one to the other and knew he
could do nothing. He was a guest here in the lands of the
Chippewa. He and his warriors were outnumbered. Even
Red Hawke was against him. "So be it," he said harshly
and, leaping to his feet, left the lodge.

"Perhaps White Falcon and his men would hunt the elk
at first light," Manitowa said.

"I'd like that," James replied, and as the powwow
seemed to be over, he rose and left the tepee.

"Lad, you've got a passel of trouble with that Lean Elk,"
Angus observed as they walked down to the lakeshore.
"He's meaner than Wawatam, and I dinna kin anyone could
be meaner than him."

"I'll stay out of his way," James answered absently. He'd
just spotted Swan Necklace amongst a group of young
women who were filling birchbark water containers. He
paused to watch. She was laughing, her face flushed and
happy. He'd never seen her among her own kind before.
She stood out from the other girls. Although she was small

and shorter than most of them, they seemed to flock around her as if she were the center of their group.

"James?" Angus said. He'd walked on for a pace or two before realizing James was not beside him. Now he stood regarding his friend. Knowingly he glanced in the direction James was looking, noting the presence of Swan Necklace among the girls. Unaware they were being watched, the girls climbed the steep shoreline and walked back toward the lodges, each carrying a birchbark container of water. As if released from a spell, James joined Angus.

"You've always known she was promised," Angus said.

"Aye, I've always known it," James said.

"The rules are still the same, lad. If you try to win her, you might bring shame on her, even death. Lean Elk looks the kind of brave who wouldn't tolerate someone taking what's his."

"If she'd been promised to me, I'd not tolerate it either," James said. "I'm tired, Angus. It was a long trip. I think I'll rest." He turned toward the lodge where men were sheltered.

"Yeah, me, too," the Scotsman said. "We've got an early hunt in the morning."

The warriors hunted on foot, spreading out and moving through the forest as silent as a spirit. James had learned to move in this manner as well, and now he moved swiftly, confidently, pausing only when he found a print. Shemung had returned his long rifle to him, and now he carried it in one hand while his legs moved in tireless pursuit of a stag.

He was the first to bring down game that day. His shot brought other hunters who prayed over the fallen stag and, at his nod, knelt to cut the warm heart from the valiant beast and pass it around. All took a bite of it, for such was the way of warriors. James shut away any thought of the Ottawas and the hardships he'd endured. He'd survived. Now, standing here looking around the circle of Chippewa and Cree warriors, he felt a certain kinship. He would continue to survive and he would find some way to take Swan Necklace away from Lean Elk.

The hunt continued and James went to help others, driving game back toward those hunters who'd not yet succeeded. This endeavor brought him close to Red Hawke, which had been his intent in the first place. When they stopped to rest, James spoke to the chief.

"I have heard Red Hawke is a wise and fair chief," he began.

"Who has told you this?" Red Hawke had settled on the ground to rest. He was beginning to feel his age.

"Swan Necklace. She spoke often of her father and of how much she respected him."

"It is good for a daughter to respect her father and follow his word."

James frowned. The wily chief had cut off that attempt. He tried again. "Swan Necklace has said that Red Hawke not only is wise in his words, but that he listens to the words of others."

Red Hawke glanced at him in surprise. The white man could be wily, too. "What others?" he asked.

"If a daughter were to speak to her father and tell him of her love for another man, would he not listen?"

Red Hawke stared at James without answering. Finally he shook his head. "If Swan Necklace had spoken to me months ago, I would have listened, but she did not." He turned to look at James. "She has not spoken to me of her love for someone else since I have come to the Chippewa village."

"She's afraid to say anything," James said urgently. "She doesn't want to dishonor you. She knows she has been promised to Lean Elk."

"That is true. She has been," Red Hawke said, and got to his feet. "I have rested enough."

"But she does not love Lean Elk," James said, moving to stand in front of the chief.

"How do you know this? Has she spoken to a stranger when she has not spoken to her own father?"

"Nay." James shook his head.

"Then you cannot know how she feels," Red Hawke said, stepping around him.

"I know she loves me," James cried. "And I love her."

Red Hawke turned back to face the white man. "I do not know what this word 'love' means."

"It means she pleases me and I want her for my wife," James answered. "I want to live with her and raise children with her." He'd had much time to think in the camp of the Ottawa. Now he said these things without hesitation.

Red Hawke listened until he stopped speaking, then shook his head. "Many white men take our women," he said slowly. "When they are finished with their time here and return to their own lands in the big ships with wings, they do not take their wives with them. They leave them behind. This does not seem like a good thing to me."

"I will not abandon her," James said. "I will live here in her land, your land, if need be."

"You will give up your people, your lands, for Swan Necklace?"

"Yes," James answered. His gaze was steady and sure as it met Red Hawke's.

The chief shook his head again. "This cannot be," he said slowly. "Swan Necklace is already promised to Lean Elk."

"No!" James cried. Red Hawke held up his hand.

"Red Hawke does not break his promise." He stood considering for a few minutes, then finally nodded as if he'd made up his mind. "Tonight Swan Necklace will become Lean Elk's wife. I have spoken." Without glancing at James, Red Hawke disappeared into the forest.

James clenched his fists. "Swan Necklace!" he whispered. He turned back toward the village, leaving his game behind. Desperately he ran, mindless of the branches tearing at him. He ran easily, swiftly, covering a great deal of ground. Finally he saw the shimmer of sun on water and knew he was near the lake. He turned along the shore and ran swiftly toward the village. Still some distance from the camp, he heard the bright chatter of women and swerved toward them. Several women and girls were busy picking berries. James ran toward them, his eyes searching out the bright dark head of a small woman.

"Swan Necklace!" he called, startling some of the women so they dropped their baskets. The women moved out of his way as he ran past. Suddenly he saw her. Her head was raised expectantly. When she saw him, she smiled, then glanced around at the other women and cast her gaze to the ground. James had no time for such proprieties. He grabbed her arm and pulled her away from the group of women.

"White Falcon," she called in surprise. "What is it?" Her basket tumbled out of her hands and the berries spilled. She glanced at the fallen basket, but he gave her no time to retrieve it. He pulled her away to privacy behind a bush.

"I cannot stay here with you," she whispered, trying to pull away from him. "It is not seemly for a woman promised to another to go off alone and unchaperoned."

"Swan Necklace!" He shook her slightly. "You must come away with me, now."

"Come away with you?"

"Your father says you are to become Lean Elk's wife tonight."

"Tonight?" Her expression was stricken.

"You can't become that man's wife. Come with me. We'll go somewhere, back to Montreal. We'll go to Fort *d'Étroit*. We must hurry." He took hold of her arm and started to drag her toward the lakeshore, where they might find a canoe.

"Wait, White Falcon," she cried, straining against him so he was forced to stop and face her. "I cannot go with you."

"What are you saying?" he asked in a calm voice that belied his agitation.

"I am promised to Lean Elk. If I run away, I will so dishonor my father, he could no longer be chief of his tribe. He would be shamed. I cannot do that to him."

"You can't marry Lean Elk."

"I must! You have known this all along."

"Swan Necklace." James yanked her against him and crushed her soft lips with his mouth. She made no struggle to get away from him. He felt her mouth open, felt the surrender in her kiss, and his blood flamed. "You belong to me, Swan Necklace," he whispered, raining kisses on her cheeks and brow and finally on her mouth again. "You can never belong to another man. I love you. You love me."

She was crying. Tears streamed down her cheeks, yet she made no sound. "I belong to Lean Elk," she said in a small voice that cut him more painfully than any knife ever had done. "I cannot belong to you." She pulled away from him, forcing a smile through her tears. "I will always remember that you wanted me as your woman."

"Swan Necklace, no!" he whispered desperately, but she was already gone, whirling away from him and running through the woods toward the village. James started to run after her, but a woman stepped in front of him.

"You must let her go," the woman said. Behind her stood another woman with strong features and a pretty girl about Swan Necklace's age. "If you pursue her, you will embarrass her in front of her husband-to-be. You may even brand her a woman without morals, which would shame her when she goes to her new home. You white men do not understand the ways of the Cree. You come here and make your home among us, but you do not understand our honor."

"Nay, ma'am. I do not," he said.

"I am called Red Sky," the woman said. "I am the wife of Red Hawke. Hear me, white man. You must leave Swan Necklace alone or you will dishonor her if you have not already."

Red Sky picked up Swan Necklace's fallen basket and stood. Her eyes were calm as she spoke again. "Swan Necklace is lost to you, White Falcon. You must accept this."

She turned toward the path to the village and the other women followed her, casting curious glances over their shoulders. James watched them leave. He couldn't breathe, he was in such pain. He felt rage and helplessness. They numbed him. Raising his hands to the sky, he shouted, a wild, haunted cry that could be heard down in the village and along the lakeshore.

Chapter 9

SWAN NECKLACE WAS IN such pain, she couldn't speak. She sat on the sandy shore looking out over the great body of water and wondered that the world could continue looking so normal when her life had brought her such despair. She found no comfort in the lapping of waves at her feet or the sough of wind through the trees at her back. In the distant blue of the sky, a flock of geese called to one another, formed their flying wedge, and winged their way southward. Summer was drawing to an end. It had been a summer of hope and temptation for her. Now that must end as well. She must marry Lean Elk and travel northward to the land of his people. She would never see White Falcon again. A breeze came up from the lake, ruffling the water and fanning her pale cheeks. She sat unmoving, her heart like a stone within her.

Red Sky followed her stepdaughter and watched from afar, seeing the hopelessness in the set of her shoulders. Although she'd heard Swan Necklace deny White Falcon, she'd seen the flare of emotion in the young girl's eyes and understood how deep a young love can be. She had felt such for Red Hawke when she was but a girl like Swan Necklace. Red Hawke had never seemed to look her way, and she'd thought she would surely die from grief. The day he'd paused by the river to speak with her, she'd known for the first time that he desired her as his wife. What joy she'd felt, for seldom does a young girl move from one emotion to another without great passion. Red Sky shook her head sadly, for as much as she cared for her stepdaughter and understood the young girl's feelings, she could do nothing to help her.

Even Yellow Leaf was touched by the meeting between Swan Necklace and White Falcon. She had seen in her friend an emotion so raw, it had been painful to observe. Yellow Leaf thought of the other young men in her village. She'd flirted with them, exalting in her power to make them stammer and act silly, but she'd never once felt the passion that passed between Swan Necklace and White Falcon. Even with Wye, she had not yet had that awakening as a woman. Now she sat quietly by Walking Woman's fire, wondering if such a feeling would ever be hers and wondering if it would be better if it were not.

The village was abuzz with the meeting between the two lovers. Women gossiped beside their campfires, and warriors grunted in disbelief. Women always made much of such things. Lean Elk was not so tolerant. When he heard of White Falcon's actions, he flew into a rage.

"I will kill White Falcon for his betrayal," Lean Elk shouted.

"You have forgotten that it was White Falcon who returned Swan Necklace to us," Red Hawke said.

"And now he tries to take her from me," Lean Elk snapped. "He is a dog, a cur who sneaks among the bushes to steal another warrior's wife."

"Swan Necklace rejected his suit," Red Hawke reminded him. "Why do you fear White Falcon's power over her?"

The warrior swung round and glared at him. "I do not fear White Falcon," he said grimly. "But he has offered me an insult, and I must defend my honor by killing him."

"Or by being killed," Red Hawke answered.

Lean Elk's gaze was dark and intimidating, but Red Hawke was not a man to back down to any man. "We are guests here in the village of Manitowa. Do not be unwise and start trouble that may spread beyond the fight between you and White Falcon. Swan Necklace has acted in an honorable manner with him. He is unaware of our customs. Forgive this deed and do not listen to the gossip of old women."

"You speak as an old woman, Red Hawke," Lean Elk sneered. "I will fight the white man known as White Falcon because I do not fear to defend my honor." Grabbing up a knife, Lean Elk strode through the village square, knocking aside all who wandered into his path.

No one seemed to know of White Falcon's whereabouts. Lean Elk went among the white voyageurs, pushing the men aside, in the belief that White Falcon had hidden himself among them.

"There's no need for you to look for him here," Angus snapped. "He's not a man what would run and hide from the likes of you. When he hears you're looking for him, he'll find you."

"I do not believe this," Lean Elk snarled. "This man known as White Falcon is a coward. He is afraid to fight Lean Elk."

"That's a lie," Wye cried, getting to his feet. "White Falcon can whip you or any man."

Lean Elk leaped toward the voyageur, his knife raised. The other men gathered around him, their meaty fists raised, their eyes belligerent. Wye was their favorite. Lean Elk hesitated. He had come alone and he was outmanned. The voyageurs were a rough, mean-looking lot. In that moment of hesitation, Angus stepped forward.

"Put your knife away, you savage devil," he bellowed. "There're too many of us. There's not a man here who wouldn't fight for the honor of White Falcon. We saw how he fought the Ottawa warriors to save his men. He killed many Ottawa warriors before they took him captive, and even then his bravery won him a release from captivity. You'd do well to go away and forget this grudge you bear him."

"I shall never do that. He has dishonored Lean Elk by

speaking to his woman. I will kill White Falcon when I see him."

"Swan Necklace ain't your woman yet, Lean Elk," Angus snapped, "and White Falcon would never do anything to dishonor her."

"You lie! He sought her out in the berry fields and tried to steal her."

"If he'd wanted to kidnap her, he'd a' succeeded," Angus said. "It's 'cause he's an honorable man that she's still here and about to become your wife tonight. Go back to your warriors, Lean Elk, and count your blessings."

Lean Elk regarded the ring of hostile faces. Slowly he sheathed his knife. His jaw muscles flexed and his dark eyes were bright with hatred.

"Tell White Falcon that Lean Elk will hunt him down and kill him," he said, and stalked away.

"Think he means it, Angus?" Wye asked, watching the warrior disappear toward his own lodge.

"Aye, he does," Angus said. "James has made himself a bad enemy."

"He's not alone," Lyle said. "I'll fight by his side if he needs me."

"*Oui, moi aussi,*" another man cried. "*C'est affaire d'honneur.*"

"A matter of principle," other men echoed.

One man did not join in this affirmation of support. Garth Buckley had watched Lean Elk closely, and now he walked away so he might think.

Lean Elk was furious. When he left the voyageurs, he stalked through the village, butting into people and kicking kettles of food from the cooking fires. A trail of protests followed his progress. He paid little heed to those people he hurt or inconvenienced. At the end of the square he came abreast of a young warrior who didn't leap aside quickly enough. Lean Elk shouted and lashed out at him, knocking him to the ground. The warrior rolled away and regained his feet. Lean Elk rounded on him again.

"Get out of my way, dog," he cried in his most insulting

manner. The young warrior swallowed and looked around the group of villagers who'd gathered. He knew he shouldn't ignore this insulting challenge issued to him, but Netnokwa was a peaceful man and not given to fighting. Even while courting Little Bird, he'd remained gentle and affable. Now he saw that Lean Elk was a far more experienced warrior than he and knew that he would lose in any altercation.

"I am called Netnokwa," he said nervously. "I am sorry I gave offense by stepping in your way, Lean Elk."

Lean Elk stared at him, the blink of his flat black eyes like those of a deadly serpent about to strike. Netnokwa felt a shiver run up his back.

"Your words do not take away the offense," Lean Elk snapped, drawing his knife.

"I—I do not wish to fight you, Lean Elk. You are a guest in the Chippewa village." Netnokwa looked around. He caught Little Bird's gaze and saw the disappointment there. He knew one reason she had not agreed to become his wife was that she wished to have a great warrior for a husband, one who commanded respect and admiration from his comrades. Netnokwa knew he was not as flamboyant as some of the other warriors. He'd never gained that veneer of arrogance and pride that each warrior displayed as naturally as the male pheasant flaunted his bright plumage. Nevertheless, he had thought himself brave until now. Little Bird's doubts about him made him question his own courage. So he stood before the fearsome Chipewyan war chief and felt the thudding beat of his pulse in his ears and knew he must fight or forever lose Little Bird.

Reluctantly he drew his knife and began to circle. Lean Elk's anger had begun to cool. He'd been about to sheathe his weapon and move on. Now, at the sight of the young brave's daring to draw his knife and meet his challenge, his anger rose again. He must meet the fool in combat or lose face among his own men. The muscles in his legs twitched, but otherwise he did not show fear. Suddenly Lean Elk leaped forward; his knife flashed, arcing through the air and entering the young warrior's chest. Blood gushed from the wound and Netnokwa fell back on the ground.

"No," Little Bird cried, running forward. Lean Elk stood over the fallen warrior, his bloody knife poised. He felt no elation. The young warrior had been too inexperienced to provide any real trial. Lean Elk was sorry he'd killed him, when his real anger had been for the white man.

"Netnokwa!" Little Bird whispered.

"He is dead, woman. Take him away and weep your tears over him." Lean Elk stepped away from the body and, with a final glare around the circle of onlookers, stalked away.

Netnokwa's mother ran into the square, summoned there by Little Bird's cry. When she saw her son on the ground, she tore at her clothes and hair and began to wail. Villagers came forward and carried the gentle young man back to his mother's lodge, where she found her son still lived. Walking Woman was sent for and she worked over the young brave to stem the flow of life from his body.

Now word of Lean Elk's deed spread through the village. Manitowa and Red Hawke conferred.

"This cannot happen in my village," Manitowa declared. "Lean Elk is a guest, yet he has behaved as an enemy."

"I understand the anger of my friend Manitowa," Red Hawke replied. "I, too, am angry at Lean Elk's actions. I cannot undo his bad deed, but I offer you this gift as a token of my regret." Red Hawke handed over his long rifle, a much-prized possession.

Manitowa took the rifle and examined it at great length. Finally he nodded in acceptance. "My friend Red Hawke is a man of honor," he said graciously. The two men smoked together, then Red Hawke withdrew to his own lodge, where Red Sky waited.

"Lean Elk is a man of great anger," she said slowly. She knew she must wind her way carefully. Red Hawke merely grunted and lowered himself before the lodge fire. Red Sky brought him a drink made from the twigs of the wild chokecherry plant and sweetened with maple sugar, which had been a gift from Walking Woman. Quietly she waited until Red Hawke had sipped his drink. When she was sure he was pleased with it, she settled herself beside him and took up a skin that she was embroidering with porcupine quills. For a while they were quiet. At last she forced herself to speak.

"I have seen Swan Necklace's face when she looks at Lean Elk," Red Sky said quietly. "It is filled with anxiety. Yet when she looks upon White Falcon, she smiles and her expression is filled with joy."

"What do you wish to tell me, my wife?" Red Hawke said, turning his gaze to Red Sky. She sighed and put aside her needlework.

"She does not wish to marry Lean Elk."

"Has she told you this?"

"No," Red Sky admitted. "But I see in her eyes, she is unhappy. I hear her cry when she thinks she is alone. She does this for you, Red Hawke. She is a dutiful daughter."

"You have raised my daughter well, Red Sky." He brushed her hand with his own. She smiled and lowered her gaze, coloring at the unaccustomed compliment. She knew Red Hawke thought well of her efforts, but he was not a man of flowery words. She hadn't minded. She understood her husband, just as she understood now that he was trying to lead her astray of their subject.

"Swan Necklace is a good and loving daughter and she would sacrifice her own happiness to please you."

Red Hawke stirred. "You speak of happiness," he said. "This is a new notion brought by the white man. Contentment should be found in pleasing one's parents. You did this when you were a girl. You became my wife as your parents wished."

"I became the wife of Red Hawke to please myself," she answered shyly. Red Hawke put down his cup and stared at her. She could not bear his scrutiny, so she rose gracefully and fled the lodge, her cheeks aflame.

Left alone, Red Hawke contemplated what he must do. He had hoped the marriage of Swan Necklace would win a peaceful alliance with the Chipewyan nation, but now, seeing the evidence of Lean Elk's intemperate rage, Red Hawke felt doubt. He wondered, too, if he should send his daughter into a strange land to live with such a violent man as Lean Elk. Yet he had given his word, and even now the women were preparing a wedding feast. Red Sky had brought a beautiful wedding dress for Swan Necklace. It was made of three deerskins, which Red Sky had carefully bleached in the sun before decorating with cowrie shells and fringes of fur from the black squirrel. It was a dress worthy of a chief's daughter, and such Swan Necklace was. Now Red Hawke wondered if Lean Elk, who, as a guest, could not even show courtesy to his host's men, would show respect to a mere woman. If Lean Elk could not hold Swan Necklace in high esteem, what good would their alliance be? Red Hawke pondered the fate of his daughter and of his tribe.

Red Sky waited outside their lodge. She saw her husband's dilemma and wondered what he would decide. Patiently she waited. After some time, Red Hawke left the lodge and paused to look at his wife.

"The marriage will take place as planned," he said, and without explaining himself further, walked away. Red Sky bit her lip to hold back her disappointment. She feared for Swan Necklace's well-being if she were to go with such a man as Lean Elk. Yet she knew Swan Necklace had no other recourse than to obey her father. Sadly Red Sky took out the beautiful dress she'd made for her stepdaughter and found the matching embroidered moccasins. Swan Necklace would be such a beautiful bride, Lean Elk's heart would have to be moved by her, Red Sky decided, and set herself to make it so.

Swan Necklace's heart was breaking as she prepared for the evening feast and her wedding to Lean Elk. She, too, had heard of Lean Elk's unprovoked attack on Netnokwa, and she'd gone to Little Bird's lodge to express her sorrow. The two girls had clung together and wept.

"I am frightened for you, Swan Necklace," Little Bird cried.

"There is no need to be. I will be safe," Swan Necklace said, although in truth she was very frightened.

"Why don't you run away?" Yellow Leaf exclaimed when Swan Necklace returned to Walking Woman's lodge. "You could find White Falcon and he would take you away from Lean Elk."

"I must do as my father wishes," Swan Necklace whispered. "Besides, if I went away with White Falcon, Lean Elk would find us and kill him."

"Perhaps White Falcon would kill Lean Elk," Yellow Leaf said.

"Perhaps. But I do not wish to take that chance," Swan Necklace replied, and turned away, not wanting to speak anymore of White Falcon or her pending marriage to Lean Elk. Dusk was falling over the lake and village. Campfires glowed brightly throughout the village. Flares of pitch had been set about the village square in readiness for dancing and feasting. Despite their anger at Lean Elk's behavior, the villagers were prepared to celebrate the marriage of Red Hawke's daughter. Besides, witnesses had told how Netnokwa had pulled his knife in answer to Lean Elk's challenge. All agreed the young warrior had acted foolishly against the more experienced, fierce Chipewyan warrior, but he had allowed himself to be provoked into the fight. Netnokwa's mother and Little Bird were not attending the festivities. Some people whispered that the fight was a bad omen for this union between Lean Elk and Swan Necklace.

The marriage council had been called. Garbed in her wedding finery, Swan Necklace sat waiting for the time to attend the ceremony. It was to be given with great ritual since she was the daughter of a chief. Red Sky had drawn a series of small black dots of ground charcoal on her face and white lines with paint made from powdered shells. From the bag of paint brought as a gift for Swan Necklace, Red Sky drew out the precious red hematite, which had been ground and mixed with bear grease for easier application. Carefully she painted a large red circle on Swan Necklace's forehead and each cheek. At last she drew back, satisfied with her handiwork.

"You are very pleasing," she said, and turned away from the misery she saw in Swan Necklace's eyes. She had done all she could on her stepdaughter's behalf.

"Red Sky, what if Lean Elk is not pleased with me?" Swan Necklace whispered her dread.

"He will be. You must not be afraid, Swan Necklace."

"He nearly killed Netnokwa, who was very gentle and angered no one. What if he becomes angry with me?"

Red Sky did not know what to answer. This had been her own fear for Swan Necklace. She forced a smile. "You are the daughter of a great chief. Lean Elk knows that if he harms you, he must answer to Red Hawke."

"Red Hawke fears Lean Elk and the Chipewyans," Swan Necklace said. "That is why he wishes this alliance."

"Red Hawke fears no man," Red Sky insisted. "He is a brave and wise chief. He has led the Cree people well."

"I know this, Red Sky. But my father grows older. I have seen the weakness that comes upon him in the morning. What will become of me if Red Hawke dies? What will become of all the Crees? Will Lean Elk continue to honor the alliance between our tribes?"

"You must not think these things or you will bring them about," Red Sky said sharply. The vision of Red Hawke weak and dying took her breath away. She was sympathetic to Swan Necklace's fears, but now she grew impatient with the girl for pointing out the very thing she herself had tried to ignore. "Red Hawke will live many winters. He will see his son become a great warrior." Red Sky curved her arms around her inflated stomach and glared at Swan Necklace as if she dared her to defy her prophecy.

Swan Necklace forced a smile. "And when I have a son, they will play together and be great friends." She made herself laugh and the haunted look left Red Sky's dark eyes. The two women laughed together, then hugged. Someone approached the lodge.

"It is time," Red Sky said.

"I will miss my mother," Swan Necklace said.

"My heart will be heavy without the presence of my daughter," Red Sky answered. The two women rose, checked their attire, and left the lodge.

Most of the villagers had gathered in the square, where a fire had been lit. Lean Elk and White Bird, a warrior he'd chosen to act as his sponsor, stood on one side of the fire. Red Hawke waved Swan Necklace forward. Frantically she looked around the square, seeking the face of one person. Angus and the other voyageurs were present.

Garth Buckley stood slightly apart, his eyes glittering in a way that once would have made her shiver with fear. Now he meant nothing to her. Her fear was centered on the tall man on the other side of the fire. Red Sky guided her forward and they took their places. At a nod from Red Hawke, Red Sky spoke, her voice clear and firm in the night air.

"Swan Necklace, woman of the Cree nation, is our daughter," she began. "She is pleasing to look upon and good. She has learned to make fine garments. She is an accomplished cook. She is faithful to the ceremonies of the Great Spirit."

Red Sky turned her gaze to Lean Elk and spoke more firmly. "We honor Swan Necklace. She may show temper at times, but she is kind. She may desire things you do not wish to give her, but she is never lazy or greedy. If you take her as your wife, you must be kind and patient with her."

Red Sky turned back to Swan Necklace, gripping her hand very tightly. "And now you, our fair daughter, you are about to take upon yourself the duties of a wife. You are to know the cares of a home. You must be faithful to the warrior Lean Elk. You must give him of your talents. You may find him angry at times, you may find him ill and tired from the hunt, but you must be patient. I have spoken."

Lean Elk stepped forward. The villagers gasped, for the chief would speak for himself. "I am Lean Elk, war chief of the Chipewyans. I have many enemies, but none who equal me in prowess. I am strong and brave. I kill my enemies. I have many honors from war. I will be your husband." He slapped his chest with his closed fist and stood back. His expression was fierce. The women around the square sighed with sympathy for Swan Necklace. Such a man would be difficult to live with. He was too full of himself and he'd made no promises to his new wife.

Face dark with anger, Red Hawke stepped forward and spoke to his son-in-law. "And now, Lean Elk, you are to be the husband of Swan Necklace, who is the daughter of Red Hawke, chief of the Cree nation. Be kind, be patient. There are many occasions that will make you wish to speak harsh words. Withhold them. Depart and hunt for a day before you speak. Then return and speak pleasantly, and your wife will be glad to see you. A good husband does not speak unkindly but by his industry and thoughtfulness proves himself capable of being a husband and a father. I have spoken." Lean Elk's eyes blazed with anger as he regarded his father-in-law. Red Hawke had made it clear he would not have his daughter mistreated.

Now Lean Elk and Swan Necklace were brought to the center near the fire and made to stand facing each other. Someone ordered Lean Elk to bow down. For a long moment he glared into Swan Necklace's eyes and she flushed and turned away, her heart hammering within her chest. What she had seen in her new husband's eyes was rage and a promise of retribution for the liberties Red Hawke had taken in the wedding ceremony. Stiffly he bowed his head, and Swan Necklace threw her two braids around his head. The shaman intoned prayers and drew back.

"These two are one," he cried.

Lean Elk straightened abruptly so that Swan Necklace backed away from him, a look of fear crossing her face. He was supposed to give her a bouquet of wildflowers now, but his hands were empty. After glaring at her, he gripped her upper arm and propelled her toward the campfire, where a place had been reserved for the newlyweds. Swan

Necklace was made to sit behind Lean Elk. Meekly she accepted her position, fighting to hold back tears of mortification at his treatment of her. Dishes were brought of meats and vegetables, wild berry cakes and nutmeats. Barrels of rum had been bought from a trader, and now cups were passed around. The warriors drank deeply; laughter grew loud.

From his place in the woods, James had watched the wedding ceremony, listening to the words of Red Sky and Red Hawke. His love for Swan Necklace seemed overwhelming. He would have cherished her and never would he have spoken harshly. He would have protected her, and even now, at the first sign from her, he would race forward and steal her from Lean Elk and make her his own, but she'd made it very clear this could not be. He saw the way Lean Elk looked at her, and he wanted to leap into the square and cut the warrior's heart from his chest and feed it to the dogs.

He saw the look of terror on Swan Necklace's face and his lips tightened. When Lean Elk led Swan Necklace to the campfire, James turned away. He could watch no more. He made his way down to the lake and sat gazing out over the moonlit water. He felt empty. He had no idea what he would do now. Perhaps return to Scotland. He had no further desire to travel into the wilderness. He wasn't afraid of it; he simply hadn't the heart without Swan Necklace at his side.

"James," a voice called, and Angus came to sit beside him. "Why do you sit out here alone, lad? Why do you not join the feast?"

"Your jest is ill placed," James replied. "I have no wish to join this celebration."

"Aye, but she was a bonny bride, lad," Angus said. "I can see why you want her for your own."

"I don't want to talk about it, Angus," James muttered. He looked out at the black water and noted the call of a loon. "Do you think we'd have time to return to Montreal before the streams freeze?"

"Aye, we could, if the snows hold off a bit and if we paddle like the devil himself is after us."

"Maybe he is," James said.

"I have no mind to return to Montreal a failure," Angus said. "We could winter with the Chippewas and continue on next year to build our fort."

"Aye, you could do that," James agreed. "But I'd not be staying with you."

"Why not, lad? The country is pretty. The Indians are friendly. Red Hawke has become our ally. We could travel with no fear of being attacked by unfriendly tribes."

"In that case, I've no need to go on," James said. "We've made friendly contact with the Indians."

Angus remained silent for a while. "I thought you a better man than this, James McLeod," he said finally. "I'm disappointed with you. You've given her up without a fight."

"Without a fight?" James declared. "She docsn't want to be my wife, man. I can't force her. It's not my way. I believe she wants to be married to Lean Elk. He's some big chief. There's a lot of status for her."

"Nay, lad. She's not wantin' to be married to the likes of him. I seen the terror on her face. She's fearful of him, and that's a fact. But she's been brought up a certain way to do as her father tells her and she's obeying."

"Well, it's the same thing," James said. "There's nothing I can do. She begged me to go away and not interfere. I'm doing what she asked."

Angus sat thinking for a long time, debating over something that could bring his friend what he wanted or bring him death. Either way, he knew the choice was not his. Red Hawke had made that clear that afternoon when he'd stopped to talk to the voyageurs. Now Angus cleared his throat.

"Them Injuns," he said, rocking himself back and forth. "They have some strange customs." He shook his head as if he hardly believed some of them himself. James remained quiet and sullen.

"Did you know they have a custom among the Chipewyans that a man can wrestle for his wife? The winner takes the wife, and the other man has to let him."

James made no answer. He was contemplating getting into a canoe and setting out for Montreal that very moment.

"Don't seem proper to me to take a chance on losing your wife like that, but the Chipewyans don't hold a woman in much account anyway. They think it's unseemly to spill blood on the ground for a mere woman."

Some of what Angus was saying penetrated James's dull shell. "What are you saying, Angus?" he inquired.

"Jaimie, lad. I'm saying that if you want Swan Necklace, you can still get her, and in a way that won't dishonor her father."

"Angus, are you saying . . . are you . . . I can?"

"You can wrestle for Swan Necklace."

"That's ludicrous."

"Aye, but that's the way of the Chipewyan. If you want to win Swan Necklace, you'd best use whatever means you can."

Before he'd finished speaking, James was running up the bank toward the village square. When he stepped into the firelight, he was breathing from his race there. He was shirtless and his chest rose and fell with each breath. His muscles rippled in the firelight. His angular face was stern, his eyes glittered with purpose. He looked dangerous, and the villagers moved aside for him until nothing stood between him and the people seated beside the campfire. Red Hawke glanced up and repressed a smile. The white trapper had carried his message well. Manitowa regarded the white warrior with some concern. Swan Necklace's eyes grew large and she clasped her hands in her lap. Only Lean Elk seemed pleased by James's appearance. Lithely he sprang to his feet.

"What do you wish, white eyes?" he demanded.

"I, White Falcon, have come to challenge Lean Elk," James called.

Lean Elk reached for his knife. "I accept any challenge

the white eyes makes." He leaped over the fire pit to land in front of James.

"This isn't a battle to death," James said. "The victor does not claim the heart of his enemy as reward."

"What do you wish, white eyes?" Lean Elk asked.

"Your wife!" James's lips barely moved as he said the words, but they were heard all around the square. Swan Necklace sprang to her feet. Lean Elk's face grew ugly.

"You will never have her," he snarled.

So swiftly Lean Elk hardly knew what he was about, James drew his knife and tossed it into the ground near the fire pit. "We do not need weapons for this fight," he called. "Or is Lean Elk afraid to meet another warrior without his knife?"

Lean Elk glared at him, then threw his knife toward the fire pit. It landed upright and quivering in the dirt beside James's knife. Crouched, the two men faced each other, circling warily. James watched Lean Elk's eyes. The other warrior never even blinked, but once his eyes narrowed slightly and James readied himself for the attack. Lean Elk leaped at him. James spun away and turned on Lean Elk, flipping him in the air. The war chief came down on his back. The impact stunned him. James launched himself at him, but the wily Indian rolled away and sprang to his feet. James scrambled up and once again the two men circled.

James began the second attack, leaping forward and grabbing Lean Elk in a choking hold about the neck. Lean Elk kicked out at James, loosening the hold, and they both went down in the dust. The villagers moved back so the two struggling men would have more room. Swan Necklace stood beside the fire, too stunned to do anything, her heart in her throat so she was unable even to cry out. She saw muscles strain, heard fists hit against flesh, heard the grunt of two men who fought for her, one out of a sense of possession and one out of love.

Lean Elk was thrown. He landed heavily on his left arm and lay in the dust, stunned. James staggered toward him. "Have you had enough?" he called. Lean Elk made no answer, nor did he move. Assuming he'd surrendered, James turned away. In that instant Lean Elk reached out for the knife he had thrown away earlier. Swan Necklace found her voice now.

"White Falcon," she called out, and he spun around, throwing himself to the ground as Lean Elk's knife whistled over his head. A villager cried out and sank to the ground, Lean Elk's knife buried in his shoulder. James leaped forward and wrestled Lean Elk to the ground. The warrior struggled feebly. James clamped his arm around Lean Elk's neck and arched his head backward until he heard a grunt of pain.

"Do you give up, Lean Elk?" he cried.

Lean Elk gritted his teeth and growled low in his throat. His eyes were those of an animal, wild and untamable. James increased the pressure.

"Do you concede that Swan Necklace belongs to me now?" Still the warrior made no answer. His muscles quivered as he sought to break James's hold, and the veins in his temples bulged. James held him fast, pulling his head back until it seemed his neck would surely snap.

"Do you surrender all rights to Swan Necklace," James demanded, "and concede I have won her fair and square? Do you?"

Lean Elk grunted his surrender.

"Say it so all who are present might hear," James demanded.

"The Cree woman is yours," Lean Elk gasped, and James released his hold on him. Lean Elk leaped to his feet and glared around at the circle of faces.

"I could kill you for this, white eyes," he snarled.

"But such is not the custom of your people," Red Hawke said. "You have told me so yourself. No warrior would spill the blood of another over a woman won fairly in a wrestling match."

"So it is done," Lean Elk replied bitterly. His hate-filled gaze moved to Swan Necklace. She shrank back from the rage she saw in his face. Lean Elk's gaze went on to James.

"Someday, white eyes," he said curtly, "we will meet again. There will be another reason for me to take your life, and so I will do." With a final baleful glare, he retrieved his knife from the friends of the man he'd accidently injured and, without a backward glance, stalked away. Silently his warriors followed. The villagers were speechless, walking to the edge of the shore to watch as Lean Elk and his warriors gained their canoes and paddled out into the lake. Swiftly the canoes glided away around the curve of the bay and were lost to view. The villagers looked at one another and smiled. With a shout they went back to their feasts and dancing.

"I am sorry to have brought this shame upon you, my father," Swan Necklace said to Red Hawke.

He put his arm around Red Sky and they laughed together. "You have brought no shame to me, my daughter," he replied. "You became the wife of Lean Elk as was promised, but Lean Elk lost you to White Falcon in a wrestling match. It is his own fault to indulge in this foolish custom."

"Then you do not object?" Swan Necklace asked, hardly daring to hope.

"You belong to White Falcon now," Red Hawke replied. "It is not for me to object or approve. Go, my daughter, and seek out this white warrior who has bested Lean Elk to win you."

Swan Necklace pushed through the milling villagers, searching for White Falcon. When she saw him, she stood still and gazed at him. He was dirty. His sharp cheekbones were scraped and bleeding from his struggle, but he had never looked more handsome. He turned and saw her. His eyes filled with joy.

"Swan Necklace!" he cried, and stepped toward her, uncertain if she was angry or not. "Lean Elk is gone."

"I know," she answered softly. "I am White Falcon's woman now." He smiled then and his long legs used up the space between them. She was in his arms and his mouth was on hers, hungry and seeking. She answered him in kind. For the first time in months, they could express their love wholeheartedly and without shame.

Red Sky watched her stepdaughter and White Falcon. Her fine brow wrinkled. "You know this is not the end of it with Lean Elk," she said to her husband.

"That is true," he sighed. "I could only show White Falcon how to win Swan Necklace from Lean Elk. I cannot show him how to keep her." Red Hawke turned away to his lodge. Despite the dangers that lay ahead for them from the events of this day, he was pleased.

Chapter 10

"**Y**OU'RE HURT," SWAN NECKLACE said, and led White Falcon to a secluded haven along the lakeshore, gently shoving him down on the sand. Taking a soft piece of doeskin, she knelt and washed his battered face. Her small hands were tender, her fingers brushing his skin in a way that made his pulse leap. She was unaware of the effect she had on him.

James snatched up her hand and pressed it to his lips. "I thought I'd lost you forever," he said.

"And I you, White Falcon," she answered. She rested her cheek against his bowed head. For a moment they held each other, rejoicing in being together.

"I am your woman now, White Falcon," she said in a small voice that he had to strain to hear. He raised his head and looked at her. Moonlight gilded the sweet curve of her cheeks and mouth. Her beautiful eyes were lost in shadows, but her girlishly rounded brow was smooth and clear, her face a pale oval in the shadows. James touched the shells adorning her ears, smoothed back the sleek, black hair, and slipped lower to clasp her around the waist.

"You are my woman," he said. "You belong to me."

"I belong to you," she echoed.

"No other man can ever claim you?"

"No other man ever will," she vowed. Suddenly she was grateful for the white man's custom of claiming only one wife. She studied his face, the proud beak of a nose, the high, prominent cheekbones, and the tall, lean body that possessed the strength and power to best even Lean Elk. She shivered as she thought of that body possessing her. She was still virginal, and although she well knew the ways of men and women when they mated, she felt a tremor of trepidation.

She saw the hunger on his face, and to forestall the moment, she quickly disentangled herself and loosened the soft doeskin garment that had been her wedding dress. She heard his quick intake of breath as she stood naked before him. The moonlight caressed her small, perfectly shaped body, highlighting the curve of breast, the flare of hips, and the fine, straight slope of thigh and calf.

"You are a bonny lass," he whispered raggedly.

"So is White Falcon," she answered earnestly. He bit back a grin at her attempt to use his language. Later he would tell her the difference between a lad and a lass, or maybe he'd just show her. At that thought, his eyes darkened with desire. Reading the passion in his gaze, Swan Necklace turned, flipping a coquettish glance over her bare shoulder, and waded into the cool water made silver by the starshine. Her small feet barely disturbed the still surface. She waded out beyond her waist and glided into a swim, her arms flashing, creating a silvery spray of water with each stroke. Her wet head was as sleek as an otter's. James thought he'd never seen anything as beautiful as this girl. There were some back home who might call her savage or wild, but she was the gentlest creature he'd ever met and she awakened a fire in him that could never be called gentle.

He drew off the ragged leggings he'd worn from the Ottawa camp and stepped into the water. It lapped around his ankles. Standing in the moonlight, feeling its glow against his skin, James was aware of his own nakedness, of his readiness to claim the girl who swam just beyond his reach. He raised his head and looked at the star-studded sky. He felt invincible and at the same time humbled. He was part of the sky and the lake and the girl. He was part of the land

and the men who celebrated back in the village. Never had he felt his manliness so potently, never had he felt his very humanness so clearly. Was this the magic of which the red men spoke?

Swan Necklace stopped swimming and watched White Falcon standing at the edge of the lake. His long, dark hair fell to his shoulders, his magnificent lean body seemed carved of stone. She belonged to this man. She reveled in the knowledge. Slowly, sensuously, she swam toward him. He came to meet her, his strokes long and even, his shadowed gaze fixed on her with an intensity that woke a curling heat deep within her.

When they met, they treaded water and gazed into each other's eyes. No words were spoken. None were needed. James reached for her, pulling her close so her smooth, bare breasts brushed against his chest. His lips claimed hers, hungry and demanding, not to be denied ever again. His long arms wrapped around her, pinning her wet, sleek form to his, crushing her small breasts. She felt his erection even in the cold water and was inflamed by it. They kissed and sank beneath the water and rose to gasp in a breath of air before kissing again. He couldn't seem to stop touching and kissing her. She was like some exotic, potent drug found in the dark, mysterious forests. He pulled her closer to shore until his feet found purchase in the soft sand, lifted her high above him and took one of her nipples in his mouth, suckling hungrily.

Swan Necklace's body shook in a spasm of delight. She arched against him, cradling his head in a silent gesture of love, while his hungry mouth claimed her other pert nipple. She gasped. His hands settled on her hips, anchoring her against him. Her legs wrapped around his waist. He settled her so her hot center was at the tip of his throbbing penis. With one mighty thrust, he claimed her. Swan Necklace bit her lips against the pain, burying her head against his neck.

"I'm sorry to give you pain, my love," he whispered against her mouth. "It will be better now, I promise."

"I do not mind the pain," she fibbed. It had been greater

than she'd expected, but now she felt the bigness of him filling her and she forgot the discomfort. He didn't move again until she was ready, and then he thrust against her, his big hands covering her smooth, rounded buttocks, holding her captive so she couldn't have escaped even if she'd wanted to.

But now Swan Necklace felt the power of this man's passion and she had no wish to run away, ever. She felt the cool, sensuous lap of water at her shoulders and breasts and the hot spilling seed of the man within her. She closed her eyes and clamped her legs tighter about him, feeling the waves of her fulfillment.

James stood as if made of stone. His arms were still strong around her, his muscular legs held them both afloat in the water, but his lean body had arched away from her as if in pain, before he'd folded her close again. He didn't speak, couldn't speak, she perceived, and was entranced by his reaction to her. She had pleased him mightily, she saw, but even more, he had pleased her. She had thought she loved him as much as possible; now she saw there were whole new layers to these emotions between a man and a woman, and she would be subjected to each of them until she would be forever caught in her feelings for him. The thought was not displeasing to her.

Slowly he raised his head and looked into her eyes. "You are a wee, bonny lass," he whispered, and the strange words were soothing to her. She hid her face against his neck in sudden shyness. James laughed and carried her to shore with her legs still wrapped around him and his member still within her. She tried to get down, but he wouldn't let her. He fell onto the soft sand and cradled her against him, nibbling at her ear and cheek until passion flared between them again and he took her there in the soft, warm sand. Afterward, exhausted and trembling, they lay together until the damp mist drifted in from the lake and she shivered against him. Instantly he rose and picked her up in his arms. She'd never felt so cherished, so protected, so adored.

"There is a lodge set aside for us," she whispered, and

didn't reveal it had been intended for Lean Elk and her to share. She directed him toward the bridal lodge. Inside, a small fire had been kept burning. Its embers glowed. At one side was a fine pallet of soft furs Red Sky and Swan Necklace had prepared earlier that day. Swan Necklace smiled, remembering how heavy her heart had been as she made her bridal bed. She hadn't known then she would share it with White Falcon. He placed her on the bed and smiled down at her. His gaze was full of love. Lying down beside her, James pulled a warm fur around them, and Swan Necklace lay against his shoulder thinking what happiness she felt at being with this man.

"You're quiet, lass," he whispered. "Have I hurt you?"

"A content woman has no need to chatter, my husband," she replied.

"Then I shall strive to make you more content," he said, and reached for her.

"I am content enough for one night, White Falcon," she whispered shyly.

James drew back and looked at her. "Aye, lass, I've used you roughly for a virgin. I'll be gentler in the future." He cradled her against his side. Swan Necklace thought over his words.

"White Falcon?" she whispered. "There is no need to change."

She heard his sleeping chuckle and he clamped her to him more tightly. He would be a most possessive husband, she saw. She lay awake long after he slept. She thought back over the day's events, and the more she thought, the less content she became, so that the dawn was just touching the horizon before she fell into an exhausted sleep.

"Good morning, wife," White Falcon said, gazing down at her. His face was freshly shaven and he had bathed. Water trickled from his wet hair, dropping on her face and breasts. She mumbled a protest and he laughed teasingly. "Have I married a *da*?"

"What is this *da*?" she asked in wonderment.

"Aye, well you might ask if you've a mind to be a goody

wife to me." He smiled, leaving her in suspense before answering her question. "A *da* is a sluggard, an indolent
wench."

"Wench?" Swan Necklace repeated.

"A woman who lies abed."

"I am not this—this wench, White Falcon. I will be a
good wife to you. I will rise early and bring fresh water and
build the fire and tan the hides you bring. I will gather food
so we will never go hungry in the time of hard, crusting
snow. I will . . ." She ran out of steam, remembering her
last thought before she fell asleep the night before. De-
jected, she sat on the pallet and turned her back to him, letting her dark hair fall forward to cover her face.

"I do not blame White Falcon for thinking so little of his
new wife," she said in a small voice. "He won her in a
wrestling match, so he must think her a thing of small
worth."

James laughed until he realized she was serious. Taking
her shoulders, he turned her to face him. "I find you of
great worth," he replied.

"A wife who is but a wager between two men cannot
mean much," she answered. "Lean Elk held me in low esteem or he would not have risked losing me, so it is small
wonder that you do not hold me in high esteem."

"That isn't true, Swan Necklace," James cried, catching
her close. "I love you, lass. Didn't last night prove that to
you?"

"Men mate with women when there is no emotion such
as the white men call 'love,' " she replied stoically. James
laughed and pulled back from her, studying her face. "I
cherish Swan Necklace above all else," he said, but when
she remained sullen and unresponsive, he sighed and rose
to his feet.

"I will dress at once and tend to my husband's needs,"
Swan Necklace said, rising and drawing on her deerskin
garment. James watched, openly admiring the sleek line of
his wife's body, the shadowy contours of her breasts and
hips that called to him, but he feared she might yet expe-

rience some soreness from their first mating, and he forced himself to patience.

When she was dressed, Swan Necklace cast him a troubled glance and left the lodge. When he followed her outdoors, she had already gathered wood and was preparing a fire. For a while he sat and watched her, just because he now had that right. Finally, perceiving such scrutiny made her nervous, he rose and made his way down to the village.

Manitowa hailed him, motioning him to his lodge. Curious, James followed the old chief. Inside the lodge, all was neat and in place and a small fire burned in the center fire pit. Walking Woman was an admirable wife and took great pride in rising early to attend to the needs of her family. Now Manitowa motioned James to be seated while he rummaged in a stack of birchbark *mukkuks*. Finally he drew out a small object wrapped in deerskin and handed it to James.

"I have not given you a wedding present," he said, and waited with a pleased look while James slowly unwrapped the object. The last of the hide covering fell away and James gasped. His heart beat wildly. In his hand lay the precious magnetic compass he'd brought from Montreal. Its flat round face marked the four corners, and the needle wavered with the slightest movement of his hand. Manitowa chuckled, obviously pleased with James's reaction.

"The magnetic compass. I thought it was lost," he said in wonder. "I asked Shemung about it and he simply shrugged as if he didn't know what I was talking about."

"Shemung traded it to me for a barrel of white man's whiskey," Manitowa revealed. "I do not understand this thing, so I give it back to you."

"Thank you, Manitowa," James said. "With this we can continue our journeys to the West."

"Is this what White Falcon wishes to do?"

"Aye, it is," he said. "I have promised the governor in Montreal that I will find new trails to the beaver streams in the West. I must keep my promise."

"Aye!" Manitowa nodded. "Soon will come the months of wind and snow. The rivers will freeze. We can no longer use our canoes. We must walk on shoes made specially for the snow. White Falcon and his men are welcome to stay with Manitowa for the winter."

"We are grateful for Manitowa's hospitality, but we will likely travel on with Red Hawke and his people."

"He prepares even now for his journey," Manitowa said.

James held aloft the magnetic compass. "You have given me a valuable gift, Manitowa," he said. "Someday I will repay you."

"You have rid us of Lean Elk; that is enough," Manitowa replied with some humor.

When James quit Manitowa's lodge, he went at once to the lodge where his men stayed. Most of them were still in their pallets, their faces slack in sleep, their features blurred from the excess of too much rum and food at the wedding celebration.

"Wake up," James shouted, kicking the booted feet of the nearest man. When they were all sitting, bleary-eyed, belligerently regarding him, he smiled. "Red Hawke is leaving soon to return to his winter camp. I propose we go with him."

"But we have no food, no clothes, and no trade goods," Garth Buckley protested. Several of the other men nodded.

"Aye, that's true," James said, "but how many of you want to return to Montreal with our tails between our legs and admit our failure?" The men looked at each other. None spoke.

"If we go on with Red Hawke and his people, we'll be given food and clothes. We'll learn to hunt off the land, the way the Indians do. If they can last a winter out here, then by God, so can we."

"You've a *fille de joie* to keep you warm at night," Buckley spoke up again.

Guy d'Chaney spoke up. *"Gardez le bouche!"* His eyes were hostile as he faced the stockier Buckley.

James looked from one man to the other, his expression becoming stern and unyielding.

"Do you have something to explain, Buckley?" he demanded.

The Frenchman shrugged. "A slip of the tongue, *monsieur*, nothing more." James studied the other man with narrowed eyes.

Uneasily Buckley glanced around the group of voyageurs. "If it is the wish of everyone to go on, I will go with you."

"We'll have some trouble navigating without a compass," Angus said. "Mind you, we can do it, but it would've been a lot easier with our compass and with goods to trade to the other Indian tribes."

"I've been thinking about that," James said. He took the compass out of his pocket and held it up for all to see. "A wedding gift from Manitowa. As for the rest of our goods . . ." He shrugged. "Shemung and his warriors have them. Although Shemung released Angus and me, I figure I still have the right to reclaim my goods. How many of you are in the mood to attack the Ottawa camp before they move out?"

"They beat us before," Buckley cried. "They'll beat us again."

"They came upon us when we weren't prepared," Angus called. "I figure I can hold off ten of them devils myself."

"I can handle another ten," Wye called. "Especially if one of 'em's Wawatam."

"We don't have to worry about that warrior," James said quietly. "His own people took care of him." He squatted beside the fire and read the faces of his men. "Make no mistake about this, some of us may be killed. We will have no rifles, only our knives and bows and arrows we borrow from the Chippewa. The Chippewa are at peace with the Ottawa. They won't fight with us."

The men looked troubled.

James continued. "But Angus and I know the ways of the village. We know where they've stashed our goods. We know who has our rifles. We can sneak into the village at night, retrieve our supplies, and try to ease our way out without being discovered."

"What about their sentries? Won't they have lookouts?"

"Aye," James replied. "Angus and I know where they are. We'll silence them, but not kill them."

"*Mon*, it sounds impossible," Buckley protested.

"It might be, but it's worth taking a chance. Who's with me on this?" He looked around at the circle of men. They looked considerably better than he'd hoped for. Their clothes were ragged and dirty, but their wounds had healed and they'd eaten well in the Chippewa camp. They looked fit enough except for the slackness of inactivity.

One by one the men indicated their willingness to join him. James nodded his head in satisfaction. "We go tonight," he said.

"That's a bit soon," someone grumbled.

"The Chippewa are getting ready to move back to their winter camps. Soon the Ottawa will do the same. If we're to do this, we must do it tonight." There were no more objections. With a final nod, James left the lodge and made his way to the Cree lodges. When he found Red Hawke, he greeted his new father-in-law.

"All is well with White Falcon?" Red Hawke inquired politely.

"Aye." James nodded. "I have spoken with Manitowa, who tells me you plan to return to your winter camp soon."

"We will leave at first light," Red Hawke said. "Does White Falcon and his men wish to travel with us?"

"Aye," James said with some relief. He was rapidly gaining a deep respect for the proud chief. "My men are concerned because we have no winter clothes and we have no food except that which we hunt with bow and arrow."

"White Falcon is a good hunter," Red Hawke replied. "He will add meat to our winter fare. His wife, Swan Necklace, will make him warm furs for the cold months. The white voyageurs must take Indian wives as White Falcon has done. Their wives will gather food and make life comfortable for them."

"Red Hawke is very wise," James said. "But there are no unwed Cree women among your party."

"There are Chippewa women in Manitowa's camp who seek husbands," Red Hawke replied. James saw the glimmer of humor deep in the old chief's eyes.

James grinned. "So there are," he said. "So there are. We will be ready to join you at first light." Quickly James left the lodge and made his way back to the lodge of his men. When he revealed his conversation with Red Hawke, the men looked at each other. Several of the younger ones scrambled from their pallets and hurried away. Wye was among them, and James noticed he made straight for Yellow Leaf's lodge.

James sauntered back to the lodge he shared with Swan Necklace. When he arrived he saw a kettle of savory-smelling stew was boiling over a tidy fire. Swan Necklace sat at one side, a fur across her lap. Her fingers were busy embroidering a quill pattern. Her sleek head was bent over her task and she did not look up as he approached.

James paused and studied her. She seemed subdued and aloof, not at all like the Swan Necklace he'd come to know. When he spoke, she turned her head away and he saw the runnels tears had made down her cheeks.

"Swan Necklace, why do you cry?" he asked, lowering himself to the ground beside her. "Are you unhappy that you're my wife?"

Silently she shook her head.

"Do you wish to have Lean Elk again?" he asked.

Again the silent shake of her head.

"Have I displeased you in some way?"

The movement was barely perceptible, but it was there.

"Then why do you sit and weep?" he demanded in exasperation. He was surprised to find this moodiness in Swan Necklace. Having a sister, he was well used to the vagaries of women, but he'd not expected it of Swan Necklace. Helpless in the face of a woman's tears, he waited while she dried her face and raised her head. Her eyes were dark and melancholy, the mischievous lights dimmed.

"I am sad, my husband," she began in a low voice, "because I am a woman of so little worth. White Falcon can never feel proud to have such a wife as me. He must hide me away and pretend I do not exist."

"What are you saying, Swan Necklace? Ah, you're not still going on about the fact that I won you in a wrestling match, are you?"

She bowed her head and said nothing.

"I could have lost my life, you know," James cried. Still she said nothing. "I risked my life for you because you mean so much to me. That seems a bloody high enough value to place on you."

"It is not the same," she sighed.

"Why isn't it?" he demanded, irritated at something beyond his patience.

"You do not understand the ways of my people," she whispered.

"I'm trying to," he said with some asperity. "You'll have to forgive me, Swan Necklace, it I'm not the husband you expect me to be."

"White Falcon is a bonny husband," she cried.

James couldn't repress a smile at her use of his language. "And Swan Necklace is a bonny wife," he said, reaching for her. "White Falcon is pleased with his wife, Swan Necklace." His mouth claimed hers. She was soft and yielding in his arms. He forgot about food and carried her inside their lodge.

"White Falcon, the sun is still shining," she cried in consternation at his intentions.

"Aye, wife, the sun is still shining, but I want to show my wife how pleased I am with her." He placed her on the rug pallet and stood over her, his gray eyes taking in every detail of her. She blushed beneath his gaze until he stripped away his leggings and she saw his arousal. Her eyes grew round and suddenly she leaped up as if to run away. He caught her before she reached the door, wrapping his long arms around her waist, pinning her to him, so his hard arousal scraped against her mound. Her giggle turned to a gasp and her hands trembled as she stripped away her clothing until she stood before him naked and beautiful. Her eyes were wide and trusting, her small mouth full and inviting.

Slowly, wonderingly, he reached for her. She was so perfect, he shook with a desperate need not to rush, but to go slowly and savor every moment of discovery between them. Her small hands came up to touch his battered face and he seized her, holding her, thinking how close he'd come to losing her to Lean Elk.

"White Falcon?" she whispered.

He scooped her up in his arms and carried her back to their pallet. Bright sunlight spilled through the door. He should close it for privacy, but he had a sudden need to see her in the daylight. When her arms reached for him, to pull him down to her, he pushed them aside and straddled her while he gently kneaded her breasts.

He saw the change that came over her as she accepted that first awakening that comes to each man and woman no matter how often they couple, that first surrendering to the sensuality that claims the body and then the mind. His hands moved down to the delicate bones of her rib cage, the tiny waist, and the flaring of hips.

Her eyes were closed now. Her expression was one of relinquishment, a giving up of self to this other world of pleasure. He released her legs and scooped his hand between her thighs, searching for and finding the moist bud. She jerked and her eyes flew open. There was a look of startlement. Her eyes were dark and deep and glowing. He touched her again, watching her face, enjoying her expression of astonishment and then of acceptance. She bent her knees, opening herself to his touch, and he stroked her with increasing vigor until she gasped and tried to close herself again, but he was there and ready.

He moved between her slim thighs, pressing his hardened penis into her, feeling her tightness, her hotness, stroking her with his body as he had with his hand, so she arched against him and her cry startled the blue heron fishing in the shallows. He heard the flap of wings and swore he was himself a great bird soaring over the lake, until his heart started beating again and he began to breathe and he realized, with gratitude, he was just a man.

He lay too sated to move. Swan Necklace stirred beneath him and he rolled to one side. A wonderful lethargy claimed him. He wanted only to drowse in the late afternoon sun. Forgotten were his plans to raid the Ottawa camp, gone were his plans to join Red Hawke at first light. He lay as if dead, until a tiny sob caught his dulled ear and he sat upright.

"Swan Necklace?"

"I am an unworthy wife," she sobbed.

"Bloody hell!" James shouted, leaping to his feet and glaring down at her.

"Are you going to beat me now?" she asked fearfully.

"Beat you? Swan Necklace, I just bedded with you. Didn't that mean anything? Didn't you feel what was between us?"

"Aye, White Falcon, I did, but men take women to bed without paying a bridal price. They pay only a small bead necklace or a kettle. I am not even worth a kettle."

"Swan Necklace! You must stop this. I have nothing to trade." He reached for his leggings, and the leather cloth containing the precious compass fell at his feet. The compass spilled out onto the furs.

"White Falcon," Swan Necklace cried. "The Great Spirit has provided you with something to trade for me."

"I can't trade this, Swan Necklace. This is the magnetic compass I must use to travel through the wilderness. It helps me find my way."

"This?" she asked, picking it up and moving it so the needle jumped first one way and then the other. "How can this show you the way around the Mother Earth?"

James took the compass and pointed it north. "Do you see that needle? How it points to the north? We have only to follow that needle and it will lead us home."

Swan Necklace listened carefully to his words, then took

the compass and turned it. "But the needle moves around, White Falcon. You must not trust this. It lies to you," she said.

James laughed, glad to have her diverted. "You can always trust it," he said. "It will always tell which way is north. It's magic!"

"But you have no need of such magic. The Mother Earth tells us these things and they are always constant."

"Not as good a magic as this."

"Yes, White Falcon. Come with me." She leaped up and threw on her clothes, then taking his hand, she led him some distance into the woods.

"Do you see the moss growing here at the back of this tree?" she asked, pointing to a clump of lichen. "It grows only on the north side of the tree. The sun does not reach here, so the moss can grow in peace." She rose and pointed to the high branches of an oak tree.

"Do you see how the branches are more in number and are larger on one side of this tree than on the other? The branches are thickest on the south side of the tree. They do not jump from one side of the tree to the other like the needle in your compass." James was growing amused at her comparison.

"See the tops of the pine trees?" Swan Necklace cried. "They lean toward the rising of the sun." She turned and looked at him. "If White Falcon is ever lost in the woods, he can look to these things and find his way."

Suddenly he realized she was teaching him the ways of her world, much as a mother would teach her child so he would not become lost. Her small face was so earnest, her eyes so solemn, that he hadn't the heart to laugh at her. He walked to her and smoothed a hand down the long, silken drape of her hair.

"White Falcon will remember these things when he is alone in the woods and he will think of Swan Necklace with great pleasure," he said.

She smiled, then pulled away from him. "Though I am a wife of little worth, I will try to be a good wife," she whispered, then with a sob, whirled and ran away through the woods.

"Swan Necklace," he cried, but she didn't halt in her headlong flight. Perplexed, James made his way back through the woods alone. The compass felt very heavy at his waist.

Chapter 11

THAT EVENING A final feast was planned. Red Hawke and his people would be leaving the village the next morning, and in a few weeks, after rice and crops were harvested, the Chippewas would leave their summer camp. Swan Necklace prepared a kettle of food to be taken to the village square. She was silent and subdued as she worked. Troubled, James watched her move gracefully around the campfire. He could not give up the compass. It was too important to their journeys, yet he must find some way to assuage his wife's offended pride.

Swan Necklace disappeared into the lodge and, after a short while, returned with her face painted and her hair decorated with bits of fur and shell ornaments. Taking the kettle off the fire, she turned to him, waiting meekly for him to rise and accompany her to the village.

"Let me take that for you," he said, reaching for the heavy kettle.

"No!" she exclaimed, drawing away from him. "Do not shame me, White Falcon. The other women will think I am of even less worth if I do not carry my own burdens." She darted away toward the square.

Cursing under his breath, James followed. During the festivities, he watched as Swan Necklace moved among the other women, chatting and blushing at their teasing remarks. She seemed happy enough, he told himself, yet he denoted a sadness in her eyes.

The gathering had become quite festive. New friendships had been formed over the past weeks since the Crees first came to Manitowa's camp. Those new friendships would continue in the years ahead. The two tribes, so similar in their language and customs, had found a new kinship. Furthermore, several Chippewa maidens had been persuaded to join the white voyageurs in the coming journey. They, too, would travel with them and live in the Cree village.

James saw Wye with Yellow Leaf. The young voyageur's face was beaming with pride. Yellow Leaf and Swan Necklace hugged each other, wildly excited at the prospect of sharing the coming adventures. Wye watched the two young women with a newly acquired indulgence, his chest puffed out, his chin high, but when Yellow Leaf turned and spoke to him, he dropped his superior male facade and leaped to do her bidding.

"Bah, look at him. He's gone all barmy!" Angus cried in disgust. The other men snickered. Some of them had their arms around comely maidens.

"You haven't chosen yourself a woman, Angus," James said.

"I ain't seen one I couldn't live without," Angus snapped.

"Mais oui, mon ami," Buckley cried. "We all know he'd have to wrestle for the woman he wants."

"Shut up, Buckley," Maurice snapped.

James looked at the faces of his men, then back at Angus. "What does he mean, old friend?"

" 'Tis naught but the braying of a jackass," Angus answered.

"No, no, my friend," Buckley said, shaking a finger to emphasize his point. "I've seen with my own eyes how this man watches the little Swan Necklace. I have told him he must wrestle with you. You have won her in a wrestling match, so she can be won back by someone else."

"Pay no heed to what he says, James," Angus cried.

"Is this true, Angus? You have feelings for Swan Necklace?" James's gray eyes were nearly black as he studied the trapper's face. Angus glanced away, then back to meet James's steely gaze.

"Aye, true enough," he admitted. "Not a man here who doesn't feel the same way, and why not? She's nursed our wounds, worried over us, and cooked for us. She's gentle and good and a wee bonny lass. Who would not be caring about her? But she's too young for me, James, and she's never seen another man except you on this trip. Ain't no doubt, you're the one she wants. You've naught to fear from me."

His words were truly spoken and his gaze never wavered, so James knew he need never have a concern about Angus's intentions regarding Swan Necklace, but Buckley's attitude was another thing. James glanced around the circle again, knowing the men were behind him, but that they, too, thought less of Swan Necklace for the way she'd been won. Without another word he strode away from his men.

"You fool. Why can't you keep your mouth shut?" Maurice declared to Buckley. "Angus is right. You're naught but a jackass, a *sot*, an eem-be-zeele!" Maurice shook his finger in Buckley's face as he drew out the last word. The other men and their mates tittered with amusement, but Buckley's face grew mottled and furious.

"I think you like Swan Necklace yourself," Maurice scoffed, and turned his back on the big man. Buckley lunged after him. The other men quickly placed themselves between the two men, aligning themselves with the feisty little Frenchman who'd dared to speak up to Buckley. Buckley glanced at their expressions and backed away, his face surly.

"I have no need of any man's leavings," he exclaimed. "I have me my own woman."

"Then why don't you go to her and stop causing trouble?" Angus called.

With a final defiant snarl, Buckley turned and made his way toward the circle of dancing women. Unceremoniously he pushed his way forward and grabbed Little Bird's arm, hauling her away from the others. Startled, she looked at the bearded trapper. He was not as handsome as the young voyageur Wye or as warriorlike as White Falcon, but he had given her many beads and he'd whispered many fine promises in her ear. If she became the wife of one of the white trappers, she would enjoy the same prestige as Swan Necklace and Yellow Leaf. So thinking, Little Bird smiled up at the trapper and did not protest when he fumbled with her hide dress, roughly caressing her breasts through the soft buckskin.

From his pallet Netnokwa watched as Buckley and the girl talked. When Little Bird nodded and accepted the white man's embrace, Netnokwa looked away. He knew he'd lost Little Bird with his mawkish shyness and his careful nature. She thought him womanly, especially after his defeat by Lean Elk. She preferred men who were bold and fearless. He couldn't blame her. Such were the ways of their people. Bitterly he gritted his teeth and gazed at the stars overhead. He prayed to the spirits to give him strength to spring up and claim Little Bird as his own, but the spirits weren't listening to him. Even they had turned their faces from him. Netnokwa turned away and pretended not to see Little Bird walk with the white trapper. It was hard to claim a woman's heart when he was forced to lie on his pallet like a toothless old man.

Manitowa himself looked saddened at the prospect of losing not only his new friends but several comely women from his tribe. The old chief sat with great dignity at the front of the square, Red Hawke beside him.

Troubled by what his men had revealed, James made his way across the square and came to a halt before the two chiefs. When the music from the drums stopped, he stepped forward and greeted them.

"I have come to speak to Red Hawke," he said.

"Speak, White Falcon," Manitowa replied.

"White Falcon has earned Swan Necklace from Lean Elk in a fair fight," James began.

Red Hawke frowned. "White Falcon is not pleased with Swan Necklace?"

"White Falcon is very pleased with Swan Necklace," James said. "White Falcon is proud of his new wife and wishes to show Red Hawke and the rest of the village his esteem for Swan Necklace."

Swan Necklace had crept forward, her eyes wary as she observed these events. Now, as James pulled the leather cloth from the pouch at his waist, she smiled and, squaring her shoulders, stepped into the circle of light.

"White Falcon has nothing of value to give Red Hawke as a bride price for Swan Necklace," James said, both hands covering the leather-wrapped object as if he entertained last-minute doubts, "nothing except this gift which Manitowa gave me today." His fingers worked quickly now that he had committed himself. He threw back the leather covering, revealing the magnetic compass with its gold case. A sigh of wonder went up from the villagers.

"Mon Dieu!" muttered Buckley to the other men. "He's giving away the compass!" Wordlessly, the men watched the transaction taking place.

"This is an instrument of the white man," James explained. "It is very important and contains much good magic. Without it the white man has trouble finding his way through the forests." He held it out to Red Hawke. "Willingly I give it to Red Hawke for his daughter, Swan Necklace."

With great dignity, Red Hawke accepted the compass, holding it reverently, watching in amazement as the needle jumped and spun. With the delight of a child he turned it this way and that, then held it up for his people to see.

"Never has such a high price been paid for a wife," he cried so all in the village square heard it. "Swan Necklace must be pleasing, indeed. For this you could have two wives."

"I wish no other wife but Swan Necklace," James explained.

The women in the village *ooh*ed and *ahh*ed among themselves. It was indeed an honor that White Falcon would choose no other wife, but they'd heard this was the way of the white men. Still they cast sympathetic glances at Swan Necklace. If White Falcon took no other wives, then she must do all the work herself and there would be no sister wives with whom to talk or to take care of her when she fell ill.

There were many disadvantages to being an only wife. But Swan Necklace thought of none of that. She knew only that she couldn't be the wife of another man, nor could she share White Falcon with another wife. He had paid his magic compass as a bride price for her. He must surely hold her in high esteem as he claimed. She edged forward and put a timid hand on his arm. White Falcon turned and smiled at her.

Red Hawke spoke once more. "White Falcon has given Red Hawke a great honor that he should value my daughter so highly. White Falcon is now my son."

"I am honored, Red Hawke," James said solemnly.

Red Hawke turned to Manitowa and held out the compass. "Manitowa has been a friend to Red Hawke and his family. He has helped with the rescue of Swan Necklace and of the white men who brought her back to her tribe. He sent a message that my daughter was safe with his tribe and he has accepted us here in his village as if we were of the same clan. I will always count Manitowa as my blood brother and I wish to honor him with this gift of the white man's magic. He gave it to White Falcon and now it comes full circle back to him. Just as this compass has returned to Manitowa, so too will the friendship he has shown Red Hawke and his people."

Manitowa took the compass, pleased to be a part of this expression of valor and goodwill, pleased to have back the white man's magic that had so mystified him. He stood and began an elaborate speech.

James half listened. His eyes were pinned on the compass. He'd thought in giving it to his father-in-law to have it both ways, to please Swan Necklace and still to have access to the compass if need be. Now Red Hawke had given the compass away yet again. It would remain in the Chippewa village while they traveled on without it. Well, so be it. The deed was done and, by the expression on Swan Necklace's face, she was pleased at his actions. As soon as Manitowa had completed his speech and the villagers had begun to dance again, James drew Swan Necklace aside.

"Tomorrow morning we leave with your father," he said. "You must have everything ready and if we do not return by the time he leaves, you must go on without me."

Her happy smile died away. Her dark gaze darted over his face. "White Falcon is leaving?" she asked in a small, pain-filled voice.

"Only for a few hours," he reassured her. "But if we haven't returned by the time your father leaves, go on with him. Do not wait for me."

"I will go with you now," she cried.

"No, listen to me, Swan Necklace," he said gripping her arms. "My men and I go to the Ottawa village to steal back our goods."

"You will be killed," Swan Necklace cried, clinging to his arm.

"Trust me, Swan Necklace," he said. "We will be careful, but we must have our trade goods back. Otherwise, it does us little good to go into the wilderness. We cannot trade with other Indian tribes. We will go empty-handed. No one will lead us to the beaver creeks or trade their pelts to us."

"I will lead you," Swan Necklace said.

James scowled. "I know where Shemung has hidden our goods. These things belong to us. Would you value me as a husband if I did not protect that which belongs to me?"

Silently she shook her head, but her expression was so woeful, he relented a bit.

"We may not even waken the Ottawa," he sought to reassure her.

"They are fierce fighters and they hate the white eyes,"

she cried. "They have no honor even among themselves. They will kill you if they capture you again."

James remembered how the villagers had fallen upon Wawatam and repressed a shudder. "They won't capture me again," he said quietly. "At least, not alive."

"No!" Swan Necklace wailed.

James gripped her shoulders. "You must be brave and believe in me," he said urgently. "I will return to you, I promise." He kissed her quickly, his lips hard and unyielding. She knew his thoughts were already ahead on the raid of the Ottawa village. Silently she watched him go, tears sliding down her cheeks.

Like silent wraiths the men slipped into their canoes and pushed away from shore. Their paddles made no sound in the water as the birchbark vessels glided away into the darkening shadows. Swan Necklace watched long after the boats were lost from view, straining to hear the splash of an oar against water or the soft voice of her husband calling instructions to his men, but there was nothing. The night mist had swallowed them up as surely as if they'd never existed.

She turned away from the lake, back toward the brightness of the village square, but the gaiety and laughter she heard there did not draw her. How could she return to the feasting and dancing, knowing White Falcon had gone to risk his life among the Ottawas? The voyageurs had told no one of their intentions. Only their new wives knew of their raid and each one had been urged to secrecy.

Now Swan Necklace saw those girls slip away to their tepees so as not to give away the absence of their husbands. Sighing, she turned to the lodge she'd shared for one short night with White Falcon. She would not sleep. She knew that, but she would do as he asked her.

She lay on the fur pallet, remembering how he'd held her the night before, remembering the powerful passion of their mating. Her small hand smoothed across her flat stomach and she wondered if she carried his seed even now. If he died and the Great Spirit had not seen the wisdom of granting her White Falcon's son, she would throw herself from the highest cliff into the water. Then she pushed such thoughts from her mind. It was best not to anger the Great Spirit with such thoughts or he would make them real. Still, she spent the rest of the night turning on her pallet, unable to sleep.

The Ottawa villagers had no such trouble. The village was silent and dark, its fires burned down to glowing coals. James and his men left their canoes hidden along the lakeshore some distance back. Silently they crept forward, staying on the sandy shore when ever possible. The mists had obscured the moonlight so they were not so easily seen. As they neared the village, they left the beach, leaving only Wye behind to guard the canoes and obtain additional vessels from the Ottawas.

James and the men went inward through the forests, slower now, taking care not to make any unexpected noise that might give them away. They moved beyond the village, turning northward again, making their way to the base of a rocky abutment. Water rushed over the ledge and into a basin below before forming a small stream that flowed into the lake. James looked around, marking the area by a large oak, pacing off the clearing with long strides until he came to what he wanted.

"Here!" he called softly to his men. "This is where he has a cache. We dig here." The men grabbed up sticks and began digging in the loamy soil. The roar of the waterfall covered any sound they made. Still, they were cautious, for the village was close by. Quickly they unearthed the cache of goods still in their heavy canvas pouches. They hauled them out and headed back through the woods toward the shoreline. Several trips were made before all the goods were retrieved.

"Where's that fool Wye?" Buckley grumbled, looking around. The young voyageur was nowhere in sight. They waited, crouching low against the sand, uneasy at the delay.

"Do you figure the lad's been captured?" Angus whispered at James's elbow. Slowly, James shook his head. He didn't want to believe anything bad could happen to Wye. Suddenly, out of the shadows glided a figure.

"Wye, where the devil have you been?" the men demanded.

"Shhh!" Wye signaled. He knelt down beside James. "I have the canoes, just there." He pointed.

James signaled the men to retrieve the canoes and bring them around to be loaded, then turned back to Wye. "Any trouble?"

"Only with a sad-looking creature who could neither talk or walk upright."

"Wawatam!" James said. He exchanged a worried glance with Angus. "What happened?"

Wye shrugged. "He just stood watching me for the longest time. I figured he was one of those crazy Injuns they let hang around for good luck or whatever."

"He's not," James said. "He may have been crippled by his own people, but he's still mean as a bear. Did he try to attack you?"

Wye shook his head. "It was real eerie-like," he said. "He didn't move to stop me, just squatted there on shore watching me as I slashed the rest of the canoes. Then he tried following me. I didn't want to lead him back here, so I went up onshore to knock him down or something, but when I approached he ran away like a scared animal."

"It dinna make sense," Angus said.

"It might," James said. "He may have kept silent this far out of revenge for what they did to him."

"If'n he knowed it was you raiding the camp, he'd be raising hell, sure," Angus said.

"True enough." James glanced around.

Off to the right came a cry of warning. James cursed and leaped up, running along the shoreline toward the men loading the canoes.

"What is it?" he asked, knife drawn.

"I thought I saw someone in the bushes there," Maurice called.

"Hurry, get the supplies loaded," James ordered, and

turned toward the undergrowth. Cautiously he moved through the low-growing bushes and long grass, but found nothing. He was about to give up when a rabbit darted away through the thick grass. James turned toward the bushes the rabbit had fled.

There was another rustle; then a man leaped forward. At least James thought it was a man. The moon broke through the clouds for an instant revealing the evil face of the once-proud warrior, Wawatam. His hair had grown long now and was matted and filthy. His clothes were rags. His eyes held the wild look of an animal left wounded and dying. He opened his mouth and emitted a horrible mangled sound, a harsh cry as primal as the earth itself. Before James could silence him, Wawatam was gone, limping away through the forest with surprising speed, his ugly, guttural cry going before him. James thought to follow and end his wail, but something superstitious and basic to his Scottish upbringing sent a chill across his back and he turned to his men.

"Leave the rest," he ordered, running along the shore to warn his men. "Get in your canoes, get moving. *Voilà! Voilà!*" At the old boat command, the men scrambled into the canoes and lifted their oars. Their hearts felt strong and sure again. They were voyageurs, unmatched in derring-do and skill.

Quickly, the canoes slid through the water, leaving the shoreline behind. James clambered into the last canoe and helped shove off. The moon had disappeared behind clouds and mist. In the distance, he heard the shrill warning cry as the Ottawa camp was alerted. Too late, he thought. They're too late. We did it and without a drop of blood being shed.

But the Ottawas were not to be so easily dismissed. They raced along the shoreline, peering into the foggy mist for any glimpse of a floating vessel. Several times, warriors waded into the icy cold waters in the hopes of spying a boat. They could hear the paddles of the invaders, but they were unable to see them. The laden canoes stayed tantalizingly out of reach in the deep waters.

"We have to stay closer to shore," Buckley shouted,

"otherwise, we'll end up turning into the big lake and becoming lost."

"Stay in deep water as long as the Ottawas are following us," James instructed. "As long as we can hear the warriors on shore, we'll not make a wrong turn." They paddled thus for hours, gaining a grudging respect for the perseverance of the Ottawa warriors.

On shore Shemung urged his men onward. Their canoes had been destroyed. This was their only hope of regaining their bounty. Soon, though, they came to a high rocky cliff that cut off their trail. They must repair their canoes, if they were to leave for their winter camp in a few days. By the time the canoes were water-proof again, the raiders would have long since disappeared. With bitter defeat, they turned back toward their camp. They would not return as triumphantly as they'd hoped, bringing a store of the white man's beads and iron pots and colorful blankets. Still, they were not unhappy. They would be returning closer to the white fort and many goods could be had for a mere few pelts.

Dawn rose over the horizon like a flower blooming out of darkness. Pink stained the gray sky as Red Hawke's canoes slid away from the land. Manitowa and his villagers stood on shore waving farewell to their new friends. Pipes had been smoked, gifts exchanged, marriage ceremonies performed, tepees dismantled, and canoes loaded. The quietness of the hour mirrored the sadness of their parting. Swan Necklace cast a last lingering gaze along the shimmering water to the west, searching for the slightest hint of an approaching canoe, but there was nothing. The water lay undisturbed in silvered perfection.

"Swan Necklace, where are White Falcon and the men?" Yellow Leaf called from her canoe.

"I do not know," Swan Necklace answered.

"They are dead," Little Bird cried.

"No, they are not dead," Swan Necklace said. "I would know if White Falcon were dead."

"Then where are they?" Little Bird wailed.

"You must have faith," Red Hawke admonished them. "If White Falcon said he would return, then he will." The girls fell silent at his gentle rebuke. His words also gave them courage, so they faced forward in their canoes and took up paddles. Yellow Leaf turned once to wave a final farewell to her mother and father and baby sister. Walking Woman stood on the shore watching as the canoe bearing her oldest daughter glided away from her.

The sun climbed from beneath the rim of the horizon and rose with unrelenting insistency toward its apex. As the morning passed, Swan Necklace found herself glancing over her shoulder more often, each time feeling such despair upon not seeing any sign of White Falcon that she vowed not to look again. With every stroke of the paddle, she became quiet and withdrawn.

"Swan Necklace is quiet this morning," Red Sky said to her stepdaughter. She sat behind Swan Necklace regal and relaxed. She'd seen how often Swan Necklace looked over her shoulder and had noted the slump of her body.

"White Falcon hasn't returned," Swan Necklace answered in desperation. She could voice her growing fear to her mother.

"You heard your father," Red Sky said gently. "A wife must learn to have confidence in her husband's ability. Do you not think White Falcon is a capable warrior?"

"He is," Swan Necklace said. "But he has gone to the village of the Ottawa. They are fierce fighters, without honor. They will trick him and kill him and his men."

"Perhaps not," said Red Sky. "Did White Falcon not best Lean Elk to win you from him? I have seen White Falcon fight. He is strong and wily and brave. He is a worthy opponent for the Ottawas."

"He should not have gone," Swan Necklace said morosely. "If he had concern for me, his wife, he would not have done so."

"You are being selfish, Swan Necklace," Red Sky reprimanded. "It is the way of men to fight to win back those things which are theirs and have been taken. It is the way of women to wait patiently."

"But I have been patient," Swan Necklace cried, slumping forward over her paddles. "I am so afraid he'll never return."

"Then you must learn to have a brave heart," said Red Sky. She looked at her stepdaughter. "It is good for a woman to have strong feelings for her husband, but she must hold a small part of herself free of such feelings, or else she will not be able to deal with her pain should she lose him."

Swan Necklace's head came up; her eyes were those of a startled deer. "Then you think White Falcon is lost? The Ottawas have killed him?" Her voice rose shrilly.

"No, my dear child," Red Sky said. "I only say that warriors must go to war against our enemies; they must make raids and hunt far into the wilderness for food. They are often in danger and still they go, for they must. And we—" she shrugged her shoulders eloquently "—we must do as all women do. We must wait and welcome our men when they return and grieve for them when they do not. If you do not accept this, your life as a woman will be fraught with terror. You must be brave and strong regardless of whether or not White Falcon comes."

"I hear my mother's words," Swan Necklace said softly, "but I cannot accept them. I am too new to this guise of being a wife. I will study what you have told me and I will strive to be more like you, Red Sky."

Red Sky smiled and leaned forward to cup Swan Necklace's chin in her hand. She'd always loved this girl with her gentle nature and steadfast loyalty. Swan Necklace was a daughter of whom any woman could be proud. Swan Necklace pressed her cheek against Red Sky's hand and opened her mouth to express her gratitude for her stepmother's wisdom, but from the corner of her eye she caught a movement upon the distant water. Her head snapped up and her gaze filled with hope.

"Stop," she called to her father and the warriors who drove the canoe with their paddles.

"What is it, Swan Necklace?" Red Hawke asked.

Silently she pointed back in the direction they'd come. The speck on the watery horizon had grown larger now. They could begin to make out the shapes of the canoes and men plying their oars.

"It's White Falcon," Swan Necklace cried joyously. Red Sky glanced at her face. It was transformed. Her dark eyes shone as if a light had been ignited.

Red Hawke signaled to his men to halt and they waited for the canoes to catch up to them. "They have recovered their trade goods," he said. "See how the canoes ride low in the water."

Swan Necklace said nothing. Anxiously she peered back at the boats until she discerned White Falcon's figure seated in the prow of the lead canoe.

"There!" she cried. Once again Red Sky studied her step-daughter, sympathizing with the very young, who give of themselves too unreservedly. She'd tried to warn the younger woman, just as her own mother had tried to warn her years before. Red Sky smiled to herself. Some women were meant to give more completely than others. She'd been one. Swan Necklace was another.

The canoes were close by now. James held his paddle aloft in a gesture of triumph. The voyageurs thumped the sides of their canoes and cried out shrilly. The Cree warriors called back. With quick, deep strokes, the voyageurs were among them. James guided his canoe close to Red Hawke and reached out for Swan Necklace. Laughing, she leaped into his canoe, her arms going around his waist, her cheek resting on his shoulder. Other voyageurs had paddled close so their new wives might join them in their canoes. There were cries of greeting among them.

"You have returned, White Falcon," Red Hawke said, "a man of greater wealth than when you left last night."

"Aye, Red Hawke," James said, setting Swan Necklace away from him so he might address her father. She couldn't take her gaze from him. One small hand touched his thigh as if she couldn't bear not to be connected to him in some way.

"We've recovered most of our trade goods, and not a drop of blood was shed on either side," said James.

"You have counted a great coup against the Ottawas," Red Hawke observed. "Still you have taken no lives, so the Ottawas will carry no hatred for White Falcon and his men."

"I'd hoped for that," James said. "We are here to make friends with the Indians, the Ottawas, the Chippewas, and the Cree. We have no wish to war with them."

"You have acted wisely in many things, my son," Red Hawke replied. "Now you will come with us. Soon the winter months will be upon us." He pointed to a wedge of geese flying overhead. "We must go to the west to make our winter camp. You and your men must stay and help us gather food. When our village is secure, I will give you men to guide you to the Red River land."

"White Falcon is grateful to his father," James answered. Taking up his paddle, he turned his canoe in to the line following Red Hawke's craft. He felt Swan Necklace's small hand on his thigh and felt a thrill of elation. He and his men had succeeded in the dangerous task they'd set for themselves, and now they were once again moving forward on their journey to the interior beaver streams. But an even greater cause for elation was the feel of the small, brown hand on his thigh.

Chapter 12

THE VOYAGEURS WERE elated to be on their journey again. They expressed it in the strong voicing of their rowing songs. The Cree warriors listened, bemused and awed at the lusty power of the white men, certain that they were calling upon the magic of their white spirits to give their arms strength for rowing. Good-naturedly they raced their laden canoes, undaunted by their cargoes, for all were equally burdened. Eventually they settled down to the sobering task of pushing their heavy canoes through the waters, following the narrow passage from the North Channel to Lake Superior.

They camped that first night on a small island not unlike the one where James and his party had been attacked by the Ottawas. The next day they rose and traveled on to the final narrow waterway that led into the larger lake, portaging around the raging falls where one lake level dropped to the next. They were grateful when they reached the dark, forested shores of Lake Superior.

Soon campfires were lit from the smoldering punk brought by the women from the Chippewa village, preserved in dried fungus rolled tightly into cylinders and placed inside hollow corncobs. Swan Necklace worked with the other women gathering slender sapling poles to form a frame and placing brush and branches over them to provide them with a shelter.

When James had finished his meal, he found a soft fur pallet awaiting him beneath a sturdy shelter that would keep out rain and dew. Swan Necklace waited for him, her eyes shining, her slender arms reaching for him. James thought he'd never known such contentment. The awesome challenge of this land touched him as an adventurer, the beauty of the Indian woman touched him as a man. He found delight in all and rose each morning vigorous and renewed, ready to explore what that day brought him.

Red Hawke had come to have a high regard for his new son-in-law's skills as a hunter and defender. White Falcon was bold and brave and determined to protect his own. He possessed many qualities the Crees held in high esteem. His strength and power were tempered by wisdom and a respect for others. This respect for other living creatures was part of the Cree way, part of the kindredness the red men felt for all that lived upon the Mother Earth. Although White Falcon was not of the Indian nations, he possessed a soul and humanness many of the greedy white men who'd come here to their lands did not seem to own.

One day as they pushed westward along the southern shore of the lake, they were hailed from behind. At once the warriors drew close to shore and reached for their weapons. The cry came again and they relaxed their vigilance. Only one canoe was following them. Two rowers could be seen.

"What is it, my father?" Swan Necklace asked.

The chief shook his head. "Perhaps Manitowa has thought of something and is sending us a message."

James remained silent, but he felt a tightening of his muscles. Some instinct told him the message brought to them would not be a happy one. He thought of all the things that could have happened since they left the Chippewa village. Had the Ottawa attacked their neighbor out of retaliation for what he and his men had done? He shuddered to think he'd caused a war between the two nations.

As the canoe approached, they could make out the figures of Netnokwa and Walking Woman.

"Mother!" cried Yellow Leaf, her expression joyous, her cry happy. Then slowly, seeing her mother's stiff bearing, the joy faded from her face and she waited silently until the canoe came amidst their own. Now all could see that Walking Woman's hair was in disarray, her face dirty, her clothes rent. Knife slashes had been made in her arms and legs and cheeks as is done when one is mourning.

"Walking Woman, Netnokwa. What has happened?" Red Hawke asked.

"Walking Woman, my friend," Red Sky said softly. "Is all well with your family?"

Walking Woman looked around at the faces of her friends and slowly shook her head. "The first moon after you left us," she began in a voice that cracked from her repeated wails of grief, "Lean Elk and his warriors came in the darkness as we slept. He knew where the guards were posted and tricked them into believing he came as a friend. He and his braves killed many of our warriors before they even rose from their sleeping mats." She paused and bit the inside of her lip to keep from crying in front of her friends. "They also killed many of our women and children before they could flee into the woods and hide."

"Your child, Grasshopper?" Red Sky asked gently.

"Manitowa?" Red Hawke asked.

"Both dead," Walking Woman said dully. Seated in her canoe, Yellow Leaf had listened to the fate of her family. Now she set up a wailing. "Manitowa was struck down by Lean Elk himself as he begged for the life of his people."

"No!" James cried, striking the side of the canoe with his fist. The news Walking Woman brought was much worse than anything he'd expected, and he blamed himself. "I should have killed him that night," he swore savagely.

"We did not know he would retaliate in such a dishonorable way," Red Hawke said.

"Look at what he did to Netnokwa." James pointed to the scarred warrior whose wounds were still fresh and puckered angrily. "He would have killed the man for no other reason than his anger with me. I was too soft. I let him go and now women and children have been killed because of it."

"You cannot blame yourself, White Falcon," Red Hawke insisted. "You are not responsible for another man's decision to so dishonor himself. The Chipewyans are a fierce tribe from the north. Their ways are harsh and undisciplined. They do not think as the Chippewa and the Cree, who are brothers." He turned back to Walking Woman. "We will avenge the death of our friend Manitowa and his people."

"It is for that reason that I have come," Walking Woman said. She dug into a pouch and brought out a leather wrapping, holding it toward James. "Before he died, Manitowa gave me this and instructed me to bring it to White Falcon. With this he charges you to seek revenge against Lean Elk for his deed."

"I have no need for a gift to do as Manitowa wished on his dying breath," James replied.

Walking Woman opened the flaps of the leather wrapping, revealing the magnetic compass. "You will need the white man's magic to find Lean Elk in the land to the west," she replied. She held the compass out to him and James took it.

"I shall do as Manitowa has asked," he replied gravely.

"White Falcon is a brave and honorable warrior," Walking Woman said. "Manitowa's honor will not be forgotten."

"I will never forget my friend Manitowa," James replied.

"Do you return to your village now?" Red Sky asked.

Walking Woman shook her head. "Those who survived Lean Elk's attack have gathered what they could and returned to their winter village. They have already chosen a new chief. I will not return to my people until I hear that Manitowa's enemies have been defeated."

"Walking Woman will be a guest in our lodge." Red Sky spoke impulsively, then glanced at her husband for confirmation.

Red Hawke nodded. "We will be honored to have Walking Woman as our guest," he replied. "Netnokwa is also welcome to stay with us as well."

The young warrior had remained silent until now. "I wish to travel with White Falcon and seek my revenge against Lean Elk when the time comes," the warrior said. There was new purpose in his gaze and the tightening of his lips. Gone was the womanly gentleness.

"You are welcome," James said. "Lean Elk would not have stayed in the land of the Chippewa, and he knows the Ottawas are friends to the Chippewa, so he could not go there."

"White Falcon speaks wisely," Red Hawke said. "Lean Elk will try to return to his own land or—" he paused and looked around "—or he will try to overtake and attack us."

"If that's the case, why haven't they done so yet?" Buckley asked. "Netnokwa and Walking Woman have caught up with us. Why hasn't Lean Elk?"

"We know these waters. We know the shorter trails through the islands in the North Bay," Netnokwa said.

"What if he got lost back there?" Angus asked. "If not for Swan Necklace, we'd have surely not found the passage through the first time."

"Aye, that's true," James said. "He's still back there somewhere." They all gazed toward the east, thinking of the tortuous route they'd taken through the passage from one lake to the next.

"We must be prepared," Red Hawke said. "Come, there is little time for us to linger here. We will go to our winter grounds, and there we will prepare for any attack Lean Elk and the Chipewyans make against us."

They took up their paddles again and the canoes aligned themselves. Netnokwa maneuvered his canoe close to the one bearing Little Bird. His eyes were fierce as he gazed at the young woman he'd once loved.

"It is well you chose the white man," he said, nodding his head toward Garth Buckley. "If you had stayed in the village, you might have been killed."

Little Bird hung her head, not knowing what to say. She

was now the wife of the French voyageur. She'd already experienced the crudity and roughness of his mating. She'd already learned not to cry out in pain, for it only brought more pain at her husband's hands. She already regretted her hasty decision, but how could she tell Netnokwa that now?

Garth Buckley thumped the Indian canoe with his paddle. "*Mon Dieu*, pass on by," he warned, and without another glance at Little Bird, Netnokwa paddled his canoe away and fell into line near James. They were quiet as they paddled now, thinking of their friends the Chippewas and of Lean Elk's vengeance. No one thought to blame James for their danger, although he did himself. The Crees recognized that he'd acted in accordance with Chipewyan law. Lean Elk himself was the one who'd chosen to act outside his own law. He'd chosen to become a renegade.

Despite their concerns, they arrived at the southwest corner of the lake in easy fashion and paused for a few days so the women might harvest the wild rice to be found along the lakeshore. The slender stalks were weighted by the heavy ripe grains.

"*Mon*, this is foolhardy," Buckley raged. "Lean Elk and his men will catch up with us if we linger here."

"It is necessary to harvest the wild rice at this time," Red Hawke said. "In the time of the hunger moon, we will be glad to have the rice."

"I say we go on," Buckley insisted. "We have no wish to be killed by Lean Elk's men. Who knows if they're not here now, watching us this very moment."

"Are ye fearful, man?" Angus asked.

Buckley turned on him, his mouth open to give the old Scotsman a tongue-lashing, but he caught the derisive glance of the other voyageurs and the Cree warriors.

"I'm worried only for the women and children," he said quickly.

"We must gather the rice," Swan Necklace said. "To live now and die later of starvation is not a fate I wish."

"Nor I," cried Wye. The words were echoed around the campsite.

"Lean Elk does not know of these rice fields. He will believe we are far to the north. That is why I have led us here. We will set guards," Red Hawke said. "If the Great Spirit is with us, Lean Elk will not find us."

The days that followed were idyllic. The air was warm and still, with no hint of rain or wind to disturb the fields or dislodge the kernels. The men went along to guard the women and to pole the boats, which was heavy work. James poled Swan Necklace's canoe, amused by her pride in having her husband help her with such work.

On their way to the Chippewa village, Red Sky and the other Cree women had camped here. Seeing the bountiful rice fields, they had marked them well. Some of the women had even used basswood fiber to tie portions of the rice into small sheaves and cover the heads with other untwisted strips of fiber, forming hard balls which had been left to ripen. Now they moved into the rice fields, using their rice hoops to draw the sheaves over the boat and shake out the fat grains. These would be kept separate from the rest of the crop, for the kernels would be heavier and would need more boiling.

The free rice or that left unbound was harvested with two rice sticks, simply by drawing the stalks over the boat with one rice stick and using the other to knock the kernels free. The kernels were allowed to drop into the bottom of the canoe.

A good rice gatherer could use either hand with equal dexterity, working from either side of the boat. She could also dislodge the ripe grains without disturbing the unripe kernels. Thus they could return in a few days and harvest again.

James watched Swan Necklace working rhythmically, marveling at the stamina and strength of her slight build. By midafternoon each woman had filled her canoe with rice grains. James was astounded by their industry and complimented Swan Necklace profusely. She accepted his praise with quiet pride. Back at camp, the women spread the rice on sheets of birchbark placed in the sun so the grains could

dry but not become heated from the direct sun rays. Swan
Necklace and Yellow Leaf were given the task of stirring
the rice frequently so it would dry evenly.

The following day the rice was gathered into large kettles
and placed at a slant over a fire. Once again Swan Necklace and Yellow Leaf seated themselves beside the fire with
large, flat paddles with which to stir. This was a task they'd
shared before. Considerable skill was needed to parch the
rice kernels without burning them, so at first they did not
talk, but soon they grew more comfortable at their task.
The other women were busy spreading the new rice to dry,
and the men had gone off to hunt.

"Are you happy with your husband, Swan Necklace?"
asked Yellow Leaf.

"Aye." Swan Necklace's face softened as she thought of
the nights she spent with White Falcon on their sleeping
mat. He was a tireless lover, only momentarily satiated by
their matings. She smiled to herself, then remembered her
friend. "Are you happy with your new husband, Yellow
Leaf?" she asked hesitantly. She couldn't bear to think her
best friend might be unhappy in her union when she herself
knew such joy.

"Aye," Yellow Leaf replied primly. "Wye is a considerate
man." She glanced at her friend from beneath her lashes,
then an impish grin appeared. The two girls fell into gales
of laughter and had to be admonished by Red Sky not to let
the rice burn. Quickly they returned to the job at hand. In
quiet voices they shared their experiences as new wives,
discreetly skirting the real questions in their minds about
the prowess of their own husbands as lovers.

"Sometimes Wye does things," Yellow Leaf said timo-
rously.

"What things?" asked Swan Necklace.

Yellow Leaf blushed and, giggling, turned her head
away. While they talked, Little Bird came upon them and
sat to one side.

"Why do you laugh so?" she asked.

"We are happy," Yellow Leaf answered. "Are you not happy?"

Little Bird looked away, and they saw the shadow of a bruise on her slender neck. Both girls sobered.

"Do you think white men are very different from our own warriors?" Little Bird asked softly. Her gaze was fixed on the figure of Netnokwa as he knelt beside one of the canoes to patch a seam.

"I do not know," Swan Necklace answered. "I have not lain with a Cree warrior. I do not wish to now that I have known White Falcon."

"Nor I," Yellow Leaf said quickly.

"I wish to," Little Bird said. "I wish to know if a gentle warrior is also gentle in mating."

"It is too late for you to wonder such things," Swan Necklace admonished the young woman. "You have made your choice. If you do not abide by it, you will bring anger and discontent within our camp."

"At least I will not bring death to those who befriend me as you have done," Little Bird said, leaping to her feet.

Swan Necklace sprang up, her face twisted in anger.

"Your words are unwise, Little Bird," she said. "I would not repeat them, for they are lies."

"You forget that I have lost my own father because of you," Little Bird said. "If you had not made yourself known to White Falcon, he would not have fought Lean Elk for you, and he in turn would not have attacked our camp." Her words were true, and Swan Necklace was left speechless at the accusations.

Yellow Leaf rose and faced Little Bird. "You forget that my sister and my father were killed by Lean Elk's attack. Still I do not hurl such angry accusations at Swan Necklace. She is not at fault for the attack. You heard Red Hawke. Lean Elk has gone against the laws of his own tribe in spilling blood over this. It is unseemly for you to say Swan Necklace has brought this about."

"It is unseemly for Swan Necklace to put so many people in danger so she may sleep with the white man," Little Bird snapped.

"He is my husband," Swan Necklace answered. "Just as Buckley is your husband. You must accept this."

Little Bird hung her head. "I have spoken angry words to you, Swan Necklace. You do not deserve them."

"I have forgotten them," Swan Necklace answered. "I know Buckley is not kind to you. I see the marks where he has hit you. I will speak to White Falcon. Perhaps he can make Buckley stop."

"I would be grateful," Little Bird said, and hid her face so they would not see her tears. Swan Necklace and Yellow Leaf exchanged glances and stepped forward to hug their friend. Little Bird hugged them back, grateful to have their friendship still, despite her harsh words.

"Girls, the rice," Red Sky said sternly, and all three jumped apart and hurried to stir the rice.

Now that the rice was fully parched, the husks were loosened and could be easily removed. The rice was taken from the kettle, allowed to cool, and carried to another part of the camp where wooden mortars with sloping sides had been set up. Here women pounded the rice with wooden pestles that were somewhat pointed at the end. The women didn't pound the rice so much as they allowed the pestle to drop of its own weight. This loosened the husks without breaking the kernels. Swan Necklace and the other young girls were allowed to winnow the grain, pouring it slowly and carefully onto a birchbark tray so a lake breeze could blow away the chaff. Finally the men put on clean moccasins and trod on the grains to finish loosening any remaining husks. James was among those who did so, and Swan Necklace stood to one side watching him stamp the rice. He leaned his weight upon the posts provided for that purpose and moved his body with an undulating, sensuous grace that reminded her of his movements against her in the night. His gray eyes gazed into hers boldly and she blushed and looked away. That night when he came to their tepee, she went into his arms with a fierce hunger of her own that surprised and awed him.

They tarried for several days harvesting the grain and readying it so it could be stored against the meagerness of the winter months. There had been no sign of Lean Elk. They began to relax. The men still went into the rice streams with the women, but now to pole the heavy canoes while the women harvested. This was their final day of gathering wild rice. Tomorrow they would move inland to the rivers that flowed into the big lake. An air of gaiety pervaded the camp, and the people were lighthearted as they worked.

The sun was warm on their heads as James poled the boat along. He'd removed his shirt, and his chest was brown and muscular. Swan Necklace had glanced at him appreciatively more than once. Lazily he thought of taking her back to their lodge and spending the afternoon in exploring the sweet curves of her body.

"Haven't you gathered enough rice?" he asked somewhat impatiently. The canoe was nearly filled again with the brown-hulled grains.

"Soon," she said, sparing him a smile. "Our people will not go hungry this winter, and when White Falcon and his men go into the wilderness to find the beaver streams, we will take plenty of rice, so we need never worry about food."

"We?" he asked, raising one eyebrow. "Does my wife plan to travel with me through the wilderness?"

"Aye, White Falcon," she answered seriously. "I will be at your side always."

"Such travel will be very dangerous. I would prefer you stay safely in camp with your father."

"I am used to danger and I'm used to the hardships of travel. Did I not lead you this far?"

"But you were . . ."

"I was not yet your wife," she finished for him. "You must not hold me too tightly, White Falcon. I will be always at your side. . . ." she paused. Voices could be heard in the distance. Swan Necklace tried to peer over the edge of the grass, but could see nothing.

From his stand in the boat, James scanned the flat, watery fields, and what he witnessed made his blood run cold. Enemy canoes had slipped into the rice fields.

"Lean Elk," James muttered. He crouched and signaled behind him for Swan Necklace to do the same and remain silent. He peered through the long grass looking for the rest of the Cree warriors and his own men.

They were at a disadvantage, spread out as they were in the marshy waters. The canoes were heavily laden with the gathered rice, and paddles were useless. Only poles would move them ponderously along. Swiftly James assessed what must be done. He must somehow rally his men, so they might stave off the attack. He reached for the pole and pushed his heavy craft through the narrow, watery path they'd made. A muffled cry came from the other end of the canoe, causing him to swing around.

Everything happened so swiftly, his brain barely registered the chain of events. A Chipewyan canoe had glided close to theirs, hidden until now by the thick, hot grasses. Now a warrior leaped forward, grabbing Swan Necklace by her hair and jerking her backward into his canoe. At the same time, Lean Elk reared up, his tomahawk raised. The distance of the canoe separated the two men. Lean Elk threw his tomahawk. James saw the shadow of it descend toward him, followed by a searing pain in his side. Ignoring it, he scrambled across the canoe toward Lean Elk. He didn't see the other warrior's club raised to strike him. He felt the explosion of pain and a welling blackness.

"Swan Necklace," he shouted hoarsely. He heard her scream. He carried the memory of it with him as he fell forward onto the rice.

He didn't know how long he was unconscious, long enough for Lean Elk to make his getaway, long enough for all his men to withdraw from the rice fields, leaving behind sobbing women and the smell of death, long enough for Lean Elk to take Swan Necklace. Her scream rang in his ears as he opened his eyes and looked around. He could smell the dry, pungent odor of the wild rice in his nostrils, feel its giving softness surrounding him. He fought his way upright and saw the blood staining the rice Swan Necklace had so patiently gathered.

He stood up, felt the tremors in his legs, felt his body resisting this movement when it had received such a nearly fatal blow. There was warmth at his side and he felt the gaping wound. Blood poured down his leggings. He picked up the shirt he'd discarded earlier and bound it around his middle, then reached for the pole. The canoe was heavy with the bloodstained rice. Desperately he knelt and began shoveling the rice over the side. Sweat dripped from his brow and he tasted bile in his throat. He was losing blood and felt the weakness creeping over him. He refused to give in to it. With half the rice thrown out, the canoe rode higher in the water. He pushed his way along the water paths, passing canoes where women wailed over the fallen bodies of the men.

He passed the canoe where Red Sky lay crumpled, her life's blood draining from her. "Red Sky!" he shouted, but she made no answer. Her face bore the serene expression it always had, one slender, brown hand curved around her swelling stomach in a protective gesture, her dark eyes reflecting the sky she could no longer see.

He didn't pause except to motion to the men who were able to follow. Swiftly the men organized themselves, dumping the rice from canoes so they could move more freely. Throwing aside the poles, they brought out paddles.

"They headed north," one warrior called. The men pressed forward, striving to speed their crafts along at a rate far greater than human muscle and sinew could attain. Seated in the front canoe, James grimly ignored his throbbing wound. His arms churned rhythmically, his paddle bit deep into the cold lake water. With each stroke he sought to reach Swan Necklace, sought to rescue her from her ruthless captor, sought to keep her alive by his very will.

His lungs burned for air, his heart pounded in his chest; his every thought was of rescuing Swan Necklace.

"There!" Turtle, one of the Cree warriors, pointed. The pursuers increased their efforts. Lean Elk and his renegades tried to outrun them, but rage over the attack, the desire to regain their women, and the need for revenge lent extra strength to James and the other men. Slowly they closed the distance between the canoes.

The Chipewyans stopped paddling, bringing up their weapons to fire on their pursuers, but in the rocking canoes, their aim was bad. A ball crashed into the bow of a Cree canoe, but high enough above the waterline as to offer no danger. The canoe sprinted ahead. Soon James and the Cree warriors were among their attackers. They brought their canoes alongside and a hand-to-hand combat was waged. Canoes were overturned in the struggle and the men continued their battle in the water. The women belonging to the Cree warriors and voyageurs tried to leap out of the canoes; some jumped into the water. Some fought their kidnappers, creating a further diversion. James angled his boat directly toward that of Lean Elk.

"White Falcon!" Swan Necklace called, and he felt his throat muscles close at the sound of her voice. She was alive! He renewed his efforts and brought the canoe around, cutting off Lean Elk's escape. The Chipewyan warrior snarled and raised his knife.

"White Falcon!" Swan Necklace screamed, and stood up.

"Swan Necklace, no!" he shouted. He saw the knife enter her slender body, saw the spreading stain of blood against her white caribou-skin dress as she slumped against the raised prow, half in and half out of the canoe. Her eyelids fluttered closed and one hand trailed in the water.

James raised his rifle and fired without taking time to aim. He felt its discharge, heard the report, and heard Lean Elk's terrible laughter. He had missed. Now James paddled closer, his knife drawn and at the ready. He had to get to Swan Necklace before her life's blood drained away. He had to hold her and command her to live.

Savagery and pain were reflected in his face. Lean Elk saw it and for the first time remembered the tales he'd already heard of this white man's prowess as a warrior. He'd achieved what he set out to do. He'd avenged himself for the insult paid him by Swan Necklace and her white man. She lay dead before him. The white man could no longer claim what had once been Lean Elk's.

With a flip of his arm, he tumbled Swan Necklace's body into the lake and, taking up his paddles, evaded the white man's attack. He would return. Someday he would return and kill the white man who'd dared to best him and take his wife.

Swan Necklace's body floated facedown, her dark, silken hair fanning out around her in the water.

"Swan Necklace," James called hoarsely. He forgot Lean Elk in his need to get to Swan Necklace. He threw down his rifle and leaped into the water, swimming in long, powerful strokes to her. Quickly he turned her over, raising her face out of the water so she could breathe. "Swan Necklace," he called, shaking her head slightly. She made no sound. Her body was limp. Angus pushed his canoe close by.

"Hand her up to me, lad," he called, and between the two men, they soon had her in the canoe.

James pulled himself on board and bent over her. "Swan Necklace, speak to me," he cried, tapping her cheek.

"She's taken in water, lad. Turn her over," Angus said. They turned her onto her stomach. Water flowed from her mouth. Her lashes lay black and shiny against her pale cheeks.

"Get us to shore," James ordered, grabbing up a paddle. They started out and were intercepted by Red Hawke. His face was sad, grieving. When he saw his daughter, he shook his head.

"She's been wounded and pushed into the lake," James shouted without pausing.

"Take her to Walking Woman," Red Hawke ordered.

James nodded. He continued his frenzied paddling until he felt the sand scrape the bottom of the canoe. Springing out, he drew the canoe up onshore. Angus had already gathered Swan Necklace up from the bottom of the boat. Now James took the slight body from him and ran through the bushes to the copse of hardwood trees where they'd made camp. Walking Woman was already there tending other wounded people. She looked up when James ran into the clearing.

"It's Swan Necklace," he shouted. "She's been wounded and she was thrown into the lake."

"Bring her into my lodge," Walking Woman said, indicating a pallet. Gently James placed the slight form on a fur and knelt anxiously at the side.

Walking Woman knelt beside him and cut away the bloodstained portion of the caribou dress. When James saw the ugly, gaping wound, he choked back a curse. Walking Woman glanced at him. His teeth were clenched, as were his fists. He looked like a man about to fly apart.

"You must leave," she said softly.

"No!" He looked startled by her request.

"You must. I am a shaman. I will do my best for her." Walking Woman spoke strongly. He studied her face, then slowly he nodded.

"She'll be all right, won't she?" he asked. "She'll live."

Walking Woman glanced at the still girl. There was no sign of life. "Only the Great Spirit knows," she answered softly. "Today many Cree and Chippewas have died. Perhaps Swan Necklace will be one more." She was unprepared for his painful grip on her arm. Alarmed, she stared into his eyes. He was a man crazed.

"She can't die," he said, shaking Walking Woman's arm slightly. "Do you understand? She can't die!"

"The Great Spirit decides such matters," she said. "Now, go. Your anger will disturb the spirits and they will not come to help her make this fight."

After a moment's hesitation, he rose and left the lodge. Walking Woman bent over Swan Necklace. She had not lied to White Falcon. This day the Great Spirit had claimed many. Red Sky had been among them. Now her daughter might also walk the path to the world beyond. Walking Woman felt tears slide down her cheeks as she began working on the slim young body that lay so still.

Chapter 13

JAMES STAGGERED FROM Walking Woman's lodge. His side throbbed with pain, his knees trembled with weakness. He should have his wound attended, he thought vaguely, but he felt no inclination to do so. His thoughts were all for Swan Necklace. He thought of that small body lying beside him during the night, soft and sweet and trusting. He thought of her laughter and the lights in her eyes when she was pleased. He thought of her bravery and her pride in herself. He remembered her passion, her womanliness, her moodiness, her anger, and her laughter. The thoughts brought fear to his heart. He couldn't bear to live without this small bundle of womankind who'd somehow snared his heart.

He'd never thought he'd come to care so fiercely for another human being, and now as he considered Swan Necklace, he realized he could never accept a life without her. But she wouldn't die, she couldn't. If the Great Spirit hadn't meant for James to have Swan Necklace as his woman, it would not have let him win her in battle against Lean Elk. Their mating seemed destined from the first moment he saw her being sold as a slave. He hadn't recognized then what had happened to him, but he did now. And understanding the depth of his love for Swan Necklace, he had to believe she would recover. The Great Spirit wouldn't let her die now!

And what did that do to his plans to one day return home
to Scotland? He would take her with him or he'd live out
his days here in the wilderness. Perhaps he'd take her to
Scotland to meet his mum and da. He could imagine such
a meeting. Swan Necklace, beautiful and serene in her
white caribou dress with all its fine decorations, and Mum
wiping her work-hardened hands on an apron as she went
to hug her new daughter-in-law. They'd all be a little bit
stiff at first, uncertain of how to talk to an Indian princess,
but Abby would overcome that, asking impertinent questions and drawing that tinkling laughter from Swan Necklace.

He was getting daft in the head, James thought. He'd lost
too much blood and he could feel the warm seepage at his
side. Too weak to stand, he slid down to the ground and sat
with his head bowed while he tried to cling to the happy
picture he'd created of Swan Necklace and his family. Why
should he think of Mum now? he wondered, and slowly
shook his head in disbelief at himself. Because he was hurt,
and Mum always came to tend him when he was ill. No
one else intruded on his grief. Too many people were ex-
pressing their own grief or struggling to overcome their
wounds and the shock of the attack.

Red Hawke looked around his camp at his wounded and
beaten people. He was to blame for this, he thought. He
had somehow offended the Great Spirit. He had left his village, taken a small entourage of his people and traveled a
great distance to rescue his daughter. Somehow the Great
Spirit had found disfavor in that. Now Red Hawke's people
were vulnerable, many of the men severely wounded. Like
others in his camp, Red Hawke had lost his favorite wife,
his unborn son, and he might even yet lose his daughter.
He'd seen how pale her face, how limp her body, when
White Falcon carried her to Walking Woman's lodge.

Standing among the trees, Red Hawke stared out at the
great expanse of lake and wondered what he could have
done to anger the Great Spirit against them. He must be pu-
rified and perform a ceremony to the Great Spirit. But first

he must take his people to safety. Sitting here as they were now, they were open to further attacks from Lean Elk. Slowly he walked through the camp, cajoling his people and urging them to rise and break camp. They must move on. He came upon White Falcon and saw that his life was leaving his body. Quickly he sent for Angus. The burly Scotsman came running to the aid of his friend.

"Jaimie, lad, ye'll not give up now," he admonished, pressing a cup of rum to his pale lips.

James sipped and shook his head. "I'm all right, just resting," he said. "Soon Swan Necklace and I must leave. We're going to Scotland. I want to show her to my mum."

"Lad, ye're out of yere mind," Angus muttered while he cut away the rawhide shirt and looked at the gaping wound in James's side. His face expressed his shock when he saw the jagged, torn flesh.

"Will he live?" Red Hawke asked.

"I don't know," Angus replied.

"Have you no white man's magic to make him better?"

"Chief, if I had some, I'd sure use it and I'd share with you for all your wounded. Right now I have to close up this wound or he's going to die."

"I will summon Walking Woman," Red Hawke replied. "She has good medicine."

"I appreciate that, Chief," Angus said.

Walking Woman came and saw the wound and had White Falcon carried to her lodge, where he was placed beside Swan Necklace.

"Is she alive?" he asked weakly when he saw her still body. She lay with her eyes closed, her small hands folded on her chest.

"She is," Walking Woman said, and knelt to tend him. Chanting a song to the spirits, she cleansed the wound and pulled the jagged edges together, covering them with the crushed leaves of the wild plum, then she bound it tightly with soft, thin pieces of doeskin that were kept for this purpose.

He had remained conscious during all of her ministrations, but she saw the sweat on his brow and the pale clamminess of his skin. She prepared a tonic from her small hoard of prairie sage and patiently dribbled it between his lips. She was pleased when at last he closed his eyes and slept. Leaving the lodge, she went to join the gathering of people around Red Hawke.

"We must move inland along the river," the old chief said. "We cannot remain here. Lean Elk and his men will return, and finding us weak from our wounds, he will kill the rest of us."

"What makes ye so certain Lean Elk will return?" Angus asked. "After he wounded Swan Necklace, he seemed content enough to withdraw."

"Our own warriors had arrived," Red Hawke replied. "The chances of his men being killed were far greater. No Indian leader will deliberately lead his men into a battle that will take their lives." He paused. "I have watched as the white eyes adopt the ways of the Indians. This is good. But there are many Indian ways that are not yet understood by the white man. It is no disgrace for the Indian to withdraw to save the life of himself or his men. Lean Elk will return and attack when we least expect him as he has done this time. He will look for us to the north, believing we are trying to reach the rest of our people. Therefore, we must flee to the west. We will follow the river."

"Many of our people are badly wounded," Walking Woman spoke up. "They should not be moved."

"We cannot wait," Red Hawke replied. "We will bury our dead and leave this place, never to return to it." The Crees looked around the gathering. They had thought it a place of sunshine and goodness, but evil spirits had found them here. They would never return, no matter how abundant the rice fields.

Gravely the people broke apart and prepared their dead for the burial rituals. Normally friends and families would come from near and far to attend the funeral gathering, but there was no time to send out news. There was no time for ceremonies and feasts, and it would be far too dangerous to tarry for such a burial ceremony, which could last several days.

With a minimum of prayers and ceremony, the bodies of the dead were placed in temporary graves. Later they would be retrieved and brought to the village for a final interment during the Feast of the Dead, which was held every three years.

Somber and grieving, the rest of the people who were not too severely wounded gathered up their belongings and the cache of rice they'd harvested with such light hearts and packed their canoes. The wounded were carried to the canoes, and the paddlers took up their oars.

James was awakened by all this activity and watched as the Indians prepared to move westward. A narrow, deep stream had moved past the camp and emptied into the lake. They would follow this upstream, for eventually it would lead them to the Little Fork River. By a series of streams and rivers they would eventually make their way to the area of the Upper and Lower Red Lakes, where they would make their winter camp.

Anxiously James watched as Swan Necklace was brought down to the canoes. He cursed at the warriors, exhorting them to be more careful with her. They cast him a dark, pitying glance and turned away to help with the rest of the canoes. From his canoe, James watched Swan Necklace's face intently, looking for any sign of life, the flicker of an eyelash, the twitch of a muscle. She was as perfect in her coma as she was in all things.

Weakness overcame him and he lay back in his canoe, tears sliding down the sides of his face at his own helplessness, but what could he do? How could he reach through the darkness that claimed her and bring her back to him? Angus and Wye clambered into the boat and picked up paddles. Yellow Leaf settled near his head so she could bathe his flushed face if need be. Other tribe members took their places and silently the canoes glided away from shore, slipping through the edge of the rice fields and paddling against the flow of water that swept down the deep stream.

They took care to stay to the middle of the stream so as to leave no record of their passing. They pushed westward, pausing only when there was darkness and no one could see. Wearily they unloaded the canoes, trying not to think of what this day, begun in such brightness and hope, had taken from them.

Netnokwa came to lift Swan Necklace from her canoe. James had brushed aside any offer of help from Wye and was forcing himself to move from his own canoe. He glanced up as Netnokwa gathered Swan Necklace up in his arms, and for that reason he heard the tiny moan that she emitted. Ignoring his own weakness, he splashed through the water until he stood beside Netnokwa.

"She made a sound," he said hoarsely.

"Her *manitou* is calling her back," Netnokwa said, and carried her to shore. James stumbled after him, his hand pressed to the wound at his side. He could feel the warm gush of blood and knew he'd opened the edges Walking Woman had so patiently fitted together. He couldn't lie down, though, not until he was sure Swan Necklace was indeed returning to consciousness. He must be there beside her when she opened her eyes. When Netnokwa placed her on a bed of dry leaves and stepped away, James lay down beside her, his gaze fixed on her pale face, but she made no other sound.

"Swan Necklace," he whispered, and placed his lips against her cold cheek, breathing in the familiar scent of her. She made no answer, and at Walking Woman's scolding, he lay back and rested.

"You will make your wound bleed again and it will never heal. You will lose too much blood and be weak. It will take you many moons to regain your strength," she admonished.

"I will be well soon," he answered. "I will be well enough to go with Red Hawke to avenge this attack on our people."

Walking Woman heard his words and remained silent about his claim to the Cree people. This white man was different from the others she'd met. She'd seen it in his wisdom, his bravery, and his stamina. Now she saw it in his heart and spirit, which were truly those of a Cree. He watched with jealous, anxious eyes as she tended Swan Necklace, checking her wound and applying more crushed leaves.

The people lay down on makeshift pallets without erecting brush wickiups, for they had no wish for Lean Elk's men to find evidence of their camp. Likewise they did not make a campfire, but contented themselves with dried jerky. Through the long, dark night, warriors took turns watching the stream trail they'd just traveled. When the first streaks of gray appeared on the horizon, they quietly roused the camp. Canoes were repacked, and by the time the gray dawn had brightened enough to show them the way, they were traveling upstream.

Much as James had wished it, he was not beside Swan Necklace when she first woke. His canoe had fallen behind. Angus and Wye were bringing up the rear and watching carefully for signs of anyone following them. Lying in the bottom of the canoe, Swan Necklace opened her eyes and studied the bright sky moving above her. She listened to the minute splash of paddles dipping into water and knew she was in a canoe, but was it Lean Elk's or her own people's?

"Swan Necklace is better," Walking Woman said, and the girl drew a weak breath, feeling relief wash through her. She was with her own people. Her first elation died away as pain claimed her from her chest to the back of her head. Carefully she moved her head and felt the pain explode behind her eyes.

"I have been very ill?" she asked.

"The spirits took you away from us for a while," Walking Woman replied. "But now they have returned you and White Falcon will rejoice."

"White Falcon? He is well?" Swan Necklace demanded.

"Aye, Swan Necklace. Even now he rests in the last canoe, pining for you. He scowls at anyone who comes near you, and woe to any who might cause you pain."

Swan Necklace smiled and closed her eyes and slept again. Walking Woman felt her cheeks and found the fever had burned itself away. When Swan Necklace woke again, White Falcon was bending over her. His eyes were dark with worry.

"Swan Necklace?" he whispered as if the sound of her name might cause her more pain. She smiled up at him and saw the tension ease from his face.

"I knew you would save me from Lean Elk," she murmured softly.

"From Beelzebub himself," James vowed, but she was too tired to ask him who Beelzebub was. She gripped his hand tightly and slept again.

"Walking Woman?" James asked worriedly.

"She will need much sleep to regain her strength," Walking Woman said. "Maybe now that you know she's going to live, you can allow yourself the rest you need. You are not healing as swiftly as you could."

"I'm all right," he said gruffly, but when they stopped to rest for the night, he sprawled on the robe beside Swan Necklace, carefully so as not to disturb her, but close enough to touch some part of her. Soon Walking Woman noted with satisfaction he slept as deeply and easily as Swan Necklace herself did. If only she had been as successful with some of the other wounded and dying of the villagers, she thought regretfully, and went away to mourn over the loss of her husband and child and her friend Red Sky.

They traveled with little rest, pushing westward. The autumn storms would soon be upon them. They needed to gather a store of food and build permanent shelters. Only death waited for anyone trapped in the open with no permanent lodges prepared. Red Hawke urged his small, ragtag band onward, and soon enough they reached the Little Fork River. Here they came to a small valley surrounded by rolling timbered ridges fertile in wild plants and small game. Gratefully the band pulled their canoes to shore and made camp, making campfires and cutting brush for their temporary lodges. They'd been without campfires for several nights, and their spirits were as weary as their bodies.

Red Hawke watched his people move about the camp. Some of the men took up their bows and arrows and moved into the hills to hunt for game. The women were busy setting snares for birds and rabbits. Even the wounded who were able sat on the riverbank fishing.

Red Hawke nodded his head in approval and felt emotions well in his chest. He had not forgotten his responsibilities to these people, and his own need to assuage the anger the Great Spirit had shown against him.

In the three days they stayed in one camp, Swan Necklace gained much in strength. Many times she offered to rise and help the women who were gathering roots and acorns, which they pounded into flour. Each time, Walking Woman pushed her back on her pallet.

"Where is Red Sky?" Swan Necklace asked one day. "Why has she not been to see me?" She had asked this before, but Walking Woman had not answered, but now she turned to face the girl.

"You must not speak her name again," Walking Woman said, and Swan Necklace gasped in pain. It was the custom of her people not to speak the name of the dead. To do so would bring bad luck to the living. Swan Necklace turned away and sobbed quietly. She did not ask again to help the other women, but lay on her pallet, lost in grief as she remembered the kindnesses Red Sky had shown her. Red Sky had been the only mother she could remember.

Even White Falcon was not there to comfort her. He had gone into the hills with the men. At first all believed he had gone there to hunt game, but he soon disappeared in the woods and could not be found. Netnokwa was the one who first mentioned the purpose of his disappearance.

"White Falcon has gone into the wilderness to seek his totem spirit," he said.

"But why would he do that?" asked Turtle. "Has he not already had his vision and been claimed by the white falcon?"

"That is what Swan Necklace has said," replied Two Otter, a wise and brave warrior who'd come to like the white man known as White Falcon. "Perhaps we should ask her." So the men went to the tepee of Walking Woman and spoke to Swan Necklace. She told them of the night she heard the wings of a bird rising over the river and of the vision James had described later.

"He does not know the ways of our people," Turtle declared. "How would he know how to prepare himself for this ritual?"

"I do not know," said Two Otter, "but I feel certain he has done this."

"White Falcon knows many things about our ways without being told," Swan Necklace replied. The men nodded thoughtfully and went away. Now she no longer grieved for Red Sky; she lay on her pallet and worried over White Falcon.

High in the hills, James had found a place where he could see the small valley and the river cutting its way to the west. He wasn't certain why he'd come here, what he'd hoped to gain, but he'd been driven here by a quest to find the power needed to overcome Lean Elk. He remembered the things the other warriors talked about and he seated himself in an open place and looked to the sky. He remembered the night the white falcon had come to him and the feeling of oneness with the Mother Earth and the comfort it brought.

Now he sought more than that. He sought a communion with the spirits that ruled this green, savage land, the spirits that could take from him all that he desired or give to him the strength and wisdom to wrest it away. He must never be so complacent as he had been at the rice fields. He must always be on guard to protect Swan Necklace and his men.

So began his rites of purification. He prayed, groping toward some great unknown that had thus far eluded him. His voice came out small and rusty. He took a deep breath and began again, letting his song echo through the trees and ra-

vines. As he chanted, he closed his mind to all things, even
his men and Swan Necklace, and concentrated on the unseen spirits around him. He sang and thought of the mysteries of life and death and of his destiny here in this vast
land. He thought of what he was and what he should be as
a man.

Far into the night he chanted the words of his soul, and
as the new light sprang to the eastern horizon, he slumped
forward in a spell. When he woke, the sun was in his face
so he could not see and a falcon flew in its golden light.
Images shifted and suddenly James saw his former life in
Scotland, the croft where he and his family lived, the face
of his mother. He heard Abigail's cry. The light moved and
he was looking ahead to what the future held for him. He
saw death and danger. He saw Swan Necklace's face, all
smiling and glowing. He even saw his own death and tried
to turn away from the image, so painful was it, but the falcon flew in the light and he could not look away. This was
his destiny, his future. He was one with the spirits who
dwelled in this land. He understood that the people who
made their homes here were the true tamers, not the greedy
white men who pushed into the country, robbing her
streams of furs, demeaning the beauty and bounty of this
country. For the first time, James saw how puny were the
intents of such men, how petty their needs, how stingy their
souls, and he whimpered to the Great Spirits that he, White
Falcon, was not of such ilk.

Even as this knowledge came to him, he collapsed forward onto the ground. The white falcon disappeared and
the blinding light left him. He closed his eyes and slept
again, and when he woke, he was cold and in need of food.
He made his way down to the valley where Swan Necklace
waited.

"White Falcon," she cried when she saw him moving
across the clearing toward her. She tried to rise, but fell
back against a tree. White Falcon ran forward and scooped
her up in his arms.

"You are too weak," he said, sitting on the ground and

cradling her in his arms. "You must be still until your wound is healed."

"As you have done, my husband?" she asked mischievously. "Where have you been?"

"I went into the hills to seek a vision," he replied. "I have made enemies here in this country. I must have the help of the Great Spirit if I am to overcome them and protect you."

"Did your *manitou* speak to you?" she asked softly, fearfully almost. She was still uncertain if the spirits would favor a white man so. Her heart squeezed with happiness when he nodded. She did not ask him more about his vision. Some must not be spoken of; that which could would be told her when White Falcon was ready. Contentedly she leaned against his shoulder and thought how brave and true her husband was. It gave her great joy in a time of sorrow.

When Red Hawke came down from the mountains, he walked through his camp and spoke to his people. They could tell he'd spoken to his totem spirit, for his face was serene. They knew he'd been troubled by Lean Elk's attack and taken the blame for it upon his shoulders. They knew, too, he'd been concerned that winter approached and they were so far from their own people. They were worried by this as well. Now they saw that Red Hawke had returned with answers for all their worries. When he urged them to join him at the campfire, they hurried to do so and listened attentively as he spoke.

"The Great Spirit has guided us to this valley," he said. "Here we must prepare for winter. Here we will be safe."

The people looked at each other, torn between disappointment that Red Hawke would not even now try to travel to their home on the Canadian plains northwest of Lake Winnipeg, and relief that they could rest and make a permanent winter settlement. Attentively they listened as Red Hawke spoke eloquently of his concerns for their safety and the Great Spirit's reassurance that here in this small, protected valley, they were safe from Lean Elk and their enemies.

That night the people feasted and their chief joined in, partaking of the bountiful gathering of his people.

"Looks like we're here for the winter," Wye said as the voyageurs sat in their own circle considering what they would do for the winter. He stretched out his long legs, displaying the new moccasins Yellow Leaf had made for him. Like James, several of the men had taken to wearing the Indian moccasins. At first they'd done so out of convenience, for their boots were waterlogged and cracked. Then they had learned the meaning of wearing the Cree moccasins. To wear them signified a willingness to take on the tribe's customs and laws as their own. Most of the men who'd chosen wives readily changed. Buckley was one of the men who had not.

"Aye," Angus said now in answer to Wye's observation, "and we're lucky, lad, to be here. The winters here are fearsome. A man can freeze to death standing up in a blizzard. Besides, there are beaver streams around here we can explore."

"I'm not complaining," Wye said with a soft smile. His glances toward his wife were frequent and warm. Yellow Leaf blushed and quickly served him food before hurrying off to join her friends.

"Aye, the game is good here," Maurice said. "We'll not starve nor go cold with wives such as some of us have."

"Speak for yourself," Buckley said, spitting out a mouthful of rabbit and turning to strike his wife. She cowered before him, her eyes huge in her face, before she hung her head in shame and moved away from them.

"You treat her too harshly," James snapped.

"She is my wife, not yours," Buckley answered. "She is lazy and incompetent."

"I have not observed this," James said. "She always works very hard."

"Her food is not fit to eat," Buckley complained.

James stared at the portly man, then reached across and seized a piece of rabbit from his plate. "I find it tasty," he said.

Buckley's face turned ugly with anger, then sly. "Perhaps you would like to trade wives, then, *n'est-ce pas?*" he asked cunningly.

James's face turned dark with anger and he got to his feet. "Mind your tongue, Buckley."

"As you have minded yours in criticizing the way I treat my wife," the man snapped. "Don't interfere in my marriage, McLeod." James took a step forward.

"James," Angus said. "You're too weak to fight, lad. Besides, he has a point. It's not for us to get between a man and his wife." James relaxed his stance. With a mocking laugh Buckley rose and walked down toward the canoes.

"It doesn't set well with me to see a man misuse his wife," James muttered beneath his breath.

"Nor I, lad," Angus replied, "but the lady chose him for her husband when she had a chance at Netnokwa."

"She didn't know what she was letting herself in for," James snapped.

"Nay, she didn't," Angus said. "But it's not for us to intervene. It's between the two of them."

James slumped back against a stump and thought of Little Bird and Garth Buckley. Because the young woman was a friend of Swan Necklace's, her plight bothered him more. He couldn't imagine cuffing Swan Necklace as Buckley had done Little Bird. He couldn't bear the thought of facing the pain in her eyes, should he even raise his voice to her.

The evening grew still; the people had feasted well on the fish and game. Now they settled back to talk and contemplate the new turn of events Red Hawke had brought them. They would not return to their old village this year. They would not see aunts and uncles and friends. They would make their home here and rely on the company of each other. This they could and would do, and the meeting with their family would be all the sweeter the following year for the long absence.

James talked with his men, planning what must be done. They were anxious to move on, but James wasn't well enough to travel, so they would linger here with the Crees for a few more weeks gathering food and furs, readying themselves for the move west. When the ice was heavy on the rivers and streams, they would move on to the Red River area they'd first aimed for. James was expected to rendezvous with Governor Amherst at Fort Williams sometime before spring. All the men seemed comfortable with the new directions their journey had taken. They sat about the fire and talked. Soon some of the Cree warriors had joined them. Buckley made his way back to the fire, too, and no one snubbed him, for all of them understood a man's need for companionship in this vast, wide land.

The talk turned to many things, religion among them, and Turtle, sly as well as brave, told them of how the priests had come and told the red man the story of how Adam sinned against the Great Spirit by eating of the forbidden apple.

"This is what our priests believe," Angus said. "It is written in our Bible."

"Ah," said Turtle, smiling mischievously. "Then I shall never commit this sin. I have always thought it wrong to eat the wild apples our women find. It is far better they make a fine drink of them." The warriors laughed and soon the voyageurs joined in.

James left the campfire and made his way back to Walking Woman's lodge, where Swan Necklace lay resting. A small fire burned near the entrance of the makeshift tepee. Swan Necklace lay in her robes to one side. Her face was radiant in the firelight. James sat beside her.

"You seem sad tonight, my husband," she said.

"Not sad, content," he answered. In truth, he was troubled by a nagging hunger for his wife, but he would not tell her that. He sat watching the flickering flames, tamping down his desire. Then he felt Swan Necklace's small hand creep into his.

"I feel very lonely without my husband," she whispered, and drew aside her robes. "Come join me, White Falcon."

Disconcerted, he looked at her. "You are not recovered," he began hesitantly.

"I am recovered enough," she said, and smiled invitingly. James glanced around, uncertain as to what to do. The lodge was empty. Walking Woman was at the main camp-fire with her friends. They had the lodge to themselves.

"I do not wish to hurt you," he mumbled, clenching his fists.

"You won't. Come, White Falcon." She smiled with that eternal mystery that only women seemed to possess and slowly removed her dress. Her young breasts gleamed, pert and smooth. His mouth hungered to suckle the dark rosy nipples. With a groan he reached for her. She came to him without reservations as she always had done. Carefully he held her, using his every muscle and sinew not to press his weight on her.

Her arms urged him down to her and he found the warm, moist center of her. He heard her gasp of pleasure and felt the pulsating convulsions of her body surrounding him. He was snared in a world of pleasure so intense and consuming, he trembled and forgot his caution. Even the vision he'd experienced in the hills didn't compare with this moment in Swan Necklace's arms. When the tremors of passion were spent, he gathered her close and prayed to the Great Spirit and to his own stern Scottish God that nothing would ever take her from him.

Chapter 14

NOW THAT THEY'D accepted the location of their winter home, the people began to build more permanent dwellings. While traveling, the women had erected conical dwellings of poles covered over with bark and brush. Some did not even bother with the long poles, but bent several small saplings over and covered them with brush. Although these temporary dwellings had been adequate, the people longed for the permanency of a regular dwelling. Now the men went about the task of downing trees to form the four crotched corner posts of each lodge, and poles and saplings to form the sides of the dwelling. The women set to work stripping elm trees of their bark. Usually such a task was done in the spring and summer, but they had little choice. Winter would soon be upon them, and if they did not work quickly, they wouldn't be prepared.

Taking great care, the women stripped the bark away in sheets nearly as wide as a short woman and as long as a tall man. The bark was then placed in water to season it and weighted down on all corners to hold it flat while it dried.

James was still too weak to help bring down the trees, so he worked with his ax sharpening the ends of the corner posts so they could be driven into the ground. Swan Neck-lace had settled nearby, winding long strips of tough inner bark into a stout cord to be used in binding the bark pieces in place. Now and then she smiled at James. Neither of

them could forget the pleasure of their mating the previou
night. Even Walking Woman had commented just tha
morning that her patients looked much recovered.

The preparations of the lodges took several days, but on
by one they went up. James noted that the lodges were stur
dily built, with a familiar cribbing of support poles not un
like those used by Scottish crofters. By the time the bar
was ready to bc placed over the frame, James was mucl
improved and helped out readily, listening carefully a
Black Bear advised him to apply the bark lengthwise an
not up and down as it had grown. They pushed the bar
down between the inner and outer clamp poles so i
pinched together tightly, then the women set about sewin
the edges together. Bearskin pelts were hung over the high
wide doorways. Thongs allowed the pelt to be tied to jamb
posts while the occupants slept. Inside the lodge, they buil
bunks on crotched poles, laid them across with crotches an
crossbars, and covered the whole with several layers o
bark and finally soft pelts.

James was surprised at the comfort these dwellings of
fered. He'd heard of the blizzards in this part of the countr
and wondered how the people would survive the harsh win
ters. Now he saw how carefully the Indians planned for ev
erything.

James and Swan Necklace would share a larger lodg
with Red Hawke. Most of the lodges stood about twenty b
sixteen feet. Red Hawke's was twice that size, looking lik
two smaller lodges placed end to end. Since he was th
chief, he would hold council meetings in his lodge, and i
must accommodate all the people comfortably. Inside hi
lodge ran a long hallway where mats of reeds and husk ha
been placed for their guests to sit upon. In the center of th
hall was a fireplace where food was to be cooked. In th
roof above the fire pit, a hole had been left with panels tha
could be opened or closed. Hanging from each bunk be
were buckskin curtains.

James regarded this arrangement and was grateful for th
privacy the bunks and their curtains would provide. He'

wondered how he was to make love to Swan Necklace
under the very nose of her father. Giggling, she glanced at
him. She'd known exactly what he was thinking. James
chased her from the lodge, catching her up in his arms before they both collapsed on the ground to hold their wounds
and moan. Walking Woman passed them and shook her
head in mock disapproval. She was pleased by the love and
respect James showed Swan Necklace. The two young lovers were unable to hide their happiness in each other. This
heartened the villagers. In the midst of so much sorrow and
hardship, they were touched by the love and joy they felt.
James's regard for Swan Necklace also overcame their anger for Little Bird's mistreatment at the hands of her new
husband. Turning their faces away from the ugly scenes of
brutality as politeness dictated they must do, they nonethe-
less felt anger toward the bullish voyageur. Even Angus
and the other men had grown sick of Garth Buckley's behavior toward his young wife. Many times they voiced their
protest when he struck her, but Buckley always challenged
them and they turned away, forced to respect his right to
privacy in his own marriage.

Swan Necklace was stronger now and happily rejoined
her friends in the daily tasks of preserving food. White Falcon had also recovered from his wounds, so he joined the
men in their hunting forays. Proudly Swan Necklace
watched him leave camp each morning with the other men
and anxiously she waited to greet him each evening. She
was touched by the way his gaze swung around the camp
searching for her and the way his eyes darkened when he
caught his first glimpse of her. Despite her sorrow over Red
Sky's death, Swan Necklace felt she'd never known such
completeness.

"My daughter smiles with happiness," Walking Woman
said as Swan Necklace worked over a kettle of boiling water.

"Aye, Walking Woman, I am happy," she said shyly. She
bent to add another twig to the fire. Butternuts had been
pounded in a wooden mortar and tossed into the kettle of

water. She had already skimmed away the shells, which floated to the top, and had brought the mixture to a boil, skimming it frequently. "This is ready," she said, setting the kettle to one side. A milky fluid had formed; when cooled, it would become an oily paste to be eaten with bread and hominy.

Walking Woman smiled at Swan Necklace's careful preparations. "Swan Necklace is a good worker," she said. "She is also a good cook. White Falcon is lucky to have such a wife as Swan Necklace."

"I am lucky to have such a warrior as White Falcon for a husband," Swan Necklace answered serenely.

"Yellow Leaf says the same." Walking Woman nodded reflectively. "Little Bird is not so lucky," she said, and spat into the fire to show her disgust with Garth Buckley.

'I have spoken to White Falcon about this," Swan Necklace said, fearful Walking Woman might think her callous of her friend's plight. "He and his men have tried to stop Buckley, but . . ." She shrugged helplessly.

Walking Woman nodded. "It is the way of our people to say nothing in such a case. What is between Little Bird and the white man she took for a husband must remain between them. Only Little Bird can change this."

Swan Necklace knew Walking Woman spoke of Little Bird's right to leave her abusive husband. Slowly she shook her head. "She is frightened of Buckley," she said slowly. "He has threatened her that he will kill her if she tries to end their union."

"There are those who would not let this happen," Walking Woman said.

"Little Bird is afraid. She has no brother or father to uphold her honor. I have told her White Falcon will act as her family." She ceased speaking and shook her head. "I do not know why she continues with Buckley. I thought when Netnokwa came to the camp that she would see the foolishness of her choice and turn away from the white man."

"I have seen this many times among our people," Walking Woman replied sadly. "The Indian woman believes

marriage to the white man gives her more stature among
her own people. She travels at her husband's side and gains
many gifts."

"That is not why I have chosen to go with White Falcon,
nor Yellow Leaf to go with Wye," Swan Necklace said
stiffly.

Walking Woman saw she had offended the young
woman. "I believe your words," she said. "I have seen the
way you look at White Falcon and the way his eyes seek
you out the moment he returns to camp." Walking Woman
smiled. "Once it was this way with Manitowa and me."

"And with Red Sky and my father," Swan Necklace said
sadly. She remembered Red Sky's smiling face and the
laughter she evoked from the more serious-minded Red
Hawke.

The two woman looked at each other, aware they had
committed the forbidden in speaking of their dead, then
looked away, blinking their eyes against the sudden press of
tears.

"I will ask White Falcon to speak to Buckley about his
treatment of Little Bird," Swan Necklace said.

"It is good you do this," Walking Woman said, and went
off to join the other women as they spread chestnuts to dry.
Like the acorns, the chestnuts could be ground into a coarse
flour and made into bread. When ground corn was added,
the bread was very good.

That night, resting in White Falcon's arms after making
love, Swan Necklace spoke to him about Buckley as she
had promised Walking Woman. "I see the pain my friend
Little Bird bears in silence," she said sadly. "I hear her
weep and my heart weeps with her. She has never known
the happiness I have with you, White Falcon."

"Aye, lass, I've seen him beat her and I've spoken to
him about it. He only tells me to mind my own business.
I have no right to interfere between him and his wife."

"That is the way of my people as well," Swan Necklace
whispered.

"I will speak to him again," White Falcon said. "But cannot Little Bird do something to help herself?"

"I will speak to her," Swan Necklace said. "Thank you, my husband, for your concern for my friend."

James gathered her close. What if Swan Necklace had become Buckley's wife? He shuddered at the thought. "I'd kill him," he muttered.

"White Falcon?" Swan Necklace asked, pulling away from him in alarm. "You will kill Buckley?"

"No," he said, shaking his head. "I will talk to Buckley."

"You are a good man, White Falcon," she sighed, leaning against him. He felt the warm softness of her breast, and his caress turned possessive.

"I'm not good, I'm bad," he said, nuzzling her ear. "I'm very bad."

"That's not true, White Falcon," Swan Necklace cried earnestly, drawing back to gaze at him. "You are a good man. You are not like Buckley. Who has said this about you, that you are bad? I will speak to them. I won't let anyone speak of you in this manner. I will tell them—" His kiss cut off her words.

"I meant that I'm going to be a bad man and make love to you," he explained when they could breathe again.

"It is not bad to make love to your wife, White Falcon." She giggled at his silliness.

"Well, it should be," White Falcon said, reaching for her. She pushed him away, puzzled at his words.

"I do not understand. In the white man's world, is it wrong to mate?"

James sighed. He'd had one thought in mind, but he could see Swan Necklace was intent upon discussing this phenomenon. "No, it is not wrong to mate in the white man's world. It is wrong for the wife to ask too many questions when her husband wants to mate," he explained with mock severity. She stared at him with wide eyes. Her bottom lip quivered.

"I am sorry, White Falcon," she replied. "I did not mean

to displease you." She sat huddled on her mat, her shoulders sagging, her head bowed.

"You have not displeased me, Swan Necklace," he said. "You could never displease me." Immediately her head came up; her eyes shone, her smile was tremulous.

"I please you?" she cried, and threw herself at him, hugging him exuberantly and pressing small kisses on his jaw.

"Swan Necklace," he laughed. "You know you please me."

She sat back and grinned at him. "I know," she agreed.

"Then why do you pretend you think differently?"

She grinned again and glanced down at her hands, folded so sweetly in her lap. "My heart is gladdened to hear White Falcon say I please him," she confessed.

James bit back laughter. "Do I not tell you often enough?" he asked softly.

"I would like to hear it more," she replied.

"Then I will tell you every hour of every day," he declared, dragging her onto his lap. Willingly she came, wrapping her arms around his neck and resting against his shoulder. "You please me, Swan Necklace, with your laughter and your teasing, by the hard work you do, by the home you have made for us and the food you prepare and the way you touch me and . . ."

Eyes gleaming, he bent forward and whispered in her ear the other ways in which she pleased him. Swan Necklace blushed and tried to rise, but he clasped her to him, claiming her lips in a kiss. His tongue swirled over her lips, tasting the sweetness within, and she stopped struggling and clung to him.

"Shall I tell you more of the ways in which you please me?" he whispered gruffly. Her heart was thumping in her chest, and her breaths were quick and shallow. Quickly she shook her head.

"Nay, White Falcon. I have heard enough for tonight," she whispered, and pushed him back on the mat. Straddling him, she leaned forward and nipped his bottom lip playfully. Her eyes gleamed in the dark shadows. James felt his pulse quicken. The laughter was gone between them now. Only their hunger for each other could be felt. They reached for each other and in the hours that followed, Swan Necklace found new ways to please White Falcon.

In spite of her happiness, Swan Necklace did not forget her friend Little Bird. The young women went along the riverbanks and into the flat bottomlands in search of roots. They found a plentiful supply of roots from the wild bean vine. Swan Necklace had gathered these strings of small, potatolike roots for the voyageurs when they first began their journey in the spring, but now the young women had to dig them up with sticks. As the girls bent to their tasks, Swan Necklace sought some way to approach Little Bird. Today the girl sported new bruises and a cut lip. She did not meet anyone's gaze directly and her shoulders sagged with this new shame.

"Little Bird, why do you not leave Buckley?" she asked, kneeling beside the girl.

Little Bird looked away and jabbed at the ground with her digging stick. "I do not wish to speak of this with you," she said coldly.

"I'm sorry," Swan Necklace said. "I have no wish to bring embarrassment to you, but I see the marks Buckley has left upon you. This is not the way of men and women."

"Maybe not for you and White Falcon, but many men hit their wives," Little Bird said. "Buckley has feelings for me."

"They are not good feelings," Swan Necklace said stubbornly.

"You have no right to say this," Little Bird said, outraged.

"I'm sorry. I wish only to help."

"Do not speak of this to me," Little Bird said, and moved away, digging furiously at the hard ground. Swan Necklace moved beside Yellow Leaf and continued gathering roots.

"You have tried," Yellow Leaf said. "You can do no more."

"I do not feel better at the thought," Swan Necklace answered. The girls continued with their foraging for food.

"Swan Necklace, Yellow Leaf," called Little Bird. She stood near the riverbank. "Look at this."

The two girls hurried to Little Bird's side.

"There are boot prints of the white eyes," she said, pointing to the soft mud of the bank. Swan Necklace and Yellow Leaf studied the prints.

"Were they made by White Falcon's men?" Yellow Leaf asked. "Some of them still wear the white man boots."

"Only three of them," Swan Necklace said, squatting to peer at the prints more intently. "The boots of the voyageurs do not make prints like these. See how the marks in the heels are different."

"Are you sure?" Yellow Leaf asked.

Swan Necklace looked at Little Bird. "Do Buckley's boots make marks like these?" she asked.

"I don't know," Little Bird said, and glanced away from them. Nearly everyone in the village knew the signs made by the moccasins of their own people. Being aware of these signs helped them to ascertain if enemies had approached the village. Little Bird had been taught this as well. But she'd acted evasive.

Swan Necklace stood up. "We must tell my father." They made their way back to the village and told Red Hawke what they had seen. He nodded his head.

"Our braves have seen the marks of these men, when they were hunting," he said. "They are trappers who have come in search of the beaver pelts. Our warriors followed them for some distance as they passed through."

"Why did they not stop and join White Falcon's men?" Swan Necklace asked.

The old chief shook his head. "There are many beaver streams to the west, and many men who come seeking their furs. These men do not speak as White Falcon and the English do. Their words are different. They come from the land south of the Great Lakes."

"Then we won't see them again?"

"They have passed through our valley," Red Hawke reassured them.

The girls went back to their tasks of gathering food. The older women showed them where to find the roots of wild calla lilies. They found a pond, and Little Bird and Yellow Leaf swam to the bottom to gather the roots of the yellow pond lily, while Swan Necklace waited on the bank, chafing at her infirmities. In their ramblings they found fireballs, the onion-shaped root that was very hot and could be used for seasonings. The women also gathered the inner bark from the tops of pine trees, which gave a sweet sap, and moss that grew on white pine trees, which was very nourishing. Once dried, it would store well and later could be boiled in a fish or meat broth. Soon the *mukkuks* were filled with food against the winter season. Strings of wild potatoes and dried corn were hung from the posts in the new lodges.

While the women gathered herbs and roots, the men hunted in earnest for game in the surrounding hills. Unable to hunt as he wished, James listened closely to everything the Indian men had to offer about the hunting. He was a little skeptical when he heard them speak of talking to the animals.

"I do not understand," he said to Black Bear as they sat by the fire one evening. "How do the Indians talk to the spirits of animals?"

"The animals are our brothers. The Great Spirit made them as he has made us. Therefore the animals understand man, and man must understand animals. We are all one."

"That is how we kill the bear," Turtle said. "Bears are next to man. When they are hurt they stand up on their two hind legs and cry. They are not as brave as men, so we explain to them that we need their meat and their warm furs for our beds."

"So the bear, hearing the wisdom of your words, understands and lies down and dies for you?" James asked, amused at this simplistic tale. "I have met a bear on the path, and I told him such things, but he didn't listen."

"Ah, the bear that fought you and Shemung." Turtle recalled the tale that had won James's release from the Ottawa. "The bear ran away, did he not?" He grinned at his logic. "The bear listens and the hunter is able to swing his ax into its foreshoulder."

"Ah, it is the ax and not the words that defeat the bear."

"You may laugh at our ways, if you wish, White Falcon," Turtle replied cheerfully. "Our words are not important. It is what we think as we say them. The animals understand what we think. It is in this way that we defeat the bear and all the other animals."

Suddenly Turtle's words reminded him of the things Swan Necklace had told him many moons before when they first started their trip. "I am sorry I laughed at your words, Turtle," he said. "I will remember what you have told me when we hunt the bear and elk."

He had good reason to be grateful for Turtle's words some days later. He and Angus were hunting deer. Angus had gone around to drive the deer down to James. Suddenly James heard a terrible cry. He rushed through the trees and found his friend lying on the ground, bleeding.

"Careful, lad," Angus called. "Black bear."

On the trail a black bear reared back on his hind legs, his paws tearing at the air in obvious pain. Angus's knife protruded from its shoulder.

"Are you all right?" James asked cautiously.

"All right enough after being swiped by the monster. Have a care, lad. My bullet didn't do anything but make him mad, and you can see how my knife fared. He'll get you, too."

Remembering the story Black Bear and Turtle had told him, James put aside his long rifle and reached for his ax.

"Did you try talking to him?" he asked.

"Nay. I dinna try that," Angus said, laughing a little in spite of the danger. Hefting the ax, James crept toward the raging animal. "I am sorry to do this, brother bear," he said in a low voice. "But you have injured my friend and I must take him back to the village. I also need your furs for my bed and your meat to feed my people." The bear roared in pain.

"I hear your cry and know you are in pain. Soon that pain will be gone," James said, his ax raised. The bear roared again and turned away, his paw brushing at the knife lodged in his shoulder. James leaped forward, driving his ax deep into the bear's shoulder. With a wild cry the beast swung around. He lashed out with his paw, knocking James to the ground. James fell and rolled away until he came up against a tree. Leaping to his feet, he faced the bear. Although he'd wounded the bear with his first strike, the animal was more enraged than ever. He stood on his hind legs, bellowing his rage to the sky. At the first opening, James leaped forward. This blow was much better placed. The ax bit deep and the bear fell to the ground, twitching and bleeding.

"You got him, lad," Angus cried. He limped over to look at the bear. "Do you reckon the talking to him helped?"

James laughed. "I'm sure Turtle will think so." He placed a horn to his lips and sounded a call that soon brought the other hunters to their site. Turtle and Black Bear exchanged glances.

"You have listened well, my brother," Turtle said to James.

"My brothers have taught me well in this way of talking to animals," James replied. "But we did not find this bear to be a cowardly warrior."

The men laughed and set about helping to skin the bear and cut the meat into large chunks to be carried back to camp. Triumphantly they returned. The villagers rushed forward to admire the bearskin and listen to the tale of its taking. A man who killed a bear was thought to be very brave indeed and could count coups for his deed. Proudly Swan Necklace claimed the bearskin. It would make a warm covering for their bed. White Falcon shared the meat with all the villagers, for such were the ways of the Crees. Swan Necklace and Walking Woman gathered the thick bear fat, which would be used for all manner of things, cooking, cosmetics, and so on. Proudly she shared her bounty with the other women. To do so showed her confidence that White Falcon was a good provider and would bring her more.

When caribou, elk, and deer were brought in, the women cut the meat into strips and smoked it over low fires, while they began the arduous task of tanning the hides. New warm robes and heavy shirts would be needed for the winter months. After hunting all day, the men would loll around the fires partaking of the meals their wives had prepared and resting, for they would hunt again the next day, and always there were some warriors who were left to guard the camp against unexpected attackers. Red Hawke was determined not to be caught unawares again.

In addition to the game the men brought in, the women's snares yielded rabbits and birds. Nothing was wasted. The rabbits were roasted over the fires or cut up and made into tasty stews. Their furs were tanned and prepared for the sewing of warm mittens and hoods. The birds were roasted on sticks and their feathers carefully saved for the making of ceremonial war bonnets or other ornamentation. Fish were smoked and stored against the day when the frozen rivers would not offer enough fish to feed them all. An air of urgency guided them as they prepared for the months of the freezing moon.

White Falcon and his men accompanied the Cree warriors on every hunt. They were busy now gathering extra food to take with them to Red River. The white men had come to accept the ways of the Indians in preparing for the hunts. There were many taboos to be avoided. One of them was the eating of any food that smelled, such as leeks or wild onions. Likewise, tobacco had to be avoided. The hunters purged themselves often and took cleansing baths in the river, after which they rubbed their bodies with the leaves from sweet ferns or other grasses.

"They're trying to kill the human odor on them," Angus explained.

During their spare time in camp, while they sat talking and smoking, the men also worked diligently on their weapons, making sure they had plenty of arrows. Bullets from the white man's long guns were not to be wasted on game. The hills about had been well hunted, and the hunters were considering a prolonged hunt.

"Will you go with them?" Swan Necklace asked when she heard.

"Aye, I must," James replied. "I have no wish to stay in camp and not do my share. Besides, we are preparing to travel to Red River before the deep snow falls."

"We will need warriors to stay here and protect the camp," Swan Necklace said. "Can you not do this? Can't you wait until spring before you go to the Red River?"

"My men and I must go. I must rendezvous with Governor Amherst this winter. I wish to tell him we have established a fort. To do this, we must prepare and take plenty of furs and food to see us through the winter," James replied slowly.

"Please, White Falcon, stay here. I am afraid for you."

"Why?"

"We saw boot prints of strangers along the riverbank," she said.

"Are you sure?" James gripped her shoulders. "When did you see them?"

"Yesterday. Little Bird and Yellow Leaf saw them, too."

"Men from the Northwest Fur Company!" James said, clenching his fists. "Damn!"

"Why does this trouble you?" she asked, puzzled at his reaction. "Red Hawke said they passed through the valley on their way to the beaver streams in the West. They will not trouble us."

"They passed through several days ago, or so we thought. Now you've found prints. They haven't gone."

"Why would they stay here in the valley?"

"The beaver streams here are rich. These men are trying to horn in on the fur trade," he said. "The worst of it is, they're unscrupulous men without any morals. When you and the other women are out gathering, be careful."

"Would these men harm us?" whispered Swan Necklace.

"They might," James said. "I know they will poach our traps and cause plenty of mischief."

"Then you will stay in camp and guard us?" Swan Necklace exclaimed, feeling triumphant.

"I will speak to Red Hawke," he replied absently.

But when James spoke to Red Hawke, he was met with the old man's disbelief of any real danger. The white men were trappers, as were James and his men. If they were to fear danger from the new arrivals, then why not from the Hudson Bay trappers as well? James couldn't argue against such logic. Red Hawke further pointed out that the Cree could do nothing against these new arrivals as they would bring the wrath of the white father down on them.

"Will you at least agree to set extra guards?" James insisted.

Remembering the death and anguish Lean Elk had brought on them, Red Hawke agreed. "Will White Falcon stay to guard the camp?" he asked.

"Swan Necklace wants me to stay," James answered. "She seems fearful that something will happen to me on this hunt."

A slight grin appeared on the austere face of the old chief. "And White Falcon fears that someone will come into the camp and harm Swan Necklace." His expression turned somber again. "To hold too tightly to one's treasures tempts the spirits against us," he said, and James knew he was thinking of the loss of Red Sky and his unborn child.

"I will try to remember this, Red Hawke," James said. "Perhaps I am being foolish to worry over these Northwesterners, as they call themselves. I've been told they're upstarts and scoundrels of the worst sort. Maybe I'm worrying needlessly. I will trust your judgment. I will go on this hunt, for we need the food for our Red River fort."

"The decision is yours to make, White Falcon," Red Hawke replied.

Seeing the way things had gone, Swan Necklace became philosophical about the hunt. Like all good wives, she made up a package for her husband containing spare dry moccasins, hunting charms, and plenty of pemmican. With a brave smile she bade him farewell, although she clung to him when he kissed her.

As the hunters trudged away in the chilled dawn of early morning, James turned several times to catch a last glimpse of Swan Necklace. She looked so tiny and helpless, wrapped in her robes against the autumn chill. When they reached the top of the hill, the last point from which they could view the village, James raised his hand and let out a shrill whoop of farewell.

Standing with the women, Swan Necklace heard his cry and felt its wild echo in her own heart. She blinked to hold back the tears. It would be unseemly to weep before the other women. When the hunters disappeared over the crest of the hill, she sighed and turned back toward her lodge. The day ahead seemed empty and without joy. She had planned to stay busy tanning the hides White Falcon had already brought in, but she did not go to her task with an elated heart as she might have if he were in the village.

"Don't worry, Swan Necklace, they will soon return, and with much meat for the village," Yellow Leaf said. She and Little Bird fell into step beside their friend.

"I know," she answered, "but I shall miss White Falcon."

"And I shall miss Wye," Yellow Leaf admitted. Little Bird remained silent. Buckley was one of the men left to guard the camp. Neither girl could help thinking how much better it would have been for Little Bird if Buckley had gone hunting for several days and Netnokwa, the Chippewa warrior, had been left behind. It was plain to them all that Netnokwa still had feelings for Little Bird. Now neither girl knew what to say to Little Bird. The older girl walked stiffly beside them, needing their friendship and support in her difficult situation, but resentful that she did not possess a husband whom she could love and miss as they did.

Swan Necklace spent the whole day laboring over the elk

hide. She had already removed the hair with a lye mixture made from wood ash and soaked the pelt in water for several days. Now she removed the pelt from the water and draped it over a beam that had been driven into the ground for that purpose. Using a scraper made from an elk horn, she began scraping away the particles of flesh, fat, and sinew, then she turned the pelt and, using a beaming tool made of wood with an iron blade, scraped away the hair. She used great care to work the pelt evenly, leaving no thin spots.

This hide, once softened, would be made into a beautiful shirt for White Falcon. Even as she worked at this arduous task, she thought of the design she would embroider upon the shirt. She would use the symbol for the falcon and she would use porcupine quills and the bell hair of the moose. She would dye the quills red from the bloodroot for bravery, and white from the kaolin clay found along certain riverbanks and highly prized as a symbol of riches and generosity. White Falcon was all those things and more. This would be a very fine shirt, the finest she knew how to make.

Swan Necklace smiled. Working the skin had made her feel closer to White Falcon, as if he were not going so far away for so long. All day she worked on the pelt, scraping it and washing it before stretching it over a wooden frame and rubbing it with a paste made of deer brains and moss. Her shoulders had begun to ache with fatigue by the time she removed the pelt from the frame and put it to soak in water.

Putting away her things, she went for a walk along the riverbank, taking care not to go too far as White Falcon had instructed her before he left. When she reached a favored spot, she sat on the grass and watched the sunlight on the water, remembering how White Falcon had made love to her the night before. There had been an urgency to his caresses as if he, too, hated the thought of their coming separation. Now, tonight, she must lie upon their pallet alone.

Would he think of her tonight? she wondered, and sighing, rose to make her way back to camp.

She almost missed the booted prints, so intent were her thoughts on her missing husband. Only at the last moment did her glance happen on the tracks. Feeling alarm wash over her, Swan Necklace looked around. All was quiet. The birds sang sweetly in the trees and the afternoon sun lit the riverbank with a warm golden glow. All seemed normal.

Cautiously she knelt and studied the tracks. They were recent. Perhaps they had been made that very day. Swan Necklace's brow furrowed with worry. They were made by two men. One boot track was the same as those they'd found on the riverbank before, but the second set of tracks was different. Swan Necklace counted the marks of the nails in the print of the heel. She had seen that print many times. These were the boots worn by the men from Montreal.

Swan Necklace raised her head and glanced around. Only two men had been left in camp who made a track like that. Why would Buckley or Maurice be meeting with the Northwestern trappers when he'd been left behind to protect them from these intruders? She studied the ground.

There was no sign of a struggle between the two men. They had stood close together as if wishing to speak without being overheard, and they had parted and gone in separate directions. Troubled, Swan Necklace rose to her feet and made her way back to the village.

Chapter 15

THE HUNTERS TRAVELED swiftly through the forests, taking care to make little sound. Several times they paused and scouts were sent ahead. Turtle had been placed in charge of this hunt, and he observed all the rituals and precautions. When the scouts returned and shook their heads, they continued their journey without talking. James and the white trappers had been instructed before they left the village to think no songs, as the animals loved the Indian songs and were able to hear them if ever they were thought.

That night they paused to rest, partaking sparingly of the pemmican their wives had packed for them. No fires were lit and little talk was exchanged. The men communicated when necessary by sign language.

"They're sure serious about all this, aren't they?" Wye whispered.

"Aye," Angus answered gruffly. "Whether or not they eat this winter depends on their success at hunting. I reckon if we had empty stomachs and saw the pinched faces of our wives and children, we'd get real careful, too."

Wye made no answer, but he thought of Yellow Leaf having no food to eat and he rolled himself into his furs, determined to make a better effort on the morrow.

The next morning they traveled farther west, leaving the forests behind them and moving out onto a narrow prairie.

Once again they paused and the scouts were sent ahead. They crouched in the long grass, studying the flatland. After some time the scouts returned, silently signaling them onward. With renewed precaution the hunters spread out and crept forward, keeping downwind of the game.

Suddenly James saw a herd of a dozen or more deer. He heard Netnokwa's intake of breath. Such a number would feed their people for many moons. Slowly the men crept forward. When all the hunters were in place, Turtle signaled to them and they rose from their hiding places, their bows drawn. Arrows flew through the air. The deer raised their heads, startled. Instinctively they leaped forward, but for some of them it was too late.

The arrows struck deep into the hearts of the stags. Their muscles twitched, carrying them forward in a last graceful leap. As the last bit of life drained from their bodies, doe and stag alike tried to run. Confused by the smell of death, those animals that hadn't been hit reared and tried to run away, but another flurry of arrows brought them down. When the hunters were finished, only three of the herd had escaped unharmed. The rest lay on the open prairie or had managed to limp to the wooded rise, where they died.

Black Bear and Turtle let out yelps of pleasure, then sobered and offered a prayer to the Great Spirit for this gift. Immediately the deer were skinned while still warm with life and their flesh cut off in sheets. A fire was built and the strips set to drying.

That night as the men gathered around the campfires, laughing and feasting on roasted chunks of fresh venison, James lay on his pallet and watched the stars while he thought of Swan Necklace. He'd been away from her two nights, and it seemed a lifetime. He thought of her sweet face and the shine of her eyes when she looked at him. His body hungered for her. He tried to imagine what she would be doing at this exact moment. He could picture her sprawled on her mat, her dark hair feathered around her, her lashes curving against her smooth cheek. He fell asleep remembering the feel of her soft lips against his.

* * *

The night owl called from the trees. A frost had covered the ground. In the lodge Swan Necklace shared with her father, a small fire glowed. Red Hawke passed the pipe to Two Beaver, one of his council who were gathered. When the calumet had been passed around the circle and come back to Red Hawke, he laid it aside and glanced around the familiar faces. His heart felt very heavy, for he feared the people of his camp were once again in danger.

"Yesterday," he began, carefully choosing his words, "my daughter found the tracks of white men near the village. These white men are strangers to us, and yet someone among our camp knows them. He has met these strangers and talked to them."

"Who?" the council men asked. "Why does he not tell us about these strangers?"

"That is a wise question, White Bull, but I have no answer," Red Hawke replied. "The one who knows these strangers has not made himself known to me, nor has he explained why these strangers come near our village but do not enter and greet us properly. The strange white men are trappers like White Falcon and his men. They are from a band called Northwesterners."

"Are they friends of White Falcon?" Two Beaver asked.

Red Hawke shook his head. "White Falcon has said these men are dangerous."

Concerned, the councilmen looked at one another. "At least we have warriors here to protect the village. Even White Falcon has left two of his men. Buckley and Maurice."

"One of these white men has met with the strangers," Red Hawke explained.

"Who is he? We will ask him," Two Beaver declared.

"I do not know," Red Hawke answered. This revelation produced concern among the men of the council. "What are we to do?"

White Bull, who was one of the younger members of the council and a brave warrior who feared little, scoffed. "We are not in danger," he said. "We have men enough here to protect the village. We will set extra guards and we will watch the two white men who are supposed to be our friends."

Red Hawke nodded in approval. "So be it," he said, and passed the pipe a final time before the council broke up.

Seated on her cot, Swan Necklace had listened to the words of the council. Now she thought of what White Bull had said. He was a wise, patient man as well as a fierce warrior. That was why he'd been chosen to sit on the council. Now, considering his words about the two voyageurs, she feared for Maurice. She had little doubt Buckley was the one who had met with the strange trappers and had kept it a secret from Red Hawke and the rest of them. Such behavior was suspect. Maurice would not have behaved in such a manner. She was certain of it. Sighing, she prepared for bed.

Her sleep was troubled. She longed for the return of the hunters. If White Falcon were here, he'd soothe away her fears quickly enough. She lay in her bunk and thought of their last night together. He'd been so tender and loving. Even now the memory brought a surge of happiness to her. Swan Necklace grew drowsy thinking of White Falcon. The village was quiet. The women had withdrawn to their bunks for the night.

Swan Necklace wasn't sure what startled her awake, some sound, some movement. She lay without moving. Only her eyes moved as she strained to see through the dark shadows. She'd drawn the buckskin curtain over her bunk when she retired; now she lay straining to hear.

Someone was in the lodge. She was sure of it. Without thinking, she rolled from her bed, silently dropping below the platform that held her fur pallet. Beneath the bunk, pits had been dug where Swan Necklace and White Falcon stored extra weapons and belongings. Now she felt around frantically, searching for a weapon. Her groping fingers found a knife. She gripped it tight and waited, drawing a long, shallow breath.

Shadows flickered against the lodge wall as someone passed the fireplace. Suddenly booted feet stood beside her own bunk. A hulking shadow bent over the bed she'd just left. Holding her breath, she drew back.

"Ain't nobody in this one," a voice whispered. The boots moved away. There was a muffled cry from the other end of the lodge.

"Father!" Swan Necklace whispered, and crawled from beneath the bunk. Knife at the ready, she made her way toward her father's sleeping area. She could hear sounds of a struggle. Red Hawke was fighting someone. Swan Necklace sprang forward, knife raised, but she couldn't be sure which of the struggling figures was her father and which was not. She flung herself on the back of the nearest figure and had the satisfaction of finding it was one of the intruders. She slashed out with her knife and heard the grunt of pain. The intruder spun around, trying to throw her off his back.

"Aieeh, Sean. Help me. There's a devil on me back." Someone cursed behind her. Swan Necklace felt rough hands clawing at her. She was flung to one side and tumbled against one of the posts. Pain exploded in her head and darkness closed over her.

Some time passed before she regained consciousness. She jerked and opened her eyes. The lodge was dark except for the glow of coals from the center fire. Her head ached where it had struck the post. She put her hand up and discovered a large bump, but there was no sticky warmth of blood.

The lodge was empty. The intruders were gone and there was no sign of Red Hawke. Swan Necklace struggled to her feet and rushed into the village square, crying out a warning. Immediately Two Beaver and White Bull came out of their lodges.

"Someone's kidnapped Red Hawke," she cried. White Bull ran among the lodges calling to his chief. Maurice came out of his lodge. His wife, Little Rain, followed close behind.

"What is it, Swan Necklace? What has happened?" he demanded.

"Red Hawke's gone!" she answered. "Two white men came into our lodge and took him."

"How do you know they were white men?" Maurice asked.

"They wore boots," she said. "And when one of them spoke, his voice was that of a white man, yet it was different."

"You mean his accent was different?" Maurice said.

"White Falcon has said these men are Northwesterners. What does this mean? Why would they want to take Red Hawke?"

"I don't know, but we'll get him back. I promise you." He hurried back to his lodge to get his weapons. She saw that even in his haste, he'd slipped his feet into his white man boots. She thought of Garth Buckley and looked around the square for him. Just when she thought he wasn't present, he stepped forward and met her accusing glare without looking away.

"Where were you?" she demanded.

"Someone was in camp," he replied. "I chased them down along the riverbank. Is everyone all right?"

"Why didn't you sound an alarm, man? Red Hawke's been kidnapped," Maurice exclaimed angrily. "Did you catch any glimpse of who they were?"

Letting his mouth fall open in response to Maurice's declaration, Buckley hesitated a full minute, shaking his head as though speechless. "It was too dark to see them clearly," he said. "My impression was they were Indians. Do you think that devil Lean Elk got him?"

Swan Necklace stared at him in disbelief, wondering why he should so mislead the others. "I saw them," she said clearly. "They were white men. White Falcon says they are from the Northwest Fur Company."

Buckley swung around. "You don't know that. Are you sure your father's even missing? Maybe Red Hawke went out on one of those vision quests. You know what a stubborn old man he is."

Swan Necklace bit back a retort at his casual criticism of her father. Buckley might see her father as a stubborn old man, but she knew him to be steadfast, loyal, and tenacious, qualities that had made him a well-loved chief. Now she turned her back on Buckley and faced Maurice.

"White Bull and Two Beaver are even now searching for my father," she told the voyageur.

"Don't worry, Swan Necklace," Maurice said, touching her arm briefly in a gesture of reassurance. "We will find Red Hawke. If it was the Northwesterners who came into our camp and took him, then they don't mean him harm. Otherwise they would have killed him at once."

"I have told myself this is so," Swan Necklace answered, gratefully.

He turned to Buckley. "You followed whoever it was to the river? Which way did they go?"

"To the east," Buckley said emphatically.

Little Rain stepped forward and put her arms around Swan Necklace for a moment as Maurice hurried away into the darkness to join the search. Buckley glanced at Swan Necklace.

"We'll find your papa for you, *mon ami*," he said, and stalked away, making a great show of collecting his weapons and preparing for the search. When he had left the square, Swan Necklace turned to Yellow Leaf, who stood to one side with tears running down her cheek. She had taken the loss of her own father with surprising strength, but now at the thought of Red Hawke's kidnapping, she seemed to be grieving all over again. She put her arms around Swan Necklace.

Silently Little Bird watched the two girls, her expression closed. She made no move toward Swan Necklace to offer her comfort. When Swan Necklace glanced at her, Little Bird quickly averted her head, then walked back to her lodge.

"Will you come with me, Yellow Leaf?" Swan Necklace

whispered. Immediately Yellow Leaf raised her head and looked at Swan Necklace.

"Where are you going?" she asked, following Swan Necklace back to her lodge. Swan Necklace gathered up a spit from the fire pit and hurried toward the river. "Where are you going?" Yellow Leaf repeated. She followed her friend into the darkness.

Without looking to the left or right, Swan Necklace made her way down to the river, then turned westward along the north bank. The small brand she carried gave off just enough light to show them where to step.

"Careful, do not step there," she said when they'd gone a little distance. She knelt and studied the trail.

"What is it, Swan Necklace? What are you looking for?" Yellow Leaf asked.

"See the boot marks left in the mud?" Swan Necklace asked, pointing.

Yellow Leaf squatted down beside her. "I see them."

"Remember when we found the other prints before the men left for the hunt?"

"These are the same," Yellow Leaf exclaimed.

"Aye, these prints are the same except for this one." She pointed to one of the prints. "See how the nail marks are different?"

Yellow Leaf nodded. "What does this mean?"

"This print is the same as the ones made by the trappers from Montreal," Swan Necklace said. "These prints are from the boots of the Northwesterners."

"Are you saying one of White Falcon's men has helped kidnap Red Hawke?" Yellow Leaf's eyes were wide with disbelief.

Swan Necklace nodded. "I think so. I saw these prints together two days ago." She paused studying the line of bootprints which led down to the water. Obviously the men had taken Red Hawke away in a canoe. "Let us go back to the village and get White Bull." The two women turned back toward the village, taking care not to step on the line of tracks.

They had not gone very far when a figure blocked the trail.

"Who is it?" Swan Necklace asked, pausing. She held the burning brand higher, but its glow was too weak to cast a light very far. "Who's there?" Swan Necklace repeated but the figure remained silent. Yellow Leaf whimpered behind her.

"Our warriors are close by," Swan Necklace cried. "Move aside and let us pass." The shadows shifted and the figure seemed to have moved closer to them. Swan Necklace backed up, bumping into Yellow Leaf who yelped and jumped backward. The figure edged closer. Suddenly from the darkness came the snap of a twig. Swan Necklace's head turned.

"We're over here," she cried. Triumphantly she turned toward the shadowy figure, but it had disappeared. Puzzled she glanced at Yellow Leaf.

"Did you call out, Swan Necklace?" White Bull asked coming along the trail.

"White Bull, come and see what we've found," Swan Necklace cried. The warrior knelt and studied the muddy ground.

"They brought Red Hawke this way," he said, pointing to a moccasin print.

"Yes, those are Red Hawke's moccasin prints," Swan Necklace agreed. "These boot prints were made by the Northwest Fur trappers, and these were made by one of our white trappers."

White Bull sat back and considered her words. "Red Hawke spoke of these tonight."

There was a commotion along the trail and Buckley and Maurice arrived, followed by Two Beaver. "Have you found something, then?" Maurice asked, looking at the river.

White Bull glanced at Swan Necklace. She barely moved her head in answer to his unspoken question. She was certain Maurice had nothing to do with the kidnapping of her father.

Buckley had hung back; now he pushed forward. "*Mon Dieu!* We'll never find them if they took the river."

"We'll find them," Maurice said grimly.

"We have found the tracks the white men left behind." White Bull looked from Maurice to Buckley. "We have also found the print of a traitor who has helped our enemy steal Red Hawke."

Maurice studied White Bull's face. "I'm not sure I like what you're saying," he said. "You aren't accusing the white warriors of being traitors, are you?"

"We have found boot prints mingled with those of the kidnappers," Swan Necklace said.

Maurice gazed at her long and hard, then stepped forward, driving his foot against the soft ground.

"I have not passed this way tonight," he said. "See if the mark you speak of is made by my boot." She saw the anger warring within him and knew he was hurt by their lack of belief in his loyalty. Suddenly Buckley moved forward.

"*Mais oui*, this means nothing," he said. "I myself passed along this trail but a short time ago in my search for Red Hawke. These extra boot prints are probably mine, *n'est-ce pas?*"

"That explains it, then," Maurice said.

White Bull looked relieved. "We have wasted much time here," he said. "Come, we will use the canoes." They turned away, running swiftly along the path. Swan Necklace watched them go, her expression troubled.

"None of our husbands is a traitor as you feared," Yellow Leaf said stiffly. "I am happy for this. Little Bird would have been much shamed by her husband if what you accused was true."

"I am sorry I spoke," Swan Necklace said. "But look at the prints. They do not overlap as they would have if someone had walked here later. They are side by side on the path." Yellow Leaf studied the tracks.

"Such tracks could happen," she insisted.

Swan Necklace's shoulders slumped. "Perhaps you are right."

They arrived at the riverbank just as the canoes pushed away. Swan Necklace noticed that half the warriors would search downriver, half would go upriver. She thought of where they had found the landing site of the Northwesterners' canoes. It had been on the upriver side of the village. Surely the kidnappers would not have risked paddling past the village before landing their canoes. Hadn't White Bull understood this? Buckley had lied. She must warn someone.

"White Bull," she cried, running down to the river edge. "White Bull, wait. I have something to say to you."

The warrior had already stepped into his canoe, and his men had taken up their paddles. Now he turned to regard her with a stony expression. "Go to your lodge, Swan Necklace," he ordered. "This is the work of warriors, not women." With one mighty stroke of his paddle he thrust the canoe away from shore, heading upriver.

Swan Necklace stood watching them disappear around the river bend and felt her cheeks suffuse with color. White Bull's reprimand had been harshly made, and all the women who stood onshore had heard it. Shamed, she turned and made her way back to her lodge. Even Yellow Leaf did not follow, for she felt anger toward Swan Necklace for her accusations against the white warriors.

All day Swan Necklace sat in her lodge, until darkness fell and Walking Woman came to her door.

"Swan Necklace must forget her shame and grief and rejoin us," she said.

"I cannot," Swan Necklace replied. "I know I spoke out to White Bull in an unseemly manner, but he would not listen to my warning. It may cost my father his life."

"White Bull has returned and waits in his lodge to speak to you," Walking Woman replied.

"Have they found my father?"

Walking Woman shook her head. "I do not think so, but he has sent me to bring you to him."

"I cannot go, Walking Woman," Swan Necklace cried. "I

cannot apologize for my behavior and my suspicions. If only White Falcon were here."

"But he is not," Walking Woman said. "White Bull has sent a messenger to find the hunters."

Swan Necklace's expression changed to one of hope. "I will go to White Bull, then," she said. "I will tell him I am grateful for his search for Red Hawke."

Walking Woman nodded approvingly. Swan Necklace rose from her place by the fire pit, threw water against her face, and made sure her hair was neatly arranged in braids. It would not do to appear disheveled and in mourning. She must believe and act as if Red Hawke was alive. She made her way to White Bull's lodge and was surprised to see other men of the council were seated around his fire. Did this mean, then, that Red Hawke was dead? Had the council chosen White Bull to be their new chief? With trembling knees she waited for White Bull to acknowledge her presence. She kept her eyes cast down to the ground in a manner that would not offend the councilmen.

"Come, Swan Necklace." White Bull waved her forward, indicating she was to take a seat to one side of the fire. Swan Necklace did as she was bade and waited.

"We have found the camp of those who kidnapped Red Hawke. They are Northwesterners as Swan Necklace has said," he revealed.

"Was Red Hawke there? Is he alive?" Swan Necklace exclaimed, then blushed and fell silent. She should have waited until White Bull revealed all he wished, but the old councilman didn't seem irritated by her outburst.

"Red Hawke is there," he said.

Swan Necklace gripped her hands tightly to remain silent and not demand why the warriors had not rescued her father. White Bull nodded his head approvingly at her discipline.

"There are too many trappers," he said. "We are outnumbered and Red Hawke is well guarded. They are treating him well, bringing him food and water, so he is in no danger. There is time to wait for the rest of our warriors to return from their hunting. I have sent a messenger to summon them home. We have left two warriors to keep watch over the trappers' camp and to report to us if there are any changes."

"Red Hawke will be very grateful to his old friend for his care in this," Swan Necklace said. "I, too, am in the debt of White Bull."

White Bull nodded in acknowledgement of her words. "This matter is for the ears of Swan Necklace and the council only," he said, staring at her sternly. "This is best for the safety of Red Hawke."

At first Swan Necklace didn't understand what he meant. Then his words registered. White Bull also suspected a traitor in their midst.

"No one is to know that you've found the trappers' camp," she repeated. "I will follow White Bull's orders." She rose and, with a final glance around the circle of faces, left the lodge.

The hunting had been exceptionally good and their packs were heavy with dried meat and pelts as the hunters turned homeward. It had been three days since they'd come upon the herd of deer. Besides the deer, they had also brought down two elk. Now, despite their burdens, they moved swiftly along the trail. Each man thought of the feast the village would have when they arrived. Each man thought of his wife and the comfort of his fire and pipe. There were tales to be shared around the campfires, songs and much merriment to indulge in. When they grew tired the men pressed on, for each wished to reach the village before nightfall.

Turtle led them along the trail. He'd been a good leader on the hunt. His stature among the other warriors had increased greatly. A cry sounded through the trees. Turtle came to an abrupt halt and motioned his men to silence. The hunters lowered their packs to the ground and crouched, reaching for their weapons.

Silently they waited. The call came again and the warriors relaxed, having recognized the cry of one of their own. Two warriors came along the trail and the hunters stepped out to meet them, grateful for the extra shoulders to carry their packets of meat. But Running Deer and River Fox didn't return their triumphant greeting. Their faces were somber.

"White Bull has sent us," they said. "Red Hawke's been taken."

The other warriors gathered round to hear the sketchy details of the abduction. "White Bull says to come at once," River Fox finished.

James and Turtle exchanged glances.

"We'll split up," James said. Turtle grunted his approval. "Angus, you and the rest of our men stay behind. Bury what meat you can't carry."

"I'm coming with you," Wye said. James studied the young voyageur. Like him, Wye had adopted the moccasins and leggings of the Chippewa. His hair had grown longer and was caught back by a rawhide thong around his forehead. James regarded the young man's expression and nodded. Like his leader, Wye had taken on more and more of the ways of the warriors.

Very quickly the group had divided into those who would stay and those who would go ahead. Without a glance backward, the younger warriors who would answer White Bull's summons sprinted away toward the river village. James ran lightly, pacing himself easily with the other warriors. He thought of Swan Necklace. River Fox and Running Deer had said she was unharmed, but he couldn't rest easy until he saw for himself. As he ran he thought of the white men who had kidnapped Red Hawke. What reason would they have to capture an important chief? Amherst had warned him back in Montreal that the Northwest Fur Company was taking any steps to win the Indian tribes over to them. They'd often used whiskey to their advantage and to the detriment of the tribes. Taking Red Hawke had only angered the Crees against them.

Late in the afternoon they topped the last hill and began

the descent through the forest to the new village. They could smell the campfires long before they moved out of the trees and caught sight of the lodges. Turtle let out a cry to warn the villagers they were approaching. As they had expected, the villagers came out of their lodges, leaving their tasks to welcome the hunters.

Striding toward the village, James strained to catch his first glimpse of Swan Necklace. The moment she saw him she ran forward and threw herself at him. He caught her up, pressing her small, warm body against his hard chest. His lips claimed hers in a hungry kiss that he wouldn't end, until he heard her whimper of protest. Her slim arms wound around his neck and she pressed her cheek against his jaw; he felt her tremble.

"White Falcon," she whispered tenderly, and never in any homecoming had he felt such love for a human being. All around them other wives had rushed forward to greet their husbands. Now with their embraces done, the warriors moved through the village toward White Bull. Still Swan Necklace clung to him. Gently James pulled away from her and hurried toward the lodge of White Bull.

Stepping inside, he pulled the pelt over the door and took his place among the other warriors. The villagers gathered outside, subdued and uneasy.

Within his lodge, White Bull passed the pipe. Each man smoked and passed it on. When all had smoked, White Bull cleared his throat.

"We know where Red Hawke is being held," he said. "We needed only to have our warriors return. Now we can rescue him." He glanced at White Falcon. "We will not take the white eyes with us."

"Red Hawke is our friend," James snapped. "We will help bring him to his people."

White Bull shook his head. "We are not certain of this, White Falcon," he said. "Swan Necklace believes one of your men helped the white trappers to kidnap our chief."

"That's preposterous!" James exclaimed.

"You do not believe your wife's words?" White Bull asked.

"I would trust Swan Necklace's words over all others," James declared. "But I do not believe any one of my men would repay Red Hawke's hospitality in this manner. He is our friend."

"Let her come forward and tell you of what she knows," White Bull ordered, and a brave rose and went to fetch Swan Necklace from among the waiting women. She entered the lodge, blinking against the dark shadows after the brightness without. James watched her move across the lodge, her small shoulders squared, her expression unreadable.

"Tell us of what you found along the riverbank, Swan Necklace," White Bull instructed her, and she turned to James, speaking to him as she repeated her suspicions.

"What man do you suspect?" he demanded.

"Buckley," she replied. She saw the flicker of doubt in his eyes. She'd warned him of Buckley too many times. James gazed into her eyes, wondering if this accusation was brought about by a desire to rid Little Bird of her abusive husband.

"White Falcon does not believe me?" she challenged, and he felt ashamed of his doubts.

"Aye, I believe my wife," he said. "Have Buckley brought before the council. He must be made to answer these accusations. If he has harmed Red Hawke, he will die."

Two Beaver hurried away and soon returned with Buckley in tow. The barrel-chested voyageur looked around the gathered assembly. He'd never been present at a council fire before. Now he rubbed one meaty fist against his thigh and grinned nervously at James.

"*Mon ami*, you have returned," he said. "I have done my best to guard the camp."

James stared into Buckley's smiling face. "What has happened to Red Hawke?" he asked in a low voice.

"*Mon Dieu!* You have not heard?" the voyageur exclaimed. "He was kidnapped by the bastard Nor'westerners."

"What about the boot prints?"

Buckley's face grew ugly. He glared at Swan Necklace. "You have been listening to a squaw's tales," he sneered. "The women whisper of this ugly accusation your wife has made against us. Swan Necklace forgets how we fought to save her skin. Now she repays us with lies, casting doubt on the white men in her father's camp. She is trying to turn Red Hawke against us."

James leaped to his feet. "Have a care, Buckley. I've warned you before."

"You listen to a squaw's suspicions against your own men."

"I listen to my wife's suspicions," said James. "Do you know these men from the Northwest Fur Company?"

Buckley leaned back and shrugged his shoulders. "*Mais non*, I have worked with many men. How can I be sure I don't know these men until I have seen them?"

"How did your boot prints happen to be with those of the Nor'westerners?" James demanded.

"I searched along that trail after Red Hawke was kidnapped," Buckley said reasonably.

"If I find you've had anything to do with Red Hawke's kidnapping, I'll kill you, Buckley. You'd better pray he's not found dead so he can clear you of these charges."

Without waiting for a response, James stalked to the door of the lodge. There he paused and looked back at the council.

"It is time we rescue Red Hawke," he said. He glanced at Buckley. "My men will stay in camp, each to guard the other. I go alone with the Cree warriors."

"So be it," said White Bull. The men rose and made their way down to the river. The women and children were somber as they watched the men push the canoes into the water. Swan Necklace did not go forward to bid White Falcon farewell. As he took up his paddle, he turned to look at her. She stood on the riverbank and watched until the canoes were no longer in sight.

Chapter 16

THE CAMP OF the Northwest trappers was a makeshift affair, with skimpy shelters made of tree stumps and brush and none of the skill of the Crees. A large campfire burned in the middle of the clearing. Its smoke curled toward the treetops, and James thought scathingly of how wasteful were the white man ways. Swan Necklace and her people had taught him well. Around the camp hung racks with drying deer and caribou skins. There were no beaver pelts. Like the Crees and Chippewas, these new trappers were waiting for the winter pelts, which would be richer and thicker.

The day had been cool. Now as evening approached and the sun's weak autumn rays disappeared over the western rim, a coldness lay over the land, crisping the grass with white frost and cooling a man's breath almost before it left his body. Men sat close to their campfires repairing traps, smoking, and talking. They were at ease and seemed unaware that they were surrounded by hostile Indians.

Turtle motioned to his warriors and they crept closer, their guns at the ready. They had already determined which shelter held Red Hawke. They had observed a trapper carrying a bowl of food to the lean-to. Each warrior had already marked the location of weapons within the camp.

The plans were that James and Black Bear would creep into camp and try to spirit Red Hawke away before the trappers knew he was gone. Turtle and his men would remain hidden, ready to come forward if necessary.

With a final nod, James crept forward. Black Bear followed silently. The sparse trees provided some cover before they reached the clearing. Once there, James went down on his belly and crawled along the ground, pausing at the slightest sound from the camp. When he reached the lean-to where Red Hawke was kept, he sprang to his feet, seeking shelter behind the rough abode. Black Bear joined him and they waited to see if there was any outcry. All remained silent.

James signaled Black Bear to go one way and he turned the other. They would approach the opening to the lean-to from both sides, hoping to catch the guard unawares. Silently they crept along. A twig snapped. Black Bear froze. James glared at him over his shoulder. The trapper guarding Red Hawke remained hunched before the lean-to, unsuspecting. After a time, Black Bear and James edged forward.

"Hey there, what're you doing?" a voice rang out across the clearing. James froze. They'd been spotted. The trapper was running toward them, raising the alarm. Sounding the cry of a hawk, Turtle signaled the warriors to battle. With wild cries, they leaped forward, firing as they ran. The trappers were caught unawares. Leaping up, they reached for their weapons. The trapper who'd sounded the alarm whirled around, then turned back toward his lean-to where his rifle was standing.

When their own guns had been fired, the warriors reached for their knives and tomahawks. In the excitement a tripod bearing a kettle of stew was tipped over into the fire. It sizzled and burned. A brush shelter was knocked over; another caught fire. When Red Hawke heard the struggle without, he leaped to his feet. The guard raised his gun and aimed at the old man's chest. James and Black Bear filled the entrance at the same time, their knives driving deep into the guard's back. The trapper's body jerked backward and slid to the ground. James leaped forward and cut Red Hawke's bonds.

"I knew you would come, White Falcon," Red Hawke said. "Black Bear, my friend." James clasped the chief's shoulder in a show of friendship and concern, then turned away to help in the fighting. Black Bear had already leaped into the fray. Grabbing up the unfired gun of the trapper they'd killed, James turned toward the edge of the camp.

James ran in a wide circle to avoid the gunfire and came up on them from the side. He fired and saw a man go down. Pulling his knife, he leaped forward, throwing himself into the midst of trappers. His knife bit deep into the shoulder of one and the thigh of another. Both men scrambled away, disappearing into the forest. A trapper crouched at the end of the log, frantically reloading his long gun.

James leaped over the last body toward him. The man screamed and scrambled backward, eyes bulging in fear. Something about the frightened man, something about the smell and sound of death, made James hesitate.

"You ain't an Injun," the trapper exclaimed.

"No, I'm a trapper like you," James said. "I'm from the Hudson Bay Company," He thought of what else to tell the man, that he wouldn't be killed, that they had wanted only to get back their chief. In his moment of hesitation, the trapper fumbled with the breech on his rifle and brought the barrel up level with James's chest. James was armed only with a knife. It was no match for a bullet. He cursed himself for his softness. The man's eyes narrowed. There was no remorse, no hesitation in his movements, although he was about to kill another white man. James consigned himself to death. His last thought was of Swan Necklace.

Someone cried out shrilly and the man staggered, a look of surprise crossing his face. Slowly he sank to the ground and fell face forward, a Cree tomahawk buried between his shoulder blades. James looked around and saw Turtle watching him.

"Sometimes even men of our own clan can be our enemies," Turtle said, and retrieved his tomahawk.

The fighting had stopped. Several trappers had gotten away into the woods, but three lay sprawled in death. There had been no chance to take prisoners, so fiercely had they fought. Now Turtle and the other warriors set about raiding the camp. There were two reasons for doing this. They would gain many useful items that would be welcomed in the Cree village, and without the means to procure food, those trappers who had gotten away would be forced to return to their own forts and not the valley. Cheerfully the men gathered up weapons and ammunition, kettles, metal utensils, and even the deerskins drying on their frames, although they were not so expertly tanned as those done by the Cree women.

With their canoes loaded with their bounty, the men set fire to the brush shelters of the trappers and paddled away, sounding their shrieks of triumph. By nightfall they were back in their own village. Swan Necklace ran down to the banks the moment she heard the warriors' cry. Long before the canoes landed, she'd made out the tall upright figure of White Falcon. The women and children rushed forward to help pull the canoes up on land, then began unloading the bounty the warriors had brought back.

"Father," Swan Necklace cried, and ran to embrace Red Hawke. "You are safe."

"Aye, I am unharmed," he said, embracing his daughter. "You were not taken, my child. I worried you'd been killed when you fought them."

"No, Father, I hid under the bunks."

"Aiee!" he said softly, bobbing his head and grinning. At the cries of others he turned to greet each of his villagers who gathered around him. Swan Necklace turned to James. She had no words to say. She had turned to her father first, and James accepted this. She had known James was safe, and that was all that mattered. Now that Red Hawke was among his people again, she could turn to James with all the love and gratitude in her heart.

James pulled her into his arms, feeling the warmth and softness of her, smelling the sweet, fragrant herbs she used in her hair and to clean her body. All heartrendingly dear and familiar. He sighed, rocking her against him, raising his head to stare at the pale sky in a wordless prayer of thanks-giving. Homecomings had been this sweet back in Scotland, but standing here on a wild riverbank in a strange country, he feared he would never see his homeland again. He'd found a new home in this small Indian woman.

The hunters and warriors went to the river to bathe the stains of travel from their bodies. The women hurried to prepare food for the warriors and for the hunters who had arrived that afternoon with the meat packets. Their chief had been returned. Their village was safe once more from intruders and they had much food against the lean winter months. Their hearts were elated.

Fires glowed, a welcoming sight in each lodge, and the hunters and warriors moved from one lodge to another, telling of their adventures in finding the deer and in rescuing Red Hawke. There was much laughter and merriment. One of the warriors who'd been wounded in the raid on the trappers' camp sat in a place of honor beside Chief Red Hawke and was given choice pieces of meat and vegetables from the food kettles.

The children listened to the men's brave tales with shining eyes that grew sleepy much too soon. Mothers tucked them into their bunks and turned once more to listen to the stories. Some of them would be repeated many times, because they deserved to be. Some stories would be told only by those who'd told them first, but the people would not forget. These tales would become part of their heritage, part of their history. Buckley had joined them in their celebrations. Red Hawke had been unable to say whether Buckley was part of the kidnapping plot. He was cleared of the accusations by lack of evidence. But in her heart, Swan Necklace knew he had sought to harm her father and the villagers.

Seated at the fire with Red Hawke, James signaled to Swan Necklace, who rose and left the lodge. James slipped away from the other warriors and went to join her. She stood along the edge of the river, silhouetted by the pale moon against the silvery black water. Reminded of those first weeks when they'd traveled together, James went to her and put an arm around her shoulders, pulling her back against him.

"What does my wife dream of, standing here at the river?" he asked, nuzzling her temple. She'd loosened her hair and it fell around her like a black silken curtain. She turned her head so his lips were against her cheek.

"I dream of my brave husband, White Falcon," she replied. "I am very grateful he has rescued my father, Red Hawke. There is much cause for celebration in our village tonight."

"Much cause," he replied, enjoying the feel of his lips against her smooth, warm skin. Her womanly scent filled his head. "But now I am very tired and would like to return to my lodge and lie with my wife."

"You will not rest if I go with you," Swan Necklace replied archly.

James laughed, raising his glance toward the distant moon. "Nay, I will not rest," he promised, and bent his head to claim a kiss.

"Are you not too tired, my husband?" Swan Necklace tried again, although she trembled with longing. "You have spent many days on the trail. You have carried home much meat and furs and you have fought a battle."

"I have not fought the battle I wished," he murmured against her cheek. She gave in then, turning to him, raising her mouth to his, flowering for him. He felt her trembling and lifted her in his arms and turned toward their lodge.

"White Falcon," Wye called to him from one of the lodges where everyone had gathered for yet another feast and more stories, but James did not answer. He carried Swan Necklace to their lodge and entered, moving through the shadows cast by the dying embers of their fire. The merrymakers had been there and moved on to other lodges, but the warmth and the laughter of their happiness lingered. James placed Swan Necklace on her feet before the fire pit, then slowly undressed her, letting his hands slide over her skin until she shivered with anticipation. He saw the hunger in her eyes. Quickly he threw aside his own buckskins and drew her to him, moving her body against his own, so he could feel the smoothness of her, so he could anticipate the coupling that was about to occur.

Swan Necklace felt a wild, joyous abandon sweep over her. This was White Falcon, her husband. She felt much pride in him, but here alone in their lodge, she felt something deeper. She felt a giving of herself more profoundly than she'd ever thought existed between man and woman. For a moment she felt fearful that she loved this man too much so that the spirits would be jealous and take him away.

"White Falcon," she cried, throwing her arms around his waist and hugging herself to him.

"What is it, Swan Necklace?" he asked softly. "You're trembling."

"I grow frightened when I think I might have lost you."

He chuckled and swooped her up in his arms, carrying her to their bed. Gently he placed her on the furs and hovered over her, his eyes adoring her. "You'll never lose me," he promised. "I will be with you always."

"Do not say this. If the spirits hear, they might grow angry that a mere man and woman would—"

"Would dare to dream they could command their own destiny?"

Silently she nodded.

"Do not be afraid, Swan Necklace," he said. "I will always be beside you. No spirits, neither yours or mine, can separate us, in life or in death."

He claimed her then, his mouth hungry on her body, his hands gentle and relentless so she cried out many times in ecstasy. When at last he settled his long, hard body over hers, she was too limp and satiated to counter until his first thrust wakened new depths to her passion. She moved beneath him, stroke for stroke, until their cries mingled and even those passing their lodge heard, smiled, and hurried away to give them privacy.

* * *

Winter came, creeping on white-clad feet, covering the ponds and streams with the first thin layers of ice, scraping the last ragged leaf from the black branches. An early snowfall filled the hollows and valleys of the land. Gleeful voices echoed through the muffled landscape as children slid down snow-covered slopes on hairless pelts. Mounded with snow, the lodges took on a new appearance. Inside, they were dark and warm. Now the women did their work indoors, tanning the hides of the occasional caribou or elk by the light of the fire.

Fishermen speared bluegills through holes cut in the ice, and the women cooked the fish in stews thickened with dried moss. The quest for food continued throughout the winter, and stores were used for those days when hunters failed to bring in fresh meat. Hunters had been setting traps in the beaver streams since the first frost. The Cree warriors and the voyageurs had set out to find their own streams and each day checked their traps, wading in deep, freezing water to retrieve their animals. At night they returned to their lodges, where their wives provided warm, dry moccasins stuffed with dried moss for added warmth. James and his men waited only for the streams and rivers to freeze before they began their journey westward.

Now that food had been procured and permanent lodgings made, the warriors set about building themselves a sweathouse. Its domed surface was covered over with bark, grass mats, and fur pelts to hold the heat inside. In the center of the sweathouse a pit had been dug and a bucket and dipper made of bark set nearby. When the sweathouse was completed, Red Hawke signaled to James to follow him. They were joined by Turtle, Angus, Black Bear, and Wye. At the sweat lodge, James and his men followed Red Hawke's instructions and helped the warriors build a roaring fire. Turtle brought nearly two dozen round stones from the riverbank and placed them in the glowing coals. The men gathered around the fire and talked while the stones heated. At some point Red Hawke gave the signal and the men stripped and rubbed snow over themselves.

"Brrr, I'm not sure I'm up to this," Angus said. He'd barely gotten used to taking baths in the icy waters of the river. Wye laughed and threw aside his buckskins in a show of bravado. He and Turtle even got into a snow fight. When their bodies glistened and James feared the melted snow would freeze, encasing them in a thin layer of ice, Red Hawke signaled to the young warriors. The stones in the fire were glowing red now and Black Bear and Turtle used crooked sticks to carry them into the sweathouse, where they placed them in the pit.

"Come, White Falcon," Red Hawke said, motioning him and his men inside. James and the others followed him into the small, cramped structure, bending nearly double, for the ceiling was not very high.

"Sit here," Red Hawke instructed James, and the tall Scotsman bent his knees and sat on a mat beside his father-in-law. He watched with interest as the other men took their places. The stones had already heated the interior so the air was stiflingly hot. Turtle reached for the dipper and poured water over the stones.

Instantly there was a hissing cloud of steam. James drew in his breath and tried to hold it as the air became saturated with steam. Breathing became difficult; the pores of his body opened and perspiration poured from him. He gasped. From outside came the sound of the medicine man chanting his prayers that would drive the evil spirits of disease and poison from the body.

"Stay as long as you wish," Red Hawke instructed the newcomers to this purification. Wye and Angus looked at each other, faces glistening, chests rising and falling from the effort to breathe. None of the white men wanted to be the first to leave the sweat lodge, so they huddled as close to the walls as they could, hoping to find some crack that would let in fresh air, but the lodge had been well made. Red Hawke sat serene and seemingly untouched by the sweat bath except for the moisture that rolled down his body. James gritted his teeth and tried to draw shallow breaths. At times he thought he might faint, but a languorous tingle washed over his body. His chin dropped forward onto his chest, his hands rested on his knees, palms open. He felt transported to another plane. He could still hear the medicine man's song, still feel the moist heat of the sweat lodge, but he was no longer bothered by it.

"It is time to leave," Red Hawke said, rising and flinging open the door. Wye and Angus charged for the door, struggling through it.

"To the river," Turtle cried, and he and Black Bear raced down the bank and threw themselves into the water where the ice had been chopped away. Even Red Hawke was making his way to the river, and after a few tentative steps, Wye raced down and plunged into the icy water as the warriors had done.

"I canna do this, lad," Angus protested. His bony knees were red as he danced from one bare foot to the other in the snow.

"I think we must," James said. "Come on, man. We'll do it." With a wild Highland yell, he raced down the riverbank and leaped into the water. Turtle and Black Bear were already back on the bank, calling encouragement. Angus jogged down and plunged in, his face a mask of dislike for this particular ritual. Warm furs had been brought to the riverbank, and the men came out of the water and wrapped themselves in them before making their way back to their lodges, where they went to bed immediately.

Swan Necklace watched her father and husband return from the river, each trying mightily not to show his chills and discomfort. She had made them a hot drink of sassafras and gave each of them a cup. They drank it down quickly and hurried to their beds. She bit back a smile and banked the fire. Shedding her dress, she slipped beneath the furs next to White Falcon, wrapping her arms and legs around him to lend her warmth to him. He held her tightly and sighed.

He was more Indian than white man, he thought contentedly, and wondered how Amherst would take that when they met at Fort Williams in a few weeks.

* * *

Now that the streams had frozen over, travel was easier. James was determined that before he rendezvoused with Amherst, he would have explored some part of the westward lands. He and his men prepared to leave the Cree village. They would be gone for several weeks. Swan Necklace and the other women would travel with them, acting as guides. Several warriors would journey with them as well.

They set out following the riverbank, moving clumsily on the wide, flat shoes the women had made of rounded frames strung with rawhide, but once they became accustomed to them, they picked up speed. They traveled swiftly, stopping for camp only when darkness fell around them and rising again long before the first light broke on the eastern rim. At night they huddled in their makeshift shelters, gathering warmth from the bodies of their wives.

James worried about Swan Necklace, cursing himself for giving in and letting her come, but she met each day with better grace than he. She seemed to thrive under the harsh conditions of their travel. For three weeks they traveled westward, then turned northward, pushing deep into land that was rich in streams and forests.

"Look there, Jaimie, lad," Angus cried. "Look at the dams and beaver huts. 'Tis a good place to settle."

"Aye, I'm thinking you're right, Angus," James replied, checking his compass and map. They'd advanced farther west than he'd hoped after their months of delay. "This is the Red River," James told his men. "This is where Governor Amherst wanted a new fort begun."

The men glanced at each other, suddenly silent in the face of the task before them. James felt their uneasiness and looked each man fully in the eye. "We'll begin tomorrow," he said quietly.

The next morning the trappers and warriors began cutting down trees to build a small fortified cabin for themselves. There was little time to dawdle, for the main snows of winter would be upon them in a few weeks and they wanted to be safely settled before then. Not all the men were content.

"I am a voyageur," Buckley shouted the first day. "I am not a man who cuts down trees or builds forts. I am not a trapper. I am a man who paddles boats."

"You signed on for this journey, Buckley," James snapped. "You were told in the beginning you'd be helping to establish a fort out here."

"But, monsieur, such a man as you want is not a voyageur. He is a *coureur de bois*, a woods runner, an *engage*. *Moi*, I am a voyageur. I was hired to paddle the canoe."

"You were hired to do whatever it takes to establish a fortress here at Red River," James snapped. "Now, get back to work." With a baleful glance, Buckley went back to swinging his ax at a tree. That night the sound of blows came from Buckley's shelter, and the next morning Little Bird appeared with her face bruised and swollen.

"White Falcon, we must do something," Swan Necklace wept.

"Aye, I will," James said, and strode across the clearing to where the burly voyageur sat on a stump eating his breakfast. James lashed out with his foot and the stump toppled backward, upsetting Buckley into the snow. He scrambled to his feet and faced James.

"What are you doing?" he demanded, eyes flashing.

James circled him, crouched and ready to take on the thickset man. "I'm going to beat you, Buckley, as you beat Little Bird."

"*Non, non*, monsieur. I have no quarrel with you."

"Any man who beats his wife as you have beat Little Bird has a quarrel with me," James replied. He struck Buckley on the chin with his fist. Buckley's head snapped back and he staggered.

"How does it feel, Buckley, to be pounded by someone?"

Buckley took his meaty hand from his jaw and tried hard to bring up a smile. "I have no wish to fight you, James," he said.

James's fist struck again. Buckley's nose spurted blood.

The voyageur's expression grew ugly. He swiped at his nose, smearing blood across his jowled face. With lumbering steps he charged James. James leaped aside and grabbed hold of the man's shirtfront, his fist drawn back to strike him yet again. Little Bird had come up from the river, where she'd gone to gather water. Now she ran forward, her dark eyes rolling with fear.

"White Falcon," she beseeched, pleading for clemency for her husband.

James had no stomach to beat a man who would not fight back. He shoved Buckley, who staggered backward and fell to the ground. The Frenchman lay there without bothering to get up. Little Bird ran to help him and wipe the blood from his face with a soft doeskin. Buckley knocked aside her hands, glaring at her murderously.

James saw the fury in the other man's eyes and knew this beating would only bring further cruelty to Little Bird. Sickened by such brutality, he turned away and as quickly turned back.

"Little Bird will return with us to the Cree village when we go," he said. "Until then she will stay in the shelter with Swan Necklace and me."

"*Mon Dieu*," Buckley cried. "Such is not to be. She is my wife."

"She will no longer be your wife," James cried. "She will return to her own people. You have abused her enough."

"What if she don't want to go?" Buckley asked defiantly.

Startled, James looked from Buckley to the battered young woman. Swan Necklace had crept forward.

"Little Bird?" she asked tentatively.

Little Bird looked around the circle of watching faces, her eyes reflecting her fear and anxiety. She was thoroughly cowed by Buckley. Slowly she shook her head. "I do not wish to return to my people," she said quietly.

"*Voilà!*" Buckley cried as if he'd just accomplished a great miracle. He leaped to his feet and faced James. Little

Bird remained kneeling on the ground, her eyes downcast, her face pale and sad.

"Why do you not return with us?" Swan Necklace asked softly.

Little Bird did not answer at once. She drew a deep breath as if resolving herself. Finally she spoke in a small voice. "I carry Buckley's son," she replied. Her dark gaze flew to the face of Netnokwa, who had remained silent throughout the incident. The young warrior gazed into Little Bird's eyes and finally turned away, moving into the trees as if he could no longer bear human company. Buckley stood with a triumphant grin on his face. Swan Necklace went to James.

"I am sorry I have brought you into this," she said softly, and sadly went back to her shelter. She could do no more for her friend Little Bird. Buckley's laugh boomed out as James turned away. Little Bird got to her feet and passed too close to Buckley. He reached out and grabbed hold of her hair.

"White Falcon!" he called, his voice filled with contempt. "See how I treat my woman." He slapped Little Bird with his open palm. She spun around and fell to the ground again. "I do not let my woman tell me what to do."

James's fists balled and he took a step back toward the voyageur. Angus got there first. He tried using reasoning over fists.

"Have a care, man," he said. "Mayhap she's carrying your son."

"It does not matter," Buckley replied. "They're like animals, these Indians. They can take it, all right. Look!" He aimed a kick at Little Bird's stomach. Instinctively she curled into a ball, bringing up her knees to protect her stomach and the baby she carried.

"See what I mean?" Buckley sneered. "Instincts like an animal." His grin disappeared. "Go on. Get up from there and bring me some water," he ordered. Little Bird crawled out of reach of his boots before getting to her feet again and scurrying away. The other men turned away, ashamed of the way Buckley had treated his woman.

With all the hands working, they soon had a small log cabin raised on the banks of the river. Over the roof poles they laid birchbark and covered it over with the tarps from their packs. It would be crowded for the first winter, but come spring there would be new people arriving and new cabins would go up.

Now that the cabin was built, James prepared to return to the Cree village. Red Hawke would join them on the two-week trek northeast to Fort Williams on the northern shores of Lake Superior. Only Wye and some of the Cree warriors would return with him. The rest of the voyageurs, seven in number, and their wives and three Cree warriors would remain at the new fort. Angus would be in charge until James's return. He and the others would spend the winter months trapping beaver and defending the territory from trappers from the Northwest Fur Company.

"Take care, old friend. I will miss having you at my side," James said as he walked beside Angus along the frozen river. Now that the time for parting had come, he felt an unaccountable sadness.

"Get on with you, lad. I'll be here come spring when you return, and you'll be bringing more men and supplies. You're the one to take care. I'll have a sturdy cabin and several good men with strong arms to back me up. You'll have naught but Cree warriors."

"I'd rather fight beside them than with any man, barring you," James said.

"Aye, they are a brave, cunning lot," Angus replied. "But for the women, give me a Chippewa."

"You wouldn't be thinking of Walking Woman, would you?" James teased, thinking of something Swan Necklace had told him.

"She's as bonny a female as ever I've seen," Angus replied. "In some ways she reminds me of my mum."

"I wasn't sure you had one," James couldn't resist teasing his friend. "You should have asked Walking Woman to come with you," he said with some surprise. He'd been unaware that there was an attraction between Angus and Walking Woman.

Angus remained silent for a moment. "If it's to be, Walking Woman will come," he said, and James knew he wished to say no more about the matter.

"There have been some more signs of Indians."

"Perhaps they're friendly. I'll try to make contact with them. Little Bird and the other women will be a big help there."

"Still, don't take any chances, and watch out for Little Bird. I regret having to leave Buckley with you," James said.

"Aye, Swan Necklace was right those many moons ago in Montreal. She warned us about him. Do you go on the morrow, then, lad?"

"Aye. I must if we're to make Fort Williams before the heavy snows. We'll winter there."

Angus nodded. "All right, then. I'll see you in the spring."

"Aye, in the spring," James echoed.

Chapter 17

"**H**AIL, THE FORT," James called as they halted before the stockade at Fort Williams. Red Hawke stood on one side of James, Swan Necklace on the other. Behind them were Wye and Yellow Leaf and a small band of Cree warriors.

"Who hails?" came a cry from within the log fortifications. A man on the parapets peered over the edge of the walls.

"James McLeod, chief factor of Fort Hope on the Red River. I'm here to see the governor." He waited as this information was called down to the guards below. Finally the thick oaken door was thrown open. James motioned to Red Hawke and Swan Necklace and stepped into the fort.

A guard stopped them, thrusting his gun across their chests to bar their way. Startled, James glared at the man. "No Injuns in the fort," the man said gruffly.

"These are not *Injuns*," James said, matching the man's scathing tones. "These are my wife, Swan Necklace, and my father-in-law, Red Hawke, chief of the Cree."

"Orders is orders," the man said adamantly.

"Then tell the governor that James McLeod and his family wait for him here." James's expression was fierce enough to back the man down. The guard nodded to another man, who took off at a lope toward the rough log buildings set at the back of the fortifications. Fuming,

James stalked back and forth in front of the gate. Red Hawke remained calm; Swan Necklace watched James with wide, uncertain eyes. Soon enough, two figures emerged from one of the buildings and jogged toward the gate.

"James, you've made it, then," Amherst cried, holding out his hand in welcome. He came to a halt and glanced at Red Hawke and Swan Necklace. "I see you've brought company."

"Aye," James said in clipped tones. "My wife, Swan Necklace, and my father-in-law, Chief Red Hawke."

"Chief Red Hawke, welcome to Fort Williams," said Amherst. He turned back to James. "Come to my quarters. We'll talk."

"And Red Hawke and Swan Necklace?" James asked.

"Yes, yes, come along." Amherst led them to the log building and ushered them inside. The room was sparsely furnished with a bed in one corner and a rough-hewn plank placed over stumps to serve as a desk. A bear rug covered the plank floor. Extra shirts hung on pegs driven into one wall. In one corner, seated at another makeshift and cluttered desk, was a young clerk, who bobbed his head when introduced and returned at once to his ledgers.

The governor pulled forward two stools and offered them to James and Red Hawke. Swan Necklace was left to stand. Seating himself behind the makeshift desk, Amherst took on the mien of authority.

"Now, James McLeod, tell me what has happened since I last saw you."

James began, telling of the attack of the Ottawas, their rescue by the Chippewa, and their present relationship with Chief Red Hawke's people. Amherst was an astute man, often interrupting James's narrative to ask a question of Red Hawke. When necessary, Swan Necklace acted as interpreter for both men.

"You've done well, James," Amherst said finally. "I'll ready a convoy of trappers to accompany you back to Fort Hope come spring."

"Thank you, sir," James replied. "We'll also need supplies. Many of our goods were lost in the skirmish with Shemung and his Ottawa band last summer. If we're to make friends with the Indians west of Red River, we'll need trade goods."

"Yes, yes, I suppose so," Amherst said. "I suppose a bit of ribbon and beads smooths the way." His tone was belittling. He caught sight of Red Hawke's face and cleared his throat. "Francis." The young clerk jerked his head up and swallowed nervously.

"Yes, sir."

"Take Swan Necklace and Red Hawke down to the kitchen and see they're given some food. See if there's some pie or cake or something."

"Yes, sir. Right this way, er, Miss Swan Necklace." The clerk led the two Indians away. James watched Amherst from between narrowed eyes. The Englishman seemed to have changed, or maybe it was he himself who had changed over the winter among the Indians.

"It's not for the beads and wampum alone the Indians help us, sir," he said stiffly. "Many trappers have married Indian women. They're all family now."

"I know all about this marriage *à la façon du pays*," he said, shaking his head. "Marriage in the custom of the country. I'm not entirely against it. The Indian women provide the men with the means of satisfying certain base needs, and they've proven handy in acting as interpreters with their kinsmen, but we must keep our perspective, man. These are savages. Once we've finished our jobs here, the men will return to their own countries and take proper wives."

"How can they if they've already taken wives here?" James demanded.

"They've not taken vows in the holy church," Amherst said. "Not even you have done this. Swan Necklace is your mistress, not your wife."

"I have taken her as my wife according to the customs of her tribe."

"Exactly. But those marriages are not recognized by the

company. And it's just as well for you. Ah, James, why do we speak of this? Come, let us have a drink." He drew out a bottle of brandy and offered it to James, who declined. Affronted, Amherst set the bottle on his desk untasted.

"It was a damnable custom started by the French," he said, and James knew he still spoke of the marriages between the trappers and Indian women. "There've been some new rules, James, since you were last in Montreal. The company has written they do not wish their men to marry native women. They will not pay for the upkeep of these so-called country wives or for the progeny of such a union." James's head roared as if he stood under a waterfall. "That's why we've made a rule at all the forts. Indian wives must be kept outside the forts." Amherst glanced at James.

"You're an intelligent man, James. Surely you see the expediency of this."

"No, sir, I don't," James shouted. He blinked, trying to still his trembling anger. "You come into this country and use these people, then you treat them shamelessly."

"They're ignorant savages," Amherst cried.

"They're neither ignorant nor savage," James retorted.

Amherst took a deep breath. "I'm trying to warn you, McLeod, for your own good. If you've a wish to succeed in this company, then you must abandon your country wife. You cannot be chief factor at one of our posts and have an Indian wife. You must set an example for your men."

"I'll not be factor at your fort, then," James snapped.

Amherst looked astounded. "Think what you're doing to your career, man," he warned. "What will you do now? Live with the Indians? Live off the land like they do?"

"If I must," James said. "I can always trade my furs to the Northwest Fur Company."

"You'll be a fool to do that, a man of your caliber. They're little more than rabble and they have less love for the Indians than we do."

"But they don't lie about it and change about the way you English do," James said, and stalked out of the building. His teeth were clenched so tightly, his jaw was a clean, cutting line.

"White Falcon," Swan Necklace called, and he turned to greet her and Red Hawke. "We have had the strangest white man food," Swan Necklace cried. "It is sweet like our maple syrup, but they did not use maple syrup. Look, I have brought some for you." She held out a folded napkin upon which rested a piece of cake. James knocked it from her hand. It fell into the snow. Startled, she looked at him.

"I have no wish for white man's food," he said. "It is time we leave." He turned and stalked away. Swan Necklace glanced at her father and ran after James.

"White Falcon!" He paused and turned to face her. Her dark eyes were wide and uncertain. "Swan Necklace has displeased her husband," she said stiffly. "She has made White Falcon feel shame for his wife." Her voice broke.

"No!" he cried, catching her to him. "Never, never! You could never shame me. You are honorable and good." He pulled away and looked into her eyes. "I am ashamed of my own people, the white eyes," he said.

"Why? What have they done?" she asked, perplexed by this turn of events. He couldn't tell her of the ugly prejudices being shown her people.

He shook his head. "It doesn't matter," he said. "Come." He raised his head and included Red Hawke in his words. "Let us return to our winter village."

"We will not be staying at the fort?" Swan Necklace asked, and James shook his head. "Is it because we are Indians?" she insisted. He hated to see the pain in her eyes, yet he couldn't keep the truth from her.

Red Hawke shook his head sadly. He had witnessed the white man's prejudice before. His wise old eyes had seen much. He understood what had happened and that White Falcon was trying to protect Swan Necklace.

"The winter snows will be upon us soon," he said. "I have no wish to be trapped here in the white man's fort."

"Let us return to our people," James said, and led the way from the fort. Red Hawke followed, marveling on the differences in the white men. Some were stalwart and true like White Falcon, and some talked from both sides of their mouths, believing the Indian was too stupid to understand. He was not dismayed by this insult to the Indians. He had encountered it before from the men who closed themselves away behind walls of logs. Silently he followed White Falcon away from the fort, turning his face westward toward his village. Despite the white man's insult, his heart was light with the thought that he traveled with such a man as White Falcon.

They barely made it to the village before the winter blizzards began. The people were overjoyed to see them so soon, expecting they would have spent the winter at the fort. Walking Woman came out to greet them, her smile shy as she asked about Angus McDougall and the new fort. Swan Necklace and Yellow Leaf exchanged conspiratorial glances and went off to Walking Woman's lodge to talk of all that had occurred since they last parted.

James and the other warriors gathered to talk and plan a hunting party that would leave in a few days as soon as the blizzard was ended. James stood in their midst, listening to the laughter and bragging. These men were the same as the brothers he'd known back home, seeking land and the freedom to live as they wished. He felt a kinship more keen than any he'd known before and felt certain this was due to the mystical beliefs the Indians held.

"Will you be hunting with us, White Falcon?" Turtle asked, and James nodded.

"Aye, brother. I will hunt with you."

The winter passed peacefully. The blizzards blew down from the northwest, enclosing them in snowdrifts as high as their lodge roofs. During the breaks in the snowfall, James and the warriors hunted for fresh game to supplement their diet.

Their rice and pemmican grew low and the women stripped the inner bark from the basswood and slippery elm trees. Bark strips from maple and sassafras were cut up and boiled into a stringy soup. Even the seedpods from cattails were cleaned and used. The women set their snares and occasionally caught an unsuspecting rabbit.

When the hunters brought in a caribou or elk, there was a banquet and everyone settled around the fire pit in Red Hawke's lodge and listened to the storytellers. Lying on his bunk, James watched Swan Necklace as she brought food to her father and his guests, and felt the pride and belongingness of these people.

He lay thinking of what his life would become now that he was no longer with the Hudson Bay Company. He could live here with Swan Necklace's people and probably would, but there was a whole wide expanse of country out there waiting to be explored, and he wanted to be part of that exploration. He wanted to top a new rise and view the sweeping vistas on the other side and know there would be others to follow who would view it as well.

The thought of returning to Montreal or to one of the fortressed towns in the colonies was distasteful. He had sampled the freedom of this country. He was unfit for civilization. He thought of Angus McDougall waiting out the winter at the new fort. He'd go collect Angus come spring, and together they'd trap on their own, selling their furs to the Hudson Bay Company or to the Northwest Fur Company, whichever gave them the best price.

Having decided his future, James accepted the present with all its hardships and kinships. The time with Swan Necklace became special. He took her with him as he set his beaver traps along the frozen streams. If she didn't accompany him on a hunt, her face was the first one he searched for the moment he returned to the village. Each night he claimed her, rolling them both into a warm bear rug and feeling her small body meld to his trustingly, familiarly. His life was complete.

Spring came to them as slyly as a fox creeping through the forests. First came the drip of melting icicles, the black shine of ice, and the unexpected rivulet rushing toward the river. Mothers called their children away from the frozen river. They could no longer skate there or run on its surface throwing snowballs. Finally the river thawed, and for a few days, large chunks of ice floated by. Wedges of geese could be seen in the pale, bright sky, and the sun grew warm on the shoulders. The people of the village tarried in the ripening air, and bright voices called out plans to begin gathering sap from the maple trees.

"Will you come with us today, White Falcon?" Turtle asked as the two men stood by the river preparing to bathe.

"There is a hunt?" James asked, wondering why it hadn't been mentioned to him before.

Turtle's eyes gleamed with humor. "Swan Necklace did not tell you?"

"Tell me what, brother Turtle?"

"I will race you to the river," Turtle said, "and then we will talk." The two men threw aside their leggings and shirts and darted down to the river. Without pausing, they plunged into the cold water and set out swimming with mighty strokes to warm their blood. When they tired, they ran back onshore and drew on their clothes again. Turtle sat down to groom his hair, braiding it from a center part. James tied a rawhide thong around his forehead to hold his black, shoulder-length hair in place. If he'd had a mirror, he would have been astounded at how much like an Indian he'd become.

"So speak, Turtle. We have had our baths. Tell me where we are going."

Turtle laughed. "Does White Falcon remember the lodge we built some distance from here before the winter snows?"

"Aye. The one up in the trees along the ridge. It's too far from the village to be of any use to anyone, and you did not put sides around it, only a roof."

"Aye, my friend, that is true, but there is a reason," Turtle replied. His guttural English had taken on a burr from the time he'd spent with James. The two had become good friends. Turtle was arrogant and impatient at times, but he was also a tireless hunter, a fearless brave, and a steadfast brother. He loved nothing better than to tease James, so now James remained silent, asking no more questions about the lodge, because he knew Turtle wanted him to ask. Finally the other warrior could bear it no longer.

"Today we go to repair the lodge so the women can begin to gather sap and make sugar." He got to his feet and stomped off. Chuckling that he'd managed to best Turtle, James followed. The women followed the men to the ridge where the sugar huts had been built. Their bright voices echoed in the cold, clear air.

Trees had already been marked, territories laid out as to each person's sugar bush. When they arrived at the ridge, all set out examining their gathering areas, each of which consisted of several full-grown maple trees. The women shoveled away the snow from the open-walled lodge and began to make everything comfortable. The men checked the roof for needed repairs. Rolls of bark had been brought for that purpose, carried on their backs with a tumpline around their foreheads. Now the men drew out a ladder made of tree branches, leaned it against the sloping walls of the lodge, and began the repairs.

Beneath the roof of the lodge, where sleeping platforms had been built, they placed their sleeping mats. Down the center of the lodge, from one end to the other, the women dug a trench. In this they laid a fire. Later they would cook their sap there. The fires would be kept burning throughout the night, with the men or women taking turns rising to replenish the wood.

While they worked, the women peeled back the sheets of elm and cedar bark on the conical storage shed to reveal piles of bark dishes, *mukkuks*, and buckets that had been stored in the fall by placing them upside down. The women examined the utensils to see if any were damaged. They had also stored extra bark for the making of new ones should the need arise. A festive air settled over the gathering. James glanced at Swan Necklace often, noting her blushed cheeks and sparkling eyes.

The villagers spent their first night in the crowded lodge, sharing food and laughter. James sat watching Swan Necklace, wishing he could be alone with her. He wanted to take her into his arms and make love to her, but there were too many people. Other young couples, elated by this outing, made love in their bedrolls, but James was still reticent of such sharing.

They arose in the morning with renewed vigor. Voices rang out with happy anticipation. The tapping of trees was about to commence, but not everyone could tap them. Only the most skilled in such an art could tap the trees. Walking Woman was one of these, and Swan Necklace and Yellow Leaf watched her carefully, fully intending to one day do their own trees.

When the diagonal cut had been made, the bark removed, and the wooden spile made of slippery elm inserted, the girls placed their sap containers beneath the cut and watched avidly for the first drip of sap. Walking Woman laughed at them and moved away to the next tree.

In the afternoon, Swan Necklace and Yellow Leaf could not contain themselves but rushed back to see if the first of their taps had produced sap.

"Come and see, Walking Woman," Swan Necklace cried, holding up her container. The older woman shook her head.

"I would be very surprised if there was not sap," she said. "It would mean I had not made a good cut."

"You made an excellent cut, Walking Woman," Yellow Leaf gushed. "You are most skilled at tree tapping. I would not want anyone else but you to tap my trees."

Their praise went on until Walking Woman reminded them there were many taps from which they must gather the sap and they hurried back to work. They poured their sap into a larger bark bucket and moved on to the next tree and the next. When the bucket was filled, they filled another. James and the other men used shoulder yokes to carry the pails back to the cooking lodge.

"White Falcon, there is something you must see," Turtle said, lowering his shoulder yoke so the buckets of sap sat on the ground. Walking Woman and Otter Woman hurried forward to gather up the sap and start it cooking. When the sap had been carried into the lodge, James turned to Turtle.

"What is it, my friend?" he asked.

"This morning when I climbed up on the high ridge, I found tracks."

"Northwesterners?" James said.

Turtle shook his head. "These tracks were made by a moccasin, but they were not the moccasins of our own people."

James's face went still, his eyes grew hard. "Show me," he said. The two men put aside the yokes and hurried away toward the high ridge. A cold wind was whistling among the trees, making a thin, lonely sound. Turtle knelt and pointed at snow that had been disturbed.

"Here, White Falcon."

James knelt beside him, studying the prints. They were the seamless prints of moccasins. "Could be Chippewa," he said hopefully. "We're still on the western edge of their land."

"Aye," Turtle agreed. "But the Chippewa are our brothers. If they had come upon our camp, they would have come down to make themselves known."

James raised his head and met Turtle's gaze. Both men were thinking the same thing.

"Lean Elk has returned," James muttered.

"He has never left, my friend," Turtle said. "I have seen these tracks before and wondered that the wearer did not come into the village. When we journeyed to the new fort on the Red River, I found these tracks. I was not sure what they meant, but now I fear our old enemy has found us again and means to attack us."

"What's he waiting for?" James said. "Why hasn't he attacked the village before this? There were few warriors present when we traveled to Fort Williams. If he trailed us to Fort Hope, he knew the village was less well protected."

"Aye," Turtle said. "But Lean Elk does not wish to bring

death to the people of the village. His hatred is for you and Swan Necklace."

"Are you telling me Swan Necklace and I must leave the village?"

Turtle shook his head. "I do not say this, my friend," he answered. "Red Hawke is our chief and you are related to him. He would not let you leave, but your presence brings danger to us all."

James got to his feet and stared down at the trampled snow. "I will take Swan Necklace and go," he said. A voice rang out in the trees below. Laughter sounded. From the cooking lodge came the scent of smoke. It spiraled thinly in the cold air. "White Falcon will miss the friends he has made among the Crees," he said, swallowing hard against the lump in his throat.

"White Falcon will not go alone," Turtle said. "I will travel with you until you are safely with your men again."

James shook his head. "You will be needed here to protect your own people."

"The danger is not here," Turtle reminded him.

James stood considering his words. Finally he clasped Turtle's arm. "I am grateful to Turtle for his friendship. I will be honored if you would travel with us to Fort Hope."

"Aye, I will," Turtle said. "We will leave as soon as the women finish here. The ice floes will be gone and we can use our canoes. It will be safer to travel that way."

With their pact made, the two men turned back to the duties in the sugar camp. James still hauled sap to the cooking lodge, but he no longer tarried, not wanting to be away from Swan Necklace very long. He didn't tell her of the tracks they'd found, not wanting to dampen her enjoyment of the camp.

Later, he was to remember his decision and wish he'd been wiser. He warned Wye, and the two men took turns staying within sight and sound of the two young women. Where one could be found, there would be the other. The days passed without mishap. James overcame his shyness and made love to Swan Necklace beneath their robes, holding her close, cherishing her. No one would take her from him, he vowed. No one, not even Lean Elk.

Sometimes he was so consumed with hatred for the Indian who'd nearly killed Swan Necklace that he could barely contain himself from running into the forests in search of him. Such behavior would be foolhardy, he knew. Lean Elk didn't suspect that they were aware of his presence. James must continue to act as if everything were normal, but he could not control his thoughts. Several times Swan Necklace came upon him.

"Why do you frown so, my husband?" she asked. "Are you not pleased to be here?"

"I'm very pleased," he answered, and contrived to look and act more amiable, but she'd come to know him well and saw his ruse. She pondered over his mood and, seeing no reason for it, finally put it away from her and continued with her duties gathering sap.

Oblivious of any danger, Swan Necklace and Yellow Leaf went freely into the forest to check their taps. The snow was melting, the ground soft beneath their feet. The sap had run well and everyone felt happy and triumphant. Soon they would return to the village and prepare to travel northward back to their own lands. James had told her of his plans to stay in the Cree village. Soon he would travel to Fort Hope to tell Angus of his plans.

Swan Necklace's heart was filled with joy. So preoccupied was she with her thoughts, she was unaware anyone was present until she went round a tree. A man stood on the path, and for a moment she didn't register his identity.

"Lean Elk!" she whispered, peering into his evil face. He held a knife in his hand and his intent was clear. Stunned, she stood on the path as he sprang toward her. Then something snapped inside her and she dashed around the tree.

"White Falcon," she screamed, dodging back and forth, keeping the tree between herself and Lean Elk.

"Do not cry out for the white eyes," Lean Elk muttered. "He will not help you." He leaped forward, his knife striking out, catching her on the arm in a shallow cut. Swan

Necklace screamed and leaped away. Lean Elk ran after her, but his feet slid on the melting snow and he fell, giving her the chance to reach the safety of another tree.

Yellow Leaf came along the path and, seeing Lean Elk, screamed. Her cry was heard back in camp. James and Turtle glanced at each other and threw down their shoulder yokes, snatching up their weapons. Cursing himself, James ran through the trees toward the place he'd left Swan Necklace with Wye and Yellow Leaf. Other warriors, seeing them leave, took up their weapons and hurried after them. Wye heard the cry and, being closer, ran toward the gathering ground.

Lean Elk's eyes glittered with malice as he listened to the cries of the approaching warriors, and with a snarl he leaped away and ran back into the trees. By the time the warriors had arrived, there was no trace of Lean Elk.

'What is it?" James cried, running forward and grabbing hold of her shoulders. "Are you all right?"

"Yes. Lean Elk. Up there!" Swan Necklace gasped, pointing to the path the Chipewyan chief had taken. With a curse, James signaled to the other men to follow and dashed away up the hill. Before long they were back.

"Did you find him?" Swan Necklace cried.

James shook his head. "They left a trail, too good a trail. We thought it might be a trap to draw us away from camp." Swan Necklace said nothing, but her dark eyes were wide and fearful. Yellow Leaf cast a worried glance over her shoulder.

"Let's get packed up," James said. "We're rejoining Red Hawke and the rest of the winter camp."

They made their way back to the sugar lodge, where Walking Woman dressed Swan Necklace's wound.

"It is Lean Elk, isn't it?" she demanded, her lips pressed together grimly.

"Aye, it was," James replied. "We'll get him next time, Walking Woman, I promise. We will avenge Manitowa's death."

"That is all I wish," she said.

The women hurried to pack up the sugar they'd already harvested. In their haste, birchbark containers were left behind. By evening they'd rejoined Red Hawke and the other villagers. Almost immediately James began preparations to journey to Fort Hope. Swan Necklace would accompany him.

Red Hawke watched them pack. "You do not need to go," he said. "You will be safer if you remain with us."

"Your people won't be safe. Lean Elk will continue to seek revenge against Swan Necklace and me. If she's at Fort Hope, Lean Elk won't be able to get to her and he'll be led away from your village. They've done nothing to warrant this danger."

"Neither have White Falcon and Swan Necklace," said Red Hawke fiercely.

"I was going anyway," James replied. "I want to tell Angus that I'm not continuing with the Hudson Bay Company."

"Will White Falcon return to his Cree family?"

James paused in his preparations and looked at the old chief. In two strides he crossed the lodge and clasped Red Hawke's shoulder. "When Lean Elk is dead, we will return," he said.

Red Hawke nodded. "I will take my people back to our home in Canada."

"Swan Necklace will lead us there."

As if summoned by her name, Swan Necklace entered the lodge and looked at the two men. She had seen the love and respect grow between them, and now she felt a welling of pride. James turned away and gathered his weapons. Red Hawke looked at his daughter. Swan Necklace hurried to embrace him.

"You have lost a great deal to come rescue me, Father," she whispered. "Now I bring more danger to my people."

"You have not caused this danger, my daughter," he answered. "Lean Elk has done so. Red Sky—I was warned about him." He fell silent and she knew he was thinking of his dead wife and child. Never once had he indicated a displeasure with his daughter over events. Even now he accepted that she must leave and that Turtle and several warriors would accompany them.

"We will join you soon, Father," she said, her face buried against his strong shoulder.

"Aye," he said, and released her. He blinked rapidly and made his face calm as befit a chief, but his eyes still held sadness.

Suddenly a voice hailed them from outside. "White Falcon, come quickly." James dropped his packet and ran to the door.

Turtle pointed to the river where several heavily laden canoes approached. Though the vessels bore the marks of the Chippewa, behind the rowers sat white men. "Who are they, White Falcon?"

"I don't know," James answered. With Turtle he walked down to the river. The canoes came along the waterway and stopped before them.

"Greetings, my brothers," a white man called from the canoe.

"Greetings," Turtle replied in Cree.

The white man directed the canoes to shore and climbed out, glancing along the line of Indians who had come out to greet the visitors.

"Do any of you speak English?" he asked. No one spoke, so he turned back to one of the paddlers.

"Three Feathers, I need you to act as interpreter."

"I speak the white man's tongue," Turtle said. James remained silent. He was still stunned by the fact that the newcomer hadn't recognized him as a white man.

"Ah, good. I'm Simon Oakes. Is this the village of Red Hawke?"

Turtle glanced around. "It is," he replied abruptly.

"Excellent. I'm looking for a man called James McLeod. The Indians call him White Falcon."

"What do you wish with this man White Falcon?" Turtle demanded.

"My men and I come from the Hudson Bay Fur Company," Oakes said with a tinge of self-importance. He nodded toward the other white men still seated in the canoes. "I have a message for McLeod." He paused waiting for a response. When there was none, he turned his head, birdlike, and glanced around the assembled villagers. "Where is McLeod? Ah, there he is." He'd caught a glimpse of Wye. "I say, James McLeod." He scrambled up the bank. James stepped in front of him.

"What is the message you have?" he asked.

"Here, you. It's not meant for anyone else but James McLeod." His words slowed. "My God, man, you're not an Indian."

"No!" James's gray eyes were flat as he stared at the other man.

"I-I'm sorry, sir." The man was visibly shaken.

"What is the message you bring?" James insisted.

The man drew himself up. "Sir, I've been sent by Governor Lydell Amherst to tell you that Fort Hope has been attacked and your men killed."

Chapter 18

JAMES'S HEAD ROARED with disbelief. His look became so fierce that Simon Oakes stepped backward, preparing to flee in the belief that the man had gone mad here in the wilderness. But James's fist locked in his shirt, yanking him forward.

"What did you say?" he demanded.

"G-Governor Amherst sent me with this message, sir," the man said, remembering all the times in history when the messenger was killed for bringing bad news. James shook him slightly. "Word came in to the fort that sometime during the winter, hostile Indians attacked the new fort. All yours were killed."

"Are they sure of this?" James shouted.

"Y-Yes, sir, fairly sure. The Indians who brought in the report were scouts for the company. They're as reliable as you can expect an Indian to be." Realizing what he'd said and to whom, Oakes swallowed hard and rolled his eyes from side to side at the gathered Indians. James released him abruptly and turned away. His gaze met Swan Necklace's. She was weeping for the brave trappers she'd come to know and for Little Bird and all the other wives who'd gone with them.

"Tell Governor Amherst I appreciate his sending the message," he said stiffly.

"That's not all, sir," Oakes said, feeling emboldened now

that his life didn't seem in danger. James turned on him, his expression so fierce that Oakes might have quavered yet again, if he hadn't been made of sterner stuff. He recognized the lines of grief in James's face. "Governor Amherst sent you this letter." Oakes dug inside his vest and brought out a doeskin packet. James took it and moved to one side where he tore open the missive and read it.

Dear James,

It is with the profoundest regret that I send you this news about your men at Fort Hope. No one knows which tribe is responsible, although there is rumor that a band of renegade Chipewyans attacked the fort. There's also a question concerning men from the Northwest Fur Company, a dastardly deed, if this rumor is true.

It is my hope that our differences can be forgotten in the face of this tragedy and that you will proceed forthwith to Fort Hope, where you are appointed as chief factor. I have sent you twenty men and the supplies you spoke of when last here. Additional men and supplies will be sent in summer.

Do not fail me in this, I pray you, James. My best regards to your wife, Swan Necklace, and her father, Red Hawke.

Sincerely,

Lydell Amherst, Governor.

James crumpled the letter in his hands and turned back to Simon Oakes. "Have your men alight and rest. We leave at daybreak on the morrow."

"Yes, sir," Oakes said, saluting. He ran down to the river and motioned the canoes in to shore.

The village was somber that night. There was much to mourn. The voyageurs had become friends to the villagers. Walking Woman walked alone to her medicine lodge and sat in the darkness with no fire to warm her as she remembered a gentle bearded man who'd been kind to her.

"Lean Elk has done this," Red Hawke said. He sat before

his lodge fire surrounded by his council and by his young warriors. "It is only a matter of time before he attacks us."

James sat staring into the fire, thinking. "We must split up as we planned," he said. "It is the only way."

"White Falcon is right," replied Turtle. "If he had enough men, he would have attacked us by now. He would not have retreated at the sugar camp. He has lost men, first in his battle with us at the rice fields, and later at Fort Hope. He and his men have spent the winter in running and hiding. They are cold and hungry and weakened, driven only by Lean Elk's hatred for White Falcon and Swan Necklace. He cannot risk attacking us when we are together, and he must choose whom to attack if we separate, for he has not enough men to divide."

"Aye, Turtle speaks with a wise tongue," Two Beaver replied.

"If we separate, we will draw Lean Elk away from the village," White Falcon said.

"How can we be sure he will follow you and not attack the village when you have left?" Black Bear asked.

Swan Necklace was seated on her bunk, discreetly listening. Now she walked to the center of the lodge to face the men. "Lean Elk will follow when he sees I, too, go to the fort."

"No!" James said loudly. "At first I meant to keep you with me, but now it's not safe."

"It's not safe to stay behind. Besides, I will not have more of my people killed because of me. I will accompany you, White Falcon. I will ride in the front canoe so Lean Elk will know and follow. And in the end I will help kill him. I have spoken." Never before had she dared to speak out so in council meeting. Now she left the lodge before the men could rebuke her or order her to stay.

"She is right, White Falcon," Turtle replied. "She is the bait we must have to draw Lean Elk away from the village. You have known this."

"Aye!" James agreed.

"She will be safe with us."

James made no answer to this. Springing to his feet, he went in search of Swan Necklace. Turtle sighed and turned back to his chief.

The next morning at first light, the canoes were readied and loaded. With great show, Swan Necklace bid her father farewell and walked down to the first canoe.

"It is not fair," Yellow Leaf cried. "I wish to accompany you on this trip, but my husband has forbidden it."

"We will be back soon," Swan Necklace said.

Yellow Leaf nodded. She could not speak of her fears for her husband's life. To do so would be bad luck. Instead, she hugged Swan Necklace and gave her a special talisman she'd made herself. Simon Oakes and the new trappers clambered into their canoes, and James and Turtle got into the lead canoe. Standing on the banks, Yellow Leaf and Red Hawke tried to hide the fear in their hearts.

They traveled more swiftly than they had in the early winter, staying to the waterways where they could and portaging overland where they must. When they reached the Red River, they turned northward as they had done in the winter. The river sites looked different with the snow gone and the trees budding. As they approached the bend where the small log fort had been built, James marveled at the beauty of the setting and grieved that in the midst of such beauty, there had been death for his old friend Angus. Cautiously they approached the fort. There had been no sign that Lean Elk was following them or had even preceded them to the fort, but every man knew he was there and extra precautions had been taken all along the way.

The canoes slid up on shore, silently. Somberly the men debarked. Swan Necklace was made to wait in the canoe as James and Wye made their way toward the log cabin. There had been an attempt to burn it, but the green logs hadn't caught fire. Even the frame for the roof remained intact. Neither man spoke. Turtle and his warriors had spread out over the clearing, weapons drawn and ready.

When they reached the cabin, James saw the first of the

bodies of his men. It was half-charred and ravaged by wild animals. Wye made a gagging sound and James turned away. Other bones lay on the ground. James searched among the pitiful remains for his friend. When he found him, he knelt beside him and cursed, unable to express his pain and guilt any other way. He'd done this to them. His ambition had led him here and caused him to leave his men to go off and rendezvous with Amherst. If he'd remained here, his men might yet be alive. Wye came to kneel beside him.

"Weren't anything you could do, sir," the young voyageur said.

"Why weren't they inside the cabin where they would have been safe?" James demanded of no one in particular.

"Must be they didn't recognize the danger," Wye said. "They must'a thought the Indians were friendly. They walked right into a trap."

James cursed. "Why? Angus is no fool. He wouldn't have been so easily misled."

Wye shook his head. "We'll never know."

They buried the dead men and said a prayer over their mounded graves. The bodies of some of the men, Garth Buckley among them, hadn't been found, nor could they find all the remains of the women who'd accompanied them. They'd searched the woods around, thinking some wild animal had dragged them away, but they'd been unsuccessful.

James stood in the chilled spring air thinking of life and how quickly it was snuffed out in this dangerous land. How could a civilized man hope to live here? he raged inwardly, then Swan Necklace came to touch his arm and he saw her beautiful, flowerlike face and knew if something so delicate and fine as she could make a home here, then so could he. He took her hand and held it, drawing strength from her.

The first task was to repair the log cabin and enlarge the fort. This they set about doing, white man and warrior alike. The days were lengthening and they worked from sunup to sundown. There was no sign of Lean Elk, and James thought of Red Hawke and his band making their way northward. Had Lean Elk followed them to exact his revenge on them? James could only pray the renegade chief hadn't.

Once their fortifications were completed, they set out to find the nearby Indian village whose scouts had reported the massacre at Fort Hope. Swan Necklace went with them. James kept her at his side at all times now. When they neared the village, they let out a cry and, when it was answered, continued into the village. Chief Pawpitch came out to greet them. His eyes were guarded as he regarded James and his entourage.

"Greetings, Chief Pawpitch," James said in his halting Cree tongue. "I am called White Falcon. I have come from our great father in the East with gifts to thank you for sending us the news about the death of our men."

The chief's eyes flashed with interest. "White Falcon and his people are welcome," he said, and led the way to his lodge. Seated inside, he examined the gifts of blankets, hatchets, and kettles James had brought. "You did not bring the white man's firewater?" he asked.

"We do not possess white man's firewater," James replied. "It is not good for Indians."

"It is not good for white man, then," the chief commented, and reached for his pipe. As they smoked the chief told him of the things that had occurred through the winter and how they'd come to find the fort destroyed and the men killed.

"We do not know who has done this," Pawpitch replied. "Our warriors did not. We ourselves have suffered much at the hands of the white men. They come to our village and take our women and steal our horses. We believed they were the men from the fort and we went there to warn them, but they were already dead. Since then, our village has been raided again."

"Are you sure it's being done by white men?" James questioned closely.

"White men!" Pawpitch said adamantly. James and Turtle exchanged glances.

"Northwesterners!" James said. "We ran a bunch out last fall. Maybe they came on here. We will try to help the Chippewas with these men."

Pawpitch nodded and passed around the pipe. As they left the chief's lodge, they heard a cry. Swan Necklace looked around as a young woman ran forward.

"Little Bird!" The two girls embraced, weeping together. When the shock of her appearance had worn away, James came forward.

"Little Bird, we are grateful you are alive. What happened at the fort? How was it that the men were lured outside their fortifications?"

"I have much to tell you," she said, her glance going to Netnokwa. "Now that you are here, I will accompany you back to the fort." She hurried away and soon returned with a cradleboard into which was strapped a small, dark-haired baby. Swan Necklace's expression went all soft as she peered at the tiny face.

"He is so beautiful," she exclaimed. The two women chattered over the baby, and Swan Necklace insisted on riding in the canoe with Little Bird on the way back to the fort. Once there, she sat and watched as Little Bird nursed the baby, then helped put him to sleep on a fur pad. They had eaten their evening meal and now sat around a fire that had been built in the center of the cabin's dirt floor.

"It is time to talk now," James said. He had been patient, but he would wait no longer. Little Bird and Swan Necklace recognized this. Their faces became somber.

"It is good to be back here with my own people," Little Bird began. "There was a time when I didn't believe I would ever see any of you again." Her gaze went to Netnokwa and darted away again. "Buckley and two of the trappers, Simmons and Le Blanc, left the fort soon after you did," she said. "They left to hunt one day and never came back. The other men searched for them, but they found no sign of them. At first some of us thought a hostile tribe had attacked them and killed them, but guns and ammunition were gone, and in the winter months when food was scarce, our cache of meat was robbed and boot prints were found. Angus was very angry. He doubled the guard and we stored our meat closer to the cabin. Some days we ate only the seeds of the cattails.

"Angus was very kind to me. He watched over me after Buckley left and he helped during the birth of my son, Little Fox." She paused and smiled briefly at the mention of her son. Then her expression grew somber.

"In the spring, when the streams and rivers thawed, a group of white men came to the fort in canoes. The men thought they were White Falcon returning with men and supplies as he had promised. Everyone ran out to greet them. The strangers in the boats hid their guns until Angus and the rest of the men were close to them, then they fired on them. Our men were unarmed. They had left their weapons in the cabin. They tried to take shelter behind the trees, but the strangers were running after them and killing them."

She paused, tears streaming down her face. "Angus tried to protect me, but he was wounded. I saw him fall to the ground. I tried to rouse him, but he didn't move. I thought of Little Fox and ran to the cabin and then I saw him. Buckley was leading the attackers."

"Buckley?" James said, and looked at Swan Necklace.

"He is an evil man," she said, and patted her friend's shoulder.

Little Bird went on with her narrative as if they hadn't spoken. "He looked at me with our son in my arms and raised his rifle and shot me, then he set fire to the cabin. I managed to drag myself and Little Fox out of the cabin and hid in the woods. When the men were gone, I crawled away and made my way to the Chippewa village." Little Bird was weeping by the time she finished, and Swan Necklace thought it was for Buckley's deadly betrayal.

"You should not weep for a man such as Garth Buckley," she said. "White Falcon will seek revenge for you."

"I do not weep for Buckley," Little Bird said. "I grieve for my friend Angus. I have called him Gentle Bear."

"Do you know where Buckley and his band of cutthroats

have gone?" James asked. He couldn't think of Angus without feeling a need to wreak vengeance on someone. He'd thought Lean Elk had been responsible for this massacre, but it had been one of their own men.

"Pawpitch's warriors have found signs that went westward from here," Little Bird said. "But they have not gone too far. They wish to take over this area for themselves."

James sought out Turtle and Wye to speak to them outside the hearing of the women. "We must avenge the deaths of our comrades," he said. "I do not wish to risk the fort, but I cannot sit still while those murderers go free. We'll take half our men and leave the other half to guard the fort."

Turtle nodded. "I will send a runner to Pawpitch to bring warriors to help us. They have suffered much at the hands of these white men."

"Good man," James said, clasping Turtle's shoulder. "We'll leave as soon as they arrive."

A messenger was sent at first light, and soon Pawpitch and his braves were at the fort. Half the men were left to protect the fort. The rest piled into their canoes and followed the tributaries westward. Pawpitch's braves led the way, for they'd come upon the trappers' camp during one of their hunting parties. They'd circled wide to avoid a confrontation, but now they were eager to teach their white enemies a lesson.

By late afternoon, they were within a short distance of the camp. They pulled the canoes onshore and crept overland the rest of the distance. James was surprised to see this camp was much like that first Northwesterners' camp where Red Hawke had been held. Crouched low, he observed Buckley stalking around the camp with his customary bravado. For all his pomposity, the trapper was aware of the ways of the forest. When Turtle let out the cry of a hawk, Buckley grabbed for his rifle and spun around.

Edgy, James thought. He's expecting me. With that thought, he felt better. He knew he was going to kill Garth Buckley, and the thought was satisfying. Turtle sounded another call and they leaped from their hiding places and ran toward the camp. James ran forward, firing his long rifle, then reaching for his hatchet. He swung without mercy, driven by some inner madness, and when the battle was finished and their enemies lay around them dead, James walked among the bodies searching for Garth Buckley.

"Have you seen Little Bird?" Swan Necklace inquired of Simon Oakes. He'd been left in charge while James and the other men were gone.

"She went down to the river for water," he said. He was sharpening his knife against a grindstone. Swan Necklace glanced out the door of the stockade toward the river. Little Bird was not in sight.

"Who went with her?" she asked.

"What? Oh, I told her to go on alone since I was right here and could hear her if she had any trouble."

"You let her go to the river alone?" Swan Necklace repeated. "White Falcon has said no one is to leave the fort without a proper guard."

"Well, I'm here!" Oakes said as if she were being unreasonable.

"But Little Bird is not in sight," Swan Necklace said, her fear rising. "Did she come back when you were busy and didn't notice?"

"No, I've been sitting right here waiting for her return."

"Call some of the men," Swan Necklace cried.

"They've gone hunting. There's just Netnokwa and me."

Swan Necklace stared at him with wide eyes. "Who gave them permission to hunt?"

Oakes glanced away. "Well, we were low on fresh meat. I told 'em to go ahead. Look here, like as not, Netnokwa and Little Bird are out yonder somewheres doing a little courting. They've been eyeing each other for days now."

"Perhaps you're right," Swan Necklace said, "but we must search for them." She hurried outside the fort and looked up and down the riverbank. "You go downstream and I'll go upstream."

"Maybe we'd better wait until the others get back,"

Oakes said, wiping his hands against his breeches. He was remembering the sight of the dead bodies when they first arrived at the fort.

"*You* wait," Swan Necklace snapped, and set out along the river, searching for footprints that would indicate Little Bird had passed that way. She hadn't gone very far when she caught sight of a body lying in the grass at the edge of the woods. Before she reached him, she recognized the body of Netnokwa. She knelt beside him, searching for signs of life. He moaned and tried to sit up.

"Be still," she commanded. "You're badly wounded. Where's Little Bird?" He tried to answer but couldn't. Shaken, she got to her feet. Some distance away lay Little Bird.

"Little Bird," she whispered, turning the girl. The caribou skin over her chest was stained bright red. Little Bird's lashes fluttered against her cheeks. She opened her eyes and gazed at Swan Necklace as if from a long distance.

"Who has done this to you?" Swan Necklace whispered in despair. "Was it Lean Elk?"

"B-Bu—" Little Bird tried to speak and couldn't. Her eyes pleaded with Swan Necklace.

"What is it, my friend? What do you want of me?"

Again Little Bird's lips moved, trying to form the words, but no sound came. In her agitation, one hand fumbled to grip Swan Necklace's arm.

"Is it Little Fox?" she cried. "Do you fear for him?" Little Bird's head barely moved, but her gaze gave the answer. "He's safe. Do not fear."

Little Bird relaxed visibly, her gaze fixed on some point over Swan Necklace's shoulder. Suddenly her grip on Swan Necklace's arm tightened in a deathlike spasm.

"Beware," she cried, and slumped back. Swan Necklace had no time to think of what her warning meant. She was grabbed from behind and yanked backward. She screamed and rolled to one side. When she looked up, she saw Garth Buckley looming over her. She leaped to her feet and tried to run, but he grabbed her ankle, bringing her down hard.

She lay stunned, trying to draw a breath. Once again she tried to scramble away, but Buckley kicked her in the side and she lay still. Grabbing hold of her hair, he pulled her to her feet.

"You ain't dealing with White Falcon now," he sneered. "I don't let any woman get by me."

"What do you want?" she gasped.

"I want a canoe so I can get away. White Falcon attacked our camp two days ago and I had to slip away without much of anything, but now I've got you and we're going to take one of those canoes down yonder, you understand me?" She said nothing, so he yanked on her hair. "Do you?"

"Yes." She nodded.

"Good," he breathed in her ear. "Now, we'll just take it slow and easy. If you try to warn them up at the fort, you'll get the same thing Little Bird did."

She could barely breathe from the pain in her head and side. She stumbled down to the canoe.

"Hey!" someone shouted. Buckley turned and in one liquid movement threw his knife. Simon Oakes slid to the ground. Buckley shoved Swan Necklace into the canoe and, grabbing up a paddle, pushed it out into the middle of the river. Quickly he began paddling. The birchbark canoe leaped ahead in the water. Swan Necklace closed her eyes and tried to shut out the sight of the evil man. White Falcon, she prayed silently.

Tirelessly James paddled. They'd left for the fort the moment he realized Garth Buckley's body wasn't there. Once again the slippery trapper had eluded him. There was only one place Buckley could go, and he had a head start. Simon Oakes would know not to trust the man. He'd heard Little Bird's story. Little Bird and Swan Necklace would not be tricked by the man's poses.

It was late in the afternoon when he reached the fort. At once Turtle hailed the fort, but there was no answer. The eerie silence reminded James of their arrival after the massacre. Such a thing could not have happened again. Perhaps this time Lean Elk had come. He leaped out of the canoe and ran up to the stockade, crying Swan Necklace's name, but there was no answer. The other men had debarked and were running along the riverbank and around the clearing, searching for signs.

"White Falcon," Wye called, and James ran down the bank to the place where the young trapper stood. Wye pointed to Netnokwa, Little Bird, and Simon Oakes. "They're alive." Turtle motioned to the medicine man to tend them. James's heart was pounding.

"Swan Necklace?" he asked.

"We haven't seen any sign of her, sir," Wye replied. "But there are booted footprints down by the canoes."

"Buckley," James said flatly.

"Looks like it," Wye said.

"He's gone downstream. Let's follow him." They ran back to the canoes and, scrambling in, took up their paddles, heading east. James was like a man possessed, refusing to stop even after dark when snags or stumps on the flooded river could rip the bottom from the canoes.

"White Falcon," Turtle said, bringing his canoe alongside James's. "We must stop. The white eyes would have stopped and we could pass him in the darkness."

James stopped paddling, letting his canoe drift forward. "We'll camp for the night," he said. No fires were lit. The men chewed on pemmican and huddled on the ground without bedrolls. James neither ate nor slept. In their restless sleep, they heard him move about the shoreline. Before daybreak they were up and paddling again. They nearly passed the place where Buckley had landed. Turtle spotted the abandoned canoe and they beached their own vessels and ran along the shoreline looking for prints.

"They have gone this way, White Falcon," said Turtle. "Her prints are there, too." James felt a moment of relief. She was still alive. They set off down the trail. Buckley was following the river around a set of waterfalls. They moved silently, quickly. Turtle and the other men could barely maintain the pace James set. They were on land they'd never negotiated before. Even Pawpitch's men seemed surprised when they came over a bluff and spied an Indian camp.

"It's Lean Elk's camp," James said, and headed down the slope toward the camp. Buckley had made for Lean Elk's camp, he thought dimly. Lean Elk would kill Swan Necklace in an instant. From the camp came warning cries. The renegade warriors ran out with weapons in hand. Seeing the Cree braves bearing down on them, they ran forward to attack. Smoke filled the air as long rifles were fired. Knives flashed. Tomahawks were raised in deadly warfare.

Over the clash and fury of battle, James searched for Lean Elk. Suddenly Lean Elk was there. James sensed him before he saw him and whirled, bringing up his arm to ward off the knife blow. The two men fell to the ground, rolling down the slope toward the river as each struggled to sink his knife into the flesh of the other. James felt the tearing burn of Lean Elk's knife in his shoulder. Lean Elk sprang forward, planting his feet on either side of James and staring into his eyes.

"Know this, white man," he said. "I will yet claim Swan Necklace, and when I do, she will feel the blade of my knife as you have."

"Wh-what have you done with her?" James gasped.

Lean Elk's expression registered puzzlement. "I do not have her," he said.

"Buckley came this way with Swan Necklace. You must have seen them."

Lean Elk raised his head as if sniffing the air, as if hearing some message the forest had for him. Leaping away from James, he ran into the trees. James forced himself to his feet and retrieved his knife. His wound was bleeding profusely, but he had no time to tend it. He ran after Lean Elk, certain that the Indian would lead him to Swan Necklace. Shadows lay thick in the forest, shadows that could hide a man who might spring out and sink his knife into your heart, but James didn't slow down. Night was approaching. He would lose Lean Elk's trail in the darkness.

He stumbled on, forcing his legs to move. He was growing weaker from the loss of blood. He stumbled, tumbling down a long slope, and lay stunned, fighting to regain his breath. All around him came the night sounds of the forest.

He must wait for light again, he thought. He was of no use to Swan Necklace like this. Gritting his teeth with anger and impatience, he bound his wound, then found a log and made a bed beside it. By the first hint of dawn he was up and moving through the trees, worried that he would no longer be able to find Lean Elk's trail, but it was there clearly marked as if the Indian intended him to follow.

He came out on a high ridge. Below lay the river. He made his way down to it and halted, staring at the canoes resting onshore. Lean Elk and his men had hidden canoes here at this part of the river for a second escape should they need it.

Even as James peered down on the landing, Buckley came into sight, pushing Swan Necklace before him. She looked small and helpless. He shoved her into a canoe, cuffing her when she was slow, then stood onshore, relieving himself in full view of her. James gritted his teeth at this final insult the trapper had shown his wife and half ran, half slid down the steep ridge.

Swan Necklace saw him first. She stood up in the canoe, her face bright with hope. James motioned her to silence, but Garth Buckley turned. Stunned at the sight of James launching himself across the clearing, he brought up his rifle, firing without aiming. The bullet caught James in the thigh muscle. He went down, automatically rolling before coming to a halt.

"White Falcon," Swan Necklace screamed, and clambered out of the canoe. Buckley was already reloading, pouring powder down the barrel and ramming home a ball. In one swift movement James drew his knife from his sheath and threw it at Buckley. It pierced his neck and he fell to the ground, mortally wounded. Swan Necklace paused on the edge of the river, her gaze going from her kidnapper to White Falcon.

With a cry, she ran up the bank, intending to go to
James, but Lean Elk leaped forward, blocking her way.
Eyes wide with fear, she took a step backward, her gaze going to White Falcon in a silent plea for help. Holding his
wounded leg, James struggled to get to his feet. He had no
other weapon.

Swan Necklace tried to dodge around Lean Elk, but he
grabbed hold of her, twisting her around so she was between James and him. He held his knife at her throat; his
eyes reflected a terrible kind of triumph.

"Lean Elk." James leaned against a tree, trying to gain
strength to launch himself across the space at Lean Elk, but
even if he weren't wounded, he knew it was no good. "Let
her go, Lean Elk. It's me you want."

"No, white eyes. I will kill you both. I have waited for
you to follow me so you could see her blood flow before
your very eyes." The point of his knife pressed against her
throat. A trickle of blood flowed. Swan Necklace whimpered in fear.

"Why do you wish to kill Swan Necklace?" James cried,
groping for anything to delay Lean Elk in his intentions.
"She did not choose to come with me. I wrestled you for
her and won. That's not her fault."

"She has brought much badness to my life. Once I was
a great chief of my people, but I traveled to another land to
rescue Swan Necklace, only to find she was willing to give
herself to a white eyes. I have broken the customs of my
people. I have offended the spirits. I have spilled blood
over a mere woman. For this my people will turn their
backs on me. I cannot go back to my tribe. For this Swan
Necklace must die."

James saw there was nothing he could say to dissuade
Lean Elk. His eyes filled with tears as he looked at the
woman he loved. Her gaze held all the sadness and all the
love a human soul could contain.

Suddenly the cry of a hawk sounded through the woods.
Turtle had followed them! James felt a moment of hope,
then it died in his chest before it was full-born. Turtle

would never reach them in time. The cry came again, piercing and urgent.

Lean Elk raised his head and studied the treetops. His hold on Swan Necklace loosened slightly. Her hand came up to push against his arm as her foot lashed out, kicking him in the shin. For one breathtaking moment she was free, the knife no longer at her throat. She threw herself to one side. Lean Elk lashed out with the knife, but she rolled away.

James moved, ignoring the dull pain that shot through his leg, throwing himself at Lean Elk, grabbing the arm that would plunge the knife into Swan Necklace's back. The two men struggled, sliding down the bank and into the water. The swiftly flowing current carried them downriver.

James heard Swan Necklace's cry and knew it was for him. He was weakened by his wounds, but her cry gave him added strength. He fought with Lean Elk, wresting the knife from his hand. He felt the water pulling him down. With his last ounce of strength he plunged the knife downward. Lean Elk's face registered surprise. He gasped for air, drawing water deep into his lungs. James saw the convulsive grasp for fleeting life and then Lean Elk was gone, carried away by the current.

James felt the pull of the river current, the cold, dark allure of the water and the peace it offered, then he remembered Swan Necklace waiting on the shore and he kicked against the dark tide and strained upward toward light and air.

"White Falcon!" Her cry filled his mind. She was alive. He felt her joy. "He's there. Help him!" Turtle pushed Buckley's canoe out into the stream and paddled out to him.

"Take my hand," Turtle ordered, and James reached up and grasped the red man's hand and was pulled into the canoe. He was unaware of the red-tinged water that drained away from him. He was home, among his friends. He heard Swan Necklace's cry and felt her beside him. He was home with Swan Necklace. James closed his eyes and slept.

Epilogue

Swan Necklace stood at the edge of the river and watched the line of canoes approach the fort. New voyageurs had brought supplies and families to the Red River settlement. Tall and handsome in his dark suit and shiny boots, James McLeod stood on the bank waiting to greet the new arrivals. For today she thought of him as James instead of White Falcon.

Swan Necklace herself wore a dress brought all the way from Montreal. It was made of silk and was adorned with lace and ribbons. She felt very pretty in it, but James had said he found her more desirable in her caribou dress. Still, she wanted to make a good impression on the white trappers, clerks, and *engages* who were coming to the settlement.

In the past year the fort had increased significantly in size, with many new buildings being added. With James as chief factor of Fort Hope, their lives had been peaceful and prosperous. They had journeyed north into Canada to the land of the Cree so Swan Necklace might see her people once more, but she had known her heart would forever be with White Falcon. Walking Woman had traveled back with them and now lived at the fort. Her presence was a comfort to Swan Necklace. Now she came down to the riverbank carrying Little Fox.

From their places on the river shore, Little Bird and

Netnokwa turned and waved at them. The gentle warrior had taken Little Fox as his own son. Little Bird was radiant as she looked at her husband. She had learned the hard way to prize her husband's gentle ways and kind heart. Yellow Leaf and Wye stood beside them. Wye barely took his eyes off his young wife, for she was heavy with their first child.

Swan Necklace sighed with happiness over the turn of events for her friends. To her surprise, James had arranged for a bishop to come and perform the white man's ceremony over them all.

"This is for your own good," he had told her. "No one can ever say you are not my wife, and if something should happen to me, you have only to go to the company and they will provide for you and our children."

Swan Necklace had been touched by his concern, but she knew if anything happened to White Falcon, she would return to her own people and raise their sons in the ways of the Cree.

The canoes had reached the landing now, and James stepped forward to greet the first boatload.

"Look, Little Fox," she exclaimed. "See how handsome White Falcon looks today." The boy gurgled his delight and reached for her. Swan Necklace took him from Walking Woman and turned back to the event at the river.

"Today is a special day," Walking Woman said.

"Aye, it is," Swan Necklace said, then turned her head and looked at the older woman in surprise. "Walking Woman is too wise," she retorted. The older woman chuckled.

"You have not told him yet?"

"Tonight," Swan Necklace promised. "Tonight I will tell him he is to have a child. He will be pleased."

"Aye, he will," Walking Woman said.

Down on the landing the speeches of welcome had been completed. James had introduced the newcomers to Wye and the other men. Now he looked around, searching the crowd of onlookers until he spied her. He waved, signaling her to come down. Swan Necklace felt her heart fill with happiness. It was always so between them. Swan Necklace handed Little Fox to Walking Woman, then hesitated.

"Go, my child. He wants you there beside him."

Swan Necklace made her way down the riverbank toward the landing. People turned in expectation. She saw their surprise at seeing she was a full-blooded Indian. Surprise turned to admiration as she greeted them charmingly. She knew she was very beautiful even to the white man. She moved easily among the white trappers and their families, taking her place beside her husband. His arm went around her, pulling her close as he introduced her.

"This is my wife, Swan Necklace," he said with quiet pride, and she smiled and greeted their guests with natural grace. The newcomers were captivated by her. In the years ahead, all up and down the land, as far as Montreal, her name would become legendary. She was Swan Necklace, wife of White Falcon.